ASHES OF REGRET

FROM THE WORLD OF THE

MISBEGOTTEN

BY

SEARBY GRAY

MudHouse Publishing

Title: Ashes of Regret

Fiction > Fantasy > Dark Fantasy, Urban Fantasy, Mythology, Mythical Creatures

Identifiers: ISBN 979-8-9865731-2-0 (print)

Cover Design by Sarah Waites

The Illustrated Page Book Design

Printed in the United States of America

To Lyn,

this book would not exist without your support and encouragement.

And,

To Sylvia,

this world should be a better place for our daughters. We'll burn it all down if it isn't.

Content Warning: Self-Harm

AFTER THE FIRESTORM
Kur
New Tigris
Ashur's Firepit
Marduk's Territory
New Babylon
Chicago
Bâltimore
DO NOT ENTER
Inanna's Theater
Hiraeth
An's Territory
Nammu's Territory
Euphrates
Alchemists' Camp
Nippur
New Wonderland
Atlantic Ocean
Enlil's Desert
Ki's Island

ONE

The fox yelped from inside the Skeleton Woods and Tamaki's stomach clenched. She'd found the carnivorous vines wrapped through the vixen's bones a week ago. Every night since then, the male fox called for his lost mate like a wailing baby. Tamaki could no longer ignore him. Sad as it was—for them both—she was his only hope. Red foxes mated for life. Poor bastard. Tamaki understood his pain and loneliness.

Without a soul to see her expert technique, she swung through the branches of the Empress Paulownia tree, parkour-style, ducking under leaves and pushing off of branches. The sensation of warmth she still didn't fully understand traveled from her calloused palms into the tree and then back again. The lifeforce inside of Tamaki automatically connected with the lifeforce inside the tree. She'd been teaching herself how to use this energy -- *etemmu* – on purpose, whether moving branches of the tree or encouraging new branches to start. Her grandmother, Obaa-chan, could no longer guide Tamaki. She'd been murdered by religious fanatics soon after the firestorms.

Firestorms fell on the summer solstice. One moment Tamaki was working at a bookstore café that had more cats than customers, half-heartedly studying for classes at the community college in between orders, but mostly waiting for the summer concert series so she could lose herself in rocking out to loud music and getting cheap beer with a fake ID. The next moment she was sprinting out of the bookstore, dodging falling debris as the ground shook and the sky broke open. The firestorms came, literal balls of hungry flames dropping down again and again in explosions of power. Tamaki and Obaa-chan found each other and were able to hide in the bomb shelter of a school. Roads crumpled from the heat. Cell phones worked sporadically, if at all. It was a war zone, but no one knew who was attacking. So many people died, either from the fire or from lack of medical care. The survivors scattered, searching for safety.

There was no safety.

Tamaki dropped down from the tall tree whose curved branches served as her home. She crossed the field to the west that led to the woods her every instinct told her to stay out of. As the waist-high weeds swished against her capri pants, she turned back to savor the view. Hiraeth's cabin windows framed the Appalachian Mountains near what used to be Harper's Ferry. Idyllic and peaceful. And empty. She took a breath, turned back around, and tread toward the dark forest of twisted vegetation. The pungent smell of decay wafted out like fingertips reaching for her, drawing her in. The forest hid mutations, some might even say monsters. Tamaki had a theory, well, Scott the park ranger had had a theory, that *etemmu* could become corrupted if it didn't flow along ley lines. Thus, the creation of the Skeleton Woods. Regardless of whether the theory was right, the place was scary. Tamaki frowned and attempted to steel herself, determined to help the fox.

First, Tamaki checked the sky. She had to be fast. In and out; this was no place to be after dark. Later, after the firestorm, Tamaki and Obaa-chan found out that each cyclone of the firestorm had contained a Mesopotamian deity breaking free from their celestial prison. Later they found out that the gods were creating their own city-states, setting up territories like a game of Risk. Later, they realized that human survivors were choosing to worship some of the ancient gods – gods who rejoiced in pain and suffering. It was Hotheads, those devoted to the god Ashur, who'd murdered Obaa-chan.

This was, Scott had told her, a neutral place. A kind of Switzerland under the rule of a god who practiced benign neglect. Sure, the weather changed on a day-to-day basis depending on the mood of the resident god, The Weatherman. It could be snowing one day, hot and humid the next, but it could be worse. The cloud cover, however, never burned off during the day. The best one could hope for was a grayish light that turned everything sepia. Blame Shamash, the sun god, for dying.

The fox cried again, a clear call for help.

Standing a few feet away from the tangled branches that guarded the entrance to the Skeleton Woods, Tamaki took a deep breath and dropped her hand to her knife. Maybe the fox had wandered into a metal trap from pre-firestorm days. Or maybe there was something like the two-headed moose wandering through. She closed her eyes and opened her senses to the plants.

Some would call it magic, but the women of Tamaki's family had passed down the tradition of Alchemists — humans who'd learned the secret art of the gods. Obaa-chan had taught her that all people have a divine life force and the ability to develop natural talents through meditation and ritual. Until the firestorms on the summer solstice, Tamaki had outgrown believing the fantastic stories; instead, she'd dismissed her grandmother's "growing hands" as being a good gardener and knowing which fertilizer to use.

To manipulate *etemmu* and manifest a physical change, she needed to relax, to have her mind in the present. That was one thing Obaa-chan had repeated. *You can't change the future; you can't change the past. Regrets and hopes are distractions. You must fully accept the present. That is when change occurs.* What was alchemy if not change?

No more delay. Unable to sense anything specific from the woods, Tamaki shoved through the curtain of branches to enter the woods. Pressure scraped along her limbs. The dead branches gave way to thick vines. Thorns plucked at her clothing as the vines fell back into place, vines that belonged to a jungle rather than an old-growth forest.

She was inside the Skeleton Woods.

The light on this side of the curtain of vines was reduced, noises muffled. The ground was mushy, swampish, and accompanied by a putrid odor. Fungus, brown and slimy with orange tips, grew straight while the trees leaned and listed as their roots rotted from below or the vines encircled their trunks with a chokehold. It was hard to get her bearings, although she had a clear line of sight on the black-barked tree marking the vixen's skeleton. Reluctantly, Tamaki moved closer to investigate. The male fox would be close by.

The tree's branches twisted like a picture of Dante's suicides that she remembered from high school. White bones that she'd last seen forming a perfect skeleton had been pulled apart by the carnivorous vines that had covered the vixen's body either while she slept or while she lay injured, unable to get away from their deadly embrace. Tamaki whistled; she wanted the fox to appear so they could leave. Quickly.

A strangled yelp, the cry of a creature so helpless that it would answer any call.

Her heart thudded so hard it made Tamaki's hands shake as she stared at the vines. They'd continued growing, sightlessly searching for their next meal. Tamaki followed their green path to the left, grunting as she ducked under a decomposing tree. The ground sucked at her foot with a smacking sound. The vines grew thicker closer to their base. Hopefully, her knife would be able to saw through them.

And there it was. A nest of these vines thick as her ankle growing out in all directions. Movement to the right attracted her notice. The red fox looked up with panicked eyes rolling in his head. A vine squeezed around his middle, holding him captive, and tendrils grew into his handsome pelt. He exposed neat teeth with flecks of green, marks on the vine visible from where he'd tried to bite his way free. Tamaki pulled out her blade and stepped over two green arms to the one that immobilized the fox.

Reaching out, Tamaki touched the vine's arm and then yanked her hand back, wiping it on her capris. This plant did not give off the clean energy of a pre-firestorm plant. Instead, it felt like a sentient chaos that wanted to consume. Still, she recognized the feeling of power in the vine. Her Empress Paulownia tree's roots reached past the cabin toward the creek, a ley line, and the tree's xylem delivered energy along with water and minerals. Tamaki could manipulate the tree so she should be able to manipulate these vines into letting go of the fox.

Licking her lips, Tamaki imagined that she was an outline of a person with a glowing center, and able to interact with the glow inside the vines. She inhaled and then, on the exhale, pushed the warmth from her chest down her arms to her hands. Her face and abdomen grew warm and Tamaki lengthened her spine, rising up through the crown of her head. She was medium height – taller than her Japanese mother but shorter than her Caucasian father – and had an athletic frame, but all the physicality melted away when she focused on becoming energy.

Tamaki placed her hands on the vine and dug her fingers into it, pushing her warmth into the plant, urging it to go limp like a wet noodle. Everything felt natural like she was connected to the life energy within the vine. It grew heavy in her hands, obedient to her will.

She had felt this way once before, under her grandmother's tutelage in the ceremony to initiate Tamaki into her family's secrets. Obaa-chan had taught Tamaki to feel the light, detach from her physical body, and push the light through her hands. A young Tamaki had opened her eyes, delighted to see the blue flowers of the iris plant blooming with joyous abandon, peeling down in a dancer's backbend. Proud, Tamaki had studied the resulting blue streak in her own black hair, a blue streak that matched both her mother's and grandmother's. It was soon after that ceremony that her mother, always an inconsistent presence, hadn't come around anymore. Tamaki had decided that the flower and her hair was some type of trick. Not like she could ask her mother; the abandonment hurt so much. Wasn't she a good enough daughter? The wound scabbed over, but it never healed.

Tamaki gave a bitter laugh and the warmth slipped. She was losing the connection with the plant. *Think of good memories*, she told herself. But the old anger returned, the sense of injustice, the underlying fear of being alone because she was worthless. She needed to clear her mind. Return to a sense of peace. But the more she tried to hold onto the feeling of light, the more it slipped away.

The vine seemed to awaken, snapping back to a rigid structure.

No! Tamaki let go of the vine and banged her fists against her thighs. She couldn't do it.

A bird launched from a higher branch with a raucous cry. Tamaki looked up through the tall trees. A large raven flew toward the river, its long narrow wings ending in the typical pinion shape at the tips, the wedge-shaped tail acting as a rudder in the air. The sky was getting darker. She didn't want to be in this jungle of meat-eating plants when night fell.

Just a plant, she told herself, as if that would make it true. *And there's more than one way to rescue the fox.* Tamaki grabbed the vine with her left hand and sawed with her right. *Action is better than worry. Can't get caught in your head. That's where a thousand deaths lie.*

The whole nest quivered. The tendrils curling into the fox's pelt trembled at the attack. Retaliation? Her knife passed through the fibrous outside; the inside was more difficult to cut. Jelly-like, it closed back over her blade, resealing any cut. It smelled fermented, rotting in its own juices.

The fox whined. The nest was undulating now. She wanted to burn the whole plant, but hadn't brought the tools. That would have to be another day. If there was another day. She had no doubt that black, greasy energy would be released from it; *etemmu* gone rancid, and the energy vultures would come flying.

The fox squirmed, maybe trying to help, or maybe trying to escape as he felt the vine going slack. Tamaki was halfway through when she heard movements in the underbrush all around. The vines were retracting like long green snakes crawling in the cursed forest, slithering back to the nest to defend its heart. Frantic, Tamaki redoubled her sawing efforts. One last cut and she was through the main vine. The fox stumbled to his feet, unsteady.

Sweat dripped down the side of her face as Tamaki studied the problem. Tendrils still corkscrewed into the fox's body. "Hold on," she said to the fox, her voice rusty from disuse. It was becoming hard to see in the dark twilight. "I'm going to get you out of here. I promise."

She grabbed the nearest tendril and twisted it out. The fox cried and tried to step away, but fell down.

"Oh, God. I'm so sorry." She stared in horror at the barbed tip of the plant tendril, covered in fox blood. First the vines encircled to capture prey and then the barbs went in, sucking out nutrients. Drawing out life and feasting on *etemmu*. She couldn't rip these out, they had to be massaged or persuaded from the inside.

She needed a boost from her power; she had to try again.

Tamaki didn't have Saki the turtle-penguin to help her stay calm, but she slowed her breathing and pictured herself without form, a being of light and power, letting *etemmu* move from her heart down to her hands, pressure from inside pushing the tendrils out. The inner goo burned her hands, but it was a distant sensation. Pleasure filled Tamaki as the remaining barbs vibrated, pulling out. And then a rush of unclean energy pushed back, rancid green jelly covering her right hand. Tamaki gasped and opened her eyes as she lost concentration. She'd failed, again.

Tamaki took a breath, trying to steady herself. A vague sensation of pressure on her leg made her look down. While she'd been in the trance one of the recalled vines had encircled her calf, the brown hairs working their way through the thin cloth of her capris.

"Oh, hells no." Horrified, Tamaki plunged her knife tip straight down into the vine and yanked it back out. Green jelly spurted. The cut vine released her leg and flailed in the air, but there was another behind it and another one behind that one.

Plan B. Tamaki grabbed the fox, ten pounds maybe of starving, matted fur. She yanked it up into her arms and heard another of the tendrils rip out. The fox barked in pain.

"I'm sorry." There wasn't time to cut the tendrils, not with the falling darkness and the slithering sounds in the forest, the green snake vines gathering around, reaching and grabbing, trapping them here.

Clutching the fox to her chest, Tamaki sprinted, brambles scratching and clawing at her, trying to hold her for the snakes. Her right hand burned with the juice of the vine, a poison bite. Up ahead she could catch glimpses of the field and beyond that the cabin. She buried her face in the fox's fur, feeling the roughness of the tendrils against her cheek. There was a stitch in her side, and she was breathing hard, but she was going to make it. All she had to do was pound through the curtain of brambles. A few more steps and she'd be out in the open.

Then the green tip slithered around her waist, clinched around itself, and yanked her back into the darkness like a living rope. Tamaki knocked its questing tip with her elbow, jabbed backward with the knife, the other hand clutching the fox. More vines wrapped around her right leg. Pain exploded as the barb pierced her skin, screwing itself into her flesh.

Tamaki cried out for help, but there was never anyone to help her. A helpless rage filled her.

"Get off me," she screamed, shoving her knife back into its holder. She used her right hand to reach down to the barb. Her fingers slipped in her blood; she was scared. Beyond the pain, she felt the connection, but it was hard to hold onto, like a song in the middle of a thunderstorm. Within the pain, though, was an electricity. It was closer, easier to reach. Desperate, Tamaki veered toward the pain.

Power exploded through her.

Tamaki gripped the barb and sent a blast of *etemmu* through her hand. The irritant shriveled so that she could pluck it out and throw it away. The heat inside her body was almost unbearable, but it felt so good. Tamaki was lost within it, watching as the power moved her body: watching as she turned to face the green snake vines without fear, setting the quivering fox down so she could grab vines with both hands and send surges of power down the vines back to the plant's heart, thrusting the shriveled vines away and picking up the fox.

Tamaki jumped through the curtain of thorny brambles – the hedge appeared to pull away from her – and waded through the field toward the cabin without looking back.

The fox whined, a soft exhalation against her neck. She thought of it as a 'thank you.'

"I'll take care of you," Tamaki said. "But then I have to go." She needed to move on. That was the only way to survive. Rachel and her son Adam had welcomed Tamaki after she'd escaped from the Hotheads, but they had gone to Baltimore to find a cure that might or might not exist for Adam's cancer. Her Obaa-chan was dead. The soldiers of New Babylon – an expanding military territory 𒁹𒈗𒂊 in former Pittsburgh —— knew she was here.

Approaching the cabin's door, Tamaki looked over her shoulder at the path into the forest that led to the blueberry clearing. That was why she kept delaying. Because there was a teeny tiny hope inside that there was something of Scott left. As long as she didn't enter the clearing to check, she had the hope.

Scott. His name conjured images in her mind. The New Babylon soldiers arriving and then Scott, the red-haired park ranger, rushing into the clearing, excited because he'd scored some plums and coffee. She saw his face when the soldiers attacked, heard their laugh when he was hanged, and remembered being shoved to the ground when she'd tried to protect him.

A few hours difference and she'd have been cuddled next to Scott on the porch swing right now, holding hands. She would have made fun of his scavenging skills in bringing back a rotten plum. Taken a bite and let the fermented juice drip down her chin. Maybe he would have licked it off. Maybe they would have had their second kiss while sitting on that porch swing over there and it would have seemed like an evening from before the end of the world.

A soft whuff of breath at her neck startled Tamaki out of the fantasy.

"We're here, foxy," she said, glad for the distraction. One of the problems with being alone: it was easy to get lost in one's head.

Carrying him into the cabin, Tamaki set the fox down on the living room floor and reached for a blanket off the couch. She needed to get water from the rain barrel outside and wash them both off, check the fox's

broken barbs and decide how to get them out.

The surge of power was wearing off.

Suddenly the room spun as vertigo gripped Tamaki. She threw her arms out to the side for balance. An overwhelming sense of loss swept through her. Her heart thumped. She closed her eyes and fell.

TWO

When Tamaki struggled up through a nightmare of twisting green snakes, she opened her eyes to the safety of *Hiraeth*'s family room. Rachel and her husband had designed the house to be a cozy retreat. Rachel's art supplies covered the desk in the corner and the throw rug was colorful and bright. A leather sectional couch wrapped the room. The fox curled into an orange donut atop a pile of blankets on the couch, his snout pointed towards her, brown eyes watching. She pressed her palm against her heart where the mysterious pain had occurred before she'd passed out. It was tender, but not like something was broken. Maybe poison from the vines. She gave an internal shrug and examined the cut in her calf where the tendril had coiled into her flesh.

"Nasty," she said, looking at the jagged scab. She pulled herself up by using the ledge of the double-sided fireplace and limped to the bathroom closet for a first aid kit. "This is for you and me both, Foxy." Then she went to the kitchen and grabbed supplies.

Coming back into the family room, Tamaki grunted as she sat down in front of the fox. She popped open the can of tuna and offered it as a distraction while she looked at the fox's wounds. He sniffed, his little nose twitching before hunger won out. He used sharp teeth to remove a chunk of meat and eat it. When he reached forward with a paw to hold the can in place and bent his head for another bite, Tamaki shifted her focus to his wound.

Like in her leg, the tendrils had gone deep into the fox. One hole had scabbed over, but the other hole had closed and swollen. It was hot to the touch. She guessed that the green jelly was trapped under the fox's skin and creating an infection, killing him.

She reached for a long match stored by the fireplace, struck it, and then used the flame to clean her knife. The green gunk from the vines had dried into a sticky web, but the flame burned it clean. She used a nearby throw blanket to rub the knife blade until it gleamed.

Then, with the fox's attention on getting the last bit of meat out of the can, Tamaki touched the warm blade of her knife to the fox's infected wound. The skin broke open and green-tinged pus poured out.

The fox tried to leap away from the pain, but Tamaki pressed him into the blankets. She coughed at the stinging, rotting smell that emerged. The same corrupted energy that had poured from the two-headed moose when its carcass burned.

The fox whined, his brown eyes rolling to look at her.

"I know that hurt," she said. "But now you can get better." She poured hydrogen peroxide over the wound.

The fox yipped and struggled to its feet, but he was too exhausted. His legs shook.

"Shh," she soothed. Some connection still existed between them beyond a wild animal and a strange human. Wrapping the towel around her hand in case she was wrong and he decided to bite, Tamaki urged the fox back down.

Then she watched with satisfaction as white bubbles overflowed from the wound. She unwrapped the towel and used it to sop up the mess. Tamaki remembered that Adam had been recovering from leukemia when the firestorm struck Baltimore. It wasn't a coincidence there were plenty of supplies out here. "Thank you, Rachel, for being such a prepared mom."

Tamaki tended her own cut while she tried to figure out her good mood. Last night had been an incredible test, to the point where she'd wondered if she was going to even make it out of the Skeleton Woods. It was hard to remember exactly what had happened, but that fight at the edge of the forest when she'd attacked the plant… Tamaki examined her hands. She didn't know what she'd done, but it had been spectacular.

"You're welcome for rescuing you," she said to the fox, reaching for the tuna can. She froze when the fox jutted his head forward, thinking that he was about to bite. Instead, the wild fox touched the back of her hand with his damp nose.

Tamaki's shoulders relaxed. Now it was time to face a different challenge. She looked out the large picture windows at the path towards the blueberry clearing where Scott had been murdered. With a brisk rub of her hands, Tamaki set off around the cabin and collected what she would need to find out if any part of the man she'd been falling in love with still existed.

The fox followed when she left the cabin, limping in a way that made Tamaki shake her head. "Go sleep on the blankets. You shouldn't be walking around yet." It didn't make sense for him to follow her either. He wasn't a pet.

He blinked and dipped his head to lick his wound, but Tamaki snapped her fingers at him. "Don't do that." The cabin had a lot of medical supplies, but nothing specific for pets.

An insistent clicking from the Empress Paulownia made Tamaki smile as she jogged toward her tree. She clambered up through the branches. Years before, her grandmother had sent her to learn karate at a local studio, but Tamaki had hated the gi, the teachers, everything. Instead, as she'd walked to class, she'd seen some older teenagers jumping, climbing, swinging, even crawling, through obstacles. She'd offered the envelope of weekly karate money to the group and they'd included her. The system worked until the karate teacher called Obaa-chan and wanted to know why Tamaki didn't attend anymore. Her grandmother had been disappointed and Tamaki had been grounded. When she was able to go back, the group had moved on. Tamaki had watched videos and practiced by herself, but it wasn't the same.

Now she settled into a vee by Saki's platform, a living branch manipulated to create sides so the turtle-penguin wouldn't fall out. Unfortunately, Tamaki had lost focus and the end of the branch stuck straight out from the last coil like a pottery snake that had dried before the last curve.

Tamaki stroked her shell and Saki's eyes closed. Tamaki was nineteen years old and she'd guess Saki wasn't quite three months, a baby when the firestorm hit and random *etemmu* mutated her. So how old did that make Saki in turtle-penguin years? Her green shell was larger than it had been a few days ago, about seven inches across, and the random brown squiggles across the top were resolving into what, with a little imagination, could be a cursive spelling of the turtle-penguin's name.

"Hi, baby. Sorry, I left you alone all night."

Saki tilted her round penguin head and made clicking sounds through her beak. She stretched her back legs so the nails scratched against the tree with an irritating sound. The soft gray fur on the legs had been replaced by sleek feathers. Tamaki stroked the feathers with her index finger.

"Yes, you are the cutest mutation ever."

The repetitive petting motion helped Tamaki's heartbeat slow, her breathing deepen, the pressure drop away. A light wind caressed the skin showing through her ripped concert shirt. She smelled the woodsy floral scent she'd come to think of as belonging to the tree. Warmth blossomed in Tamaki's chest, a sensation both relaxing and buoying. The elephant ear-sized leaves fluttered in the canopy around her.

Saki tucked her chin and then used her flipper to push forward something oval and white that had been hidden by the bulk of her body. Marveling, Tamaki picked up an egg. It was the size of a golf ball, but the shell was soft. It would probably need warmth and time to harden, like a reptile's egg. Or maybe cold like a penguin's egg. Perfect for this territory's constantly changing weather patterns.

"You made an egg?" Completely baffled, Tamaki stared at the turtle-penguin.

Saki opened her beak in what could have been a mockery of Tamaki's expression.

Looking towards the blueberry path and then back to Saki, Tamaki made a decision. No way was she going to leave Saki and her perfect, unexpected egg in the tree as bait for some predators. Tamaki unclipped the black carrying pouch from around a nearby tree branch and eased Saki and the egg into the pouch before securing it across her front.

Then, followed by the fox, Tamaki walked the path to the blueberry clearing.

Abruptly, Tamaki's cheerfulness vanished. She wasn't ready for this – wasn't ready to confront Scott's death. Instead, Tamaki unstrapped the pouch and let Saki out on the ground, the egg perched on top so she could see it. The fox had no interest in the turtle-penguin and, with a sigh too big for his small body, used his paw to rake some leaves into a pile and then settled down for a nap.

Tamaki rubbed at the scar on her thigh – a reminder of when she'd been held by the Hotheads. No more excuses for procrastination.

Scott's bag still leaned against the base of the oak tree. Tamaki ran her fingers over the sturdy fabric, touched the metal zipper. She pulled it closer and dumped it out. His notebook with the ley lines map was gone but wouldn't have worked anyway. She needed something personal and important to him, but the flint, pocketknife, small first aid kit, and flashlight could have belonged to anyone. She unzipped the innermost pocket and shoved her hand inside, seizing on a slick paper the size of an envelope and pulling it out.

"Oh, Scott." How like him to have a printed photograph when everyone else kept theirs on phones. Scott and four other rangers stood in a line outside of a brown hut. It couldn't have been that long before the firestorm. Scott looked younger; his face eager, tall in his uniform. She felt sad for this earlier Scott. He was trained to tell kids about recycling and not feeding the wildlife. Instead, he became the last forest ranger desperately trying to keep the woods alive, pulling down vines, shoring up roots, digging up the fungus that proliferated after dirty rains fell from the pus-colored sky. Propping the picture against the bag she'd brought from the cabin, Tamaki sat down.

She remembered their kiss. Their first kiss had been their last. Tamaki struggled to breathe against the pain that twisted her insides.

A breeze whistled through the clearing. Tamaki turned her head, looking for movement. To her left was the path up to *Hiraeth*, the homestead. Puny blueberry bushes on her right. Scorch marks in the center of the clearing indicated where Scott's physical body had burned. Vegetation, some type of mountain laurel, was mangled at the other end of the clearing by the New Babylon soldiers' exodus.

Another breeze riffled over her skin like a touch, cold enough to make her shiver.

"Scott?" Tears made her face wet, although she didn't remember starting to cry. The moistened skin made her sensitive to the breeze, made it easy to believe that Scott's energy caressed her face. She put her hand to her cheek and it passed through chilled, still air.

What had been small pockets of chilled air, small wisps of breeze, grew larger, expanding. Tamaki stood up into the coldness; goosebumps raised on her skin. She turned and used her outstretched hands to find the edges between cold air and the moist, thick air of the clearing.

Words poured out. "They left me. Rachel, and Adam. They left for Baltimore because Adam's cancer came back and I don't blame them, but I'm all alone again."

Cold soothed her heated cheeks, pressed against the sides of her head like comforting palms.

She sank back down to the ground. Different air temperatures weren't definitive —— she could be fooling herself because she wanted Scott's essence to still be here. Tamaki had felt like a freak learning about manipulating energy, meditation, and ley lines while growing up in the little town in Ohio where she'd lived with Obaa-chan, but now this knowledge gave her an advantage in this world, a basic understanding that most survivors lacked. That said, her grandmother had never taught her anything about trying to communicate with a ghost.

Opening the bag she'd packed at the cabin, Tamaki arranged the mirror, lit the candles, and took out the chimes. All things she'd seen in movies or read in books. For example, jewelry could disrupt energy flow, so she took out her nose stud and tossed aside the metal knife.

"Hey, I brought a mirror in case you want to show yourself. And chimes in case you want to make some noise. Not exactly talking, but we'd be communicating. I guess I could make a Ouija board if you want to spell things." She held up the chimes. "Recognize this? Adam made it from seashells he collected in Ocean City. He was so proud. Must have told me five times about how he made them, step-by-step." She swallowed, recognizing how much she didn't want to be disappointed. "Want to jingle them? I know you can make breezes. Try to blow the chimes."

She pinched the top loop of the chimes with her thumb and index finger and looked up at the trees, checking to make sure there wasn't a natural breeze.

Please, please, she wished. *I don't want to be alone anymore.*

A familiar smell of dry grass and sandalwood made her nose itch. It was the combination of scents that she'd inhaled when hugging Scott, standing on tiptoe with her face pressed into the sweet spot between his neck and shoulder. The seashells began to move in a circle, tugging against the loop she held. Tamaki grabbed the mirror with her other hand and positioned it to look for a reflection over her shoulder.

"Move the chimes if you are Scott."

They jangled. So did her heart. A million questions fought to get out, but she made herself slow down.

"Are you trapped in this clearing or can you go anywhere?"

No ghostly breeze. "Sorry. That wasn't a yes or no question. Or, maybe you don't know. Let's try it." She set the mirror down. "Follow me." Tamaki walked over to the blueberry bushes. "Can you jangle them now?" Yes. She walked around to the path. "Can you jangle them now?" Yes.

Excited, she walked up the path halfway to the Empress Paulownia. If he could go with her back to the cabin maybe it would keep the loneliness at bay. She could wake up to his light touch on her cheek. They could be a team again.

"Can you jangle them now?" Thick, moist air all around. It didn't smell like sandalwood. She retreated to the clearing. Crappitty-crap.

"That's okay. Now we know." She sat down by the candles, biting the inside of her cheek to hide her dismay. "Can you blow these out?"

They flickered.

"Good job."

Her heart hammered in her chest and she hoped she wouldn't trip over the words of the most important question. Part of her wanted to wait until tomorrow, but she wasn't a coward.

"Do you miss me?" She held up the chimes, concentrating on not letting her handshake. "Yes or no?"

Immediately the seashells smashed together as some strings moved clockwise and others moved counterclockwise.

Tamaki released a delighted laugh, her chest lightening as if a thousand miniature balloons floated in her ribcage. "Okay, okay. I had to ask. I miss you, too." That reaction wasn't from any wind. She didn't know exactly what was here in the clearing, but there was enough of Scott that he still missed her.

She blew out the candles and stood, taking the chimes to the oak tree where the New Babylon soldiers had hanged his body.

"This way you can call me. I'm a little old-fashioned." She put her hands on her hips and cocked her head. "It shouldn't always be the girl who does the calling."

There was no answer. Maybe he didn't like her joke.

Tamaki stretched, twisting to one side and then the other to release an ache in her lower back from sitting still so long. It was getting dark, but she didn't want to leave, to return to the empty cabin so she paced in the clearing. Scott's energy was stuck here and she had no idea how to free him. There was no one to ask, no book to read. Maybe she was overthinking this. If Scott was energy, then maybe she could use her power to make a connection.

Saki had rolled her egg into the pouch and then climbed in after. The fox was still sleeping, making little whining sounds while his leg twitched as if he was running from hungry vines. With the animals accounted for, Tamaki rubbed her hands together and then sat down. She closed her eyes and reached out her awareness.

Soon she could feel the roots of the trees beneath the ground, stretching together, a network of information. Could almost smell the distinct scents of different plants. The chimes made a soft jangling. But she couldn't feel anything that was Scott.

The fox yelped.

Tamaki's eyes snapped open. He'd woken up and jumped to his feet, his teeth worrying at the wound she'd cleaned earlier. Before she could stop him, the fox had bitten the skin enough to make it bleed. Exasperated, Tamaki got up and went to the fox. She moved his snout away from the wound and smoothed the edges of skin, hoping the blood would dry into a scab to hold the wound shut. Blood seeped along the edges of his skin, coating the tips of her fingers. Could she make a 'cone of shame' for a fox to keep him from worrying at it?

Tamaki's senses, still open to finding plant *etemmu*, seized on another source. Like in the Skeleton Woods, this was nearby and unknown, although clearly not plant. It started in her fingers. She'd been so powerful fighting the vines the last time when she'd used a different source that Tamaki seized the *etemmu*. An immediate tingling in her blood intensified until she couldn't tell if it was pleasure or pain.

The sensation was intoxicating. Beyond any wine she'd ever tasted or the effects of eating a pot gummy while alone in her room or the caffeine pills she'd taken to pull all-nighters before exams. This was power. It was confidence that what she wanted to happen would, all she had to do was hang on. She was yielding to something greater than herself, becoming part of something.

Tamaki panted. Her mouth was so dry. The smell of sandalwood was all around her and her skin was cold but her blood was hot and it was so loud with the chimes jangling in a destructive cacophony. The *etemmu* hurt, but she didn't want to let go. She wouldn't.

I was born for this, she thought. *I can do what no one else can do.*

The fox whined as blood dripped out his side, no longer seeping at the edges, but a crimson faucet. Had he bitten it open again?

She pushed herself to her feet. Wind blew all around; a cyclone confined to the clearing. Tamaki shoved her hair out of her face. It was hard to think, but she knew what she wanted. The words poured from her, "I want

Scott to have a physical body again." She swallowed through a throat that was on fire. "I want him back, not trapped in this clearing."

As if her words focused her thoughts, funneled the excessive power running through her body, Tamaki was once again pushed outside of herself so that she watched as her eyes glowed a golden color.

She watched as the air coalescing around the chimes became a visible swirling cloud. The fox whined in pain. Part of her noted it was the same sound he'd made when trapped by the vines, but Tamaki was helpless while in the grip of power. She couldn't stop herself from advancing on the fox, reaching down to squeeze his jaw until his mouth opened, and then beckoning toward the swirling cloud.

Resistance came from the fox and from the cloud, similar to like poles of two magnets being placed together, but their resistance was nothing to Tamaki. She pulled on the *etemmu* source and pushed out. With a roaring sound that Tamaki felt rather than heard, they came together. For a moment Scott-fox was a photograph that had been double exposed: the image of a naked crouching human superimposed over the struggling fox. She pushed harder, forcing the images to melt together.

A sudden cawing made her look up as a raven launched from a nearby tree.

Frowning, Tamaki turned back to Scott-fox. And when the cloud was inside the fox's body, the wind died. Tamaki released the body to the ground, watching from afar as it shined. Light spilled from the wounds, from his mouth, from his eyes. Her fingers were slippery with the blood of the fox. Fire danced on her fingers, invisible burning that felt both horrible and so good. The place beneath her breastbone filled with vibration, a subvocal humming. Now she had no trouble seeing the energy fighting inside Scott-fox's body.

Tamaki poked and pushed with her mind, guided by the power. "Knit his flesh together, fill his veins with life, let his heart beat strong."

Scott-fox's body jerked and cracked. The fur smoothed out into a luscious coat. She heard a pop of a bone she hadn't known was broken snapping back into place, and then he grew about a foot longer through his spine, his shoulders filled out, and even his tail grew fluffier until he was a perfect specimen of an Australian Shepherd-sized red fox.

It was so easy. Tamaki laughed. She could do anything. She clasped her hands together, wanting to celebrate. The fear she'd been carrying fell away like a physical burden. All the wondering if Scott was here, all the debate about whether to leave, all of it was over. She'd won.

And then the fire she'd been using turned inwards. Tamaki gasped and wrapped her arms around her middle. She'd been pushing the power out. Now it flowed back through her body like razor blades slicing her open, relentlessly moving into the hollow place beneath her breastbone. It burned there, carving her into strips from the inside out. She grabbed at her chest, beat at it to make the sensation stop. Coughed until the taste of ashes filled her mouth. Finally, the fire died.

Tamaki leaned against a tree and vomited, spitting, again and again, to get the taste out. She wiped her hands on her shirt.

Across the clearing, the fox twitched.

"Scott?" Her voice came out hoarse.

The fox's eyes blinked open, a bright gold color.

"Hey!" The voice drifting from the direction of the cabin sounded male, old, and irritated. "What in *kur* is going on in there?"

THREE

Tamaki looked around the clearing, frantic. The seashell chimes had exploded. Now the strings hung empty and the shells scattered all around, including embedded into tree trunks. Meanwhile, tree branches had sheared off from the cyclone and the grass was trampled. She had blood all over her hands and the fox, fur matted with blood, sat by himself, shaking.

"Stay there," she yelled. "I'm coming." She shoved her knife back into its sheath and worked her nose stud back in as she crept up the path toward the cabin. Twilight made everything into silhouettes. Peering through the branches, she saw a man holding a small lantern in front of him, the light reflecting off of his bald head. Tamaki squinted as she glanced around the rest of the yard. He was alone.

"Hurry," he said. "I don't feel like waiting all night."

Fear caused sweat under her armpits, she could smell it, but she didn't have to show it to the stranger. She could have ignored him, but she had the feeling he wasn't going to leave. She walked out of the woods, standing tall as her 5'4" frame allowed, wanting him to know she wasn't an easy target. She rubbed through her pants at the scar the Hotheads left on her thigh in unconscious reaction to the thought.

Up close, Tamaki could see the man had a thick white beard and deep creases in his weathered face. His eyes were hidden behind black sunglasses. Was he blind? Who wore sunglasses at night? He wore a white Western shirt, an old-fashioned vest, and a bolo necktie while leaning precariously on a lacquered walking stick. She coughed. The cologne he wore caused a tickle in the back of her sore throat. Almost like an oncoming summer rain.

A raven, possibly the same one as before, landed back in her tree.

"That's Jude," the man said. "He says you've been busy."

"Jude?"

"Yeah. He flies around this area keeping an eye on things. When you see him, you can say 'hey'."

"Hey, Jude?" Tamaki narrowed her eyes. Typical old man. Thought he was funny. Probably moved to the mountains decades ago to be away from people, talked to the animals since he didn't have any friends. She could probably knock him to the ground if she needed to. He wasn't a threat.

The old man snorted as if he could hear her thoughts. "That's a nice blue stripe you've got in your hair. Very fashionable."

She curled her hand into a fist so she wouldn't touch the blue streak of hair caused by performing a transmutation ritual on her twelfth birthday, a tradition for the women in her family that traced back to before the Great Flood. Stories of the gods and the powers they wielded also passed down through each matrilineal generation until it broke with Tamaki's mother. And now the threatened return had happened: the gods were busy setting up territories, the world was awash with the primal energy of Shamash's destroyed body, and only Tamaki was left of her family. It would be funny if it weren't.

"Go away," Tamaki said. "This homestead is taken. You're not welcome here."

"No," he shouted, jabbing his walking stick at her. "I decide who's welcome here."

Tamaki rolled her eyes as she glanced over her shoulder. She needed to get back to the clearing, get back to Scott-fox.

"Got a name inked on your neck." The old man snorted. "That doesn't read Anderson or Smith or Miller."

He could read kanji? In an effort to win her Obaa-chan's approval, Tamaki had gotten a tattoo of their family name, Hayashi. Unfortunately, Obaa-chan had not been impressed. She wouldn't even look at it. Instead, she'd launched into a lecture about the danger of joining gangs even when Tamaki tried to explain that the tattoo meant "forest" and was a reference to the story Obaa-chan had told about how their family had survived the Flood by growing trees so tall that the Flood waters couldn't touch them, then making a village in the treetops until it was safe to come down. But this old man couldn't know that. He meant that she had a Japanese name.

"Ah," he said, his voice dropping back into the normal range, head tilting like he was sly. "Maybe that's not what I meant at all. Maybe I meant your aspirations to be an Alchemist."

At the word 'Alchemist,' Tamaki gulped. He did not look like an academic or someone who, pre-firestorm, had studied esoteric arts. "What do you mean?"

The raven cawed from the Empress Paulownia tree. Another raven winged in to settle on a branch and then a third. They all watched Tamaki.

"I heard about what happened in the forest and came to see who had done it. Wanted to see this little tree hugger who fancies herself able to manipulate *etemmu.*"

Guilt made Tamaki's cheeks flame, but she wasn't sure why and didn't have time to examine it. "Are you an Alchemist?" She pointed a finger at the old man's chest. "Tell me right now or–"

"Or what?"

In the silence, Tamaki heard the lack of insect music, the lack of birds settling in their nests, the lack of wind, or any movement in the trees.

It was dark and yet she could see as well as if they were in a subtle bubble of light.

"Will you do this?" The old man raised his walking stick. Thunder rolled across the sky and clouds gathered overhead. Tamaki's hair whipped her face and her clothes flapped against her body. He lowered the stick and the wind stopped.

No human could do that. Not even an Alchemist.

Tamaki's limbs froze in horror as she realized she'd made a mistake. A terrible mistake.

Tamaki snapped her palms together in front of her chest and bowed at the waist. Staring at the ground she tried to remember Obaa-chan's stories about the Misbegotten, the gods and demigods of Mesopotamia who'd walked the earth before being banished to a prison in the sky. There were so many and it hadn't seemed important at the time.

"Forgive me," she said. "I didn't know to whom I was speaking."

The old man pulled on his puffy white beard, preening under her flattery. "That's right. You didn't."

He sounded gleeful, so she kept going. "You are surely a powerful being."

Thunder rolled, the growl of an angry animal, and lightning flashed white. Rain fell hard against her skin. Overhead, the elephant-ear-sized leaves of the Empress Paulownia acted as a funnel to shower Tamaki.

"You're a sky deity," Tamaki guessed, pushing wet hair behind her ear.

"What gave me away?" He shook his walking stick until the end crooked into a lightning zag and pointed it at her. "You're just like that other one who bothered me. You don't ask the right questions."

The other one? He must mean Rachel. She'd said the local deity of this territory called himself The Weatherman, even Scott had talked about The Weatherman, but this was no demigod. Tamaki began to shake as she thought about the ravens and the Cedars of Lebanon that grew here in the post-firestorm mountains. She was talking to a first-generation Misbegotten, one of the first Nephilim. He was the god of the heavens and the original leader of the Mesopotamian pantheon before ceding power first to his son Enlil and then to Mardu.

"Glorious An, please forgive me for not recognizing you."

"Well." An placed the end of the walking stick back on the ground. The sky cleared as if he'd flipped a switch. "It's understandable." He adjusted his sunglasses. "I'm not wearing my horned crown."

"May I offer you something to eat or drink?" She straightened from the bow and rung out the bottom of her wet shirt. Hopefully, he would say "no" because, having been through the cabin's cabinets, there wasn't a lot that didn't require preparation.

"I will accept some wine."

She shook her head.

"Beer, then."

She shook her head again.

"Milk."

"Uh." She cleared her throat. "We might have some canned tuna."

"Keep it." He sighed. "It's so hard to find good worshippers in these modern times. As the Fab Four say, 'Ob-La-Di, Ob-La-Da', am I right? The point is, I wanted to see the hero who went into the forest."

"I… am honored." Tamaki clenched her fists to keep her face from revealing her elation. She was getting the recognition she deserved for saving Scott. Seconds after his death she'd pleaded for Scott to stay with a prayer that she'd heard Obaa-chan use for dying houseplants, but she hadn't dared hope that she'd be able to give him an actual body. "I didn't know what to expect, but I did the best I could."

The original raven cawed as if speaking directly to An. Three more blackbirds settled into the branches.

"But you saw a creature in trouble and went in to rescue him and then had a tremendous fight."

She pictured the destroyed clearing and gave a little laugh. "It was tough, but the result was worth it."

"Where is he now? I'd like to see him."

"Scott's in the clearing." Tamaki smiled. Of course, An would want to see Scott. Since the firestorm, Scott had been working as a spy for An and making a map of all the local ley lines.

"I meant the fox." His voice was cold as the rain. An leaned forward until she could see her reflection in his sunglasses. "The one you rescued from the vines yesterday. Jude told me you were very brave and I came to see a hero."

Tamaki's stomach clenched with fear and she felt lightheaded as she realized they'd been talking about two different things. "Yes, that was me. I did that, too."

"What is this about Scott?" His whispered words came out like pieces of hail falling.

Her knees knocked together and she hadn't known that was actually a thing, but it was happening to her now. "He, his spirit, was in there after he died and…I…." Her voice faded away.

"Go to the clearing. Say your goodbye and give him permission to die. There's nothing to be done, no choice you can make that won't cost your humanity. Mourn for him, respect the dead, and let him go." An's white beard puffed out and his shiny bald head seemed to glow as his voice filled the space around them. "There's a price for breaking the flow of fate."

The raven cawed from its branch, an echo of An's threat.

"But he's special." She pressed her palms together, frustrated that she had to defend herself for saving the fox and saving Scott. "I love him."

"He's special; you love him." An's voice went into a falsetto-mocking pitch before returning to its normal scratchiness. "Everyone is special to someone. The answer is no."

"I'll pay the price, whatever it is." Frantic, she stamped her foot.

One of the ravens began cawing again.

An listened, his frown deepening, before turning back to Tamaki. "You petulant child! How dare you commit such a sin in my territory?"

With a great rush of wind, An leaned forward and rushed past Tamaki with inhuman speed. The brush lining the path to the clearing trembled in his aftermath.

Unbalanced, Tamaki stumbled and then had to duck, covering her head, as the murder of ravens launched from the Empress Paulownia and bulleted towards the clearing.

Tamaki ran behind, arriving to see the birds settling into the oak tree. She hated them. Those stupid tattle-tale watchers.

Scott-fox still trembled, but he saw An and tried to walk toward the god. His legs went in one direction and his hind end went in the other. Whining, the fox stood there, trembling.

"What's wrong with him?" Tamaki came around the god so she stood next to the pouch. Saki's black eyes looked out from the interior. "Why can't he walk?"

An's upper lip curled with derision. "What did you think would happen? An unskilled, untalented, hack necromancer tries to make a miracle and instead creates her own Frankenstein's monster. You've shoved an immortal human soul into a dying animal and only now do you begin to wonder if that human can work the limbs of this strange body." His voice was cruel as he taunted her. "How's that alchemy working for you now?"

The fox lifted his snout to the sky and made a mournful cry.

The god's face softened as he shook his head. "Sorry, friend, but I can't bend the rules, even for you. You were murdered, Scott, and that's unfair, but you should have stayed dead."

"Fix this. Give him a new body." Tamaki dragged her gaze up the walking stick to the lightning carving and then up An's face to his sunglasses. Except the god's sunglasses weren't on. Where his eyes should be were swirls of silver and green moving at a dizzying pace. The smell of ozone filled the clearing.

"You broke the rules," An said. "No blood magic. It's a perversion of the gift granted by the Creator. Instead of working to grow your skill through discipline and dedication, blood addicts cheat by releasing control."

Tamaki dropped her gaze to avoid both An's silver and green orbs and Scott's repetition of pawing the air as if he couldn't stop.

"You do not deserve a home here and you are not worthy of the protection of my territory," An said.

She seethed at the injustice. She'd fought for Scott's life, without anyone's help, and won. That required discipline, honor, and courage besides. "But—"

"Stop talking, mortal," An roared. Not one of the birds rustled a feather.

Tears of anger threatened. She'd gone from a god calling her a hero to being evicted from the territory. Humiliation battled with shame to see which could make her feel worse. And she'd messed up with Scott too. She'd been trying to help but An wouldn't listen. Desperate for compassion, she fell to her knees and reached into the pouch to touch Saki. A soft head pressed against her hand and Tamaki closed her eyes in relief.

"Stand up for your sentencing." The god's voice was rough as thunder. "You are exiled forever."

Tamaki's hands shook as she tried to put the pouch on. The open end tipped up so that Saki's egg rolled onto the ground. The white oval gleamed in the trampled grass like a miniature moon.

"What's that?" An leaned forward.

Jude cawed an answer.

Tamaki righted her pouch, pushed Saki down inside it, and reached for the egg with her other hand, but the egg was already floating through the air towards An's open hand.

"That's mine," Tamaki said. She had to force down her instinct to snatch it from the god. "Please."

"Nothing in my territory is yours," An said. "I own all of this."

The fox had taken halting steps toward the god. One paw thrown into the air and landed with a graceless plop, then the other front paw thrown into the air. The hind leg dragged forward and then the other.

"Scott, you are complicit, too." An reached down to place a hand on the fox's head. "Not by choice, but because of your very nature."

Scott-fox's mouth dropped open in a human expression as he looked from Tamaki to An.

The murder of ravens began to caw in a chorus that raked over Tamaki's raw nerves.

An's eyes swirled faster and faster. The leafless branches of the clearing rattled against one another with a sickening scraping sound. Power gathered around the god. Tamaki cowered, arms wrapped protectively around the pouch holding Saki while Scott-fox tried to stumble away, ears pressed back. Then An opened his mouth wider and wider as if to swallow them. His hands moved forward, fingers spread, pushing through the air. Tamaki tried to brace herself, but couldn't even scream when the wind hit.

FOUR

Helpless in An's breath, Tamaki rocketed through the air, scenery passing in a blur as she flew backward over the clearing, feet kicking through the uppermost branches of the forest. The wind lifted her higher and higher until she continued over the Appalachian Mountains. She gasped and choked, struggling against the wind like it was a living thing. A moment later, her arms and legs jerked like a puppet as current raced through her body. That must be the edge of An's territory. He was following through with his promise of exile. To her right, she could see Scott-fox tumbling head over legs in the wind.

She twisted in the wind's grip, eyes tearing in physical reaction from the speed of the air, clothing, and hair whipping against her skin. Pressure squeezed her body so it felt like her bones were forced inwards. Below, a wide river that might have been the Mississippi or might be some new, unnamed feature in the post-firestorm landscape curved around what looked like a desert. It was an abrupt shift from the mountains and greenery of An's territory, but Tamaki had no idea which god controlled this one.

An's breath tapered off. Gravity took over and her momentum slowed. Abruptly, Tamaki plummeted. Her stomach dropped like she was on a roller coaster. Tamaki flapped her arms, but the ground rushed up. After everything, they were going to die anyway. Panic set in.

Tamaki ripped off the bandage on her leg and dug her fingers into the wound from the plant's barb. She pushed her index finger into the meat of her calf, hooking and pulling at muscle. Pain burned; blood thundered in her ears.

Then a rush of power filled her chest. She recognized it this time, the sour under the sweet, but she embraced it.

"I want to live," she cried. Then she gave herself over to the *etemmu*, relished the tingling all over her body. She absorbed the rush like a shot of espresso, a drug to her system. She was confident, eager to see what would happen. Struggling to keep her eyes open against the force of falling, Tamaki spotted Scott-fox. His eyes rolled in terror and his tail was tucked against his body, although the wind pulled at his red fur.

"I want him to live, too."

Tamaki instinctively knew what to do as time slowed down. She felt pressure at the front of her head and then power pushed through her third eye as she mentally threw a line of *etemmu* to Scott, or into him, she didn't know. She imagined the line becoming a vine-like in the forest, thick and strong, as it connected the two of them. She made the vine expand into the form of a parachute, dragging against the air, slowing them down.

More digging and squeezing into the flesh of her calf. More blood. Crap, the ground was coming so fast. This wasn't going to work. She needed more blood. She scraped her fingernails against her bare chest, skin curling up under her nails. The blood fed the *etemmu* parachute, expanded the umbrella shape, but there was no more time. Against her will, Tamaki's eyes fluttered closed. She fought to stay conscious.

Tamaki hit hard, right hand bending backward with an audible snap, as her body rolled over and over, skin scoured off, hips bruising, knees banging. Sand filled her mouth and lungs when she tried to breathe. Moaning, Tamaki tried to spit from a dry mouth. Pain flared everywhere. Like a car accident, but she hadn't had the protection of a vehicle.

On her back, Tamaki coughed, ribs spasming and stared up. The landscape was flat and dry, rocks of all sizes the only embellishment, thrown like a child tossing a handful of marbles. The same bile yellow clouds covered the sun here as in An's territory. There was a smell – something herbal and musty – under the dust, but Tamaki didn't recognize it.

She coughed again. It hurt so bad she wanted to give up, but she wouldn't give An the satisfaction. Her right hand pulsed, already swelling from the break. She used her left hand to push to a seated position against a nearby boulder. Without water, they'd soon die in this place, wherever it was.

"Scott?" Her voice came out like a whisper, the dust coating her words. She had a sense of being connected to the fox but didn't see him as she looked to the left and the right. "Where are you?"

Then she glanced at her broken wrist and felt nauseous. The bone wasn't poking through her skin, but there was a bump that shouldn't be there and the entire area was swelling. Tamaki's capri pants had been shredded during the fall. Using her left hand, she ripped off a long stretch of cloth. She tucked the end between her thumb and palm and wrapped it around her wrist. It would do for the moment.

Leaning her head against the rock, Tamaki patted Saki through the padded material of the pouch. "Hi, Mama."

She heard a soft chirp before her palm hit something sharp. One-handed, she struggled to unzip the pouch. Leaning to the side, Tamaki used her teeth and left hand to pull it open. When she reached inside, Tamaki felt Saki's smooth shell. Then she felt the crack.

"No." She eased out the turtle-penguin. The cracked shell revealed a cracked spine. Dark blood smeared across the creature's belly and flippers. "Oh, Saki, my beautiful girl."

Saki tried to nuzzle Tamaki's fingers, but her head fell to the side. She chirped once and then her eyes stared blankly into the distance.

Another death.

An will pay for this. He will pay. Deity or not, he will regret this.

Fury blazed through Tamaki. She kissed Saki's face. She murmured and cooed, but Saki didn't answer. Instead, there was a faint tingle. A possibility.

Tamaki's hand shook as she held it over Saki's body. It would be so easy to bridge the short distance and dip her fingers into Saki's blood, pulling the *etemmu* out. The wish shocked her. Still, her mind kept working. If she did, the power might heal her injuries. Her wrist was broken and maybe a rib or two. With a little help, she'd be in a better position to survive this desert.

"No." Tamaki clenched her shaking hand into a fist and dismissed the idea. She sat up straight, disgusted by herself. Addiction: the dark side of blood magic. She wasn't going to do it again.

This was An's fault. He should have helped her with Scott. Instead, he'd exiled her for using blood magic, but then put her in a position – flying through the air — where she had to use it or die. The gods, the Misbegotten, she corrected herself, had power but they were mercurial and selfish. If she had that power then she'd make sure to help the ones who deserved it. Like Scott. And her grandmother. And little Saki.

Tamaki stroked Saki's broken body and shook her head. Saki had kept her company since the moment they'd found each other. The turtle-penguin had only been the size of a donut. When Tamaki had knelt to wash her face at a stream, she'd looked up to see round black eyes staring back at her. A fuzzy head quickly drawn back inside a turtle's shell.

That was when she'd been traveling south with Obaa-chan, into the mountains, and before they ran into another group of people: Hotheads. They hadn't known that Hotheads worship the god Ashur with pain. Tamaki began to shake from the memory of being attacked. Hotheads had stolen their food and then tied them up. Saki's soft clicks from the pouch had kept Tamaki company, kept her from losing herself to terror.

Then, a few days later, when the camp was empty, Obaa-chan was able to get free from her ropes. She wasn't strong and she still had dried blood down the side of her face from being attacked, but she tried to cut Tamaki free too. She didn't see when the man with his face painted red came back.

Tamaki's shoulders slumped forward and she touched Saki's broken shell. This was the moment she replayed in her mind. If she'd lunged forward and taken the knife from Obaa-chan. If her grandmother hadn't considered life sacred. If Obaa-chan had even held up the knife as a threat instead of standing there, shocked. If the man had had any kind of soul.

The Hothead smashed Obaa-chan's face against the tree, killing her. On purpose, like it didn't even matter. Then he picked up the knife and he stabbed Tamaki in the leg. Reliving the moment made Tamaki close her eyes and bang her head against the rock behind her. Anger and guilt and rage made a swirling toxic cocktail inside of her, but she shoved it down to deal with later.

Tamaki traced the letters S-A-K-I on the shell. That was when she'd learned that pain clarified everything. Her instinct to live had roared awake. She'd lunged up, surprising the man who'd thought she was a hostage to be tortured for his amusement. She had only that moment – that surprise – because he was bigger and stronger and more experienced in violence. She'd wrenched the knife away from him while her leg poured blood and then yanked the knife across his throat. His hands wrapped around the wound and she'd fled on her injured leg with the knife clutched in her hand and Saki in the pouch across her chest.

That was the secret only Saki had known. Tamaki was a killer. And it hadn't even saved her grandmother. It hadn't saved her either because the rest of the group had tracked her down and kept her captive until she escaped later with Rachel and Adam. But it was Saki who had kept her sane all the nights she'd been tied up and taunted by the Hotheads with plans for how to use her as a sacrifice to their god.

She'd named her Saki to be funny, a little joke about a turtle and a penguin getting drunk enough to make a baby. But Saki had turned out to be the sweetest companion a girl could want.

Bad jokes made Tamaki remember Scott. She looked around again and called for the fox, but there was no answer.

Knowing she didn't have much time before the backlash from using blood magic hit, Tamaki crawled to the largest boulder of the group and dug a hole in the sand at the base of it. She placed Saki's broken body in the hole and wrote 'S' in blood on the boulder, ignoring the tingling in her index finger. Then she filled the hole and stacked smaller stones on top to mark the grave. Closing her eyes, Tamaki sang with a halting, alto's voice:

> *Rock-a-bye, Saki, in the tree top.*
> *When An's wind blows, the cradle will rock*
> *But the bough won't break and the cradle won't fall.*
> *I'll hold you close, Saki, newborn egg and all.*

"I'm going to get your egg back, Saki." She sniffed hard and used the back of her hand to wipe under her nose. "I will. And I'm going to make An regret meeting me."

At first, she thought her heart was breaking, but then the pain grew under her breastbone and Tamaki moaned.

She didn't want to feel it all again. Now she knew what it was like, how long it lasted, and she didn't want it. Tamaki panted. Invisible fire burned at her calf and worked its way up her body to join the pain in her chest. She settled back against one of the boulders and stared into the distance. "This is the last time," she muttered. "Get through this and never again. I'll be good."

Fire burned through her sinuses, through the inside of her throat and up into her head like a swarm of fire ants. She rolled in the sand, whimpering, repeating 'I'll be good' while pushing at her face to make it stop.

When the pain receded, the sun had moved across the sky and Tamaki's skin was tight with sunburn. Sand scratched inside her clothing. Her pants were wet at the crotch. She'd peed herself during the aftershock of blood magic. Every movement made her head hurt. She narrowed her eyes against the glare from the sand and touched the empty pouch across her chest.

A rough, wheezing sound came from behind one of the larger boulders, an animal's whine.

Tamaki lifted her head. "Scott?"

FIVE

Impressions of light and pain and wrongness blasted through his mind. His thoughts were not his own; he was helpless in this strange body. Then the body's nose caught a subtle smell that didn't have a name, but he, or some part of this body, recognized it. Green oval leaves with a brown seed pod flickered in his brain before disappearing. He growled in frustration and the sound was both familiar and foreign. The vibration in what must be a throat, but he hadn't chosen to make that sound, didn't think he could do it again. He was a driver in a vehicle with so many buttons and no idea what would happen if he pushed any of them. And there was another driver still in here, faint maybe, but still here.

He tried to remember, but it was like watching a filmstrip that had been cut to pieces and then spliced back together with an uncaring hand. The sound of wind chimes. A young woman's face floated by with determined brown eyes, skin like a cherry tree, and a slight curl to her lip that invited a fight as she tucked a blue streak of hair behind her ear. *Tamaki Hayashi.* The name floated up from somewhere. And then someone else. An older man who was important…but then the thought was gone.

A sound from behind a pile of rocks made his ears swivel. It was like turning up the volume on a radio. He could hear everything: little pebbles falling, the scape of skin against rock, sand shifting under something's weight. *Those are the ears.* He hadn't made the choice to swivel them. That was part of the other still inside this body, but he could learn it. It was frustrating, painstaking work, but he moved the ears. Something was coming closer. The body's head turned and so he found the eyes. The image he saw was muted compared to…how it was before…but he didn't know before.

Again, that older man's face popped into his mind and black birds flew in a circle around the man's head, cawing in reproachful symphony. *The Weatherman. I used to work for him. A god. The firestorm. I was human and then I was not and now I am this.* That was the wrongness. He'd been murdered. And Tamaki had brought him back in some type of necromancy. His released soul did not match this mortal, this dying, creature. The body's stomach seized and he coughed until a yellow sick came out. It sat on top of the sand. The sensation of his throat was still there. He learned it.

Tamaki staggered from behind the rock pile, walking toward him, the direction of the sun creating a corona of light around her. He saw the jewel in her nose and the way the blue streak in her hair caught the muted sunlight. Her clothes were shredded and she had rust-colored blood all over her fingers and under her nails. Cloth had been wrapped around her wrist and she walked as if her knees hurt. A wave of relief washed through him that she was alive. Something like an elastic band pulled them together so that each step closer brought a sense of comfort. In his memory, she was smaller and brighter and he could look down at the top of her head. Now he was looking up at her.

After reaching him, Tamaki slid to the ground next to him – his tail moved itself out of the way —and rubbed her left hand through his fur. Then she pressed her face deep into his shoulder and wrapped her arms around him. "You survived."

The body recoiled, jerking away from the encircling arms. It stepped back and lowered its head, maintaining eye contact as it bared its teeth. He fought for control.

"Did I hurt you?" Tamaki's expression was puzzled. "Did you break something in the fall?"

Wild laughter bubbled through him. The fox body had reacted on instinct, but now the filmstrip memory flapped and he saw the clearing and the blood and heard An's pronouncement of exile. Heard An's disgust as he said that Tamaki had shoved an immortal soul into a dying body.

What have you done to me? The words went from his mind to hers along the invisible elastic band between them.

Tamaki's eyes widened at the communication, but then her brows drew together as she registered the meaning.

"Are you blaming me? You have no idea what I had to go through to save you."

You didn't tell me we'd be exiled. That we'd never see Rachel and Adam again. That everything we'd been working for – a safe place for ourselves and our friends – would be taken away. His tail twitched. *You didn't ask me.*

Tamaki shook her head. "It wasn't like that." Drawing a deep breath, she explained, "I said what I wanted, but I wasn't in control and making choices so there wasn't a chance to weigh what would happen. The *etemmu*, the energy, chose what to do. I was just the conduit."

So. it's not your fault because you didn't have control over the wild etemmu? The fox ducked his head and the fur along the ridge of his spine floated up in a sign of aggression. The truth of his feelings shown in body language. *I was your experiment?*

"If you're going to blame someone," Tamaki said, voice rising, "how about the New Babylon archer who shot you or the soldiers who hanged you? How about your beloved An who would have left you a ghost in a clearing? An told me to let you go, but I couldn't." Her chest heaved with emotion. "But you're right. I didn't tell you that we'd be exiled. Because no one told me until after. And because I didn't know that using blood magic was wrong. The gods have all these rules and then they punish people and it's not fair."

The last phrase made him suddenly remember his mother standing at the island of their kitchen in the house near Acadia, peeling carrots for the weekly pot roast. He was young, kneeling on a stool pulled up to the other side to watch her. When she was finished with the carrots she'd move on to the potatoes and he'd run the carrot peels outside to the rabbit hutches. Their own form of composting. He must have been complaining, probably about something that one of his four older sisters had done, but she'd pointed the peeler at him as she leaned forward and said, "I may or may not agree with you, Scotty-boy, but life isn't fair and it isn't smooth sailing. The sooner you learn that the better, because while you're stuck on how you're a victim, you won't move forward."

How did you know how to use blood magic? He pawed at the sand. It was getting warm enough to be uncomfortable.

"I wanted to give you a body and I didn't know what else to do. My grandmother didn't exactly prepare me for this."

He blinked yellow eyes at her, but the fur didn't settle.

"I need you. I don't want to be alone." She drew her knees up to her chest and rested her chin on their tops. "Scott, please."

Don't call me that. Scott's dead. He died in the clearing.

"No, you're not dead," she said tartly. "You were a spirit, but I gave you a new body. A second chance. I fixed your murder."

But, I'm not me anymore. Or, I am, but I'm different. I was a man and now I don't know what I am.

She licked dust-dry lips. "What do you want me to call you instead?"

The fox looked over his right shoulder. Moving was becoming easier, but still not instinctual. Smells wafted on the breeze. An image of a brown rabbit floated into his mind. More of the green leaves with brown pods which he now visually recognized as licorice plants. It felt something like making the halves of his brain talk to each other or being bilingual and trying to translate. The fox part of him recognizing smells and the park ranger aspect of him recognizing images.

Scout.

"Fine, Scout," she emphasized his new name as she lifted her chin in the air. "I'll tell you all about not being good enough for my Obaa-chan. You told me your family is Irish-Catholic, right? You expect confession and repentance. Here you go."

The end of his tail flicked back and forth. He would have crossed his arms across his chest if he were human. Hell, he would have left this conversation by now if he were still human.

Tamaki dropped her chin and stared down at her lap. "My grandmother was very traditional in every way. Even to believing that our family was an unbroken line back to special priestesses who had survived the flood – like Gilgamesh's flood or Noah's flood or whatever. Yes, Asia has myths about a flood, too. But my mother didn't believe it, or sometimes she did and sometimes she didn't, and in one of the moments that she didn't believe it, she married a guy who knew nothing about our family and had his own world. He was American, he was white, he was in the Army and that was his life." She sighed as she shifted position. "Like, when you're in the military, you go where and when they tell you to. And my mom bounced between these two demanding realities: living on a military post with its language and customs and being the dutiful daughter of my grandmother with her weird traditions and stories. Eventually, my mom couldn't take it anymore – both she and my grandmother told me at various times that I wasn't a planned pregnancy — and she dropped me off at my grandmother's house. She drove away and I watched her through the window. I believed her when she said she would come back. I believed her for years."

Tamaki wrapped her arms around her neck and interlaced her fingers as if creating a privacy screen. "So, I was brought up in this little house that was basically a mausoleum. I could never bring any school friends over to see it, we never had visitors. My Obaa-chan was trying to preserve everything single-handedly and she hadn't expected to be raising a child. I was a reminder of how her daughter had broken the chain of priestesses."

Tamaki's voice was muffled. "She loved me, but I was a disappointment."

He'd grown up the baby in a large family with loud, overlapping conversations, threats of being beaten with a wooden spoon that never actualized, and lots of holidays that revolved around meals. Later, when he'd escaped with backpacking and camping, he'd appreciated the silence, but never been lonely. But that was what he heard in Tamaki's voice: intense loneliness.

She dropped her arms. "She did her duty by getting me through the Alchemists' rite, but then I guess she didn't think I was worthy or smart enough or had enough talent to continue and didn't teach me anymore." She shrugged. "Whatever. But after the firestorm when Ba'al, the golden bull, came through Ohio, Obaa-chan tried to teach me again. There wasn't enough time." She shrugged again. "I'm sorry I'm not more powerful on my own, Scout. I accidentally discovered the power of pulling *etemmu* from blood when I was fighting the carnivorous plant and I used it. I didn't realize I was necromancing."

And now you're addicted to blood magic.

"No, I'm not." She held up her hands in a 'stop' gesture. "I can see how a person could be, but the agony afterward is enough to keep me from doing it anymore. There have to be more Alchemists out there who know the right way, the way my grandmother started to teach me. If I can learn from them about how to manipulate *etemmu,* then I can make you a different body or see what options we have."

You're covered in blood. It's not all yours. His nose wrinkled, but he didn't state the accusation.

"Saki's dead." Her mouth curved into a bitter smile. "Crushed. And no, I didn't use her blood."

He and the body were in agreement. Tamaki was driven, but impetuous. She wasn't to be trusted. Perhaps her grandmother had not been cruel to withhold more lessons so much as pragmatic. He suspected that Tamaki's grandmother had seen the anger and fear in her granddaughter.

"What do we do now? We can't stay here without water." Tamaki stood up. "We should go back to An's territory and get Saki's egg. He won't be expecting us back so soon."

That's ridiculous. Who are you to challenge a god? Your power comes through blood magic, which you've professed to quit. Do you think you can enter his territory again and ask nicely for Saki's egg?

"No, but you worked for him. You told me so. Take me to his temple. I'll sneak in and get the egg back." Tamaki looked up into the desert sky, but he could hear the emotion in her voice. "Don't you understand? Saki's dead. She was my best friend."

Part of him wanted to comfort her, but the other part of him wanted to shake her.

Yes, I understand how important Saki was to you, but this idea makes no sense. I was a spy for An so believe me when I say you can't sneak into his territory. You'd never even get past the ravens. Besides, I'm sure he has more warning systems in place that I don't know about. The gods are vying for to accumulate power right now and that means they are all watching each other.

"This is good." She nodded. "Tell me everything you know."

It was hard to think through all the sensations in his head: the smells and feels, the anger that she was being so unreasonable, the inclination of a park ranger to teach. He tried to organize the random thoughts.

An is in several agreements in order to keep his territory neutral. He has a previous agreement between himself, Enlil, and Enki, but An doesn't know where Enki is and so doesn't know if he can count on that. Finding Enki was one of my tasks.

"So, An isn't as powerful as he pretends." Tamaki crossed her arms over her chest as if she'd discovered a secret. "Maybe he's not staying neutral, he's staying out of the way. It makes sense. Gods need to be worshipped, but An lives in a territory without humans."

He's not pretending to be powerful. Scout didn't know how to explain his intuition. *He is.*

"Not if he doesn't have a power source."

Scout pawed at the sand in frustration. *Some of the deities want humans to worship them and others feed off of suffering and fear.*

"And sex."

What?

"Some of them gain power through either sex with humans or rituals of worship that involve sex." Tamaki stared at the fox and lifted her eyebrows. "You're not the only one who knows things. I do too."

I'm not sure how that helps you recover an egg. His tail twitched as he tried to explain one more time. *I know you've experienced the Hotheads, and been evicted by An, but you haven't actually been in a fight with a god or tried to steal from one. There's too much you don't know. That humans don't know. My advice is to forget about returning to An's territory.*

"Breaking in will be difficult, but I don't care." An errant gust of wind caused her hair to brush across her face. Tamaki smoothed it back. "An stole from me."

Good luck. The fox rose to all fours, favoring his back paw. The wind fluffed through his fur. *You can go where you wish, but our paths separate here.*

He was human enough to recognize the way her chin trembled as she looked away.

"You know, I asked if you missed me." She pointed at him. "I wouldn't have tried to give you a body if I didn't think that you," she faltered.

What did you think? His tail twitched in agitation. Something about the wind was annoying him.

A flush spread over her cheeks. "We'd talked for hours the night before the soldiers from New Babylon arrived. And then we kissed. You told me about working for An and I told you some about what happened when I was captured by the Hotheads. I thought." She looked up at the milk-spoiled sky. "I thought, maybe, that you were falling in love with me and I was falling in love with you."

We'd only just met, Tamaki. We were still getting to know each other. He thought of his parents' marriage – the kind he wanted to have. *Relationships take time. Honesty. And trust.*

"Fine, I obviously misunderstood," she said, adjusting the empty pouch across her front. "I'm sorry, Scout. This wasn't the way it was supposed to go." Tamaki didn't look back as she set off toward the far-off mountains. Dust trailed behind her, but it didn't hide her left hand coming up to touch her face and he didn't have to rotate his ears to hear her jagged breath.

The fox used a front paw to scratch behind his ear. There was food to be caught in the desert and there was water somewhere nearby – he could smell it. He had to make a decision, though, knowing that his spirit didn't belong in this body, that the gods would consider him an abomination. He could separate flesh from spirit. That is, he could die again. If he was honest, he could have told Tamaki to kill him. She probably would have used his blood in another spectacular flash of temper. That woman definitely had confidence and courage, even if she was a poor team player. But he didn't want to die again. Maybe that was part of the human condition – always wanting another chance. Even if the situation was complicated.

Scout whined as a dull headache formed in the top of his head and he rubbed the spot against his front leg as it increased. Even if he had a new body, he could still track ley lines and study the new plants and animals. He didn't want to be dead, and he didn't want to be a fox, but here he was. He'd taken this fox's place, and he didn't want the animal's sacrifice to be thrown away. He hadn't left his post as a park ranger because he'd been spying for An and keeping an eye on Rachel and Adam, but now he was released. He could go north and find out if any of his family had survived.

The headache intensified until stars floated in his vision. Was he having a stroke? Lifting his head, Scout could see Tamaki in the distance. They were about two football fields apart and she'd stopped, dropping into a crouch as if to tie her shoe, but somehow he knew that it was a farce. She was watching him.

Their connection was stretched too thin. He flicked an ear. *We're linked.*

She took a step toward him and then another. The headache decreased.

Scout left the shade of the rock to limp toward her, his back leg aching.

"Stay there," she called. "I'll come to you." She broke into a jog.

It was a relief as the elastic band connecting them contracted.

Because of the blood magic?

"I…don't know." Tamaki rubbed the dust off her cheeks as she stood in front of him. "It could be one of the rules of using blood magic or it could be because of whatever I did while we were falling and I was trying to save your life. Again."

Their paths would not be separating. Scout dropped his head to hide the snarl, though whether it was from frustration or shame he couldn't say.

"It hurts me too," Tamaki said, her voice indignant. "But if we can find a ley line and I can find other Alchemists then I can untether us and give you a new body."

We don't have much choice. He shook his head as if to quiet voices, or instincts, inside. *But I don't like it. And I don't forgive you for performing blood magic on me or that poor fox without consent.*

"I understand." She chewed on the inside of her mouth. "I want to make this right, Scout. And then we can go our separate ways."

Isn't that a song?

She snorted. "Can we find some water now? It's so dusty."

He startled. While they'd been arguing, a huge dust cloud had advanced toward them parallel to the mountain range. A sandstorm? It was moving toward them at a quick clip. Post-firestorm, it could be anything from a ship that sailed the sands to an unfriendly god.

Tamaki followed his gaze. "Oh no. Let's get behind the rocks."

Too late.

A military truck pulled up in a choking swirl of dust and sand. Two soldiers in camo and face masks jumped out. One had an automatic weapon and the other was shorter and held what looked like a black wand.

"You've crossed the border into Enlil's territory," the soldier with the gun said. "Where are your papers?"

Tamaki frowned. "Papers?" She forced a laugh and shrugged one shoulder.

"No papers?" asked the shorter soldier with the black wand.

"About that." She took a deep breath.

"You're in violation of our border and you'll now be taken into custody. Hold out your hands for restraints."

Scout barked as the soldier reached the black wand toward her.

"What is that thing?" the first soldier asked. "Looks like a fox, but he's huge and got golden eyes." He fingered his gun and then turned toward the back of the truck.

"You aren't taking me anywhere. Not again." Tamaki dodged away from the wand and circled around the back of the soldier while Scout stepped in front.

Scout's hackles raised and he bared his teeth. Instinct was moving him and that made it simpler. His mind worked to reach out to Tamaki. *We need this truck.*

She gave a nod of acknowledgment and then slammed her fist into the soldier's kidneys.

The soldier grunted, but before he could turn around Scout had lunged forward and snapped his jaws shut on the man's hand.

Tamaki made a fist and swung at the soldier again.

Suddenly the first soldier reappeared behind Tamaki holding a bag he must have been retrieving from the jeep. He threw the bag over Tamaki's head.

Tamaki struggled, pushing herself into the man's chest, knocking her head back in an attempt to headbutt his face, but the first soldier just lifted her off the ground by her elbows.

Tamaki shrieked.

Distracted, Scout let go of the soldier's hand. The soldier used the bleeding hand to hammer Scout's head hard enough that the fox lost balance.

"Stupid bitch. I'm going to be pissing blood because of her." The soldier pushed the wand into her stomach.

Tamaki's body convulsed, her booted feet jittering against the sand. Then she slumped over and the soldier let her limp body fall to the sand.

The first soldier snorted. "Not so tough now."

He leaned over with something in his hand, but Scout placed himself in front of Tamaki's prone body and growled.

Scout's instincts told him to run, to get away from these men, but the part he controlled had to make the body stay. He had no idea what would happen to his brain if he and Tamaki were separated. More than that, though, no matter how angry he was at her, he couldn't let these men take her away. He was surprised at the protectiveness that raised up in himself toward her.

The shorter man reached out with the black wand.

Scout battled with himself as it approached.

And then electricity surged through his body and Scout felt his eyes roll back as he crumpled.

SIX

The jolting made Tamaki's teeth rattle and her bones ache with new pain. She'd been in and out of consciousness several times, fatigue winning over fear, but this time she struggled to remain awake. Coarse ropes rubbed against her ankles and hands – pressing against her broken wrist — and a blindfold covered her eyes, but the smell of gasoline and a familiar vibrating movement confirmed she was in a moving vehicle, the back or trunk because her body rolled at every turn.

"Scout" she whispered, licking lips chapped by the desert air.

I'm here.

His presence calmed her. Whatever was about to happen, she wasn't alone.

"Where's here?"

After they knocked you out with that wand, they loaded us in the truck. They said something about taking us to Ekur Temple.

The truck downshifted. They must be getting close to the destination.

"We need to escape. Can you bite this blindfold off so I can see?"

I'm in a bag.

"Are you hurt?"

My hip. It's not broken, but it hurts. He exhaled in a soft woof.

The truck stopped. Metal creaked as doors opened. Rough hands pulled her out and untied the ropes around her ankles. Tamaki hissed as feeling returned to her blood-starved feet. When the blindfold was yanked off, she blinked in the sudden light. The truck was in a large parking lot with other military vehicles in neat rows. Behind them was an unpaved road out to the desert with the dust settling from their recent passage. In the distance, a stone wall circled to the left and to the right with the road straight in between. Standing to the right, another group of refugees had been unloaded from a different military truck. Tamaki noticed with bitterness that no one in that group was tied up.

"Where are we?" She didn't expect a response so she was surprised when the soldier with the assault rifle answered.

"This is Nippur." He'd pulled off his mask to reveal he was her age, maybe, with a pale, round face. Windburned cheeks and sun-bleached hair suggested he often patrolled for refugees and the reason for his mask. "The most civilized place in the world."

"Come on, Baumann," the other soldier said. He held the bag with Scout. "Let's get her and this creature to the tollbooth so we can get paid."

Baumann gripped her upper arm and steered her toward a long rectangular set of boxes that looked like a set of toll booths that opened into a dark tent. The bottom flaps of the tent's far side fluttered in the wind, offering snippets of voices and daylight beyond this gateway. Only one box was open, indicated by a green light on top. How did they have electricity here? Baumann pushed her in line behind the other group. Tamaki craned her neck to see what was happening. A man, belly straining against the buttons of his shirt under a stained white suit jacket, stood with his hand against the gate and spoke to the soldiers. Then he reached into the tollbooth and handed the soldier several thick metal cuffs. The soldier dropped to the ground and affixed a cuff around each refugee's right leg and then walked through the tollbooth. It flickered red and then went back to green. This happened each time a member of the group walked through until it was their turn.

"Straighten up," Baumann hissed. "Mr. Wilson will determine your worth."

"What does that mean? My worth for what?" Tamaki racked her memory. Enlil was the god of wind, but there was something else too. Humans worshipped the god who embodied the value they revered the most. So, An was the original head of the Sumerian pantheon because he was a mysterious supernatural power. Later generations revered Enlil more because he was the god of commerce and products became more valuable as they created trade relationships with other countries. After that, the god Marduk had emerged as the head of the Babylonian pantheon because they prized military power and conquered other populations. The god who was most worshipped became the strongest and whatever that god embodied affected the society in a cyclical pattern. *Thank you, Obaa-chan, for making me learn that.* Now she had to figure out what that meant for this city.

They stopped in front of the man in the stained white suit. Wilson wasn't just overweight, he was huge. Pouches of flesh were fixtures under his eyes and his nose had been broken at least once. Dark hair slicked back from a face that looked Mediterranean. To distract herself, Tamaki imagined him as Uncle Pennybags, the character from the board game Monopoly.

"Let's see what we've got." Reaching into his suit pocket for a pair of glasses, Mr. Wilson frowned. She wished she could raise her hackles like Scout.

"Turn her in a circle." Mr. Wilson spoke to Baumann.

She was trapped by the soldier holding Scout's bag, Baumann, and Mr. Wilson. They stared at her, the weight of their combined gaze pressing in. All three men were larger than her and she didn't know what they wanted. Her stomach clenched as her imagination filled in possible scenarios. She'd been a victim of the Hotheads and these men looked at her the same way. She had no power in this situation.

Tamaki lunged towards Mr. Wilson to break through the circle, but he grabbed her broken wrist.

Tamaki cried out at the blinding pain as her broken bones rubbed together. Tears ran down her cheeks.

Mr. Wilson pushed her back to the center. "You're lucky that we're civilized here, girl. You gave up your rights when you illegally crossed into Enlil's territory; however, we do not stoop to sexual assault or rape."

Baumann grabbed her shoulders and spun her around. Then he poked her in the center of the back so she straightened, her chest thrust forward.

Humiliated, Tamaki pressed her lips together, angry to be so grateful that she wasn't going to assaulted. She couldn't stop shaking. *I hate you all. I hate you all.*

Steady. Scout's voice was there, but he wasn't calm either.

Mr. Wilson's fingers drifted all over, lifting her chin to turn her head from side to side, brushing against the scabs on her knees, squeezing the muscles of her arms, thighs, and calves. His touch was impersonal, but invasive. It left traces like ants crawling over her skin.

"She has blood all over her face." Mr. Wilson removed his reading glasses. "What happened?"

"We found her that way."

"Hmmm. She looks strong and no physical deformities that would hinder manual labor. And she's obviously been eating well. Not much of a looker, though." He used a fingernail to pick between his teeth and shrugged. "Smile, girl, you'll get a better contract."

Tamaki lost it. Uncaring what they would do, she lunged forward, but Baumann yanked her to the side and cuffed her ear.

We'll escape, Scout soothed. *But there's too many of them right now. Hold it together.*

"She's energetic, but has a surly disposition." Mr. Wilson wiped his forehead with the handkerchief again. "I'll have to deduct for that."

"Dammit," muttered Baumann. He squeezed her in retaliation, bruising the tender part on the inside of her arm.

The inspection complete, Mr. Wilson turned toward the tollbooth.

The other soldier cleared his throat. "We have this, too." He opened the bag enough to expose Scout.

Mr. Wilson held his glasses to his face, but didn't bother putting them on. "Ugh. Shoot it before it gives us all mange. Then make it into a fur coat."

"Is this about money?" Tamaki blurted out. The words "contract" and "deduct" and "worth" had come together in her mind. Hopefully she was guessing correctly. "Because the fox is worth more alive."

For the first time Mr. Wilson looked at her as a person. "What do you mean?"

"He's my pet."

Your pet?

"Yes," Tamaki said to Mr. Wilson, but also to the fox. "He knows commands. I'll tell him to 'stay' and to 'drink' if you offer him water."

"Why is he so large?" Mr. Wilson asked. "Is he a mutation?"

"No." Tamaki shook her head. "He's a special breed imported before the firestorms. Rangerus Scottus. They're known for intelligence and loyalty."

"We can always skin him later, if he's not worth something." The soldier tried to read Mr. Wilson's face.

"But he could be valuable." Baumann shifted his weight, a hopeful expression on his round face. "Can't bring him back to life if he's dead."

Well.

"Let's see," the first guard said, taking off his mask. Older, he had work-roughened hands and loose flesh around his jowls that accented his air of disappointment with life. He made a loop with the rope and slipped the loop over the fox's head while pulling the bag away.

Immediately Scout jerked and shook his head, growling and fighting to get loose.

"You said you could control him," Baumann said, sounding panicked.

"Calm," Tamaki cried. "You're okay." The rope must feel like a noose and Scout was reliving his death. "Stand still."

Shaking, Scout stood in front of her with his head hanging. She could see that he was fighting with himself and she prayed that he, too, could hold it together.

"Sit," she instructed in a firm tone.

His haunches sank down.

"Bark the answer to seven minus five."

He yipped twice, although he wouldn't meet her eyes.

Mr. Wilson started to turn away.

"Wait!" She racked her brain for something that would be impressive, that would improve Scout's worth in the eyes of a consumer. Then she knelt down and held out her arms straight in front of her. "Say your prayers to Enlil the generous."

Scout gave her a quizzical look and then he sat up and placed his paws on her arms and tucked his nose down so he looked like a child praying at their bed.

"Aww," Baumann said. "That's so cute. Someone will definitely bid on him."

Mr. Wilson fluttered his ringed hand in the air. "Fine. But he'll carry his own debt." He leaned into the tollbooth and returned with two metal cuffs and what looked like a scanner.

The older soldier took them and snapped the metal circle around Tamaki's ankle. It was cold, about two inches wide, and pressed tight against her skin. There was a tingle of power. She had to suppress the instinct to wrestle the cuff off, knowing it might not even be possible. The soldier snapped the other circle around Scout's neck.

Son of a —

"Don't try to remove the cuff and don't try to leave the market," Mr. Wilson said. "The cuff won't hurt as long as you remain inside, but if you try to escape… well, think about an electric fence for a pit bull. This is stronger."

Tamaki lips trembled at the injustice, but she pressed them together to hide the reaction. Poker face. They couldn't affect her unless she let them.

Both soldiers reached inside their shirts and pulled out rectangles attached to lanyards. Mr. Wilson held up the scanner and numbers flicked on the soldiers' screens.

"Thank you," they both said, but Mr. Wilson was already walking away.

"They were hardly worth all the trouble." The older soldier punched Baumann in the side. "You take them up to Ekur Temple. I'm getting lunch." He walked through the tollbooth and it flashed red.

Baumann sighed as he took Scout's leash. "Come on. I have to make a stop in the market first."

"What does the red mean?" she asked. She might as well get as much information as she could.

"It's the entrance price being charged to your collar and to my wallet."

"I mean, I don't really want to enter and you work here, so I don't understand why either of us should pay."

Baumann sighed. "Don't make me put the gag back in." He poked her in the back until she moved through the tollbooth and into a tent.

She meant to be quiet after that, but emerging from the tent, she couldn't. "Holy crap!" Her best guess was that they were somewhere in west Kentucky or Arkansas, but this looked like the entrance to a giant farm fair. Colorful tents and tables dotted the sandy landscape on either side of the unpaved road and the smell of hot dogs and fried chicken and funnel cake drifted on the wind.

"Yes," Baumann said happily. "It's magnificent, isn't it? The blessed couple is merciful."

Over the road, a large metal arch spelled out New River Market in arabesque lettering. A table nearby held clothing, arranged by size from infant to extra-large. Another table had books, some with charred edges, and kitchen items. Musicians with guitars were setting up in a pavilion down one of the uneven aisles. Pottery, artwork, and carpets were all for sale. This was a place where a person could meander for hours, enjoying the sights and smells. Tamaki sniffed. Close by, a delicious coffee aroma wafted from a tent café where people drank from mugs decorated in a blue and white floral pattern. A pastry, half-eaten, revealed red jelly insides. Tamaki's stomach growled. *The end of the world, but humans still need their caffeine and sugar.*

"How does this place exist? It's only been two months since the firestorms, but you've already rebuilt?"

"I've heard how bad it is past the border," Baumann shook his head. "Makes me grateful to be here because our god and goddess care about us. Their fires burned – that's what created the desert – but then Enlil and Ninlil stepped out of the fires surrounded by light. The most holy beings I've ever seen. All the people who survived were given a choice: leave the territory with no ill-will or stay and pledge allegiance to Enlil and Ninlil. If we stayed then we'd be full citizens of Nippur and they would show us how to become rich. No brainer."

No brainer, indeed.

"Hey, Baumann, that's a great story," she said. "But the fox and I are really thirsty."

He gave her an exasperated look.

"You said this place was really civilized." She shrugged as if to say 'those are the rules.'

"Fine. We'll stop." He held her arm as he maneuvered them down one aisle and turned down another.

Tamaki looked at the vendors and the people shopping in the bazaar. They were only a few feet away and her hands were obviously bound and she was being forced to go somewhere against her will. Wouldn't anyone speak up about how wrong this was? Case in point, one woman in a silk jumpsuit sitting at the café met her eyes and turned away, adjusting her designer sunglasses in her hair and laughing at something her companion said. No one here would help her. Abruptly the tents and tables of pottery and jewelry became a crooked labyrinth that she wouldn't be able to escape even if she could get away from Baumann.

There's too many smells. Too many people.

Tamaki looked down at Scout and walked right into Baumann's back.

"Here." They'd stopped at a cabana that might have been used for parents to sit under to watch their kids play soccer before it was repurposed as a watering hole in Enlil's grand marketplace.

"The Debtor will take a dipper," Baumann told a bored-looking teenager perched on a stool. The teen scratched at her ear and then gestured to Tamaki to bring her leg forward. The cuff beeped.

"Here." The teenager held out a metal dipper – a long-handled instrument with a cup on the end – and pointed to the barrels sitting in the shade.

"I serve myself?" Tamaki was trying to figure out what she was supposed to do when her hands were tied.

Both Baumann and the teenager sighed.

"I can dip it for you, but it'll cost more."

"No," Tamaki said quickly. "I've got it." She grabbed the handle of the barrel's top and shoved it halfway across to the point it teetered, but didn't fall, into the sand. The water inside shook a little and Tamaki wanted to plunge her entire head into the barrel and feel the chilliness all around.

Baumann stepped forward and grabbed her hands. Startled, Tamaki looked up. Could everyone read her mind? She wasn't really going to do that. Who knows how much it would cost in this place?

Scout snickered. He'd sat in the shade next to the barrel, eager for his drink.

But no, Baumann was only untying the ropes that bound her wrist. "I've seen a man try to run through the cuff," he said with a shudder. "Don't do it."

She didn't answer. Instead, she plunged the dipper into the water and then brought it up, water sluicing over the cup. She slurped the water. Nothing had ever tasted so clean and wonderful. It was over too soon. She plunged the dipper in again and then held it out to Scout.

His pink tongue flicked as he greedily drank.

"Enbu!" The teenager leaped forward and shoved Tamaki. "You get one drink per payment. You owe me."

"She's a new Debtor." Baumann raised his hands in supplication. "Charge the fox and we'll be on our way."

Scowling, the teenager aimed the scanner until Scout's collar beeped. Then she grabbed the dipper from Tamaki and muttered about needing to sanitize it because of nasty foreigners.

They were several tents away before Baumann stopped them. "You are exhausting me." He yanked on Scout's leash. "For the next stop, don't touch anything. Don't talk. Don't do anything. If you do, I will have you dragged behind the pigs."

Aren't you going to ask what that means?

She shook her head. Nope. She didn't want to know.

Baumann's errand was one row over at a fancy purple tent. They pushed aside the flap and went inside. Scout's whiskers trembled as they walked through a cloud of potent patchouli. Tamaki followed his gaze to see what had to be a four-hundred-pound pig hanging off a triangular wooden frame. A fly walked across its eye and meandered toward the snout. If the incense was to hide the rotting pig smell, it hadn't worked.

"Seer," Baumann called. "I've come with a petition."

A figure drifted from the shadows at the back of the tent dressed in gauzy white and black robes that obscured any details. "To Enlil, the god of Mighty Wind, or to Ninlil, the lady of the open field?" It was the voice of a smoker and the exposed hands were wrinkled and sported rings on four fingers, but Tamaki couldn't tell more than that.

"Ninlil."

A fire pit sat in the middle of the tent with a grate on top and the roof had a section missing so the sky was visible.

"Ah, perhaps the young man has a petition for love?"

Baumann cleared his throat.

"Is this an off-brand priest?" she whispered.

"The priests in the ziggurat are very busy," Baumann whispered back, flustered. "Seers in the market are able to accept sacrifices and make prayers on the common person's behalf."

"Huh."

"A sacrifice is typically," the seer stressed the last word, "performed in private to facilitate the communication between goddess and her supplicant."

"Don't worry, she's a Debtor." Baumann winked at Tamaki. "Who would she tell? The other Debtors at Ekur Temple?"

The juxtaposition between his carefree words and his not realizing the horror of them made Tamaki dizzy. Because he'd been acting friendly, she'd thought Baumann wasn't as bad as Mr. Wilson or the other soldier. In a way, he was worse. He thought so little of her because of the metal cuff on her leg, that she wasn't even a person.

"Fair point." The seer produced a butcher knife from the folds of their robe and approached the pig. "For love, for the attention of our lady, might I suggest the pig's private parts? A worthy offering to the virgin lady who lay by the water. Her beauty and grace attracted the god Enlil and together they conceived Nanna, the moon god."

Baumann checked the balance on his lanyard and grimaced. "Uh, no."

"Perhaps the tail of this swine?" The seer's hand hesitated near the haunches. "As punishment for impregnating Ninlil before marriage, Enlil was sent to Kur, the underworld. Ninlil bravely followed him. Enlil impregnated her while dressed as the gatekeeper for Kur and she gave birth to Nergal, god of death."

Are we getting a story about gods cosplaying to keep their romantic lives interesting?

Tamaki smiled to encourage Scout, but still felt the sting of Baumann's betrayal.

"Uh," Baumann looked down at the rectangle on his lanyard. "No. Not that either."

Impatience tinged the seer's voice now. "The heart of the beast? For the one who holds your heart? What is his or her name?"

"Jessie."

"Fine, would you like the swine's heart to offer a petition for the beautiful Jessie? A worthy sacrifice to the lady who became pregnant in a romantic rendezvous with her husband while he was dressed like the man-of-the-river while they were in Kur? To the lady who welcomed her lord when he was dressed like the man-of-the-boat? Her openness to her husband," the seer was deliberate in his word choice, "is what you are asking for, correct?"

Baumann rubbed at his chin. "What about an ear? Like for listening?"

The seer cracked their knuckles but didn't say anything, finally hacking off an ear before pulling out a scanner and shooting Baumann's lanyard.

"Here is an offering," the seer said, almost throwing the ear on the grate of the firepit. "Please accept it, Ninlil."

Guess showmanship costs extra.

Baumann stepped forward and used a match from the nearby holder to light the fire underneath.

Soon the smell of cooking meat filled the tent. Gray-tinged smoke drifted toward the open hole.

"Is it white?" Baumann squinted at the smoke. "White means the goddess is pleased."

"Sometimes," the seer said, flapping their robes, "a sacrifice demands a little more…sacrifice."

To avoid answering, Tamaki glanced at Scout and was surprised to see him making a face. The smell was making her hungry, but he didn't seem to be affected the same way. A suspicion made her blurt out, "Are you a vegetarian?"

Foxes can be omnivores.

She imagined him pouting.

"It's definitely white on that side of the plume," Baumann said with confidence.

A horn sounded from somewhere nearby, the tone impossible to ignore.

"Enbu." Baumann looked panicked. "I've got to get you to the temple. Come on." He grabbed her hand and pulled her down the aisle back to the central road and took a right turn to climb the steps to an attractive metal bridge.

"Would this be the New River of New River Market?"

"Bingo."

It was flat and wide enough for two cars to pass by. At intervals along the bridge, Ficus trees in decorative planters waved their branches in the ever-present wind. Strings of colored lights wove through the rails, each globe the size of a football. Tamaki imagined it would look beautiful and inviting if there was electricity to light them.

Scout trotted over to the side. *There's a ley line in the river. That might be our escape route.*

Tamaki set her jaw against the buzzing in her head. The little bit of water had helped, but she was so dehydrated. Scout must be the same. They were in no condition to attempt an escape, but at least they could make a plan.

Beyond the river, a path led to a massive stone structure. Like the pictures she'd seen in history books, seven terraced levels of receding stories reached toward heaven with wide stairs carved in the middle. A sand-colored structure of columns, perhaps the temple, loomed from the very top.

"What is that?"

"It's obviously a ziggurat." Baumann elbowed her hard. "Now keep quiet."

Stepping down from the bridge, Tamaki saw two large statues on the ground level of the ziggurat, positioned on either side of the stairs, so that they looked out over the water, the bridge, and New River Marketplace. Made of the same sand-colored stone as the building, she hadn't noticed them at first. A male figure seated on a throne had a beard that curled at the end and wore a horned cap on his head. Across from him was the statue of a pregnant woman in a dress, presumably his wife, with long hair sculpted to the side, as if blowing in the wind. She held a flower in her hand.

Construction scaffolding was set up along both sides of the ziggurat. Unsure where she was supposed to go, Tamaki moved toward the glass door to the right of the goddess statue.

"No, that's for Citizens," said Baumann. "I have to take you around."

Curving around to the right side of the ziggurat was a packed sand path with what looked like wheel ruts. The smell of baked earth mixed with Tamaki's armpit sweat. She wondered if this area had always been this flat.

Probably from the heat of the firestorm. If Enlil used etemmu to turn the Arkansas lowlands into desert, then the heat here at the center could have melted it.

Tamaki relaxed into his voice; having a secret friend made her feel more confident. Scrub bushes she didn't recognize dotted the ground in random splotches of olive green. Baumann stepped to the side to avoid a pile of manure on the path, thus suggesting another reason for this alternate to the front entrance: transporting heavy materials. Some little animal scampered out of one hole and disappeared down another. With a pang, Tamaki remembered Saki and then the egg.

"You're late," a familiar voice said. Mr. Wilson sat in a wagon drawn by two enormous pigs. They smelled like crap and had tiny red eyes. "Put the Debtor in the wagon. I should give you both a deduction."

Baumann's cheeks turned pink. "Sorry, Mr. Wilson."

"Hurry up." Wilson waved his hand. "I don't want to miss the trial."

SEVEN

Tamaki and Scout sat in the back of the wagon drawn by massive pigs and stared at Mr. Wilson's back. He didn't seem concerned about them jumping out and running away.

"Got a look at the market with Baumann, eh?" The giant man in the white suit mopped his sweaty forehead and then turned around to look at them. "Hope you didn't get any bright ideas. You're about to see what happens to Debtors who try to get away."

Rounding the corner brought them to the back of the ziggurat. This close to the building, it was immense.

My guess is 150 feet high, similar to a 14-story hotel.

Tamaki was impressed despite herself. But, from the side, it was revealed that the majestic front of the pyramid was a façade – like something on a Hollywood movie set. The building was hollow or, if not hollow, then still a work-in-progress. Only a few floors had been framed in while the space toward the top of the pyramid was still open. Workers in hard hats scurried to sort construction materials scavenged from firestorm debris. Enough work had been accomplished that Tamaki could guess that the lowest level of the ziggurat was going to be an indoor mall. Shops with glass walls were taking shape.

The group of refugees who'd walked into the market before them stood huddled together.

For all their talk about being civilized, they need cheap labor to build their city. Scout's ears pricked up and he looked back the way they'd come. A second later Tamaki heard the pounding hooves of at least two creatures.

"Out of the way," a man demanded as he and his companion rounded the corner of the ziggurat. They rode horses, wore the camo of guards, and dragged a man between them. The horses had white foam around their mouth that testified they'd been ridden hard in the heat, but they looked like pre-firestorm horses.

A closed carriage rolled up the path behind them, wheels creaking. It was pulled by a large draft horse with tufts of white cottony sheep wool growing in random patches on its body. The driver called to the horse and then jumped down to open the carriage door and hold out his hand. A white woman in a severe black judge's robe and high heels climbed down first. Her blonde hair was pulled into a fancy chignon with two rows of diamonds intertwining. Dark eyeliner, eyelash extensions, and frosted lipstick completed her look. The man stepping out behind her also looked like a soap opera star in a judge's robe. He was tall and lean, with cold blue eyes, light brown skin, and black wavy hair.

Mr. Wilson rushed forward to greet them, "Mrs. Debossey and Mr. Bremmer."

Bremmer took the lead. "We need the accuser," he said to Mr. Wilson.

"Of course." Mr. Wilson snapped his fingers to get attention, but it was unnecessary. All eyes from the construction area were already on him. Two guards, both with those wands, lined up the workers. Tamaki noticed the silver cuffs attached to each worker's left ankle. The same as on hers. The mark of a Debtor.

Feeling nauseous, Tamaki looked to Scout. This felt too similar to his death.

Wind whistled through the construction area, making the plastic material inside the ziggurat flap with an annoying rustling sound.

One of the guards dismounted and pulled the man who'd been dragged to his feet, facing the wall of judges and Mr. Wilson. "This man owes a debt of work to Nippur for the next eleven years. He ran away rather than work for a chance at citizenship."

Mr. Wilson grunted.

Tamaki wished she could hold Scout right now, that she could bury her head in his fur and not see what was about to happen.

Mr. Bremmer steepled his fingers. "It is clear according to the code of Ur-Nammu what should be done with a Debtor who chooses to run away. He shall be tested by Enlil, supreme god of destinies, and Ninlil, beautiful queen of the breeze. Under their gaze, this man shall walk." His hands came apart and he pointed to a hazardous-looking elevator on the corner of the building.

The workers, guards, and Mr. Wilson echoed, "He shall walk."

If he makes it up there.

Scout was right. The "elevator" was more like a pulley with a plywood floor and sections of railing that had been lashed together with twine.

The prisoner rallied as he was pushed toward the pulley. "This isn't right." He pleaded to the other workers, "We're stronger than them if we all come together. I want to go back to the way it was before this god arrived."

The nearest guard lunged forward with the baton and chased the man onto the pulley.

He climbed on, whimpering, with the guard beside him. Two other guards pulled on thick ropes, hoisting the pulley past the second level, past the third, past the fourth.

Tamaki whispered, "No." Jutting out from the fifth floor was a single metal beam with nothing underneath but the packed sand they all stood on. The pulley came to a stop and the prisoner inched away from the baton and out onto the beam. He lowered himself to his hands and knees. His cries drifted down on the wind to the crowd below. Tamaki shivered. The man looked over his shoulder, said something to the guard, who shook her head.

It wouldn't be weak to look away.

But Tamaki couldn't. Even though she'd seen what the Hotheads had done and the soldiers from New Babylon had done, there was a part of Tamaki that still couldn't believe that people would be so cruel. Someone would step in to save this man. She looked at the faces of the guards, the prisoners, and the judges, but no one raised an objection.

On the ground, the guards pulled on the ropes, drawing away the prisoner's only chance to return.

Mr. Wilson began the chant, "Walk, walk, walk," and it was picked up by the crowd.

The prisoner seemed to realize he had no choice. Still crying, he inched forward until he was at the end of the beam. There, in painful slow motion, he came up in a crouch and then straightened, arms extended for balance. Wind whipped at his hair and his shirt.

"Mercy," he screamed and jumped.

Tamaki clenched her hands in fists and pressed her lips together to hold back a cry. A moment before the prisoner hit, the ground shuddered. Tamaki felt a tingle as *etemmu* was engaged by someone or something. The sand slid apart with a sound like a mouth opening until there was a lightless hole in the ground. The man fell into the maw. The ground closed over him, the sand sliding back into position.

The crowd let out a collective sigh, but Tamaki couldn't move.

"Enlil has accepted his sacrifice," Bremmer said. "We are civilized."

"We are civilized," the crowd echoed back.

Mr. Wilson and Mr. Bremmer climbed into the carriage and the driver flapped the reins to carry them away. Workers returned to building the inside of Enlil's temple. Guards took up their spots.

"Bring the new Debtors over here," Mrs. Debossey said, raising her hand like a tour guide. The refugee group shuffled forward. Tamaki, though, stood with her fists clenched. Each day in this world of gods revealed a new horror. Scout pressed against her leg.

"You too," Mrs. Debossey called with the hint of a Southern accent and a wide smile.

A nearby guard pressed the baton into Tamaki's side and leaned in close to whisper. "Maybe you need to walk."

"I'm an American citizen." Tamaki's anger gave way to fear. "I didn't do anything."

"Shut your mouth, immigrant," he whispered. "There is no America and you are nothing more than a Debtor."

Tamaki pulled away to look at the man's sneering face and pictured smashing her fist into it, but Mrs. Debossey called again. The guard pushed Tamaki forward until she stood right in front of the woman.

"Now Debtors, I'm sorry you had to see The Maw on your first day." Debossey gave an exaggerated frown. "Sometimes gods need to remind us of their power."

Yeah, right. The powers – human and god — want everyone scared. That's how their system works.

"And you are an important part of Nippur. Our great city has decided that we will allow illegal immigrants to work off their debt. Under the guidance of the generous Citizens willing to take you in, train you, and give you the dignity of working, you will, perhaps one day, be allowed to apply for citizenship. Such is the benevolence of Enlil." She placed her palms together and bowed to the ziggurat.

"Our first step to matching each Debtor with a contract is an interview to assess your skills and strengths." Debossey made a point of looking over the group. "My first interview will be with…" she locked gazes with Tamaki, "this young woman. Bring her to my office tomorrow morning after she's been cleared."

Cleared for what?

"No idea," she murmured to Scout. Then she raised her voice, "The fox stays with me. We're a package deal."

Debossey frowned delicately as she studied Scout. Then she smiled. "What a fine specimen. I look forward to hearing more of the story about this strange 'package deal'." Waving like a beauty queen, Debossey turned away and entered the ziggurat.

The guard jabbed her with the stick again and Tamaki gritted her teeth, but the experience of seeing The Maw kept her silent.

"Come on," the guard said. "Workers are housed on the third floor until auction."

Her gaze shifted to the pulley. "On that?"

"Yup."

I'm with you.

Tamaki nodded.

The guard took Scout's leash and escorted them up. The plywood felt like it would crack underneath their weight and the whole contraption swayed back and forth with each tug of the rope.

"Why," she asked as a distraction from the swaying, "am I considered a 'Debtor'? Why can't I get a job here without all the stigma?"

"Because," said the guard, tightening his hand on Scout's leash. "We've gotten our economy working, our electricity from the windmills, and you illegals break into our territory, steal our products, and attack our citizens."

Typical us-versus-them politics.

Tamaki scoffed. "I was nowhere near this city when we were picked up."

"You were on the way," he said with conviction. "There are limited resources and everybody wants ours. We have to take care of our own."

"Look, there are no signs telling people not to enter this territory so I didn't even know. I have no interest in Nippur." She pressed, "Take off the cuff and I'll run through the tollbooth and never look back."

"Stop talking," the soldier said as the pulley came to a stop. "Illegals are all liars."

Tamaki was almost relieved to have arrived until she saw what waited for them. The space was unfinished. Two guards sat at a card table set a few feet back from the edge. The rest of the space had chain-link cells set up in rows with walkways. Each cell had bottles of water, chip bags, a cot, and large foil blankets. Some had particle wood slabs attached to the chain walls between cells as a nod to privacy. The set-up reminded Tamaki of a dog kennel.

"Walk forward." The guard guided Tamaki through the middle row. She passed a teenager with a sleeve tattoo drawn on his dark skin and a girl who could be his sister or friend sitting with their backs against the chain-link, heads together, whispering. Across the walkway an older white woman in an oversized t-shirt, slacks, and bare feet paced her enclosure, muttering to herself. A white man in a stained undershirt did push-ups over and over in his cell. A sniffling sound came from the next cell on Tamaki's side. A mother in a hijab, pink under dirt stains, sat on the floor comforting a young boy. The cell beyond was empty.

Muscles tensed, Tamaki wanted to run. They were going to put her in there. She pulled away from the guard's grip and pivoted on her back heel.

Thrusting her shoulders forward, Tamaki tried to linebacker her way back to the pulley, but within two steps the guard grabbed the back of her shirt and spun her around, shoving her right through the doorway of the cell. She cradled her broken wrist to protect it.

"Try that again and I'll knock you out." The guard touched the baton at his waist. "Now, you'll take off your shoes real slow. And hand me that pouch thing."

Narrowing his eyes, the guard held the black wand while she untied her boots.

"This is mine," she said, holding onto Saki's pouch. It was the only thing she'd been able to keep since leaving home. It was the only thing she had to remind her of Saki. It hurt enough to make her say, "Please. There's nothing in there. Just memories."

"Not anymore. Belongs to Nippur."

Let it go.

Tamaki clenched her jaw and struggled not to fight as the guard took it away.

Then the guard looked down at Scout.

"Oy, we let animals in here now?" The voice came from across the walkway. The man had finally finished his workout. His skin was leather from countless sunburns and he shrugged into a vest with chains, his gray hair nearly matching the metal. He spit into the walkway. "If we were outside, I'd shoot that critter and cut his pretty little fur off."

"Looks like he isn't the first animal in here," Tamaki said, narrowing her eyes and staring until the man turned away, muttering. To the guard, she said, "The fox stays with me. Mrs. Debossey agreed that I have to take care of him." Tamaki swallowed past the pain of losing Saki, the anger at being made a Debtor, and housed in a cell. "And, Mr. Wilson said he was valuable."

Unsure, the guard looked at the other guards playing cards at the table and then gave a little shrug before untying the rope leash.

The metal clanged as the guard locked the gate.

EIGHT

Tamaki wiggled her bare feet against the brick floor, the rough texture catching at her skin. Scout walked to a corner and curled up, nose to tail. His eyes closed, but his ears swiveled, listening. Exhausted, Tamaki wanted to hide too and give in to a good angry cry, but the wire fence provided no privacy. She wouldn't give the guards the satisfaction or look weak in front of the other prisoners. At the thought of privacy, she whipped her head around the enclosure. They couldn't expect prisoners to use some type of pot. They wouldn't. Being helpless made her angry again, but it was a tired anger, a feeling that this was all too much and that anything she felt or said or did wouldn't matter. If she fought back, they'd make her walk the beam and fall into the maw like that poor man outside.

She grabbed the fence, threading fingers through the chain-link, and stared at the guards playing cards.

"Hey," she called. "Where's the bathroom?"

"Bathroom break is after dinner," a guard said. "We're not uncivilized."

"Now shut up or you'll get it," another guard said, lifting the black wand. He set it down on the table and played a card. The other guard took a long drink from a thermos.

Depends on your definition of civilized. The fox walked around the cage, sniffing here and there.

Tamaki slid down the fence, burying her face against her knees. Everything hurt: her broken wrist, her body from rolling around in the back of the truck, the scabs over her ankles, knees, and wrists. And she was dead thirsty.

Suddenly remembering what she'd seen earlier, Tamaki looked up. There was a row of three bottles of water standing by the folded foil blanket. She sprinted over, twisted the cap off, pressed her lips to the plastic, and chugged. Then she twisted the cap off the second one and looked around, finally pulling the blanket over with one hand and making a cup shape. She poured the water in and held the blanket for the fox to drink. Still thirsty, she looked at the third bottle but decided they should leave it for later.

Thank you. Scout's voice sounded relieved, even though he hadn't complained.

"You're welcome," she murmured, settling back against the fence and hiding her face in her knees.

A child's voice said, "You shouldn't have done that."

Tamaki lifted her head and saw the little boy in the next cell standing inches away, separated by their shared chain-link wall. His hair was going every which way and he had marks in the dirt on his cheek as if his mother had tried to clean his face, but his eyes were alight with curiosity.

"Why not?"

"Each bottle costs you another month of work. My mom says it's a scam." He studied her. "Eww. How come you have blood all over your face?"

Tamaki rubbed her left hand against her cheek and flecks of rust scattered: war paint falling off. She lowered her face back to her knees and hoped the kid would go away.

"Amil," the mother said, sounding embarrassed. "That's not good manners."

"Sorry." He didn't sound sorry. "Is that your fox?"

How was it that children could always cut straight to the heart of something?

She felt a tapping on her knee as the boy reached a finger through the chain-link fence. "Excuse me, did you hear me? Why do you have a fox?"

Tamaki gave up ignoring Amil and lifted her head. "We're traveling together."

"May I pet him? What's his name?"

"Let's ask him."

Amil rocked on the balls of his feet, excitement building about interacting with an animal, and once again the pain of Saki's loss ripped through her.

She cleared her throat. "Mr. Fox, may Amil pet you?"

Scout flicked an ear and opened his golden eyes. After studying the boy, he said, *I suppose.* He got to his feet and walked over in a smooth, gliding way that made him look less sore than she felt. *Tell him that red foxes can run, jump, and swim. They adapt well to diverse habitats and have an average life span of two to four years.*

She dutifully reported those facts while the boy pushed his whole hand through the hole in the fence so he could stroke the fox from shoulder to hip.

Amil pursed his lips. "Oh, well, how old is he now?"

Twenty-eight, she thought. "I'm not sure."

I'm done now. Scott-fox moved away and stretched his hips into the air. A fox performing a downward-facing-dog yoga pose. Rachel would have loved it. Another pang of loss. Where were Rachel and Adam now? She bet they'd made it to Baltimore and were safely in the hospital.

Amil's eyes followed Scott-fox.

"Alright, the fox says that's enough petting for now."

"You mean because he walked away?"

"Um. Yes." She watched Scout's ears flick as he listened. "That's generally how animals communicate."

"I've never had a pet."

Amil's mother leaned forward from her seat on the cot. "Is he bothering you with all these questions?"

Tamaki shook my head. "He's good." To Amil, she said, "I lived with my grandmother and she was allergic to cats and dogs, but I had a pet hedgehog for a while. His name was Sonic and he wasn't very friendly, but I still liked him."

Amil wrinkled his nose. "What's a hedgehog? Is that one of the new animals?"

Tamaki laughed. "It looks like a quirky little thing, but, no, hedgehogs are pre-firestorm." She touched her stomach, where the black pouch would normally hang. "My first real pet was a turtle-penguin."

His eyes lit up again. "What is that!"

"She had a turtle shell and a soft grey head and black eyes that told me when I was petting her just right." Her voice grew weak. "And I loved her very much."

"But now she's dead?"

Tamaki nodded.

"I had a sister. I loved her very much. She's dead now, too." Amil moved to sit so their bodies pressed against the chain-link. "Do you want to hold hands?"

They sat holding hands until Tamaki fell asleep.

* * *

Amil's mother woke them both when she came over. "Dinner is here."

Tamaki's stomach growled as she watched the guards moving down the line with the trays. Much like on an airplane, trays were stacked in a cooler and one guard unlocked the door, holding the baton as a warning, and the other handed in a tray and water. "Back up or you won't get anything."

"We get two."

The guard frowned. "I don't think so."

"I pay for my meal and the fox pays for his meal. We each have a cuff."

"I'll give you two, but you can be sure that I'm going to charge you each."

Tamaki would have liked to have spit the water back in the guard's face, but she was too thirsty. Between the wind that never stopped and the arid climate, her throat was dry. She twisted the bottle in her hand, reading a pre-firestorm label claiming, "added minerals for taste." She finished half in one swallow.

Amil's mother cautioned, "Drink slowly. There's nothing more to drink until morning. Meals are already included on your account, but every time you drink one of the stocked waters it adds a month to your work obligation."

"Everything in this territory is about money."

"Shhh," Amil's mother looked around with frightened eyes. "Each of the new gods is in control of some aspect of life, but Enlil is one of the most powerful. He was in charge of the whole pantheon before Marduk of Babylon took over. That's why this temple and the whole territory are supposed to be structured like the cities in ancient Sumer."

"So that's why the people in power are judges and this temple is a mall. Civilization, according to this god, is about laws and commerce. Got it."

"I'm hungry," Amil announced.

Amil's mother gave a little wave to Tamaki and then sat with her son to eat their meal.

Tamaki put the tray for Scout on the floor and then, feeling awkward, poured his water into a bowl. "I'm sorry." Was he embarrassed to be eating like an animal? Earlier she'd been so thirsty she hadn't thought about it.

The meal was basic: a short baguette with lamb, lettuce, and tomato. A tangy sauce made of yoghurt with dill and cucumber to spread over the bread. She tried to eat slowly, but it tasted so good. Tamaki tried to remember the last time she'd eaten.

Amil watched the fox. "Is he going to eat that bread? I could help him."

"Foxes are omnivores." Of course, this one was a vegetarian. They watched as Scout put a paw on the baguette and tore off a chunk with his teeth. "And I think he likes it."

Amil sighed. "Too bad."

After that they ate in silence. She could have eaten another entire baguette, but it was enough to not be starving.

The guards made the prisoners line up to use a set of bathrooms that each contained only a toilet, a sink, and soap. When the door opened, a light came on. Whatever the mechanism, she felt grateful. And then she was angry for being grateful. This psychological warfare was insidious.

Amil's mother set the trays by the locked door. Then she came next to the shared chain-link and sank down near Tamaki with her legs bent mermaid style. She smoothed her skirt over them.

"How long have you been here?" Tamaki said.

Amil's mother pursed her lips, but then gave a helpless shrug. "How should one keep time here? The auctions are once a month so less than that."

"And the light in the bathroom." Tamaki nodded her head toward the guards' table where two table lamps created a soft glow. The cords hung over the edge of the floor, presumably plugging into something on the ground. "And that. How is there electricity here?"

She gave a sad smile. "That's one of the reasons we came here. The rumor of electricity reached us, and we found out it was true. Engineers had set up wind turbines right after Enlil arrived. The wind is constant and Nippur reaps the benefit. It makes the citizens love him."

"Ah, yeah. He's quite civilized." The guard on the pulley had said something about electricity from windmills. This would be the perfect territory for it, especially if Enlil used ley lines to transport the energy into Nippur. Tamaki cracked her knuckles. "What was the other reason for coming here?"

"Ashur became the god of our territory. Many families left to get away from the Hotheads. Have you heard of them?"

"Yes." Those who worshipped Ashur loved fire, violence and blood. They tended to have ceremonies that involved sacrificing victims, fights to the death, and mutilation while under the influence of drugs. Tamaki rubbed the scar on her thigh.

"So we left, too. My daughter–"

"Amil told me." Tamaki didn't want her to have to say it, to make it real yet again.

"Every day since the firestorm has been so scary, running from place to place. We heard that Enlil's territory was safe, that we could start a new life here if we got jobs. I would do anything to not be scared again." She shook her head. "It was so hard to get to the border. And when we did, they told us–" Amil went to his mother and rubbed her back. "They told us that we were illegals and not wanted."

Tamaki looked over at Scout. If a fox could lock his jaw, that was what was happening.

"I want to work hard, I want to build a safe place for my child, I want to be a Citizen of Nippur. How is it my fault that Ashur fell to the ground where I lived? Why couldn't someone like Inanna, the goddess of love, rule our territory? Or wise Enki?"

Every story was like this. The gods were chaos and hurt humans without a thought. They were bullies and needed to be shoved back into their celestial prison. Tamaki shook her head. "I don't know."

"I've already lost my husband and daughter. I don't want to be separated from Amil."

Silence until the teenager with the tattoo, Darnell, spoke up from the cell across the walkway. "My sister, Valerie, and I came here to get away from Ashur's thugs, too. That drug they are on, whatever it is, it's like those people don't feel pain. Have you seen what they do to their own bodies?"

Yes, she'd seen.

"They do even worse to the people they catch." Valerie shivered.

"At least they feed us here," the older white woman said. She'd stopped her constant pacing. "And we can become Citizens if we do what they say."

"Come on, Marie," Valerie scoffed. "Don't tell me you don't recognize the lies of slavery."

"It's not slavery," Marie said, her voice turning shrill. "You're only saying that because-"

"Go ahead and say it." Valerie got up and walked to the edge of the cell. "Because I'm Black? Yes, I know my history and I know this country's history. So when I see people being dehumanized and turned into," she used air quotes "'Debtors and Citizens' as a form of free labor then yeah, I use pattern recognition and call it out."

"Not everything can be free," Marie insisted. "Someone has to pay and they'll match us with a contract that suits us. We won't have to worry about a place to live or what we're going to eat. It's the same as working for a check."

"Right. And look at these luxurious surroundings while we wait." Valerie held out her arms and twirled in the cell.

"It's only been two months. Enlil and Ninlil are going to take care of this city."

"You are really deluded, you know that?" Darnell crossed his arms over his chest and shook his head. "If the deal was so good then why do they have to lock us up?"

Marie opened her mouth and then shut it, pushed to her feet, and resumed her pacing around the cage. The sound of her footsteps was covered by the white noise of a wind that never stopped.

The man with the vest who'd been doing push-ups earlier scoffed, "Y'all are a bunch of whiners. You'd never last in an actual lock-up." He wore work boots, worn jeans, and a stretched-out t-shirt under the vest. A tattoo of an AK-47 wrapped his bicep so that every time the muscle moved, the gun moved.

Darnell bristled. "Shut up, Cooter. Even your name is stupid."

"Better be glad you're hiding behind a lock," Cooter said. "After saying that to me."

One of the table lamps turned off. "That's it," one of the guards called. "No more talking until morning."

"Time for bed," Amil's mom said. They each moved into routing: the mom softly singing to Amil, Marie walking one more lap before curling up and sniffling, the teenagers stretching out with wadded up clothing as pillows. Tamaki lay on the cot and stared up, cursing the wind that blew across her like an incessant fan.

NINE

When the door's hinges squealed, Tamaki sat straight up on the cot. Her heart thumped as she took in the cell. Scout and Amil both watched a middle-aged Asian woman in a tidy business suit with a clipboard standing outside the door.

"It's your interview day," Amil whispered.

"Indeed it is, young man," the woman said. "Are you excited for Contract Day? It's only one week away." Her smile and tone of voice made it sound like a holiday.

Amil gave an uncertain smile and looked to his mother for guidance. Tamaki stood up.

"Dana Lu. I'll be your accountant today," the woman said, opening the door to the cell. "Your name?"

"Tamaki Hayashi."

"Follow me, please. We'll head down to the second floor to prepare for your interview with Mrs. Debossey."

"I'm not going on that pulley-thing again." Tamaki stood in the doorway and crossed her arms.

Dana frowned. "Of course not." Her heels tapped against the uneven floor. Tamaki and Scout walked behind. "This whole area is an embarrassment. Completely uncivilized." She sighed. "We've put in work orders, but we're on a list and it's not a priority." They walked straight past the rows of cells toward the interior of the ziggurat, but turned to the left, away from the bathrooms, and came to a set of stairs, similar to a fire escape in a hotel.

Dana pivoted at the top of the stairs to usher Tamaki down and then she made a surprised sound. "Oh. Your animal is out of the cage. And there's no leash on him." She pressed back against the wall. "Does he bite?"

"He has a Debtor's collar on and I'm not going without him." Tamaki shrugged. "Besides, he's under my voice command."

Am I, though?

Tamaki let herself smile. She cherished these secret exchanges with the fox. "Just don't try to pet him."

With another glance at Scout, Dana led the way down one flight and then exited onto the second floor of the ziggurat. Like the bottom floor, this floor was still under construction, but there were actual rooms.

"Your report says you have an injury so we'll go to the doctor first."

The office had recognizable equipment: an exam table with paper covering, scale, instruments to look in ears and listen to hearts. Bleach and some type of cleaner mixed together in an astringent odor. Overall, the room had the feeling of an emergency clinic.

The doctor, an older black woman, tucked her chin. "Do I look like a veterinarian?"

Tamaki swallowed. Something about this no-nonsense woman reminded her of Obaa-chan. "Umm. He makes me feel calm."

Scout made a coughing sound and rubbed at his nose with his paw.

"So, he's your emotional support animal?"

"Yes."

The doctor's eyes narrowed in suspicion, but then she then exhaled. "I'll allow it. Now step up on the scale."

Dana took notes during the inspection. At first, Tamaki didn't understand why the doctor called out her weight and then listened to her heart because it was her wrist that was clearly broken. Then she realized this was a physical for the purpose of whoever would buy her contract. After the physical, the doctor used a scanner on Tamaki's cuff and then signed a document on Dana's clipboard.

"Let's see your wrist now." The doctor's touch was gentle, but it hurt. "You should have been brought to me at once. The swelling must be very painful."

Surprised at the compassion, Tamaki looked toward Scout. He was sniffing around the room.

"I'm going to have to reset the bones. I won't take x-rays; instead, I'll use a nerve block. You'll be awake, but you won't feel anything. It will take up to fifteen hours to wear off, though, and I'll have to charge you for the sling and the cast." She rubbed her hands together. "That'll come close, with the pain pills for after, but won't exceed your limit."

"My limit?"

"You're not bringing in any credits, so there's an automatic limit on spending." Dana smiled. "The goal is for you to work off your debt, not be a Debtor in perpetuity. Where would the incentive be to work if you didn't have a chance to earn out? So, we must control your spending for your own good."

"What if I don't want pills?" Tamaki was intimately aware of her pain and was using it to fuel her fire. No stifling the flames.

"Nonsense," Dana said. "Even Debtors deserve medical treatment. We're civilized here."

There's that word again. I don't think it means what they think it means.

"Right." Tamaki swallowed the bitterness, her throat aching with the effort. She asked the doctor, "Would I have gotten surgery if I was a Citizen, or would you still use the nerve block?"

"I'm a doctor first. My mission will always be to help people physically and mentally to the best of my ability." The doctor leaned forward, her shirt open at the collar so a necklace with a cross on it was visible. "I've worked under various hospital administrations throughout my career. This is just one more. Do you believe me?"

Strangely enough, Tamaki did. It was a relief to see that there was still humanity left in this commerce-driven territory. She nodded.

"Good. Because this shot is going to hurt before everything goes numb. Your arm will feel like dead weight and will have no other sensation. Until it wears off, your arm could catch on fire and you wouldn't realize, so you must be careful."

Tamaki nodded again. If she couldn't feel, would blood magic still work? Maybe she could scratch her arm to pieces and then she and Scout could escape.

Don't do that.

The doctor moved around the office getting ready for the procedure; she snapped purple gloves over her hands in preparation. "Move into the chair and then your support animal can be up on the exam table. You can face him so you don't watch me work."

Scout blinked golden eyes at her.

"Please," she whispered.

From a standing position, Scout leaped gracefully from the floor to the exam table and then curled his tail around his feet. He must be finding it easier inside the fox's body.

She closed her eyes. It wouldn't matter if she shortened her life by using up her *etemmu*. Not like anyone would care.

I would care.

Crap-in-a-bottle. She'd forgotten that they had a psychic link. Hey, Foxie, that was a private thought, not a conversation.

We'll think of something else, something that won't hurt you.

Numbness spread from her shoulder down toward her fingers. Alarmed, Tamaki glanced over, saw the metal tools, and then away. Sweat broke out across her forehead and she wanted to run from the room. She needed to vomit. The room smelled horrible. She was definitely going to vomit. Distressed, she dropped her head onto the exam table and breathed through her nose.

Close your eyes. Scout nosed the back of her neck. *I won't leave you.*

***

After Tamaki's arm was in a cast and the dead-feeling limb placed in a sling, they moved on to the next store for new used clothing. At least it was clean. She chose long grey pants made with some sort of sturdy fabric, new underwear and sports bra, and a black tank top with a wheat-colored pullover with a deep V-neck. It was fun trying to dress with the cast.

"You're getting close to your financial limit," Dana cautioned with that same smile.

Tamaki shrugged. She wasn't going to pay this debt so they could charge her as much as they wanted.

"But there's enough for the shower rooms." Dana held out a token. "You'll need this for the water. Don't get the cast wet. You don't have enough credits for another one."

"Soap?" Tamaki asked "Or is that extra?"

"Included in the shower."

"Hall-le-f-ing-luyah."

"Those who choose their words get better contracts," Dana said. Her smile never wavered. Tamaki wondered if it was stenciled on like permanent make-up.

The bathroom was the nicest room she'd been in so far. The whole thing was tiled and each of the four stalls had curtains. Tamaki yanked one curtain to the side. Sure enough, shampoo and conditioners dispensers were attached to the wall near the faucet. Across from the shower stalls, a bench ran the length of the room with hooks for clothing and a stack of white towels waiting nearby.

Scout jumped up on the bench and fastidiously licked his front paw. He made a show of turning his back to the room and curling up.

"Pay attention to time." Dana took a seat on the other end of the bench. "You only get one token."

Tamaki closed the curtain and stripped, delighting as the water sluiced away the dust, dirt, and dried blood, but holding the cast out of the spray. What a pain. She rubbed the conditioner in her dark hair twice so that it slid like silk through her fingers. Too soon the water pressure dropped and she had to finish.

But when she'd used the hairdryer and was dressed in her new-to-her-clothing, Tamaki had to admit that she was feeling more optimistic than she had been.

"Last stop is the food court. It's on the bottom floor."

They went down the stairs and Tamaki took a deep breath. Here, near the front of the ziggurat, she could see through the north-facing glass doors out across the New River Bridge and, beyond it, the colorful tents of the market. Both the east and west-facing sides of the ziggurat were solid. She pivoted and saw all the way at the south-facing end of the ziggurat was the entire open side where the maw had opened and where construction materials were brought. She quickly looked away from that and concentrated on the current area. They were near the Citizens' entrance and there was a coffee shop, a bakery, the smell of fresh-baked pretzels, and a buffet behind glass offering gooey macaroni and cheese, creamed spinach, rotisserie chicken, pulled pork, and lima beans with bacon.

Her stomach growled. So did Scout's.

"Macaroni and cheese," Tamaki said. "And a plate of pulled pork with lima beans." Dana took the scanner from the salesperson and charged Tamaki's cuff and then Scout's.

They sat down at a table to eat. Tamaki set the mac'n'cheese on the floor for Scout.

"I would have thought it was the opposite." Dana sounded bemused.

"Nah. He's a vegetarian."

While Tamaki attacked the pork, Dana looked around.

"This will be incredible when it's finished. And you'll want to come here as a full Citizen to enjoy all the benefits. We'll have a sweeping marble stairway over there and full immersion baths. The more labor we have, the more quickly we can build Ekur Temple. It's incredible how much we've accomplished so quickly."

Tamaki wondered if she was supposed to smile back. She shoved another spoonful of pork and lima beans into her mouth. The sauce was tangy and the beans had a delicious texture, cooked but not mushy. Scout had finished his pasta and was walking toward the doors.

It doesn't seem too far to run from these doors to cross the bridge. Getting the cuffs off will be tricky, but after that, we can blend in to the marketplace.

Dana looked around and saw Scout. "Oh, don't worry," she said, misinterpreting Tamaki's expression. "The doors won't open without a proper lanyard so your pet can't escape. We're not open to the public yet."

"Huh." Tamaki used her spoon to point at the servers in the food court. "Then how come you have shops open?"

"They're here for special occasions like catering when the contract auction is held. Otherwise, the food may be purchased by the Debtors who work for the Temple. It doesn't make sense to allow them to walk to the market. It wouldn't be productive."

The debtors who don't get a Patron have to work for the temple and then they spend their day's wages to purchase food from the only place nearby. Scout sounded angry. *This system is evil.*

"Think of Nippur like a new company," said Dana, "and you'll be investing on, forgive me, the ground floor. That's the idea of matching you to a perfect contract."

Tamaki blew hard. She'd burned her mouth from shoveling food in too fast. "What's your angle? Do you get a commission?"

I dare you to ask her if it's a pyramid scheme.

"I believe everyone who lives in our city has a role to play." Dana pushed her seat back as she stood. "And now I'll take you to Mrs. Debossey for your interview."

They walked away from the food court. Deep in the middle of the ziggurat was a finished area. Debossey's office had an area rug, a desk with two chairs in front of it, a map on the wall, and fresh flowers in a vase. An empty coffee mug sat on the corner.

Debossey stood in the back corner hanging her judge's robe in a built-in closet. She turned around, smoothing out her A-line cream skirt over a flat stomach and adjusting the stylish long-sleeved blouse. The tips of her fingernails were a pale pink and a pretty comb held her blond hair back. Little creases around her eyes appeared when she smiled.

Scout moved into a position to study the map labeled **New Fertile Valley of Enlil and his Royal Consort Ninlil**. A smaller map in the corner was of the city itself.

Looks like Enlil and Ninlil are claiming everything from what was Iowa, part of Kansas, down through Missouri, and the City of Nippur is in Arkansas. There are two rivers on either side of the territory. I bet they are both ley lines that bring power down to Nippur and act as boundaries. The city map shows the market and the temple enclosed by two semi-circular walls that have a gap at the entrance we were brought in and behind the temple. Also, there's a building marked on a hill overlooking the market, but I can't determine the significance.

Tamaki took three steps toward the wall with the map before Debossey pointed to the chair.

"Take a seat," she said to Tamaki, moving behind the desk. "You can wait outside," she said to Dana.

As the door shut behind the Asian woman, Debossey said, "She used to be my manager. Having her under me has not gotten old."

Scout jumped into the other open chair and sat up straight, tail dangling out the space between seat and back.

At least we have an idea of where we are now.

Debossey sat down in her chair with a long sigh and flicked the coffee mug. "What I wouldn't give for delivery, right?"

"I'm sure you could arrange it," Tamaki said. "You'd just have to pay with your lanyard."

"Your humor is so delightful." Debossey laughed, revealing teeth too white to be natural.
"Oh, Dana?"

Debossey waited for the woman to come into the office and then shook the empty mug at her. "Would you be a dear and get me a refill? A little bit of cream and no sugar."

Dana's smile didn't waver as she took the mug, "Of course, Mrs. Debossey."

After the door shut again, Debossey clasped her hands and leaned forward on the desk. "Do you know why I chose to interview you first?"

Tamaki shook her head.

"Because I watched your face when the Debtor was sacrificed." Debossey stared into Tamaki's eyes. "And you weren't surprised when the ground opened."

Tamaki snorted.

"It makes me wonder if you've seen a god or two before."

Sure, she thought about saying, I had an argument with one and that's how I ended up here. Instead, Tamaki nodded.

"Ahh, it changes a person." Debossey smiled and sat back in her chair. "On the night of the summer solstice, when the gods broke free from their celestial prison, I was reborn. Before I became head prophet to Ninlil, I was like a caterpillar. I won the state beauty pageant when I was nineteen, my goal after high school graduation. I was married a year later. Had one girl and one boy. Divorced after they both went to college. Entered the corporate workforce as an account manager, but I was decades out of date. I had no friends, my colleagues didn't respect me, I had nothing to offer anyone." Debossey tapped her fingers on the arms of her chair. "I cried every night because I was so miserable." She swiveled her chair back and forth. "Like the caterpillar in the cocoon, I thought my life was ending during the firestorm. Fire raining down, the houses falling into cracks in the ground, roads destroyed. And then the most beautiful goddess came to me. She chose me. The very things that I'd wanted – a romantic love and important children – were the things that Ninlil seized from her own life." Rapturous, Debossey looked up toward the ceiling of her office. "I emerged from the firestorm as a butterfly. My life is more perfect than I ever imagined because of the bliss from my goddess."

"Huh," Tamaki said. "Beauty queen to cult leader. Maybe you should write a memoir."

"I want you to understand how much I love my goddess and this city. When I choose what clothes to wear, I'm choosing how to represent Ninlil to the Citizens. When I decide policy, I'm upholding Ninlil's vision. I am the divine messenger." Debossey propped her elbows on the desk and interlaced her fingers. "I need you to realize that I will do everything I can to prove her confidence in me."

This lady is intense.

"In that vein, do you have any special skills that might benefit Ekur Temple?"

"No." Tamaki had one primary goal: get Scout into a new body and one secondary goal: get Saki's egg back. There was no way she was trying to rise through the semi-corporate ranks of Ekur Temple.

Ease up. We still don't have a plan to get out of here.

"Lies drift on the wind differently than the truth."

"Is that an actual saying?" Tamaki taunted. "Something graffitied on an ancient wall in Sumer?"

"It's a way of saying that I was a mother for many years. No one in management understood the skills I brought to the job. They thought I was outdated because I didn't know the jargon. That I wouldn't know how to negotiate when I'd wrestled my children through learning how to dress themselves, through years of homework, through becoming independent beings." Debossey tilted her head as she made a show of looking at the paper file Dana had dropped on her desk. "I had two decades of life experience and listening to my instincts. And, Tamaki Hayashi, I don't think I'm wrong that you could have a place here."

"I don't know what you mean. Doesn't every Debtor have to work for you?"

"I mean that I think you are familiar with the gods and maybe even know how to use their power. I mean that there is a position opening up soon, but hasn't been announced yet. You're getting a head start on the announcements we'll make on Auction Day."

Ask her about the announcements. Scout's ears flicked back and forth.

"Did Ninlil tell you something?"

"Oh, yes, but I won't tell you the secrets yet." Debossey looked coy. "The important thing is that I'm offering you a chance to become my protégé. All that's required is that you look up to me with the same passion that I feel for Ninlil. In return, I'll erase your debt. You'll be a full Citizen."

"I don't do," Tamaki raised her eyebrows, "sidekick."

That is a true statement, but you're making a powerful enemy and it isn't necessary. The fox's tail twitched.

Tamaki flicked her numb arm as an answer. "I'm not going to be a victim to any gods again."

"That's a shame." Debossey pursed her lips like a disappointed parent. "It really is." Then, she shrugged. "So you'll go into the General Debtor population. As such, you have no rights and will have to compete for a contract at auction." Debossey made a show of pulling out her scanner and tagging Tamaki's cuff. "Whoa! You've accrued quite a debt."

Tamaki's lips formed the words, "at auction" as she tried to take in the meaning. The phrase had been thrown around since she arrived in Enlil's territory, but now she saw the frightening reality. Her head shook in automatic negation. *I'm not for sale. I'm a human being.*

"We'll feed you twice a day," Debossey continued, "so you'll owe a debt to the city for medical, clothing, room and board, etc. that will be added to whatever you owe your patron."

"No," she said. "No." Tamaki tried to form a logical argument, but she'd never been put in a position where she had to argue her own humanity, her own worth. She didn't know where to begin or how to say that this was all fundamentally wrong. "This system is so corrupt. How is this acceptable to the people in this city?"

"Why are you surprised? Indentured servants are the logical result of capitalism. Profit determines policy. Nippur need workers. You're working for a wage that goes to paying off a debt that you accrued." Debossey took out her purse and opened it, rooting around before she produced a tube of lip gloss and applied it. "Now, Ninlil has not whispered to me about why the beloved couple chose this site for Ekur Temple, but I have to think that it's because the people who live here were already aligned with the values of commerce. After all, Arkansas's nickname is 'The Land of Opportunity.' We aren't idealists. We know how to slaughter the pig to make bacon. And, we know the cost of creating a strong economy is to let the strong rise to the top."

Tamaki felt hatred burn inside her at the look of smugness on Debossey's face.

Because the game is rigged from the beginning. Scout chewed at his front foot, the teeth making a snapping sound. Tamaki imagined he wanted to punch something.

"No one in Nippur is upset because Enlil declared that everyone originally here was a full Citizen. In ancient Sumer, kings would send bands of men out to acquire war captives to support the demand for help in agriculture, industry, and the households of the wealthy. We're doing the same thing." Debossey slid open a drawer and removed a red folder with questionnaires. "Normally at this part of the interview I'd ask if you have a high school diploma and about your last job experience, but I think I know everything about you that I need to."

Tamaki tilted her chin up.

Debossey leaned back in her chair. "Welcome to Nippur, Tamaki Hayashi. You're going to find out just how civilized we can be. I would be lying if I said I wasn't looking forward to it."

TEN

Tamaki lay on her cot and poked at the skin above the cast. She watched her finger press down. She could feel sensation from the finger doing the pressing, but there was no other reaction. "What did we learn today?"

This place sucks. It's a garbage trap and it's been deliberately set up that way by the leaders of the city. And all these refugees are screwed. What kind of person would separate that mother and child over there or that brother and sister? Scout bared his teeth. *Family and friends are all we have left in this world and the government here has chosen to mock that by having this system of payment and debt.*

"We should leave." Tamaki rolled over and had to manually position the arm. "But, we're locked in a cell, have to get past armed guards, and we're stuck three stories up with no way down but a) a pulley that holds two people at the most or b) stairs that take us deeper into the ziggurat. And, we'll be god-food if we mess up."

We need a map. I can slip through the space where the door meets the chain-link of our cell. Once we understand this place, this temple and city, we can make an escape plan.

"Okay, I like it." Tamaki looked in the next cell over where Amil's mother had wrapped her arms around her son, a protection against the cruel world. It reminded her of Rachel and Adam. Tamaki picked at a large scab above her ankle, watched as a drop of blood formed through the break, hovered at the surface, and then rolled down her instep. "It'll have to be before the contract auction, though."

Why? It might be easier once we're in a private residence and not within the temple where the gods could intervene.

"Because our plan has changed. We're still going to get you a new body. And I'm still going to figure out a way to get Saki's egg, but we have a more pressing obstacle." She wiped the blood droplet with her index finger, reabsorbing the *etemmu*. "I didn't want the plan to change, but the people here – Debossey, Wilson, that guard over there who always sneers when he says 'Debtors' — have left us no choice." She enjoyed the tingle that swept from her finger to her belly button. "You know what we're going to do?"

Break everyone out of here?

"Yup." She had a hundred reasons why they needed to rescue everyone here ranging from showing that the gods were not omnipotent to keeping Amir with his mother to causing Debossey to have a panic attack, but she didn't say any of them. She wanted Scout's honest reaction, not what she could convince him to do.

I'll sneak out tonight after the guards do their check.

"Who are you talking to?" Amir gripped the chain-link and pressed his face close so that his flesh squished. "Your fox?"

"Uh, yeah." Tamaki swung her legs around to sit up on the cot. "You look ridiculous."

"I know you do, but what am I?"

"I knew this boy, Adam." Tamaki snorted. "I think you two would have gotten along."

I hope Rachel and Adam are safe.

"Wanna play 'rock, scissors, paper'?" Amil clasped his hands and opened his eyes wide.

"Sure. But I'm not taking it easy on you because you're a kid."

Scout yawned as he curled into a donut shape on the cot with his head buried in his tail.

"He's so lazy, isn't he?" she asked Amir.

Vulpes Vulpes, he told her, *sleep at least ten hours a day while in captivity. I am in*

captivity. Thus, I sleep. He twitched his whiskers and shut his golden eyes.

Amil switched to the 'abc' game where one chose a topic and each had to go back and forth naming objects in alphabetical order, and then 'I Spy.' It was amazing that while the adults couldn't seem to shake the emotional toll of being locked up, Amil adapted with games and jokes.

When Tamaki had won three games of Tic-Tac-Toe in a row, Amil glared and said, "Enbu."

His mother gasped. "Don't say that."

The boy winked at Tamaki. When his mother was distracted, he leaned closer. "The guards say it all the time. Wanna know what it means?"

Feeling like a conspirator, Tamaki nodded and leaned close so he could whisper. "That hole out there? The one that opens up and eats people? What if it isn't Enlil's mouth?"

Tamaki stared at the boy. "Enlil's butthole. Enbu." A sacrilegious laugh escaped her. "Oh, man, that's disturbing." She shook her head. "And I'm going to use it every chance I get."

Finally, it was dinner time. Tamaki didn't have a watch, but she felt the energy along with the row change. She saw the Debtors who'd been in cells the longest start pacing, calling out guesses about what they would have to eat. She saw Amil lick his lips several times, salivating in Pavlovian response. But then she saw Amil's mother, grateful because another day in the cell was another day she had with her son.

The gods are horrible, she thought. They have no right to be in charge of anything because they don't care. The victims of their injustice are all innocent: Obaa-chan, Saki, Adam's wound from corrupted *etemmu*, the fox and Scott knotted together with blood magic, Amil and his mother.

After the trip to the bathroom, the Debtors moved toward their cots, quieting down without being told. Tamaki paced the cell feeling like a teenager planning to sneak out for a romantic rendezvous. Her arm hung heavy in the sling around her neck.

"Wait," she whispered to Scout. "You can go after a guard makes rounds." Once Scout slipped out, Tamaki would crumple the blanket to make it seem like the fox was curled up with her.

I don't want to wait. He swished his tail. *Red foxes have a reputation for intelligence and cunning.*

"You weren't exactly born a fox in the traditional way," she whispered.

One of the guards threw his cards down in disgust and stood, grabbing a lantern. Tamaki and Scout dashed for the cot and shut their eyes.

When the guard's footsteps passed by a second time, Tamaki opened one eye to watch him sit back down at the card table. One of the other guards laughed and began dealing a new hand.

"Be careful," she whispered. She didn't hear him leave; instead, her attention was on the guards. They didn't seem to notice anything was wrong.

Then, a faint voice in her head: *I'm taking the stairs by the bathroom down to the second floor.*

She felt the tugging in her mind, the headache that indicated he was getter farther away.

I went away from the shops where Dana took us. Ah. This is where the Debtors working construction stay. I'm looking into a room, not much to see. A cot like ours and a cheap nightstand. Oops, had to duck away before the woman saw me. I'm going back to the stairs. Huh. The ground floor is a mess of construction plastic, tools, and places to hide.

She felt and heard his interest, wished she could ask questions, but his voice in her head grew too faint for her to hear. The pain she'd felt in the desert came back, a headache marching through her skull that darkened her vision, her own breathing becoming a noise that she wanted to escape from. Tamaki bit at the skin around her fingernails, anything to distract from the moment. Her stomach turned. She lay on the foil blanket and sucked in air through her mouth, trying not to vomit.

Then the pain was bearable, receding with each breath, pressure rolling away like a boulder from her head.

Guess I went too far. Scout crept through the bars, body close to the ground, his golden eyes half-shut as he recovered from his own ache.

Tamaki took a deep, shuddering breath. "You think?" she whispered.

I went to the front of the temple. The bridge to New River Market was lit with colored lights. At the back—

"The place with the judges and the maw–"

Yes, the place below us. There are three statues the height of a tall human, but they aren't carved. Instead, they are a collection of piled boulders in the semblance of a body with long arms and short legs. Undersized wings on the back.

"They sound like gargoyles."

They aren't on the temple. They're in a row beyond the maw where the desert takes over, each facing a different direction.

Tamaki shrugged. "Great. A new horror to worry about."

I need to be able to go across the bridge. That's where the people are. We need to find out what the people in power – Mrs. Debossey, the man in a judge's robe, and Mr. Wilson – have planned and we need to find out where the contract auction takes place.

"We need a knife."

Scout tilted his head. *We're going to find another way.*

She gave a half-laugh. "There is no other way. Tomorrow night you'll have to go back down to the construction site and get a blade, a tool, something with a sharp edge. Then I'll slice off pieces of myself until we are free."

Don't say that.

"Why?" She raised her eyebrows. "I'm being serious. Why is using blood magic wrong if it's my own life force? It's my business if I choose to use years off the end of my life in the now to make my shorter life better."

Scout sighed. *I'm going to say it's probably two things. The first is more spiritual. If you believe, like I do, that a Creator made each human being, like crafted each of us, then by spending your life energy, you are shortening your life span and altering the Divine plan. Kind of like the argument that marijuana isn't really bad, but when you become dependent and would rather be high than anything else…then you lose time. You lose experiences. You lose being with the people you love and deepening those relationships.*

"That's definitely philosophical. What's the other reason?"

Because the obvious way around the pain of self-injury and giving up years off your own life is to use someone else's blood. Blood magic becomes a system of hurting or killing other people for power. Maybe that's where the idea of a vampire came from, right?

That put a new spin on using blood magic. Tamaki shivered. "Maybe."

From the front, a guard lifted the lantern and called back, "Quiet or we'll throw you into the god's maw."

They waited until the guards turned back to their game.

"There is no other way," she whispered again. "If I don't use the strongest power I have, then we aren't going to make it out of here."

You have power without using blood magic. Practice during the day. I believe in you.

"It works best on plants." She sighed. "But I have to be relaxed and I can't do that when I'm fighting for my life." She motioned in the air with her unbroken arm. "For our lives."

Let it come naturally, the right way.

"We don't have time." Tamaki cracked her knuckles.

Don't do that. You're going to get arthritis.

"Not true." She sighed and shifted position on the blanket. "Look, I wanted to learn parkour, but that didn't work out, so I ran in high school. Cross-country in the fall, track in the spring. It was an excuse to stay away from Obaa-chan's house. Coaches never thought I was anything special. And I didn't like it, but I got fast because I pushed myself every practice. I puked when I crossed the finish line, sometimes during the race. I hated when I was running, but I liked having run. Does that make sense? The accomplishment is worth it.

"I have ability with *etemmu* because of my mother and grandmother and my ancestors, but it's me, my perseverance that makes me special. I don't have time to baby my plant power, but I do have the willpower to grind through blood magic."

Coaches didn't think you were special? Scout sat down in front of Tamaki and lowered his head until he was staring in her face. His whiskers tickled. *In high school I was a C-student with ADHD who couldn't sit still and always had a hundred different thoughts shooting through my mind. When teachers started talking, I tried to listen, but it was like my mind would grab onto something I thought was interesting and suddenly the teacher had stopped talking and I'd missed everything she'd said. Being a park ranger was perfect for me. I didn't grind, I didn't push it. I relaxed into it and loved that every day was different, that the routine was loose. I think if you'd let yourself enjoy using etemmu, it would be better.*

Irritated, Tamaki brushed her hair behind her ear. "I know you're trying to help, but you don't know how to manipulate *etemmu* at all."

Scout tilted his head. *No, I don't specifically know, but I do know burnout.* He pushed closer until his nose rested on her stomach. *We've got to keep going, Tamaki. We'll get out of here and then we'll find a ley line and get rid of this psychic bond. As long as we stay in the game, there will be changes, and something, somehow, has to break our way.*

Only if we make it break our way, Tamaki thought. "Want me to scratch behind your ears or is that weird?"

Umm. I guess… oh, yes. Right there. That feels good. He gave a sigh and closed his eyes. *This doesn't change anything. We're still splitting up as soon as this psychic bond is gone.*

"I know." Tamaki stared at the ceiling as she scratched behind each of his ears. Worn out from the pain of the headache, she didn't let herself feel the resentment, the dissatisfaction, the bitterness of her position. Instead, she stayed away from any thoughts of the past or any worries about the future. She existed in the now. A gradual tingling in her fingers and hands made her look down. Her growing hands had activated. There were no plants nearby, but she could see a golden glow like a rope surrounding Scout and herself.

Excited, Tamaki brought her hands together and folded them. Then she stretched her hands apart. The *etemmu* rope grew longer and thinner. If she could do this again, then maybe Scout could go farther away before the headache became unbearable.

Told you so. Scout's eyes were still closed, but he flicked an ear.

ELEVEN

Scout stretched his legs out in front and lengthened his spine before giving a shake. He was more comfortable in this body now, had become familiar with how to move it. There was an uneasy alliance between the human and the fox living within him. He'd enjoyed spying for An, making the maps of ley lines and knowing that his information was helping keep the territory safe. This was even more important because if he could secure the right information then he and Tamaki could free the other Debtors as well as themselves and then they could find a ley line and he would be free. Maybe staying in this fox body wouldn't be so bad as long as he could go wherever he wanted.

Are you ready?

Tamaki nodded and took a seat on the cot, folding her legs and pulling a blanket around her shoulders. She'd lost weight in the week they'd been in the cell, but she did a routine of exercises as soon as she woke in the morning and again before she went to sleep in an effort to stay both physically and mentally strong. He admired her dedication even as he understood it was a coping method.

He felt the nudge of awareness of her fear of him being caught and killed, her fear of being thrown in the maw, and then the energy changed. If he were to describe it, he would say that she sank beneath the fear into calmness. He reminded himself that she was only nineteen, almost a decade younger than he was.

Eyes shut, Tamaki reached her hands in front of her, pulling her hands apart like pulling taffy. "Go," she whispered.

Scout flowed through the gap in the fence like a silk scarf in the wind, his tail flicking at the end of the motion. He moved through the shadows, his paws not making a sound as he passed the cells, the people inside oblivious. No headache yet. He went down the stairs to the ground floor of the ziggurat and trotted away from Debossey's office, through construction tarps, and toward the open back of the building that looked out over the maw. Cool night air made him lift his snout to catch smells: campfire smoke, machine oil, a horse's droppings.

Stars shone overhead in a navy sky. The waxing moon clearly illuminated the hulking stone figures Scout had seen the night before. Tamaki had been right, they looked like large gargoyles and they smelled like a mix of sand and *etemmu*. He wished he knew their purpose, but he could guess they were some type of guardians. Before the firestorm they might have been decorative or symbolic, but not now.

He trotted down the delivery ramp that curved around the ziggurat until he came to the front. Still no headache, but when he reached for Tamaki she felt faint, as if they were still attached, but he could no longer read her thoughts and feelings. Confident that he would know if she was being hurt, he continued over the bridge to the marketplace.

Suddenly, she was back in his head, clear and strong.

How did you do that?

"I had to switch how I was thinking. At first, I was trying to pull us apart, and then I had to pull myself down the rope to you, and now I can see through your body's eyes." There was a shuffling sensation and then Tamaki said, "So *etemmu* is lifeforce and every human and every creature has it. But deities have more. Why? Were they born with it? Or is it a knowledge thing? What is it that the gods want?"

I don't know. He stepped down off the bridge. *Does your seeing through my eyes mean your body is vulnerable?*

"It's locked in a cell. What could go wrong?"

He knew the effort it cost her to make that joke. He wondered if anyone else in her life had known Tamaki so well, had wanted to look beneath her tough exterior. Her nose stud, tattoo, and even her punk clothing were a form of self-expression. But Scout suspected they were also a rebellion against her childhood; chosen to push people away before they could leave her.

They looked at the empty marketplace: tents with the sides rolled up, chairs stacked on tables at the café, litter on the ground.

"I don't think we're going to find much here."

How about over there? According to the map on Debossey's wall, there was a place of interest to the east.

On a rise of a hill dotted with brush, a Southern-style mansion had lights shining through windows.

"Bingo."

They trotted along the riverbank and then up the hill. Scout heard and then his brain identified rodents moving in the darkness; he knew them, not by name like Scott the park ranger would have, but by smell and taste like a hunting fox. Then they were up on the wrap-around porch, peering through a window into what could only be called a parlor.

Mrs. DeBossey sat on a rose-colored couch wearing a flower-patterned dress that cinched at the waist. Refreshments covered a sideboard. Scout's nose identified fried chicken, deviled eggs, rolls, and lemonade. Mr. Wilson leaned against the wall, playing with a walking cane. Another figure was just out of sight, but when the head judge, Bremmer, stood and walked over to the sideboard, Scout crouched down.

"What are they doing?"

We'll have to get closer to hear.

They moved around the porch to the front door. It was open with only a screen door to keep out the bugs. Perfect for eavesdropping.

Mr. Wilson mopped sweat off his forehead with a handkerchief and shoved it back into a pocket. "Each time we do an auction it goes a little more smoothly. And with Ashur allowing Hotheads to terrorize his territory, we should continue having a steady flow of immigrants to become Debtors. However, the border guards are muttering that they shouldn't be charged entrance fees at the tollbooth since its part of their job. Apparently, this young guard Baumann doesn't think it's fair."

"Tell him he's lucky to be a Citizen," Debossey said, waving a hand. Her cheeks were flushed from drinking. "Next order of business."

Wilson looked down at a piece of paper. "So, we're supposed to make the special announcement at the auction?"

"Yes, that is what Enlil wishes." Bremmer placed a deviled egg on his plate. "So that is what we shall do."

"Certainly the best way to reach the most people, but the auction is only two days away. Do we have any candidates who will bring in money? And what about that lovely fox?" Mrs. Debossy said, "You won't overcharge me if I buy him, will you?"

Mr. Wilson grunted. "Do you want the girl, too?"

"No. Why would I? She looked more feral than the fox." Mrs. Debossy gave a delicate shudder. "But I do think she'd make a lovely sacrifice for the maw after the auction."

Tamaki wanted to growl at her, but Scout had control of the body. *It won't happen.*

"At least her true nature is displayed, unlike others who might look delicate," Bremmer said.

"That's quite pointed, but I won't deny it," Mrs. Debossy said. She gestured at the house, "I mean, who knew I'd go from a divorced wife of a lead defense attorney to becoming a chosen prophet and a member of Ninlil's temple committee? Nevertheless, here we are." She lifted a glass of wine. "It's not really that different."

Mr. Wilson raised his glass to touch hers, but the judge turned around from the sideboard. "We are much more civilized now. You'll do well to remember that."

"You're still the Boar," Mrs. Debossy laughed. "You take your role as head judge and 'prophet of Enlil' so seriously, as if you weren't a criminal only a few months ago."

The Boar? How did he get that nickname?

"I don't think we want to know," Tamaki said, "but I have to imagine it has something to do with all the oversized pigs around here."

Bremmer's blue eyes turned even colder as he stared at Debossey. "You would do well to remember that part of my past."

"You would do well," Debossey repeated in Bremmer's low tone. "Did you say that before you held a gun to someone's head? Like, was that your catchphrase?"

"Let's not fight," Mr. Wilson said, lifting a ringed hand into the air in a call for peace. "Money is the great motivator and our new boss-god agrees."

"Fine. Back to business." Mrs. Debossey twirled her wine glass by the stem. "This announcement is going to change everything. We'll have a head start on the other territories and need to use that wisely."

"Our information comes early because our god is Keeper of the Tablets of Destiny." Bremmer turned to face the direction of the temple and bowed. "May he prosper."

"I want to know how we can use the announcement so that we prosper," Mrs. Debossey said with a pout. "Choosing a candidate to replace

Shamash for the Seventh Seat on the Council is straightforward. We need someone who is both loyal to us and will win against the candidates from the other territories. How are we going to find humans that are able to manipulate *etemmu*?"

"That's easy," Mr. Wilson said. "We say we value that ability and let them come to Ekur Temple."

"It will also flush out those annoying Humanists," Bremmer said. "If we officially sanction humans using energy then we deflate their argument that humans are being oppressed. A better strategy than in New Babylon where they've made it illegal for their people to use *etemmu*."

"Except for those in power," Mr. Wilson scoffed. "There's no way New Babylon leaders aren't using every military advantage that they can."

"Correct," Debossey said. "So, we'll sanction that. But, knowing that the world is unbalanced until the new god or goddess is chosen… how do we use that information? All Ninlil said was that there would be rolling storms of *etemmu*. Maybe creatures from ancient myth will walk the earth again. Maybe she means new mutations will occur and chaos will be constant until the Council of Seven is complete." She walked over to refill her wine glass. "My imagination is spent."

"There's always a way to profit," Mr. Wilson said. "The gods will play their games and we shall reap the rewards." He took a swig of what smelled like whiskey.

Wind blew across Scout's fur, ruffling it the wrong way.

Bremmer, the one they'd called the Boar, stared out the screen door. "Are you expecting company, Mrs. Debossey?"

He knows we're here.

"He can't."

Enlil is the god of air; the wind is his spy.

Fear leaked from Tamaki's mind. Scout saw her mental image of the beam, could feel the metal beneath her and see the sand covering the maw. Suddenly she was separating from him.

He shook his head. She had to learn to control herself while manipulating *etemmu,* like he'd learned to control this body.

Scout snuck away from the porch and made his way down the hill, sticking close to the shadows. No one else was out and it felt like the world was his playground as he ran from place to place, sniffing and discovering. The marketplace was a cacophony of smells and Scout decided that a person could find just about anything they wanted here. He'd had experience stripping houses after the firestorm in Baltimore, so he could appreciate the hard work of repossessing. He took his time exploring so they'd be ready when it was time to escape.

As false dawn lit the sky, Scout returned to the third-floor cell, panting and tired, with a bag in his mouth.

"Fricking a-hole." Relief and anger rolled off of Tamaki as she huddled in the corner. Her hair was tucked behind her ears and her eyes were huge like she'd been staring for hours. "I thought they caught you."

No. I took off down the hill when you disappeared. Later I crept back up to the house.

"Why didn't you tell me you were safe?" She crawled toward him. "I've been sitting here, helpless, thinking that Debossey was going to throw you in the maw."

I'm sorry. I was caught up in spying, making sure I wasn't caught. It was like the human and animal part of me came together and it felt right for the first time. He opened his mouth to drop the paper bag onto the blanket. *I brought you something.*

A delicious smell drifted out and Scout realized how hungry he was. Tamaki pressed her lips together like she was going to refuse to look, but then grabbed the bag and ripped it open. Inside were three pieces of fried chicken. "Where did you get this?"

Debossey's house! She'd packed it for one of the men to take, but I got to it first. His lower jaw dropped into a grin.

Tamaki set the piece of chicken back in the bag and folded the top.

He blinked, confused. They were always hungry in the cell. *Aren't you going to eat that?*

"No, thanks." She shrugged one shoulder. "My hunger keeps me sharp."

Mine just makes me hungry. Fine. She didn't have to accept his gift. Scout stepped forward and nosed the bag open, pulling a piece of chicken out onto the foil blanket and using sharp teeth to pull meat from the bones. The skin was greasy and salty while the meat was tender. He wanted to crack the bones.

"I'm a little surprised you're eating it." Tamaki fluffed the blanket with a snapping sound. "I was under the impression that Scott was a vegetarian."

Scout stuck his nose deeper into the chicken. If he rolled over the skin, would it make it harder for Enlil to find him? Maybe he should try — as an experiment, not because the body was urging him to.

Someone hissed from across the walkway. Scout looked over to see Cooter watching them. The man shook his head and made a tsking sound as he wagged his index finger at Tamaki in the symbol of catching someone.

TWELVE

Construction sounds started soon after Tamaki had relaxed enough to even think about sleeping. She tried covering her ears to block out the banging, the shouts, the thumps, and clangs. Worse, though, she couldn't block Scout's words from her mind: *the human and animal part of me came together and it felt right for the first time.* She sighed. She'd done that to him, and it wasn't an excuse to say she hadn't known what was going to happen, that she'd gotten lost in the power of blood magic, even though that was what happened. It was done, she'd apologized, and she'd make it up to him if she could. Right now, he was her only friend and he didn't even particularly like her.

Tamaki shifted on the blanket. Scout was fast asleep, spread out this time, as if he wanted to take up his entire half of the blanket. He must be tired from running around all night. The guards were getting up from the table, night and day shift switching. The noise of construction was throwing off the routine or maybe the guards knew that the contract auction would be tomorrow. Tamaki looked in the other cells. Darnell and his sister had given up trying to sleep. Amil's mother adjusted her hijab and smoothed her dress. The older woman in the end cell, Marie, sat looking dazed as if she'd hoped that the cell was a bad dream and she wanted to go home. Cooter was staring at her, so Tamaki looked away from his cell. The bag with two pieces of chicken was hidden under her blanket. Reaching her hand under the blanket she pulled one piece out and stuffed it in her pocket. She folded the bag as tight as it would go and stuffed it under Scout's sleeping body.

"Line up for morning bathroom break," the guard called.

Tamaki was not surprised when Cooter jockeyed into position behind her in line. The noise of construction kept him from being overheard as he leaned forward against her back, his breath smelling like yellow teeth and decaying food. "Looks like your little critter goes wandering around at night. I bet the guards would be real happy to hear that. Might even knock time off my debt if I were to let them know."

Ahead of Tamaki, Darnell's sister came out of one bathroom and Darnell went in. Amil's mother came out of the other one. Tamaki was next. She glanced at the guard for permission to move forward, but he was examining the construction on the stairs between this floor and the one above.

A sudden shove from behind and then she and Cooter were in the bathroom together. He leaned against the door, trapping her inside the small room. He was enjoying this. Yeah, he hated being kept a Debtor, but as long as he could make someone else more miserable then he'd be content. This close she could see the blackheads on his nose, the food crumbs in his beard.

"Hey, little girl. So whaddya going to do to keep me from telling the guards? I bet they'd teach you a lesson with their black batons. Make an example out of you." Cooter grinned. He stepped close enough that Tamaki's back was against the stall wall, her leg pushing against the toilet bowl. She stared at the leather fringe on the bottom of his vest as he loomed over her. "You want to survive here? You got to play with me." His hand dropped to her left hip and squeezed. "You understand."

Suddenly his other hand grabbed her hair and yanked her head to one side.

His voice deepened. "I said, do you understand?"

He pulled her head down and pushed her hip at the same time until she was kneeling on the filthy bathroom floor. He pulled the toilet seat up, keeping her head secured so she was staring at the rim.

"You want to drink that water? What about after I take a piss in it?"

He shoved her head deeper into the bowl until the water was right below her cheek. Tamaki strained away, her neck at an unnatural angle, one hand trying to push against the outside of the bowl and the other pushing against his knee to make him step back.

She whimpered, but forced herself to keep her eyes open. Just like in the Skeleton Forest. No one was coming to save her. Then the smell hit and she started gagging.

"Yes," she said. "Yes, I understand."

He shoved down and her face went into the toilet water.

She jerked her face out and scrambled away as Cooter laughed. Tamaki heaved into the corner, spitting again and again as she wiped her face, shaking.

She hated this man so much; she wished she had a knife instead of a piece of chicken. A fantasy filled her mind of burying a knife in his stomach, Cooter's eyes rolling up, *etemmu* pouring into her. She'd use it to rescue everyone here. Golden ropes of *etemmu* to lower each person to the ground, to freedom. She blinked the image away. They would only be free until the guards on horseback caught each one and fed them to the maw. She couldn't allow that.

Instead, she wrapped her fingers around the chicken breast and jerked it from her pocket. Still on the ground, Tamaki thrust it toward Cooter.

"That's a good girl." He immediately took it and bit off a piece, the skin dangling from him mouth.

"Take it," she whispered. "And keep your damn mouth shut or there won't be anymore." She got to her feet, wet hair plastered to her cheek, and walked out while he was still eating.

*   *   *

Later that day, Tamaki sat on her cot, knees pulled to her chest, still breathing hard from the workout she'd pushed through. Exercising gave her a semblance of control. At least it pushed the interaction with Cooter from her mind. Except she couldn't really push it from her mind, that feeling of absolute terror as her head was pushed into the toilet bowl. The sound of him laughing as she'd gagged on the bathroom floor. The smell inside of the bowl.

She added his name to the list: An, Mr. Wilson, Debossey, Cooter.

That was for later, though. They only had twenty-four hours before the auction. Scout was still sleeping, but maybe Amil's mother could help.

"Psst." Tamaki waved her hand. "I'm sorry. I've been thinking of you as Amil's mother. What's your name?"

The woman smiled as she approached her side of the fence. "Sometimes I think of myself that way too, but my name is Anissa."

"I wish I had someone who cared about me the way you care about Amil. My mother –" Tamaki swallowed. "Never mind. I really admire you."

"I'm sorry." Anissa's dark eyes searched Tamaki's face. "Not all of us get to be children when we are young and that carries into our adulthood."

"Obviously, because I'm the weird woman who talks to the fox." Tamaki gave a mocking half-smile.

From across the walkway, Cooter whistled for their attention. He deliberately licked each of his fingers, sucking on them while he stared.

Tamaki assumed it was a reference to the grease from the chicken. "He's so creepy."

"But he'll easily find a place at auction because he's strong." Anissa looked over to where Amil was drawing in the dust. "Who will purchase the contract for a mother and her young son? I would do anything not to be split apart."

That same commitment is what made Rachel and Adam leave for Baltimore. Rachel would do anything for her son. What if Tamaki had gone to the hospital with them? Maybe they'd be back to the cabin by now, safe in An's neutral territory. Saki's egg would be in her pouch, but Scout wouldn't exist. Tamaki bit her lip. She wanted to assure Anissa that she was working on a plan, that they were going to get out of here, but she didn't want to offer false hope. Instead, she said, "How did you get here? I mean, if we were to escape, what direction would we go that isn't a desert?"

Anissa nodded. "That's all I think about. We took a boat down the Tigris-Mississippi, I guess they call it New Tigris here, but I wish we'd gone east into Inanna's territory."

"Where does Inanna control?"

"Most of what used to be Illinois. They say her temple is in the former city of Chicago. Enlil and Ninlil control the New Fertile Valley between the Tigris-Mississippi on one side and the Euphrates on the other side. Their territory cuts the former United States in half so that everyone will have to trade with them."

"Of course. Follow the money."

Anissa leaned forward to whisper, "But I've heard that they want too much. That their grip grows loose the farther north a person gets from Nippur and its sandy desert. If we can get away, there are farms and plenty of work. Amil and I could stay together. But we have these metal cuffs on our ankles. Everyone in this territory knows what that means: Debtors."

"Yeah. The cuffs are a problem." Tamaki bit at her thumbnail and then made herself stop. "Where are we, exactly, do you know?"

"This used to be Little Rock, before it became Nippur." Anissa shook her head as if at an internal joke. "I used to be a social studies teacher. If I'd had to guess why the United States would have fractured, it would have been from another civil war. Who would have bet on Mesopotamian gods?"

Tamaki imagined a map in her head with all the familiar names crossed out and new names written in with a shaky hand. Colors, maybe, to represent the new territories and which god or goddess it belonged to: Ashur in Detroit, New Babylon and Ba'al in Pennsylvania and New York, An around the intersection of Virginia, West Virginia, and Maryland. Tamaki used states because that was what she'd memorized as a kid, but if she had a geographic map it would be more accurate to look at the ley lines to determine territories of the gods.

Scout yawned, the sound turning into a high-pitched whine. Tamaki looked over her shoulder to see him stretching, then his expression changed as he sniffed at the blanket. He must smell the last piece of chicken.

Ha! You ate a piece.

Aware of Anissa watching, Tamaki put her hands on her hips. "Hey, would it be alright if Amil had a piece of fried chicken?" she said to the other woman. "I know it's not halal."

"That hasn't been an option here," said Anissa with a bitter twist to her lips. "But I believe that Allah honors the prayers we say over our food. Yes, I'll give it to Amil. He's growing and needs to stay strong. Thank you. I owe you."

"No, you don't," Tamaki said, too forcefully. "You don't owe me." She took the bag from underneath the blanket and held it open for Anissa to take the last piece, then gave a wave as if they were neighbors going back to their respective houses instead of prisoners trying not to pry into each other's lives.

Turning to give a superior look to Scout, Tamaki saw Cooter staring at her with a jealous expression. He shook his finger at her, the same gesture he'd made before, and then pointed at himself. She rolled her eyes and sank down on the foil blanket facing the fox, shoving the bag underneath.

Ha! You still gave in and ate a piece. There were three.

"I didn't. I had to pay off that redneck over there."

So you gave away the last piece to make sure I wouldn't be right about your eating it?

"I might be a little competitive."

I'm beginning to understand that. Scout rubbed his narrow jaw against his shoulder and avoided Tamaki's eyes. *We should talk about what Debossey said.*

"About throwing me in the maw or buying you for a pet? There's nothing to say." Impatient, she said, "Tonight you'll have to sneak out again. Find out where the auction is taking place–"

Probably where the construction sounds are originating.

She frowned at him for breaking her concentration. "They've had contract auctions before, so not necessarily." Standing up, Tamaki walked the edges of the cell and whispered, knowing that Scout's sensitive ears could pick it up and also that everyone probably thought she'd lost it from being jailed too long. "I need to know what is around the auction area. Are there plants I can affect? Any other sources of *etemmu* I can draw on?" She remembered the river under the footbridge, but that was probably too far away unless the auction was on the edge of the market. "We need a huge distraction so we can all get away. Finally, we need a way to get the cuffs off. If we can do that, we can pass for Citizens. Anissa said that there's a desert directly around Nippur, but beyond that is farmland. She also said there's a river. It's called the Tigris-Mississippi so maybe it follows the same course? I don't want to plan too far ahead, but we get on a boat, jump off somewhere safe, and I'll use the *etemmu* from the ley line to give you a new body. Then, I go back to An's territory and get my egg."

You've done a good job of stretching our connection. Soon you'll be able to break it. He shook his head. *But we don't need to go back to An. Haven't we learned not to piss off a god?*

"I lost Saki. I won't lose the egg. It's mine."

You're obsessed. I don't know about turtle-penguins, but female turtles cover their eggs with sand, dirt, or mud and leave them to incubate. Penguins keep their eggs warm by balancing them on their feet. Either way, the eggs take about two months to hatch, if they've been nurtured.

"So there's time." She tried to explain. "Saki was the only thing that held me together after the firestorm. After the Hotheads and my grandmother and you. Her egg… it's like a second chance. Like she left me one last present." She pivoted on her back heel to face the fox.

I don't know what An is doing with the egg, but the reality is that it probably won't hatch. He reached out a paw as if to touch her. *You need to let it go.*

"I won't abandon my egg."

Scout growled.

A flurry of commotion from the narrow stairway in the center of the ziggurat near the bathrooms made all the Debtors look that way. One of the guards got up from the card table and came to stand by Tamaki's cell. Baumann, the guard from the first day, entered the row of cells. Behind him were four women wearing loose grey robes and holding boxes of food and bottled water. The women each went to a cell and began speaking to the person inside.

Baumann approached the guard. "The Sisters of Mercy are here for their usual visit."

"No kidding." The guard spit and the glob landed inside Tamaki's cell. "I hate these losers."

The oldest woman had gray hair and creases in her brown skin. She looked over at the guard with a serene expression. "Only those who lose their life will find it."

"Ugg. A religious zealot." The guard looked like he was thinking about spitting again and Tamaki tensed to kick him through the fence.

"Ah, they're Citizens and they don't cause any problems." Baumann waved his hand like it was no big deal. "And I think it's nice."

"You better watch them." The guard wandered back to the card table and Baumann walked along the line of prisoners.

"Hey," Amil called, running to the fence. "Sister Addison. Remember me?"

A younger woman with bright pink hair and dark roots finished with Marie, the older woman in the end cage, and waved at Amil.

Amil looked at Tamaki. "They bring us food. For free."

Sister Addison stopped outside Amil's cell. "Hello, my young friend. What would you like today? An apple or an orange?" She tilted the box forward. Apples, red and green, rolled against oranges. There was a whole stack of processed cake-and-cream treats in plastic bags from the aisle of the grocery store that Obaa-chan had always skipped, walking past with a superior expression as she talked about "copious amounts of sugar and preservatives." That made Tamaki want them more.

Amil grinned. "Both."

Sister Addison grinned back at him. "Don't tell." She gave him an apple, an orange, and a cake.

"Does your mom want some hot tea? My older sister will bring the thermos by in a moment, but I can play with you while we wait." Sister Addison looked around before squatting down outside the cell. She pulled a piece of sidewalk chalk from the pocket of her grey robe and then pushed up the sleeve of her left arm. There were symbols written in charcoal.

Tamaki and Scout both moved a little closer.

"Do you remember how to draw the cat?" She pointed to it with the chalk and then handed the chalk to Amir. "Make it look like mine."

He sketched the oval body with a tail in the air, four legs as straight lines, and a circle with ears and whiskers.

"Good job. That's a pretty kitty. She's a nice girl." Sister Addison pointed to another symbol on her arm. "What about this hat? It's like what that snowman wore in the old cartoon where he danced and sang."

"Yeah, I remember that. Frosty." Amil drew the rectangle with an extended line on the bottom.

"Frosty was a nice man, wasn't he?"

"Hey," Cooter yelled, inserting his fingers through the chain fence and shaking it, "you skipped me. Don't I get my free soda?"

Soda? Tamaki moved closer to the edge of her cell and looked into the box. The metallic glint of colored aluminum flashed at her and Tamaki moaned, desperate for a rush of sugar and caffeine.

"Ladies first," Sister Addison said. Her tone suggested that she was not impressed with his theatrics. "I have one more cell before I get to you."

"That's sexist. And she's not even a lady." Cooter grabbed his crotch and gyrated at Tamaki. "I thought this was a new civilized society where gender and race don't matter. Only money matters. The great equalizer." He looked proud of himself.

"All human lives are important," the oldest Sister said, moving to Cooter's cell. "May I offer you some hot tea?"

"You got anything stronger?"

Sister Addison rolled her eyes so that only Amil and Tamaki could see.

"Alright, Amil." Addison pointed to a symbol on her arm of an 'x' inside a circle. "What does this mean?"

"A place to get help because 'x marks the spot.'"

This isn't a game. Scout's voice was excited. *I think I know what she's doing.*

"Good. And this one?" It was a symbol showing straight lines curling at the end like blowing wind.

Amil frowned and then his face cleared. "Not safe. The wind tells the secrets."

"What's taking so long over there?" The guard leaning against the card table near the pulley system crossed his arms. "I can feed the entire row of Debtors by myself in less time than you're taking." He stabbed a finger at the table. "Five more minutes before you Sisters need to leave."

Baumann walked the row, "Okay, Sisters, let's finish up."

Casting a furtive look over her shoulder, Addison poured water over her left arm and scrubbed away the marks before pulling down her sleeve and moving to stand in front of Tamaki's cell.

"What would you like to eat or drink?" The friendly face Addison had shown to Amil had disappeared.

Ask her if she ever draws a box around a horizontal line over four vertical lines.

"A Coke. Please."

While Addison looked for the soda, Tamaki whispered. "No, I'm saying that. What does that mean?"

Trust me. I'm pretty sure I know what's going on.

"And an apple."

Addison sighed as she reached back into the box.

"For the fox."

Addison peered around Tamaki and her face lit up. "Oh my gosh, he's so handsome."

It's true.

"He bites." Tamaki cleared her throat. "What's with the symbols on your arm?"

"There aren't any symbols."

"Not after you scrubbed them off." Tamaki and Addison stared at each other.

"One minute warning," Baumann announced.

The other Sisters made their way towards the stairs.

Those are hobo symbols, used after The Great Depression. She's teaching them to Debtors. Find out why.

"Why are you helping Debtors?"

"Because I believe that human lives matter." Addison pulled on her grey robe.

"I do too." Tamaki leaned forward to press against the fence. "I would take down the gods, if I could."

Addison searched her face. "Then there's a symbol you need to remember. Find other Humanists and they will help you, Debtor or Citizen." Addison pulled up the sleeve on her right arm and then she poured water over her hand and washed it away as Baumann came up. He picked up the box of remaining food and thrust it at Addison.

"Come on, time's up," Baumann said. "These Debtors are very grateful, but they need their sleep before the contract auction tomorrow."

Sister Addison looked over her shoulder at Tamaki as she was pushed through the doorway to the stairs.

The symbol had been clear: intersecting lines connected by short vertical lines. A ladder that, with a little imagination, replicated a DNA strand to represent the Humanists.

THIRTEEN

That night the guards were more vigilant than they had been before, walking the hallway between cages and shining their lanterns around. Tamaki fidgeted until Scout told her to knock it off. She couldn't respond because she didn't want to even chance that the guards would hear, which wasn't fair. Why did their telepathy only go one way? Laying on her back with her palms facing up, Tamaki tried to imagine herself as a corpse. Her only task was to breathe. Each fresh worry that appeared, she squeezed like a grape, imagining confetti shooting through her brain as it popped. When her hands tingled, she wasn't ready, which seemed an indication that she was getting better at meditation.

Keeping her eyes closed, she pictured Scout. His golden eyes and the way the black coloring around them looked like eyeliner. How his front legs were solid black, but the back legs were a mix of rust and brown. The triangle shape of the ears and the long whiskers fanning out beside a nose that was black except for the pink tip. A splash of white starting at his jaw and moving down his chest and then reappearing at the tip of his tail. His smell was close to feline, but wilder and muskier. The feel of his coat as the desert heat made him shed each day.

And then she was with him. He'd already left the cell and she had to bite back a remark about being careful, a reminder that she was the one who would be sacrificed to the maw.

The red fox is well adapted to being a predator. I'm quick, agile, have a strong jaw, and other red foxes have been known to jump over six feet. I haven't had the opportunity to test that yet, but I'm sure I can beat that because I'm awesome. Also, my hearing is more acute than yours.

"Apparently the red fox is very humble as well."

I knew when it was time to go. And, yes, I remembered the bag in case we need to bring anything back.

Instead of going down to the ground floor, they trotted up the new stairway toward the construction sounds they'd heard all day coming from the fourth floor.

"Aren't humans the most dangerous predator for a fox?"

Good thing I'm both. And neither.

Emerging from the stairwell, they took a moment to let the difference sink in. While the third floor was unfinished space with rough cells for the Debtors and a plain card table for the guards, here they were on a floor of exposed wood with colorful Persian rugs scattered around, overlapping in a palette of sophistication. More rolled up carpets were piled against the wall. Couches and love seats made a semi-circular shape. The floor extended into an octagonal atrium in the middle of the pyramid, the railing made of plexiglass so that it felt like they were suspended in space. Looking up, they noted that there was no fifth or sixth floor yet. But, high above, was the seventh floor, which must be reserved for Enlil and Ninlil. Looking down, they could see the first floor with the offices, the glassed-in future shops, and the food court where they'd eaten with Dana.

"This is going to be the showpiece of the temple, the place where special people get to congregate?"

Yes.

"Are we above the Debtor's cells? How come I can't see them?"

We're in a pyramid shape, not a rectangle. The cells are off to the side of the stairs on the floor below so that space doesn't exist on this level. Instead, there's a slanting wall right there.

"Oh." Tamaki looked at the overall design of the room again. A catwalk made of plexiglass extended from the atrium to glass doors that opened to the outside of the ziggurat. They trotted to the doors and looked out over the marketplace.

"This sucks. Even if we get away, then we have to get out of the temple and across the bridge."

Scout trotted back to the octagonal atrium and placed his paws on the railing so they could peer down to the ground floor.

No. This is a thousand times better. Think about it. If we were outside of this ziggurat on the steps, then we'd be on a triangle. The shape is intrinsically stable. We wouldn't be able to pull it apart. But look over the side. This entire atrium is held up by four columns. If any of them collapse, this whole structure will tilt. That's the distraction we need.

"Why would they build a flawed design?" Tamaki asked, suspicious.

Because the Citizens who want it are in a hurry, because the Debtors who built it don't care, and because no one accounted for a suicidal Alchemist.

"Facts." Feeling better, Tamaki focused on the plants. "Wait. Let's check those out."

Waist-high vases held plants at each of the eight corners. Tamaki recognized a Ficus tree in two planters and a lemon tree in two others. "Do you know either of the others?"

Look at the fronds. That's a date palm tree. Wind pollinated and part of traditional oasis horticulture.

"I love a fox with a brain. What about the other?" She felt his excitement before the answer came.

Smell the salt? I've never seen one in person, but I believe this is a Tamarisk, a salt cedar. They have long tap roots that allow them to access deep water tables and then they limit competition from other plants by taking up salt from groundwater, accumulating it in their foliage, and depositing it in the surface soil so other plants can't grow. I am geeking out!

"Yes, you are." She allowed a quick smile. "Now, turn that fine mind to thinking about how we can weaponize these plants for tomorrow."

They pulled a leaf from each of the plants with Scout's mouth and put it in the bag to examine later.

Then the sound of voices reached Scout's ears. A squeal of a wheel and the sound of a rope being pulled came from the open end of the fourth floor. Someone was using the pulley system. An answering lantern glowed through the glass doors from the outside of the ziggurat. Tamaki didn't know if it was him or her, but instinct sent them over to the pile of rolled up carpets and they burrowed underneath. Scout nosed a tiny gap between carpet rolls and pressed his eye to the space.

Mrs. Debossey appeared, heels clicking on the catwalk, wearing a silky white dress that hugged her curves. Next to her was the Boar, hair slicked back, wearing a suit jacket over a blue button-down dress shirt. They looked their part: attractive heads of a corporation in service to ancient gods who wanted to live in a mall-temple. Two guards followed a few steps behind, black batons at hip.

Mrs. Debossey stopped and stood with arms akimbo to critique the atrium space.

"That climb is a pain," she said. "Patrons aren't going to want to hike up four stories of ziggurat steps to purchase Debtors. And how are they going to get down after drinking cocktails? Why isn't turning the pulley into a proper elevator a priority?" She gave a dramatic sigh. "I hate being rushed. Are you sure the announcement has to be tomorrow?"

"Enlil commands," the Boar said, his face eerie in the lantern light. "It has to do with the astronomical timing beyond human comprehension."

"Of course," Mrs. Debossey said, smoothing her blonde hair back. "Guards, unload the chairs and pillows from the pulley and bring them over here. Then send the pulley back down for the raised platform."

"We've got to get out of here," Tamaki breathed in the barest of whispers. Panic beat at her throat, causing ice in her spine.

We're in a good hiding spot. They'll see us if we move.

"There's going to be such a large crowd tomorrow. Our city will prosper." Debossey sighed happily. "So, you'll channel Enlil and make the announcements. Then I've had Dana approve the patrons who wish to participate in the contract auction. They'll come in here and we'll have cocktails and appetizers brought up from the food court." Mrs. Debossey held up the lantern toward the glass doors again. "Let's have plenty of wine available." She lowered the lantern and groaned as the guards reappeared, arms full. "Yes, throw the pillows down. I'll arrange them. Apparently, I'm going to be here all night."

"Did you hear her?" Tamaki breathed. "She isn't leaving. We've got to run." It was an odd sensation to feel her own body's physical reaction to her fear and Scout's through their telepathy.

Hold steady. One pair of eyes is easier to escape than four.

"It is an honor to be the prophet for Ninlil," the Boar said.

The guards went to the opening at the back of the temple. One yelled down, "Send up the platform." A few seconds later the wheel of the pulley squealed.

"Don't patronize me," Debossey waved her hand. "I know how to throw a party. And I know how to keep my patroness happy. Wilson will reserve that dark-haired brat for me and I'll keep her fox. Toss her into the maw for my goddess and then I'll commission a diamond-studded collar for my new pet."

Wind blew through the temple, creating a whistling sound that almost had a tune. The wind blew straight through the gap in the carpets.

Okay, now we have a problem.

The Boar turned in a circle, searching for something, but Mrs. Debossey had moved closer to him and pressed her body against his, wrapping her arms around his neck. "I've got this place set up with plush carpets and soft pillows. You could channel Enlil and I could channel Ninlil. We could feel the wind around us and through us and inside us." She tilted her head back and let her mouth fall open.

"Hmm," he said, eyes still searching the semi-darkness. "Maybe tomorrow."

"Do you understand what I'm offering?" she pouted.

The Boar shoved her away, causing Mrs. Debossey to stumble on the uneven carpeting. He lunged forward and threw one rolled up carpet off the pile and then another and another.

Tamaki felt the weight of the last carpet roll removed and, although Scout had crouched into the smallest possible size, she looked up to see the Boar staring down at them with ice blue eyes.

"Do you know why they call me the Boar?" he asked. He reached into his back pocket and pulled out a butterfly knife. "I make marks with my tusks."

Scout stayed in the crouch, staring up at him.

"What are you doing?" Mrs. Debossey asked. She still sounded angry at being rejected. When he didn't answer, she shoved right next to him and also stared down at Scout. "My fox."

"It's loose in Enlil's temple. I'm killing it."

"No, you're not." Mrs. Debossey reached down and said in a baby voice, "C'mere, sweetie."

Without hesitation, Scout leaped from the hiding spot straight into the woman's arms. She cradled him. "He's mine."

"He shouldn't be loose. You have no idea what that stray animal is doing."

"He's not loose and he's not stray." She kept petting Scout. "He's up at auction and I'm going to buy him." Lifting her gaze to The Boar, Mrs. Debossey said, "Don't you dare try to tell me what to do. I'm Ninlil's chosen prophet."

Don't do anything, Tamaki. This is keeping us alive.

But Tamaki couldn't stop shaking. She could feel that butterfly knife stabbing into this body, she could feel the Boar grabbing them and breaking Scout's neck, she could feel them being thrown off the edge into the maw.

Tamaki!

It was too late, fear separated them, her consciousness rising away from Scout. She had one moment of seeing the fox's startled expression in Mrs. Debossey's arms while the Boar seemed to be looking in her direction before she was whisked back down the stairway and into the cell.

She opened her eyes and crawled on her hands and knees to the chain-link fence to look up the stairs, although it was impossible to see or hear even a whisper from above. Nothing.

Tamaki whimpered, terrified of what could be happening to Scout. Sliding her nail under a scab on her ankle, Tamaki wiped the blood with her finger and pictured Scout. She had a brief image of him sitting next to Mrs. Debossey on a velvet couch while the woman told the guards where to put the platform. The Boar was gone.

The vision faded. Pain the size of a cigarette burn bloomed under her breastbone. She picked at the scab again. It was her fault he was alone. Not sure what she could do, she at least had to know what was happening.

The guards were gone. A cardboard box with several wine bottles sat on the floor. That must have been the last load on the pulley. Mrs.

Debossey had an empty glass of wine in her hand and her eyes half-closed as she muttered to Scout. He stayed where he was, putting her to sleep.

Relieved, Tamaki didn't fight it when the vision faded. Instead, she welcomed the pain because she deserved it. She hadn't been able to stay with Scout, but he'd managed to find his way through the crisis. Exhaustion slumped her shoulders. Her eyes were so heavy, but she wouldn't sleep, not until he came back. Where was he? Surely Debossey was passed out by now.

Finally, she saw him skulking through the doorway with the bag in his mouth.

"Scout, I'm so sorry." Her whisper held all her self-loathing. "I suck."

It's okay. Debossey got into some wine so I was able to sneak down to the construction area on the ground floor. There's a hammer down there we can use to break the manacles tomorrow.

"I can't believe how resourceful you are." She wanted to shower him with compliments, let him know that she was the one unworthy to be a partner.

And I brought you a gift.

She opened the bag and removed the two leaves. "I'll try to work with these, but I can't risk anyone seeing me use *etemmu.*"

There's something else in there. The tone in his voice should have alerted her. When she thought about this moment many times after, she could hear the foreshadowing.

Tamaki reopened the paper bag. She stared down, swimming through a nauseating mix of relief and despair.

Scout, her greatest cheerleader, had given up on her. She hadn't realized how much his belief that she was strong enough to use light magic had meant to her.

Tamaki turned the steel chisel over in her hand, ran a finger along the sharp edge.

I just –

"No, I get it. You don't need to explain." They were back to the plan where to save themselves and the other prisoners, Tamaki would spend her blood, her soul, her life force.

"Ahem," Cooter cleared his throat across the hallway, made a "give me" motion with his hands.

Tamaki shook her head. "No food," she said in a stage whisper.

"That fleabag gave you something. I want my part."

"Hey!" The night guard stood up and pulled out the black stick as he walked toward the cages. "I'll shock anyone who says another word."

Cooter and Tamaki stared at each other as the guard walked closer. She didn't want to back down, that empowered a bully, but she also couldn't have the guard find the chisel. She took a step back and then another.

Cooter leaned forward until his body pressed against the fence and he held up his middle fingers. He mouthed the word "bitch" before Tamaki sank down on the blanket, hand wrapped around the handle of the chisel.

It fit perfectly.

FOURTEEN

While Scout curled up to sleep after his adventure, Tamaki examined the two leaves that Scout had brought back. She had to turn her thinking from this cell being… well, a prison. Instead, she had food and water and time to rest and exercise. Instead of counting down the minutes, she would need to use every second. Tamaki held the tamarisk leaf in her hand and closed her eyes to concentrate, to open her senses. An evergreen in the cedar family, the leaf felt like bumpy needles and they tasted like salt. She had an impression of yellow in her mind. Then Tamaki deliberately picked a scab on her knee and touched her blood and the leaf together.

Before, she'd examined the leaf from the outside as a scientist might, but the blood brought her consciousness inside the leaf so that she understood the plant, felt its survival mode, the strong taproot, and the ability to change the landscape so it could win out over other species. Yes, she could use this plant. She set aside the leaf and pulled out part of a leaflet from the date palm. Scout hadn't been able to grab the whole thing – it would have been over a foot long – but she was able to see, to taste, the faint sweetness that would form the fruit and sense the heaviness of age, it being one of the first cultivated plants in the Fertile Crescent. Yes, she whispered, you have helped humans for a very long time and now you're going to help us again.

Noise at the end of the hallway startled Tamaki. She shoved the leaves under the foil blanket. Guards, eight of them, emerged from the stairway by the bathrooms, followed by Mr. Wilson. The oversized man wore the same stained white suit and had the same handkerchief. His face was bright red from the exertion of walking up three floors and he needed to lean against the doorframe as he looked out at the cells of Debtors.

Anissa clutched Amil to her side. Tamaki saw the woman's chin tremble, but she didn't make a sound. Across the hallway, Darnell told his sister, "Even if they separate us, I will find you. Don't worry about what you have to do to survive, do it. Stay alive and I will find you." Even Cooter scrambled to his feet, looking nervous.

The guards at the card table stood, pushing their chairs back with a screeching sound. The wind, ever-present, gusted. Sand from the desert littered the opening. The day crew stood with uncertain expressions.

Mr. Wilson swirled his hand in the air. "Get the Debtors ready. A crowd is already gathering across the river. Nippur is truly the gracious host for the masses. We'll have the patrons escorted up the outside temple steps to the fourth floor. The judges have an announcement about the fall equinox or something before the auction." He used his index finger to count the Debtors. "That's all? Where are the rest?"

A guard shifted his weight, "I guess the news is getting out about how we don't want immigrants."

"You idiot! We do want immigrants because I have been busting my ass at the café rounding up patrons and now you're telling me that we don't have product." Mr. Wilson used the handkerchief to rub the sweat off his bald head.

Tamaki looked down at Scout. He flicked his ears.

The guard asked, "What do you want us to do?"

"Get the product cleaned up, quickly, and then take them outside to the steps of the temple. Keep them on display throughout the judge's ceremony. Then we'll take them inside to the patrons' area."

"Yes, sir."

The new guards stood by the stairway watching while the temple guards lined up the prisoners, rubbing each person's neck and face with a wet towel. Tamaki took the towel from the guard and did it herself, the material pulling at her skin. It felt good to be clean. Shoes were returned. Tamaki got her black pouch back, a small piece of broken-off turtle shell inside. Amil received a stuffed rabbit that never should have been taken from a child. He hugged it to his chest. Tamaki blinked away the sting of tears.

A moment later Dana appeared in a tidy shirt and skirt with a matching smile. "Well, it's contract auction day! Let me be the first to congratulate you on the first step towards paying off your debt and becoming full Citizens."

Following the temple guard, Dana rubbed lotion into the prisoners' arms, faces, and any bare skin. Then she frowned at Scout and reached for a brush. He showed his teeth and she changed her mind.

When she got to Tamaki, though, Dana grimaced. "These scabs should have been healed by now. The doctor put salve on them and it's been a week. They'll turn into scars."

"Maybe scars are beautiful," Tamaki said. "Maybe each one tells a story."

Dana sighed. "May you find the contract that suits your personality."

"Like you did?'

Dana made a mark on the paper attached to the clipboard and walked away while a guard took her place.

"We're not any different," Tamaki said to the guard's head as he knelt in front of her to check the cuff. "I graduated from high school, went to my senior prom with friends, sweated through the college placement exams." She moved her foot away from him. "What gives you the right to decide whether I should be a Debtor or not?"

His hands brought her foot back into position, settled around the clasp, and then he looked up. "Better you than me." The lock closed with a snap.

For Scout, the guard used a rope like a leash attached to the cuff again. As if that was a signal, the group of outside guards joined the temple guards. Debtors formed a single-file line to march up the stairs and out the plexiglass catwalk of the fourth floor to stand on the steps of the temple. Tamaki made sure to get between Anissa and the guard walking Scout.

The desert sun blinded after they'd been inside for so long; the heat seeped into their clothing. Tamaki pulled on her wheat-colored pullover to create air flow. Maybe she could take it off so she had on just the black tank top because even the wind was hot. The guards pushed the Debtors closer to the glass doors, so they were in some shade.

Probably so we won't look bad for the auction.

Tamaki patted her front pocket; she could feel the chisel through the material of her pants. Moving out of line like she wanted to see the crowd, Tamaki whispered to Anissa, "When the opportunity comes, grab Amil. Tools are against the wall on the ground floor. Break the cuff, look for Humanists, and get free. Don't look back."

"What do you mean?" Anissa cocked her head but kept her eyes forward. Her lips barely moved. "Is someone coming to help?"

Tamaki stepped back into line. Cooter was watching her, his eyes narrowed.

Wealthy inhabitants of Nippur crossed the footbridge of electric lights via donkeys and even by palanquin. Beyond them, in the New River Marketplace, a crowd created a sea of t-shirts, blouses, and what looked like handmade clothing. Those patrons who'd ridden donkeys dismounted and took seats under a bright yellow awning set up at the base of the ziggurat.

The Boar, dressed in black judge's robes, emerged from the glass doors of the fourth floor and walked past the Debtors to the center of the wide central steps. Mrs. Debossey joined him wearing a new pair of impossible heels and a cocktail dress. Her loose hair shimmered in the sun and the wind caressed the tendrils around her face. Not to be outdone, The Boar raised his arms in the air and cyclones spun in his palms. The crowd roared and stamped their feet.

Debossey waited for the crowd's attention and then handed the Boar a curled animal horn, perhaps a ram or some new creature.

"Citizens of Nippur," the Boar intoned, "all praise to Enlil, most high god of wind and earth." The sound, through the horn, was clear to everyone. The people across the river in the marketplace chorused back his last phrase. "We are civilized."

"The fall equinox approaches. The solstices and the equinoxes are a special time in the religious calendar, and this year is no exception. Because Enlil is the kingmaker, he holds a special position within the pantheon of gods." The judge held up one hand in a gesture toward heaven. "An exalted position."

The crowd roared.

Mr. Wilson walked through the glass doors to the outside with a glass of water in his hand. "What a ham," he muttered to the guard standing near Tamaki. "Wish he'd get to the point so we can get out of this infernal heat."

Ha! He called the Boar a ham.

The guard looked uncomfortable at the blasphemy; Tamaki frowned at Scout.

"And so, Enlil himself has spoken through the Horn of Whispers to tell us that he is ready to make a king again. But this king shall be different.

This king will sit among the gods as a peer. This king will represent Nippur on the very Council of Seven."

A strong breeze swept across the ziggurat. Even Mr. Wilson looked interested now.

"This king may be male or female, both or neither. This king may have skin of any hue. This king may be any age. But," the Boar held up a finger as the crowd began to talk, "this king must be chosen by Enlil as full of intelligence, bravery, and power."

Noise filled the air. The Boar had to hold up a hand for quiet. "For a price, the judges are willing to open the temple to candidates for special training. Only one candidate may represent our territory, but some candidates may be selected as junior temple judges."

"What a scheme." Mr. Wilson grunted in appreciation. "I love it. Bet Debossey came up with that."

"Screening will begin at the fall equinox and will be ongoing for two and a half years. Enlil will choose our candidate to compete with candidates from other territories on the third Winter Solstice from now." He had to raise his hand for silence again. "Judges cannot guarantee results, but surely those who have more training will have more of a chance to become a god. You may see me privately with questions." The Boar handed the horn to Debossey and stepped off the stage.

Excitement grew from the crowd across the river as the people talked over the opportunity. Who wouldn't want to become a king?

"There's more." Debossey lowered the horn and smiled at the crowd until they were quiet again. "Ninlil has chosen to bring me another message. Our gracious goddess gives us warning so that we might prepare while other territories will be caught unaware. While we search for a new king for the Council, the world is out of balance. There will be waves and storms of power that sweep through. Energy will be unbalanced. Creatures who have not been seen since ancient times will reappear."

The crowd began to mutter, excitement giving way to fear.

"But our goddess cares for us. And so gifts will appear among our people, gifts to harness the rogue energy. If you manifest a gift, do not be scared; instead, come to Ekur Temple and we will take care of you."

Tamaki clenched her teeth so hard her jaw ached. That wasn't true. The gods and goddesses were Misbegotten – the Nephilim offspring of angels and humans – and humans all had gifts and the ability to manipulate *etemmu*. And Debossey stood there waving like a beauty pageant queen and lying through her too-white teeth.

Mr. Wilson stepped forward to accept the speaking horn. "What an exciting prospect for our city," he said. "But we have another tradition in Nippur and let's give a hand to our patrons for supporting the rehabilitation of Debtors through our contract auction!"

At that, Mrs. Debossey signaled to the group of patrons, with their parasols raised high, to ascend the central steps of the ziggurat to the auction.

The crowd clapped and whistled while a west wind blew off the New River.

Tamaki turned to Scout. "Ready?"

Yup.

FIFTEEN

Mr. Wilson gestured to the guard to lead the Debtors inside to stand to the side of the atrium. Once there, a guard told them in a bored voice what they should do in order to "secure the best opportunity" and "win the most rewarding bid." Tamaki listened, but her mind was occupied with escape. Each Debtor would stand on the small platform while Mr. Wilson gave a brief introduction. When the patrons were ready, the bidding would start. If no bids were offered, the temple representative would decide whether to accept the Debtor's contract in exchange for kitchen work, construction, or cleaning. Otherwise, the person would serve as an offering to the maw. Then, as if they hadn't just been threatened with death, the guard took a towel, splashed some water on it, and made sure everyone still had a clean face.

Tamaki grimaced as the guard moved away. Her face stung from the rough ablutions and she felt jittery, like being backstage before a performance was about to begin and, oh yeah, she was the star. Next to her was the tamarisk tree. After working with the leaves, Tamaki knew the plant like an old friend. And over there was the elegant date palm with those beautiful fronds that looked like blades. Helicopter blades.

They want us to walk across the stage like we're in a twisted graduation ceremony.

Tamaki nodded in acknowledgment of Scout, but she was watching Cooter. He had shot a look at her before he started whispering to the nearest guard. He's telling, she thought to herself. He knows Scout's been getting out of the cage and he knows that something is about to happen. He's snitching so he'll get preferential treatment or maybe a better contract.

Why are you getting angry?

She had to make Cooter stop talking or he'd screw up the entire plan.

Tamaki's stomach gurgled, the breakfast of a fried egg and toast souring with her nerves. Looking at the nearby guard, Tamaki sidestepped so she was within arm's distance of the Tamarisk tree.

Steady.

Easy enough for him to say. Scout didn't have to cut himself and he didn't have the pressure of freeing the other prisoners. Knowing she was being defensive and unreasonable didn't make Tamaki feel any calmer, but it did give her the impetus to wrap her fingers around the blade of the chisel and pull it from her pocket. Her left hand gripped the handle. On the next exhale she jerked her right hand up, slicing open her palm with the sharp corner.

Mr. Wilson had Darnell up on the platform. He said something about "strong worker" before the pounding in Tamaki's ears matched her heartbeat and the now familiar sweep of power rushed through her like a drug. Her fear disappeared, her vision clarified, and she smiled. The heartbeat in her ears turned into an anthem. Her arm shot out and grasped the trunk of the tamarisk tree. Power sizzled. Her *etemmu* met the energy of the plant. In response, the plant exploded. The taproot burst through the bottom of the clay pot, breaking it with a sharp cracking sound, and snaked over the side of the atrium, wrapping around the support column in the quest to the ground. The plant was strong with genes bred for the desert. Tamaki had awareness through the taproot, through the sensitive hairs along its length.

She was reminded of the plant in the Skeleton Woods. She'd been scared then, but now she was the plant.

Part of her awareness was still on the atrium. She heard the gasps when the pot broke, the murmurs from the patrons and Debtors alike as people tried to figure out what had happened. On instinct, Tamaki turned to look at Cooter. His face paled and he raised his finger to point at her.

Tamaki moved through the line of Debtors. It was so easy when they were standing still and she had music playing in her head, but the music was fading and she needed more. The chisel was still in her hand. The guard to her left reached out, but Tamaki pushed his arm down like there was no resistance. Oh, she didn't want to give this up. She was a knife; an avenging knife, and she would bring justice. Lifting the chisel, Tamaki adjusted her grip. Cooter tried to turn, to get away.

She saw the panicked look on his face, felt the leather of his vest as she grabbed it and yanked him backward. He was bigger than her, but Tamaki stepped to the side and hooked his ankle so that he fell on his butt, a move they taught in women's defense classes. They also taught them to gouge eyes, but that's not what she wanted. Almost by instinct, she grabbed Cooter's arm and lifted so that the short sleeves of his white shirt slid back, exposing the hair of his armpit and the side of his ribcage. She plunged the chisel down into the flesh unprotected by his vest. The chisel only went so deep, it had struck a rib. Tamaki pulled it out. The edges of skin split open. Crimson welled up.

Tamaki held her right palm, the one she'd cut open, an inch over his wound. She could see the *etemmu* drawn into her own body. It thrummed through her veins, a vibration that made her want to have sex and write an opera and fly.

What are you doing? Scout's outraged voice screamed into her mind.

Cooter howled, but it was background noise and more in disbelief than real pain. Tamaki released his arm and he flipped over to crawl away, but there was nowhere to go in a sea of legs crushed into the atrium space.

"It was only a cut. Don't be a baby," Tamaki said, but she didn't know if she was talking to Scout or to Cooter or to herself.

"Break up the fight, but don't hurt the merchandise," someone shouted. Tamaki looked to the auction block and saw Mr. Wilson there, his face red against the very white brightness of his suit. "Go," he shouted, waving his hands at the guards. "Get her. You've got tasers."

Mrs. Debossey had pressed up against the plexiglass wall of the atrium, next to the five patrons in their colorful clothes and shocked expressions. She looked less scared than excited.

"Did you want me to smile?" Tamaki asked Mr. Wilson. "Isn't that what you said?"

There are too many guards. We need to get out of here.

Tamaki counted. Ten guards. Mr. Wilson. Neither Mrs. Debossey nor any of the patrons looked like they were going to attack.

"That if I were prettier then I'd get a better contract?"

Eyes wide, Mr. Wilson held out his hands to the guards, "Protect me."

Tamaki reached out her awareness to the taproot. It had grown down to the ground floor, encircling the support beam the whole way. She encouraged the root tip to move across the bottom floor and climb up the second support beam. That was going to take some time. She needed to do something else to stop the guards.

"This is our moment," Tamaki said, turning to face the other Debtors. The man who'd been delivered into the maw had tried the same thing, but she had to make it work. "I will not be indentured. I will not be bought or sold. I'm not a Debtor because they try to put that word on me. Instead, I will fight for my life and my freedom. Join me and together we have a chance." She used their names. "Darnell, Marie, Anissa, Jessica. This is how you stay together with your family."

Darnell, from the auction block, exchanged looks with his sister Jessica. He swallowed and then called out, "You attacked Cooter."

"He was giving away the plan." Feeling the power start to fade, Tamaki looked at Darnell's sister, too. "This is the way we survive, Jessica. You know I'm right. There are Humanists out there, people who will protect you from the gods."

Jessica looked at her brother and then they nodded in sync. Darnell grabbed Mr. Wilson by the suit jacket and shoved him into the two guards behind him.

Cooter had gotten to his feet, hand touching the gash on his ribs. "You little bitch." He swung a punch at her head.

"Shouldn't have snitched," she yelled back, ducking. She held the chisel out like it was a knife.

Scout barked.

Two guards had their tasers out and stood where she and Cooter faced off. He lunged for her and Tamaki stepped aside, letting him trip over her foot again. "Wow, twice with almost the same move." Before he could get up from the floor, she fell onto his back, used one hand to pull his head up by the hair, and brought the chisel to his throat.

Don't do this!

She needed more blood to affect the escape. Looking over her shoulder, Tamaki saw that Anissa had pulled Amil behind her, but a guard was threatening them with the taser. The older white woman, Marie, cowered on the floor and kept announcing she didn't know anything. Darnell and Jessica both fought guards. Scout had gotten away from his handler and that guard was chasing him around the atrium. The patrons stayed on their couches. They were sure of their safety. If this rebellion failed, Tamaki acknowledged, their group would all be sacrificed to the maw.

Tamaki leaned down to whisper in his ear, "Here's what I understand." She pulled the chisel across Cooter's throat.

Noooooooooo.

More power than she'd even imagined flooded through her in a pleasure so intense it was sweet pain. The gap in her chest, the place that ached when the blood magic was spent, burst. She understood then that it was a psychic abscess, filled with envy and despair and anger. For a moment it was lanced and *etemmu* shot out her fingertips. Her vision had black edges around it, a type of auspice.

"Now, my green darling," she said. "Show us how very strong you are." One with the tamarisk plant, Tamaki felt when the root squeezed itself together, like arms coming back to center, the two support columns pulled inwards. With a squeal of metal, the entire atrium shook. Then, in slow motion, the right side collapsed so that furniture slid against the plexiglass and the soldiers flapped their arms to keep balance. Now the patrons were scared, scrambling in their colorful clothes, pushing and shoving to get to the catwalk and escape the groaning atrium. Tamaki pointed her finger like a gun and shot a line of *etemmu* at each guard so that they flew over the plexiglass and plummeted down to ground floor.

Tamaki pivoted on her back heel and faced Mr. Wilson. "Did you want to introduce me to the patrons? You should hurry, because I think they're leaving." She sent a palm leaflet flying at his face, slashing up one cheek and then the other. "Smile pretty," she called as Wilson collapsed, clutching his face, then lost his balance and rolled along the tilting atrium to land amongst the piled-up furniture.

Tamaki laughed and then she saw Amil's face. At the expression of horror. It wasn't at Mr. Wilson or the guards on the floor with their torture devices out. It was at her. She sobered. Someone had to make the hard decisions. It wasn't fair that it was always her, but they'd be grateful later. She stepped closer to the date palm and pressed *etemmu* up through the trunk and out the branches to the leaves. Like her Empress Paulownia leaves, these grew in length with a sound like a rubber eraser being squeezed. Then she gave a push of power and the leaves flew away from the trunk.

"Catch it," she called to Anissa. "Each person needs one. It will float you down to the ground. Remember what I told you about the tools to remove the cuffs?"

Anissa nodded and reached out a shaking hand to grab one of the leaves. She handed it to Amil and when she let go the boy floated off the atrium. Anissa grabbed one for herself and then, fronds fluttering, the mother and son disappeared over the edge of the plexiglass. Tamaki rushed to the edge to watch them float down, safe, to the construction level.

Darnell had a palm leaf, and though he looked skeptical, he was making Marie grab one too. His eyes got big when he floated up. "I hate roller coasters," he called as he disappeared over the side. Jessica floated past a moment later.

Tamaki turned her head. Patrons and the remaining guards were on the catwalk pushing to get outside of the ziggurat. Mr. Wilson lay unconscious, Cooter was dead. She needed to grab Scout and use a frond to get to the bottom floor.

Scout barked and Tamaki saw that he was captured, struggling in Mrs. Debossy's arms.

The woman smiled. "I see you, little blood eater." Wind whipped her blonde hair so that it flowed to the side like the statue at the base of the ziggurat. Tamaki's heart skipped. This was Ninlil's prophet. And this was Ninlil's home. The atrium shifted again, the vertical weight too much for the remaining supports.

Tamaki looked to the catwalk for escape, it was clear of people now, but she still had to get Scout. When she looked back, Mrs. Debossy's eyes glowed white and wind encircled her like a cyclone until she floated above the broken atrium. In a voice that couldn't be her own, Mrs. Debossey said, "You're going to taste very good when I devour your soul."

SIXTEEN

Tamaki scrambled for the palm tree and settled on the trunk like she was riding a horse.

Scout wriggled in the blonde woman's grip, his fur blowing with the force of the wind propelling them upwards. *Everyone else is safe, I can see them from up here. You go.*

"I can't," she said aloud, choosing not to specify whether she meant because of their relationship or because of their psychic bond. Gripping the trunk with her thighs, Tamaki closed her eyes until she could understand the date palm the way she had with the tamarisk, her consciousness part of the tree. Then she threw her arms forward, fingers extended like blades. Ten giant leaflets flew toward Mrs. Debossey. The woman dropped Scout and waved her own hands in defensive windmills.

Tamaki struggled to push the leaf-blades through the air against the defensive wind around the woman even as she tamped down the fear radiating from Scout as he plummeted. Tamaki initiated the tamarisk root still clinging to the support column so that it reached out and grabbed the fox in midair, then, vine wrapped around the fox's belly, rose through the air to return Scout to the atrium.

Mrs. Debossey's wind shredded the palm fronds, green bits falling away like confetti. Tamaki launched the last three fronds from the tree and patted the trunk, "Thank you."

The tamarisk root dropped Scout onto the carpet and Tamaki directed her energy to the sturdy plant, giving it one more instruction.

"Run," she said to Scout. "Go out the catwalk, there aren't any more leaflets." The fox ran, the white on the tip of his tail bouncing as he maneuvered around the debris on the atrium.

Mrs. Debossey laughed. "You're trapped. You've used up all your weapons and you'll be screaming in pain when the blood runs out."

"Maybe," Tamaki said. "But not yet."

Suddenly, Mrs. Debossey's jaw dropped, and then she screamed. The tamarisk root had wound around her ankle and then her calf. It yanked her down until her head disappeared past the edge of the atrium.

Tamaki scrambled for the catwalk, following Scout out into the sunlight. Standing on the steps, Tamaki leaned over, pressing her hands to her knees to catch her breath.

Holy smokes and tornadoes. Scout's eyes were wide, his fur still standing up. *What was that woman?*

"Ninlil's prophet." Tamaki straightened and looked down four stories of stairs. "We can't go back inside. We need to get across the bridge so we're away from the temple and then we'll figure out how to get the metal cuff off my leg and off your neck."

The marketplace across New River was packed with people shopping. Guards on the ground were running to the back of the ziggurat, probably responding to the mess they'd left inside. "You said everyone got away?"

Yes, I saw them.

"Good." Silently Tamaki wished the former captives, especially Anissa and Amil, luck. "Once we cross the bridge, we need to walk as if we know where we're going. As if we really are Debtors on some errand."

Tamaki grabbed the handrail so she didn't pitch forward as they jogged down the stairs. Scout seemed unhurt, nimble, and light as he danced along. She felt like there was a spotlight pointed at them as they trotted down the ziggurat like ants on a picnic basket, but no one rushed out of the ziggurat to chase them. No guards blocked the bridge. No one was even on the foot bridge. Tamaki took the first step and then, paranoid, looked over her shoulder. "There he is."

The judge stood outside of the catwalk doors, black robe flapping in the wind. Mrs. Debossey was Ninlil's prophet, but the Boar worked for Enlil and he was not happy. She imagined seeing the blue ice chips that were his eyes, staring at her from so far away, but he made no move to pursue them.

Tamaki waved goodbye. It was stupid, but if she could provoke him to act, then she could stop imagining what he was about to do.

Come on, keep walking.

Tamaki trembled with exhaustion. She still had the black auspice around the edges of her vision, but soon the pain would start and she'd be vulnerable. Would it be worse or the same since she'd used Cooter's blood?

Scout circled back and wound around her ankles, a tickling sensation. *We'll melt into the crowd as soon as we cross the bridge and find a place for you to recover.*

"Being stealthy isn't working. Let's run." Tamaki ripped her gaze away from the Boar. Sweat broke out in her armpits. They sprinted across the bridge.

One person from the marketplace screamed and then another and then everyone in the market was shading their eyes and pointing to something behind them. Voices stood out against the background murmuring. "It's the *gallu* demons!" "They're hunting." "They're after the woman and the dog on the bridge." "Get out of the way. *Gallu* make no distinction when they're hunting."

Not wanting to, Tamaki looked behind them to see what a *gallu* demon was and immediately wished that she hadn't.

Enbu-covered-in-crap. Their fight to get free wasn't over.

The stone gargoyles they'd seen the other night had taken wing and, yes, she and Scout were definitely the prey. Each of the three massive gallus had a snarl carved into their faces and shouldn't be able to fly, but they flew in triangular formation, supported by the wind.

The Boar let us get here on purpose. He's going to make a spectacle of us and show how powerful Enlil truly is. That makes the people either love or fear Enlil and he gets more power.

One *gallu* landed at the end of the bridge, preventing them from running back to the ziggurat. The second landed on the other end, preventing them from crossing into the marketplace. The final one landed right in front of them. It had a body made of boulders, but this close she could see the individual sand particles, the slight variations in color. It smelled scorched like it had been baked too long and the face was intentionally horrible with a large jaw and sharp, jutting teeth. A nose to track and undersized wings that would have been cute if the whole thing wasn't so scary.

The gargoyles on the end moved toward the middle in slow, deliberate steps. There was nowhere to go.

Tamaki looked at the potted trees lining the bridge. "Tell me about Ficus."

When you cut them, there is a sticky white sap. It's related to the tree that makes rubber and–

"Got it." Tamaki glanced down at the New River, part of the Tigris-Mississippi according to Anissa. "And the river is full of *etemmu*."

Yes, I'm almost positive it's a ley line.

"Great. You distract the *gallu* for a moment."

Scout cocked his head and then nodded. He darted forward, barking and circling the *gallu* right in front of them. The *gallu* demon raised its fist and brought it down, smashing a dent into the bridge, but Scout was already dancing on the other side, tail waving. The demon turned and smashed again, powerful but slow. Tamaki squinted with her black-auspiced gaze at the creature and could see the *etemmu* that held the sand together.

Nodding, she said, "I'm sorry," to the Ficus tree and then used her chisel like a blade to cut off a branch. Immediately a milky fluid poured from the gash – a fluid used to make latex. She needed a way to get the *etemmu* from the river to infuse the sap. Then she could make a net and maybe, somehow, reverse it so she could suck the *etemmu* out of the creature and absorb it into herself. How to get the sap into the water?

She plunged her hands, right then left, into the milky fluid of the Ficus tree, allowing it to coat her fingers, palms, and back of her hands. Then Tamaki placed her left hand on the rail of the bridge and vaulted over. The power singing through her veins – the *etemmu* she'd absorbed from Cooter – made her seem to float down to the embankment. It felt like she was moving faster than everyone else.

A heavy presence behind her made Tamaki look up. The *gallu* blocking the marketplace entrance had followed her down.

Tamaki leaped down the rest of the embankment. One more leap and she landed in the water. Her hands went in and she closed her eyes to concentrate. There, that tingling was the ley line. Tamaki moved forward.

The stone creature waded into the water after her.

Thuds came from the bridge above.

A little help, please?

"Coming." Standing in the ley line of New River, water up to her neck, Tamaki began to hum. She imagined petting Saki. And then she pulled *etemmu* from the river into the latex coating her hands. Her body ached for the power and she had to fight to keep it in the latex, to pull the milky strands apart over and over to create a net.

Scout whined in pain.

Tamaki looked up to see that the fox had retreated to the edge of the bridge that she'd vaulted over. The other two *gallu* demons loomed over him.

"Duck," she screamed and spun the net through the air toward the closest demon, one strand tied around her wrist.

The net landed on the stone creature's head and his fingers were too thick to pluck away the sticky, milky strands.

The demon in the water had reached her and she had to move deeper into the ley line to evade its grasp, standing on the tips of her toes. She could see the *etemmu* from the ley line strengthened the *gallu* as it strengthened her. Tamaki shook her head. "All the better to drain you with, my dear."

Oh, this all felt so good. This is what it meant to be a god: whatever she thought she could bring into existence. No one could hurt her now. This was extreme freedom. And she was worthy of the power. So many other people were weak, but she could handle the cost.

While the demon on the bridge struggled in the net, Tamaki pulled both physically and psychically. The *etemmu* that kept the *gallu* together poured into Tamaki even as the creature lurched forward.

Scout jumped away and the *gallu* on the bridge tumbled over the side, splashing down into the New River as a series of boulders.

She used the energy she'd pulled through the net and then pointed it toward the *gallu* in front of her.

The creature opened its mouth in a roar like rocks sliding against each other. Energy ran over its body before tightening. Tamaki held out her hands and then pulled her fingers in. The *gallu's* boulders slid apart, collapsing into the water with a splash. The stone wings were the last thing to melt into the ley line.

Let go of the net! You can't hold all this power. A human body wasn't meant to.

Tamaki frowned. She didn't want to let go.

Trust me. Scout's voice was inside her mind, calm and clear. It made the noise of everything else fade away. *Release the power.*

It was hard to untie the strand of *etemmu,* but she did and the net dissolved back into the ley line, swept away with the fragments of *gallu.* She stared, feeling a concomitant sense of relief and regret. She inched toward the bank, emerging from the water even as she felt the invisible drag of the ley line calling her back. Her body tingled with power. There was still one *gallu* left on the bridge.

Suddenly a missile whined through the air overhead, shot from the marketplace and headed toward the ziggurat. Tamaki's mouth dropped open as she watched the missile and the glow of *etemmu* around it.

Looks like a short-range rocket launcher. That means the attacker is nearby.

"And the attacker is someone who can manipulate energy."

A smell like kerosene or lighter fluid drifted past on the wind. The missile struck the ziggurat between what looked like the third and fourth floor, ripping a hole into the building. Screaming erupted from the marketplace and people ran from the ziggurat. Tamaki hoped Anissa and Amil and all the other prisoners were using the distraction to get away.

The bridge shuddered as the last *gallu* demon on the bridge launched into the air, rushing toward the temple to defend it. Tamaki and Scout looked at each other and then the fox sprinted toward the end of the bridge leading to the marketplace while Tamaki climbed the embankment. The crowd had dispersed when the *gallus* appeared. Tamaki held onto the railing at the edge of the bridge to catch her breath and watch the crowd running.

Wait. One figure in a sweatshirt with the hood pulled up was not running; instead, they were watching their handiwork. The figure tossed something into the air and then turned away. The firecracker whined into the air directly over where they'd stood. It exploded into a double helix of blue and green lights before sifting back down as sparks.

"The Alchemists are Humanists," Tamaki said. "Or the Humanists are Alchemists." On the edge of collapse, she pushed away from the bridge. "We have to get to them. They're our way out of this city."

You're about to collapse.

"Scout," she whispered. "Please. We have to get out of here."

He nosed her hand. *Follow me through the market. This crowd is thin because people have taken shelter. I can take us to where the figure was.*

Every step was torture, but she stumbled through the empty rows of stalls, following the red tail waving like a banner. Scout had his nose to the ground. A shadow separated from the side of a tent. Before she could yell, strong hands gripped her shoulders. The scent of sparks and fire clung to the person.

"Turn around and go back," a man's voice whispered, "and you won't get hurt."

Two more figures in nondescript clothes with hoods pulled up emerged from the shadows.

"Sanctuary," she managed to say as she fell to her knees. "I claim sanctuary."

"Find someone in this city who can help you," he said, dismissively. "We're something else."

"Yeah, I am too," Tamaki said. The burning had started in her fingers; she didn't have long. "Watch." She motioned Scout forward and then touched the cuff around his neck. There was a spark of *etemmu* inside. Easy to snuff out.

The cuff fell off.

The man holding her shoulders couldn't hide his sound of surprise.

Tamaki touched her own cuff and it fell to the ground. "I'm one of you. An Alchemist."

"Why didn't you do that earlier?" One of the other figures crossed arms over chest.

"I was waiting for my ride." Tamaki quirked an eyebrow and smiled, holding the expression as darkness pressed in and she fell face forward into the dirt.

SEVENTEEN

Tamaki dreamed in layers. The *gallu* demons were there and the ziggurat and sometimes Cooter sat up with blood dripping down and pointed at her. Then she knew she was dreaming, but sometimes she saw Saki's egg hanging from the tree back in An's territory. The baby turtle-penguin cried in its shell, seeking warmth, seeking touch, seeking a mother, and feeling the desperation of being left behind. Tamaki didn't know if those images were dreams or visions. Those were the ones that made her chest ache in the space behind her heart.

I'm here.

Scout's voice in her mind and the weight of his body at the end of the bed gave her confidence to open her eyes. Her body ached all over and her head like cotton balls had been stuffed inside. An IV pole with what looked like saline connected to her left arm. Five other cots, empty, with folded blankets at the foot, extended in a line down the room. A window at the far end had a curtain drawn across. She moved her left foot, trying to determine if there was a cuff on it.

You've been unconscious a long time. Scout sat tall, whiskers twitching. *I was worried.* He sent her an image of herself: eyes closed and deep purple bruises underneath, hands curled into her chest, blood under her nails.

"My head is fuzzy." A disconnected pain flicked from the back of her head down her neck. "Like I can't hold onto thoughts." It should scare her, maybe it did, but she couldn't put the feeling and the reaction together. "Where are we?"

After you passed out, the Alchemists carried you to their SUV parked outside the tollbooths. We drove for hours. Now we're in the mountains. It looks like some type of campground with pre-firestorm buildings. Maybe a place where companies and churches would come for a retreat.

Tamaki moved the sheets to see that her grey pants had dried mud from the New River and she wore the blank tank top. Her pullover was folded on the table by the bed.

Someone's coming. The same man always comes. The fox looked toward the door. *Sometimes a woman is with him, but not today.*

The door opened and an older white man in an untucked flannel and baggy jeans walked in. "Ah, the patient is finally awake." He flipped the switch by the door and the overhead lights came on.

She must have looked startled because he said, "Yup, we still have electricity, although we have to ration it so it only runs at certain times. Makes an old man feel good when all the prepping pays off. A person gets called paranoid and made fun of for so long and then," he clapped his hands together. "Boom. Apocalypse." Tilting his head, the man said, "To be fair, I thought it would be something more like a global pandemic or environmental disasters caused by climate change. Gavin thought it'd be the electrical grid being hacked by another country. Hence all of our generators."

"Who are you?" Tamaki bunched her hands into the sheets. "Where am I?" She didn't feel strong enough to use *etemmu* and there were no plants in the room, but she'd strangle this man with the sheet if she had to. "Who do you worship?"

"Dr. Bill Hawsin. Most call me Haws. I've been monitoring your concussion." He chuckled and touched his rectangular framed glasses. "Guess I should be glad you aren't asking who you are."

"Where?" Tamaki shifted onto her elbows wanting to sit up. Pain flared in her head so that she whimpered.

Slow, Scout's worried voice whispered even as Haws said it out loud.

"Slow down. I'll help you if you want to sit up so bad." He held out an arm in front of her and let Tamaki pull herself up using his arm as a brace while he adjusted the pillows behind her with his other hand. She appreciated that he didn't touch her.

"Is this place like Nippur?" she asked, heart revving in anticipation. "Do you have Debtors?"

"No, it's not. But that's all I'll say. You'll have to ask Gavin your questions." Haw's speech pattern sounded Midwestern. "I'm just medical."

"Gavin who?"

"He's in charge. Should be stopping by soon enough. This is our sick room and I've been pumping you full of fluids since you arrived severely dehydrated, unresponsive, and in obvious pain, although I couldn't find any bone breaks – besides the cast you already had on your right arm — or internal bleeding. Doesn't mean it isn't there." He shrugged his shoulders. "We've got some supplies but aren't able to take MRIs, knowwhatimean? Anyway, if you're feeling better, I can take that out." He pointed to the IV. "Do I have your permission?"

Tamaki nodded.

"Good. The missus and I had to take your sweatshirt off to examine you and that fox nearly bit my arm off."

The doctor snapped on medical gloves and gestured to her arm. In a practiced fashion, he pulled out the needle and covered it with an alcohol wipe. The chemical smell burned her nose. She couldn't see the spot of blood on her arm, but the thought of it made her nauseous.

"And if you want to know more about me, I'm happy to tell you that I'm seventy-eight years young, I'm from Springfield and my wife Liza makes the best peach preserves you've ever tasted. Her canning always places at the farm fair. The secret? A little bit of habanero. You wouldn't think it, but the heat makes the sweetness better." He removed the stethoscope from around his neck. "Lemme check your heart. You complained about it hurting during your bits of coherence."

"Don't bother." Tamaki rubbed her chest and looked at the fox. "I'm used to the pain."

Scout nosed her leg and then resumed his soldier pose.

"You've been unconscious for most of three days."

Three days? She was so tired that she wouldn't mind sleeping three more, especially if she didn't have to dream. Tamaki plucked at the bed sheets. What had happened in Nippur? Would the Boar send *gallu* demons to hunt for her? Had the Debtors gotten away?

"Your little pet hasn't wandered too far." Haws replaced the stethoscope in his pocket.

"Yeah." She looked down at her ragged nails. An image flashed through her mind of standing in the New River and laughing as the *gallu* toppled into the water. "He stays close."

"Isn't that something?" Haws blinked behind his glasses. "Not what you'd expect from a wild fox. Did you raise him from a pup?"

Scout cocked his head at the door a moment before someone's knuckles rapped against it. Without waiting for an answer, a man swung the door open and entered. In his fifties, the man had rich brown hair with gray at the temple and tan skin that suggested he spent a lot of time outdoors. A camouflage jacket covered broad shoulders and he looked comfortable in crisp jeans and boots. There was an air of competence surrounding the man that suggested he'd seen it all and was ready for more. A Texas buckle marked his waist, but Tamaki's eye was drawn to the Sig-Sauer on his belt holster that he made no effort to hide.

Tamaki tensed, the muscles in her shoulders spasming. She wasn't going to be another victim like with the Hotheads, not going to be some kind of indentured servant like in Nippur.

"I believe your name is Tamaki Hayashi. That's what Dr. Haws told me you stated during one of your conscious moments." Thick southern accent, like honey over granola. "I'm Gavin Moore." He moved to the side of the doorway so that his gaze could take in the window on the far wall, Haws, Tamaki, the fox, and the door.

She didn't remember talking to Haws before. Was that part of the concussion or burnout from using blood magic?

Military. Look at how his hands hang by his sides instead of tucked in his pockets and the way he is assessing all the exits from this room.

Tamaki nodded at Scout's remark, but kept her eyes on Gavin. "You're in charge here?"

"I am." Gavin didn't hide that he was studying her. "How are you feeling?"

"Fine." She tilted her head to the side until her neck popped.

Haws made a concerning sound. "Please don't do that. You'll want to keep the head and neck as still as possible. Think of your trauma as a brain bruise."

"What is this place?" Tamaki didn't look away from Gavin. "And am I a prisoner?"

"Right to the point." He exhaled. "I can appreciate that, after what you've been through back in Little Rock, or I guess they call themselves Nippur now." The way he said the city's name showed his disdain. "But we're not like that. Kept ourselves separate and we have our own community with our own rules."

Press him.

"You've managed to not answer my question." She wanted to snap at Scout that she knew what to do but contented herself with giving him a side-eye.

"No, you are not a prisoner. You're a guest. In fact, I understand that you asked to come here." The left corner of Gavin's mouth tilted up in a half-smile that lent him a surprising charm. "If you want to leave, you'll be blindfolded to keep our camp's position a secret, and personally led away to avoid certain, um, hazards, and then we'll wish you the best."

"Hazards?" Tamaki raised an eyebrow. "You mean booby traps around here."

"Would you expect something different? You've seen some of what's out there – mutant animals, plants, Hotheads. We need to control who, or what, enters and leaves our community."

That made sense.

"I wasn't with the group that picked you up, but they told an interesting story."

"What does that mean?" Tired of verbally sparring, Tamaki let frustration tinge her words. "My head hurts and I don't want puzzles."

Dr. Haws and Gavin looked at each other. Then Gavin pulled a metal chair from near the wall into position by Tamaki's bed and sat down.

"Life is a balance, isn't it? The things you can prepare for and the things you can't." He gestured around the empty room with his left hand stiff like a knife blade, fingers pointing. "This is a community of preppers who worried about the future long before the firestorms. They stockpiled food, weapons, whatever they thought they'd need in the face of disaster. But none of us could predict those things that came down during the summer solstice. Those things that call themselves gods and goddesses." He tapped his index finger against his forehead. "We didn't imagine, even, that there would be a new kind of energy and that some people could access that energy with their minds."

"What does that have to do with me?" Tamaki swallowed. It was so hard to think. Had they seen her using blood magic or just releasing the cuffs?

Gavin tilted his head and gave her a playful smile. "I think you know how to use that energy."

Be careful. He wants something.

Tamaki shook her head. "I don't know what–"

"Maybe I should amend that." Gavin sniffed and leaned forward. "I hope," he elongated the 'o' sound, "that you know how because some of us do, too." He held a hand up to prevent her from interrupting. "Nguyen told me that you escaped from the ziggurat and that you were able to remove the cuff by using energy. He said that you claimed sanctuary."

At her nod, Gavin continued, "That's what we're building here. A place for talented humans to learn how to use this energy, to adapt to this new world. We're excited about the possibilities because unlike those sheep down in Nippur, we have survival supplies. We don't need to give ourselves over like those Hothead fools with the god Ashur. We can stand on our own feet, build our own territory. We can be whatever we want, but the first step is gathering those with the energy talent and the second is sharing what we each know to increase our communal knowledge."

Tamaki's mind spun. Gavin was talking about what her grandmother had been tasked with: the secrets of *etemmu*. These were Alchemists, but at a start-up level. Everyone and every living thing had life energy. When Shamash, the sun god, died on the summer solstice and the other deities sprang from their jail in firestorms, his *etemmu* fell everywhere as his body unraveled, igniting the ley lines and causing pools of power. It sounded like this was a community of people with new powers, but little idea of how it all worked.

From the edge of the bed, Scout sneezed and twitched his whiskers. *Sounds like a sales pitch.*

"No one is safe in this world anymore. But this community is safer."

Haws snorted and Gavin looked at him before turning back to Tamaki. "It is safer," he repeated. "Enlil claimed the middle section of what used to be America, but he can't hold it. His temple is in Nippur and that's where his followers are concentrated. We're far enough away and hidden in the mountains, so that we'll see Enlil long before he gets here. And we're not waiting. We're making plans of our own."

Brilliant. They think they can hide from wind. Oh boy.

Tamaki touched her head as a distant ache became more pronounced. "What's the price?" she asked. "For joining your community."

"You're a suspicious one, aren't you?" Gavin snorted. "To join the community at large you need a position, a day job if you will, that contributes to the greater good. Community members are entitled to all of our supplies. We have generators, clothing, housing, and food, including two meals a day."

"Sounds fair," Tamaki said.

"But." Gavin crossed one leg over the other. "To join the Alchemists, you must demonstrate the ability for energy talent. And then agree to participate in our hunting parties, which restock supplies from abandoned stores, and our patrols, which keep the community safe. Eventually, we'll set up a school here." Gavin leaned back in the chair, the picture of confidence. "Interested?"

EIGHTEEN

Scout flicked his tail against the sheets of the hospital bed. He expected Gavin and Haws to leave at any minute. Weren't they supposed to let a sick person rest? Gavin had presented his sales pitch and that was enough. Tamaki needed rest and she needed food. She'd pushed herself to the brink to escape the auction and then the *gallu* demons. These men didn't know that, though. They'd only seen her manipulate *etemmu* to remove the Debtor cuffs. Tamaki didn't need to be in a position where she could be used again. His body clenched as he fought a surge of protectiveness.

Besides, after she'd rested, he needed to speak with her alone about what had happened when they escaped the ziggurat – to congratulate her on rescuing the other Debtors and figuring out a way for the two of them to get out of Nippur before Debossey or The Boar found them. They also needed to talk about Cooter's murder. What the hell had she been thinking? But for the past three days she'd been unconscious and he hadn't known if she would wake up. Seeing her lying so still in the bed, her eyelashes dark against her smooth skin, her clavicle bone delicate under the tank top, it was hard to believe this was the same woman who'd torn apart two *gallu* demons. He'd been scared that he wouldn't have a chance to thank her. No, it was more than that. He didn't know that they were friends, exactly, but she needed someone to keep her away from the darkness. Right now, that was him. And he wasn't going to fail her, not like her mother who'd abandoned her and her father who hadn't been interested in a daughter. He could show her what friendship was supposed to be.

"Yes, we're interested." Tamaki made a face and pressed a hand to the side of her head as if to press away the pain.

What? Surprise rippled through him. *When did WE decide? I'm not your damn pet, you know.* And now he was annoyed at her again.

"We?" Gavin frowned.

"The fox stays, too. Meals included, right?"

"That's an awfully big fox," Gavin said.

Tamaki blinked. "And?"

Gavin looked at Haws and the older man shrugged. "Long as he catches mice then he's contributing to our community."

Scout's lips pulled back in a snarl.

"Do you have a garden? I'll settle both requirements at once – my community job and my energy ability." Tamaki swung her legs to the side of the bed. "Let's do it now."

"You're still recovering from a concussion." Haws held up a hand. "We know that working with energy needs your brain. And you need to eat. Your clothes were loose before being unconscious."

What are you trying to prove! Stay in bed.

"I'm too nauseas to eat." Tamaki braced herself on the bed and stood up. She let go of the bed and then swayed and reached out a hand toward the wall. In slow motion, her knees buckled and she slid down.

"Whoa, there," Haws said, grabbing under her shoulders and helping her back onto the bed. "Are you dizzy?"

"Yes," Tamaki admitted. "I don't know. I got lightheaded. My balance is off. Maybe I could eat a cracker or something small. They didn't give us much to eat in the Debtor's cell."

"Stay there." Haws ducked out of the room and then returned with a stack of plain crackers and a walking cane with a rubber tip. "Till you feel better. No rush on getting it back to me."

Tamaki frowned, but accepted the cane. Then she snickered. "You're not going to charge me a daily rate for it? Add it to my debt?"

"No," Gavin said firmly. "Although I'm glad that you've recovered enough to make jokes."

"Eat all of the crackers and see how you feel," Haws instructed. "There's no rush."

Scout flicked his tail in annoyance. He wanted to talk to Tamaki alone. She could be so stubborn and now she was fixated on proving that she was an Alchemist. Who cared what the term was? They were better off traveling alone than staying here.

"There," Tamaki said, brushing the crumbs off her hands. "Let's get moving. I want to see this garden."

"Well now, if you're sure," Haws said, rubbing his chin. "The greenhouse is my wife's project and it's gotten too much. It would be nice to hand it over to someone else."

"She can't even stand without getting dizzy." Gavin gave both humans a skeptical look. "In your medical opinion, it's okay for this young woman to be walking around?"

Scout found himself unexpectedly siding with Gavin and hoping the man would postpone the test.

"She won't be out of bed for long," Haws said, getting defensive. "She ate a little something and the fresh air will help her take a nap afterward."

"That's right." Tamaki smiled at Haws, playing into his decision. "Your wife is quite good with preserves. Maybe I could help grow peaches."

"I'm an original member of the preppers who bought this camp and I'm the doctor," Haws asserted to Gavin. "So, this would fall under my jurisdiction."

Scout studied their body language. There was something in the postures of the men, the tones of their voices. This disagreement about Tamaki was cover for something else, some deeper rift in the community.

Gavin folded his arms across his chest. "Interesting." The word had five syllables with his Southern drawl. Then he released the pose and gestured toward the open door. "Better put on that sweatshirt. It can get cold in the mountains. After you, Haws."

Scout jumped down from the bed. He'd already looked around this medical building at night when no one else was around and he needed a break from watching Tamaki's inert form.

The sickroom opened into a hallway. Haws turned right, toward a door that opened to the outside. Tamaki moved at an unhurried pace, using the cane for support and peeking into an open door on the left. Scout knew it was a replica of the room with cots where she'd been. Then they were outside, Scout pressing past her legs to trot ahead and then lifting his snout. It was nice to be away from the overwhelming medical smells.

The medical center was the last building of a horseshoe shape of camp structures that extended into the distance. Mountains framed three sides of the rectangular plateau, but the border on this side was a cliff rising high into the sky, maybe the height of a three-story building. The sky was overcast like it was everywhere, but the trees on the mountains were thick and full of leaves. The exposed rock was starkly beautiful.

Tamaki gasped and twirled in a circle. Scout could sense her appreciation of the natural beauty. It was a reminder of what he had seen in her a lifetime ago when they had first met.

"I love that reaction," Haws said with a chuckle. "This used to be a campground. We, the preppers, bought it a couple of years before the firestorm and kept most of it the same." He nodded toward the middle of the plateau. "There's the dining hall. If you follow the paths around, there's a volleyball court and an empty swimming pool, nature center, and arts'n'crafts hut. Way past, on the other end, is an amphitheater and playground. Cabins are clustered in semi-circles around firepits, but the missus and I live in the house beyond the medical center." He rocked on the balls of his feet. "This is the perfect spot."

"No doubt that's why people keep showing up," Gavin said dryly.

What is that about? Scout tilted his head.

Haws pressed his lips together and walked down the path that led towards the cliff. Soon they could see a sinuous creek emerging from the side of the mountain and flowing along the rock wall. Trees grew in an unruly mess on top and through cracks in the rock wall itself. Multicolored moss crept along the bottom of the wall in a riotous mosaic.

"That's stunning," Tamaki said.

"Even better," Gavin said, "that's freshwater. Melts from the mountains and runs down here."

Scout had a suspicion that it was a ley line, but he wasn't going to go swimming in front of them to find out.

"How you holding up, kid?"

"Fine," Tamaki murmured.

Haws was already walking back toward the medical center, but veered off on a narrower path to the right. "Come on, I don't want to be late for dinner. They won't save my place." He looked back over his shoulder at Gavin. "'Cause I'm not an Alchemist. I'm just the doctor around here. The one who keeps everyone alive."

They rounded a curve and there was a greenhouse the size of a barn straight ahead.

"That's our house over there closer to the medical center. Used to belong to the owners of the camp," Haws said. "But this was the best spot for the most sun when the camp was built, although the cloud cover doesn't move away very often anymores. And, sunsets come early because of the mountains. Guess you can see that already." The light angled inside the building and shone off the glass.

Tamaki hurried inside, her cane hitting the ground with a rhythmic beat, leaving the men to follow her. Along one side of the greenhouse were frames to grow lateral trees. Large plants in buckets were grouped in a corner like patrons waiting at a bus stop. Troughs of dirt bisected the middle space. Tamaki plunged her hand into a container and squeezed. Then she inhaled.

Scout leaped from the floor onto a stacked pile of tarps and blankets in the direct sunlight, circled three times, and then settled. He'd meant it to be a good vantage point, a way to fade into the background, but the warmth made the fox part of him want to sleep. He fought the urge to close his eyes.

"Smells good, amiright?" Haws gave a self-satisfied chuckle. "After we bought this property, we had access to fresh water and privacy, but the soil around here was crap. So, I experimented for years. Finally got the right combination of iron, zinc, manganese, copper, sulfur, and boron all blended together in the soil. Now we can grow things, but we're so damn busy surviving that no one has time. My wife switched to kitchen duty because this job is too physical with all the moving tubs here and shoveling there. That's the problem with getting old. It sucks, amiright?"

"You used water from the creek?" Tamaki's voice sounded like she was smirking. Scout guessed she was thinking about how large her Empress Paulownia had gotten back at Rachel's cabin because the roots had reached for the ley line.

Gavin said, "Are you–"

"It's my method," Tamaki said airily. "Don't question me."

"Haws?"

Scout opened his eyes a sliver. An older woman with weathered skin and high cheekbones stood in the greenhouse doorway wearing a dress with an apron covering the front. "What's going on?"

"Liza, my love. This is Tamaki, that young woman the crew brought in a few days ago. She wants to take the Alchemist test today."

Liza nodded, her dark eyes studying Tamaki. "And you've chosen the greenhouse?"

"Every community needs food."

"True enough." Liza looked around the greenhouse. "Haws and I did the setup in here so I know where everything is. What do you need?"

Scout felt panic beat wings inside Tamaki's throat, imaginary feathers filling it so she couldn't breathe. *You have growing hands. It's the first way you learned. Let your instincts take over.*

"Seeds," Tamaki said, lifting her nose in the air as she pretended to be confident. "Or whatever you are trying to grow."

Liza nodded. "Winter squash, potatoes, cabbage, kale. We even have some carrots."

"Potatoes."

Liza walked to a tub and pulled out a potato covered with eyes. She used a knife from her apron pocket to slice off a piece and hand it to Tamaki.

Gavin cleared his throat. "What are you going to do?"

"Make it grow faster than it would without my help," Tamaki said. She wrapped her left hand around the piece so the eye rubbed her palm and plunged her fist into the dirt of the nearest container. "Please pour some water over my fist."

Haws reached for the watering can on the floor and poured a stream over her hand. The water washed down her hand like a waterfall.

Scout saw Tamaki's eyes flick to Liza's pocket where the knife had disappeared and knew what she was thinking, could feel the want in her, the fear of not being strong enough.

You don't need blood magic for plants. Scout gathered himself to jump down to the floor.

Tamaki looked up at the stack of tarps, startled.

He flicked an ear at her. *Yes, I can still hear your strongest thoughts.*

She nodded and then concentrated on her left hand, ignoring the three people standing around.

Concern built inside of Scout, but he let it float away so she wouldn't feel it through their connection. Maybe it wouldn't be the worst thing if Tamaki had burned out if she'd lost the ability to manipulate *etemmu*. Maybe this would be the only way she could break the addiction to blood magic.

Sweat broke out across Tamaki's forehead. She panted with effort before giving a little laugh.

This was taking too long. He didn't know if it was her thought or his. *Breathe. Relax into it. Imagine yourself pulling on the potato, allowing it to expand.*

"So, what happens now?" Gavin said. "Do we come back in a couple of days and check it?"

Liza wiped her hands on the apron. "It takes this type of potato about seventy days to be able to eat. If you can cut that time in half, it'd be a help to the community, especially with the winter months a'coming."

Sweat broke out across Tamaki's forehead. She clenched her hand around the top of the cane for support.

Angry, Scout looked away. She was pushing herself too hard after the battle.

"Ah." Tamaki let out a sigh.

Relief flooded from Tamaki through Scout. He turned back to her. Gavin, Haws, and Liza gathered around.

Tamaki removed her hand from the dirt and shook it from side to side before turning her hand over and opening it to reveal a full potato that stretched from her middle finger to her wrist. "I guess this is okay?"

NINETEEN

Haws had insisted that she go back to the medical center and Tamaki hadn't argued. Creating the potato had felt like one of the hardest things she'd ever done. There had been a long moment when she'd reached for her power and hadn't felt anything. It had been such a shock of relief when she'd been able to conjure a spark and make the potato that she'd almost fallen over. Scout was mad, but she wasn't sure why and hadn't asked before falling into a deep sleep.

Tonight, then, would be her first introduction to the camp. Haws and Gavin came to escort her. As the group followed the path toward the dining hall in the center of the campground, Tamaki noted the flag pole. Instead of the American flag, a flag with the embroidered symbol of human DNA whipped back and forth.

"You have a custom flag?" she asked.

"Many of our prepper women can embroider, crochet, knit, all the skills you need. They get together and talk about everything while they do it. That's how we keep them happy." Haws cleared his throat. "Not to be sexist."

"Hmm," Tamaki sucked her teeth. "Sounds pretty sexist."

A large metal bell was mounted underneath it, but she wasn't close enough to read the plaque. They walked up the steps and crossed the porch to enter the dining hall. After walking across the camp, Tamaki was grateful for the cane. Her legs were starting to shake with effort.

Inside, tables and chairs were set up in rows and a long buffet table stretched across the front. Behind this table was a swinging door that revealed a brief look into the kitchen every time someone came through, pushing carts with food or setting up a station to collect dishes and utensils. Maybe a hundred, or even two hundred, people were moving around, pulling out chairs, serving themselves from the buffet. It all gave the appearance of being efficient and routine. The wooden rafters were high and the conversation rose all around. Tamaki began to feel sick. Too much stimulation.

Haws and Liza got in line first while Gavin stood next to Tamaki.

"Do you need to sit down?" Gavin asked. "You look pale."

She shook her head. First impressions mattered and she wasn't going to look weak.

A murmur went up in the room as people noticed the fox. Scout ignored them and trotted toward a wall.

"Come on, Scout," Tamaki said, embarrassed. Aware of being watched, she hoped that the fox would realize everyone in the room would be more comfortable if he at least pretended to listen to her.

I'm looking for another way out of here.

"He isn't going to bite anyone, is he?"

"No," Tamaki said, hoping it was true, "he's used to being around people."

"A lot of people here carry firearms believing that an armed society is a polite society. I'd hate to see your little guy shot."

"He won't be any trouble." Inwardly she cursed Scout for drawing attention to their arrival here. Following Gavin's lead, she picked up a tray, but he took it from her. "I'll carry it for you." Heat stained Tamaki's cheeks. She wasn't used to someone taking care of her, but she was afraid she might drop the tray if she tried to carry it and lean on the cane at the same time.

"There is a great deal of work that has gone into keeping this community viable," Gavin said. "The preppers have a board that meets and they establish teams to handle all the work in the community. Everyone helps, whether it's setting up a schoolhouse, chopping wood, or security. Haws is on the board and he'll let them know you'll be working in the greenhouse."

"Was it this way before the firestorm?"

"Yes and no." He scooped spaghetti noodles onto his plate. Metal containers held warmed marinara sauce. Beside them were two pans: roasted vegetables and meat. Glancing at a nearby table, Tamaki guessed the pitchers on each one held some type of drink. "I wasn't part of the original community, but Haws was. He said they were supposed to be this organized, but it was easy enough to make excuses when something interfered or personal conflicts arose. Now, most people are glad to put the needs of the community first."

Scout trotted back to Tamaki. *There's a door in the kitchen and the door we entered through. Also, a child tried to feed me garlic bread.*

"How many people are in this community?"

"We're growing all the time, but are starting to become more selective. The prepper board have their own list, but I want members who can use energy. That's how we're going to win this war."

Huh, he was still being cagey about direct answers. Was that his personality or a sign of distrust? And what war? With the gods?

Gavin snagged two pieces of garlic bread from a basket. "That's why I was so excited when Nguyen told us what he'd seen." He stepped away from the table, balancing both plates. "Do you remember Nguyen? I asked him to do something for me, but I don't think he's returned yet."

"I don't think so." She shook her head. "My memory is shot from the concussion."

I remember him. The rocket launcher. I wasn't very impressed.

Tamaki turned to the table where Haws and Liza had taken seats.

"Hey, you're going the wrong way." Gavin gestured with his head. "We sit on this side of the room."

We? Tamaki looked over. Only about fifteen people had taken seats at a lone table to the left.

"You're an Alchemist," he said. "You sit with us."

Aware that she was still being watched by the people in the room, Tamaki clutched the head of the cane as she approached an open spot at the end of the Alchemists' table. Scout walked beside her. She wanted to reach out to him for reassurance, but couldn't.

Gavin slid her plate in front of her. Then he moved to stand behind an open spot in the middle of the table. "Well, folks. For those who don't know, this is the young woman who made such an impression during the mission to Ekur Temple. Yesterday she tested, today she joined."

Tamaki looked down at the table, cheeks flushing, as heads swiveled to look at her. For those who don't know? Why would anyone know who she was?

Because they were talking about you while we were driving to camp so I'm sure this whole group has already discussed how you escaped the ziggurat, used energy to make the Debtor's cuff fall off, claimed sanctuary, and then passed out. All of which I would have shared with you if you hadn't rushed off to join their little club here.

Gavin reached into his pocket and tossed the potato onto the table. "Tamaki Hayashi has a gift for plants and will be working in the greenhouse." He looked down at his plate. "Not that I don't like canned vegetables, but something fresh would be… appreciated."

The table laughed the way that office workers laugh at a boss's jokes.

"We're going to teach her what we know about manipulating energy and I know she'll be a valuable asset to our team. Welcome, Tamaki."

The Alchemists stomped their feet against the floor. More sedate applause came from the other side of the room. Someone, she thought it was Haws, gave a whistle. Tamaki let herself relax into the sensation of being appreciated.

Don't let their flattery get to you. There's something more going on here.

Tamaki frowned. She'd passed their test and proven her worth. That wasn't flattery. She ate quickly – it was bland but filling — and then set the plate with half of the spaghetti on the floor for Scout. "Here."

I can still think at you while my mouth is full.

"What'd I miss?" An attractive Asian man in his early 20's slid into the seat across from her. Slender frame in an oversized gray sweater with the sleeves rolled up, neat khakis, shiny dark hair longer in the front than the back. Dark, laughing eyes that took in everything. He glanced at the potato sitting in the middle of the table and raised an eyebrow. This had to be the mysterious Alchemist who Gavin had sent on an errand.

"I'm Tamaki–"

"And I'm Nguyen." He grinned. A chain encircled his neck, but she couldn't see what the pendant was and didn't want to stare. "But we've already met."

"Right. Maybe this time I'll remember it."

"Ouch." He picked up the fork and neatly spun the pasta around his fork. The scent of sparks and fire drifted from his clothing.

Tamaki's eyes widened. This was the man who'd launched the rocket, the one who'd stopped her in New Marketplace, the one who'd accepted her request for sanctuary. "Thanks for your help in Nippur. Scout and I were having some difficulty with our escape."

"Is Scout the fox?"

"Yes."

"I'm glad I was able to help." He used his garlic bread to soak up the extra sauce. "We were there to hear the judges' announcements. Do you remember?"

"Concussion." Tamaki pointed to her head with an apologetic smile. "The whole escape is gone. All I have is bits and pieces." That should prevent too many difficult questions.

"I'll give you the quick version. Number one: creatures out of ancient myth will be reawakening. Exciting. Number two: because of the god Shamash's death, a seat is opening on the Council of Seven. I honestly thought that was going to be the most exciting news. Imagine: a god or hero will compete against representatives from other territories to become the new sun god. It could change everything. And then, number three, I had permission to use our rocket launcher if there was a complication. *Gallu* demons appeared on the bridge and Debtors made a coordinated escape. That's a complication and I shot the rocket launcher. Achievement unlocked. I thought my day couldn't get any better.

"But then," he lowered his voice, "we saw something even more exciting. A beautiful woman running through the marketplace crying for help."

"I'm pretty sure I was fighting *gallu* demons, not crying, but," she conceded, "I did need a way out of Nippur."

"I mean," he smiled. "You were running from them, but you survived and that's not nothing."

He had to slide the word 'beautiful' in there, didn't he? Scout raised his lips to reveal sharp canines. *You realize you are the only female at this table, right?*

The Alchemists had been in New Market. They hadn't seen her in the river, dismantling the *gallu*. It hurt her pride, but she'd have to leave it uncorrected. Better to be underestimated.

"Bringing you here, into the Alchemists' camp, became top priority." Nguyen grinned at her.

Tamaki snickered at his silliness and didn't remind him that she'd had to beg for sanctuary before she became a 'top priority'. It was nice to laugh after all the terrible things in An's territory and then in Nippur. "Where's here?"

"Need to know basis." He shook his finger at her. "The important part is that it's in a remote location surrounded by mountains on three sides and a cliff on the other. You're safe now and part of the human resistance."

I'm guessing we're in the Ozarks. Scout licked sauce from his whiskers.

"I passed your test, didn't I?" Tamaki set her fork down and crumpled her napkin. "Gavin said I was part of the Alchemist team. You probably missed that part because you were late."

Nguyen tapped his fingers against the table before conceding, "Ozark Mountains."

Score one for the fox.

"Thank you," she said. "You may continue with whatever you'd planned to say."

"You're confident, aren't you? I like that." He flipped his hair to the side. "You're going to like being part of our group."

"Why's that?"

He made a point of looking all around the dining hall. "Because now you get to sit with the cool kids."

Tamaki rolled her eyes. "I thought you were going to say something about how I'd never have to go back to life as a Debtor in Nippur or how I could grow my talents with using energy or about how the Alchemists will become a new family as we work together to build this community."

"You don't need me to point those things out. You already knew them." Nguyen said. "Although, it was pretty persuasive. You should write that down in pamphlet form for the recruits that come after you."

She looked down at Scout and only gradually realized that everyone around had grown quiet.

Gavin cleared his throat. "Time for the draw." He pulled a pack of playing cards from a wooden box.

Tamaki was about to crack a joke but then noticed how the rest of the men had grown serious.

"What's happening?" she whispered to Nguyen.

Gavin answered, voice pitched to reach the entire table. "We are the strongest in this community, blessed with gifts, and that puts us in a unique position. We must earn the right to sit apart, to make the decisions, and to create a community of Alchemists that will be a model for the rest of the territories." He shuffled the cards with a swishing sound and then passed the deck to the man on his right. "Every person here has agreed to be part of a hunting party."

The man – was his name Don? – looked at the cards, selected one, and passed the rest of the deck to his right. It went around the table, but Nguyen reached over Tamaki before she could take a card, took one himself, and passed it to the next man.

Each man turned the card they'd chosen to face the table and then passed them to Gavin, who fanned them out and offered the fifteen cards, facedown, to Tamaki. "Choose two. The cards represent the men who will be assigned the mission tomorrow."

Nervous, Tamaki looked around the table at the various blank, fearful, watchful expressions. She selected the first card, jack of spades, and the second, five of diamonds. Don glared at her, forehead wrinkling. It had been a random draw. Why would he hold that against her?

By the quick glances, she could tell the other man. She'd heard him called 'Stoltzus,' a heavyset middle-aged black man whose face showed no emotion at being chosen.

Individuals stood up and began taking their dishes to the other side of the room.

"That was intense," she said to Nguyen.

He nodded. "Hunting parties aren't always routine, but Gavin believes that they're necessary so that we all understand why we have to master our talents. He's changed the group since he arrived, added discipline, and I think it's for the better. Some members of the group don't like being pushed, but we don't have a lot of time to improve. Think about the announcements. Worst case is that more creatures will be attacking us. Best case is that one of us could become a god and sit on the Council of Seven."

"What do you mean 'not routine'?"

Nguyen glanced around at the open room. "I'll tell you later." Then he stood up and walked his plate toward the kitchen.

Tamaki blinked. Her first dinner as an Alchemist was over.

TWENTY

After dinner, Gavin walked her outside of the dining hall to the large bell. A plaque read *Ring the Bells that Still can Ring – Leonard Cohen.* "This is our emergency signal. If you hear it, we're under attack."

"Noted."

Liza and Haws walked outside, waving goodbye to the couple who'd sat with them.

"Liza," Gavin said, "it makes the most sense to put Tamaki in your guest room. That way she's still under Haws' care and she's next to her community service in the greenhouse."

"Guess I don't really have a choice," Liza said. Her dark eyes narrowed. "Where are your things?"

Gavin saw Nguyen and raised a hand to catch his attention. "I'll see y'all later." He and Nguyen walked away, heads together as they discussed something.

Tamaki shook her head at Liza. "Got nothing but my fox."

"Oh, he won't stay in my house."

"He stays with me."

Haws looked back and forth between the women, but Liza put her hands on her hips. "I'll have a guest because of the original community agreement, but there are no rules about accepting animals. We don't have enough supplies."

"It's the missus's house." Haws cleared his throat. "Maybe your fox can stay in the greenhouse."

Tamaki forced a smile. "Maybe." If the room had a window then she'd open it for Scout immediately. Otherwise, she'd smuggle him under her sweatshirt like an inept shoplifter.

They walked back to the house, Haws trying to restart the conversation until they fell into an awkward, tense silence.

The guest room itself was fine. It was on the second floor, small, and the bed had a lumpy mattress, but the quilt was handmade. A trunk at the foot of the bed held more quilts and Tamaki wondered if Liza had made them. The dresser was nicked but serviceable and the middle drawer had an old potpourri sachet that gave off a faint odor of lavender and mint. Tamaki shut the drawer. It wasn't like she had anything to put into it. Then she locked the door, propped her cane under the handle, and opened the window that looked toward the woods. Scout walked along the roof of the porch and then leaped into the bedroom.

Tamaki left the window cracked for the breeze and then flopped down on the bed, exhausted. "Enbu, it feels good to lay down."

We should go.

"I need time to recover." She pushed up on one elbow. "It's not just feeling dizzy or being overwhelmed with sound like in the dining hall. I almost couldn't manipulate *etemmu*. That potato should have been easy; instead, I didn't know if I'd be able to do anything. I act confident, Scout, maybe even arrogant, but I thought the one creature who could read my mind would know the truth."

If you weren't trying to fit in here then you wouldn't have had to make a potato grow in the first place.

"This is so much better than Nippur, isn't it? We don't have to pay for anything, we're not prisoners. All we have to do is play along with this 'community game' while we figure out where we are and what we need to do. We have a room to stay in and meals three times a day. This is a breathing space for us."

I don't trust them. Something's going on beneath the surface. They all want something.

"Everyone wants something. That's the human condition." She leaned back. "Take me, for instance, I want to sleep without nightmares."

Scout sighed. *We should talk about the nightmares. About Cooter.*

"What about him?"

You killed another person. Did you plan to do it or was it in the middle of the fight?

"I saved us all." The familiar anger pulsed in the empty space behind her heart. "We wouldn't have escaped without me."

She didn't want to remember the fight: random images during her dreams were enough. Somehow thinking faster than she'd ever thought before, but also trying to control an uncontrollable force rushing out of her while she grappled with the waves of *etemmu*. "I wasn't strong enough on my own."

We would have figured something out.

"That's a bold statement." She laughed, a rusty sound. "And an easy one to make when we're past the decision."

I'm trying to help you.

"That's funny. You were the one who brought me the chisel." She lay back against the pillows and stared at the ceiling, the way she used to do in the cell in Nippur. She wanted to get up and walk outside, to be free to go where she wanted, but she was so tired. "You're the one who gave up on us figuring anything else out."

Scout ducked his head.

"I know that you are morally opposed to killing." Tamaki clenched her jaw. "But there wasn't another way out. I had to give in to blood magic. And now you are free, I am free, Amil and his mother and Darnell and his sister — they would have lived their lives as indentured servants or been sacrificed to an uncaring god. Because of me, because of us, they are free."

I understand that, but giving in to blood magic, not being in control, was your excuse for turning me into a fox.

"I *was* out of control. That's what happens. Sorry I'm not perfect at knowing how to use blood magic!"

At what point are you going to take control and be responsible for what you choose to do? He looked away and sneezed twice before turning back to her. *I would hope that YOU'RE morally opposed to killing. Cooter was down, he was no longer a threat. You KILLED him, not for safety but for power. Yes, it worked, but who's going to die next time we're in trouble?*

"A lot of people have died since the damned gods returned. I'm trying to make sure that it's not us. Besides, Cooter deserved it. He --"

Scout's eyes locked with hers. *He deserved it? Was this killing someone in the middle of a fight or was this murder? Are you a judge and executioner like the Boar?*

"I didn't mean that," she backpedaled. By now she knew that Scout would never understand how much she hated Cooter after he'd held her head in the toilet. There was no point in telling him. Better to continue keeping that a secret. "But stop interrogating me about the word choice of killing versus murder. We would have been killed if we hadn't gotten free. Or is it murdered? You're making my head hurt."

Scout growled. *I'm not trying to make your head hurt, but its an important distinction because sometimes you aren't honest with yourself or with me.*

Her throat ached and she wanted to curl into a ball, but she forced the words out. "You want honesty? If you went back to An then he would 'fix' you by pulling your soul out of the fox body. I don't know what would happen to the fox, but I know you would die."

He glared at her.

"I promised you a new body. Think about it. How am I supposed to do that right now? Kill one of the people here and shove you in? Am I supposed to put you into a tree like a modern dryad?"

Scout pulled back from her, golden eyes glowing.

"Yeah. Not optimal, right? I'm finally with some other people who know how to manipulate *etemmu*. We can find out what options we have without begging or paying a god. We have to keep your secret about being a human and we have to keep my secret about being a necromancer. While keeping those secrets, we have to learn everything they know about *etemmu,* and then we can leave."

Then maybe you should keep your voice down. Scout paced the tiny room. She could tell he was furious, but everything she'd said was the truth.

She'd already been whispering – that breathy tone she'd perfected in Nippur's cell – but she made her voice even softer. "Already our bond is growing weaker."

He stopped pacing to look at her.

It was true. Maybe because they'd practiced it back in Nippur or maybe because time had passed since she'd made the connection when they were being expelled from An's territory. She didn't know why.

At least one thing is going right. I'm going to explore this campground. Without waiting for a reply, Scout went to the window and used his nose to open it wider. Then he hopped from the porch roof onto a tree branch. His red tail made a question mark before he disappeared.

Tamaki turned to her side so she could see the trees through the window and then closed her eyes. A tear slid from her eye across the bridge of her nose and she hugged a pillow closer to her body.

*   *   *

She woke at sunrise, glad that her window faced east as she watched the sky turn yellow and pink behind the trees. Gradually she became aware of an unmoving shadow outside her window.

"Scout." She'd never really had a friend before. She didn't know how this was supposed to work when you'd hurt each other so much with slashes of truth. So, she asked, "What happens now?"

A deep sigh. *I care about you, I really do. And for better or worse, we're a team. I'm not going anywhere, but I can't ignore some things and I'm going to hold you responsible when you cross the line.*

"I get it," she whispered. "I'm trying to be good."

I know that, too.

"Please come inside."

He must be sixty or seventy pounds, she thought, watching him jump lightly through the window into the bedroom. That's why everyone was surprised when they saw him. That, and his golden eyes.

I don't want to see you hurt. He walked to her bed and laid his snout flat on the quilt, rolling his eyes to look at her. *Not from the people here, not from addiction, but especially not from yourself. I was scared when I saw you in that hospital bed.*

The pain in her throat loosened with the words: "I care about you, too."

Where do we go from here? He turned the question back on her.

Tamaki adjusted so she was curled around his snout and could look into his golden eyes. "Hold on for a little longer and I will figure out how to be good and how to be powerful, not one or the other. Believe in me and I will fix us both."

Believe in me and I will show you that this community is hiding something. He moved his head off the bed and settled by the window. *Hopefully before this place breaks us both.*

TWENTY-ONE

Over the next week, Tamaki stayed in the greenhouse as much as possible. It wasn't just to avoid Liza, although that was a bonus, but because the silence was soothing. She went to bed early and she used the cane for assistance and she threw herself into the greenhouse work to drown out the confusing, frustrating arguments she kept having with herself over blood magic and Scout. No using *etemmu*. Instead, she pulled weeds, mixed soil, looked through the gardening manuals stacked in a back corner, and talked to the plants already growing. It was good work, rewarding work, and gradually the stress that had lived in her body for so long began to ebb away. Sometimes, though, she felt a tingle in her hands, a reminder that when she was stronger, she could deepen her connection with the plants. There were other moments, too, that she didn't like to think about. Moments when a little itch skittered under her skin.

At meals, Tamaki sat at the end of the row with Scout. Nguyen was often late or sat beside Gavin, but she began to learn the names of the others. Nate was the youngest at sixteen. Don was florid-faced and annoying. Gerry was a Firestarter and accidentally started fires whenever he was surprised or nervous.

After sketching out a new design for the greenhouse, Tamaki headed to her room for a nap. Scout trotted beside her. They peeked inside the front door; the house was empty. Haws was in the infirmary and Liza was probably in the dining hall starting preparations for dinner. Glad of the privacy, Tamaki climbed the stairs to the bedroom and locked the door behind Scout.

The hinges of the front door squealed, but no one called out. Tamaki and Scout looked at each other.

Expecting anyone?

Tamaki shook her head.

Soft sounds followed as someone crept up the stairs. There was a bathroom across the hall and an empty bedroom beside it, but no other rooms on this floor so no reason for anyone to come up. Scout jumped off the bed and crawled underneath it while Tamaki moved to the corner of the room so that the open door would partially hide her.

The latch of the lock turned. They had a key. Tamaki's breath quickened. She no longer had a knife and the cane was on top of the dresser.

Liza tiptoed into the guest bedroom looking over her shoulder and then heading to the dresser. She opened each of the empty drawers and then shut them. Then she pulled back the covers and looked under the pillows. Finding nothing, Liza leaned over and thrust her hands between the mattress and box spring.

Tamaki stepped forward into the center of the room. "That's about enough."

"Didn't know you were in here." Liza's cheeks turned pink, but she kept her composure as she stood up and smoothed the apron she always wore over a dress. "You should be out in the greenhouse working. That's what I'd be doing if you hadn't taken that job from me."

Tamaki tilted her head. "Haws said you chose to move to the kitchen because it was easier work for you than hauling around dirt."

"That's neither here nor there."

Declining to point out how that didn't make sense, Tamaki asked the real question, "Why don't you like me?"

Liza narrowed her eyes as she put her hands on her hips. "You aren't one of us."

"I qualified to be an Alchemist. You were there." Tamaki pulled on the blue stripe in her hair behind her ear. "Remember the potato?"

"That's not what I mean. Us preppers have been together for a decade. We got things worked out about how it's gonna be and then you lot come in with your brain talent or whatever and suddenly you're getting the best of everything when you didn't even do any of the original work."

"You're jealous of people with 'brain talent'?'" Tamaki rolled her eyes. "That is so petty."

Liza glared. "I'd have smacked a child of mine for speaking with such disrespect."

"Glad I'm not your kid."

Liza stepped around the edge of the bed toward Tamaki and raised her hand.

Scout shot out from his spot under the bed and growled. A dust bunny clung to one whisker.

Liza shrieked and backed against the wall. "I told you not to bring that mutant creature in here!"

Heavy footsteps crossed the hallway.

Scout advanced on Liza, hackles up.

"You're a brat. I bet you've always been one." Liza inched toward the door, away from the angry fox. "I hope you go to Hell."

"According to the Mesopotamians, it's called Kur," Tamaki said, ever helpful. "Is that what you mean?"

"Hey there, ladies." Gavin appeared in the doorway. "How are you this fine evening?"

"Help!" Liza turned a panicked expression to Gavin. "Her beast is attacking me and that girl stood there watching."

Gavin moved to the side. "Go on through, Liza. I'll take care of this."

"I want her and that devil-animal out of my house."

"I'll take care of it." He watched her leave and looked to Tamaki. "What was all that about?"

"Nothing." Tamaki straightened her shoulders. "Thanks for breaking it up, though."

"That's not why I came. I want to know why you skipped the Alchemists' meeting this afternoon. Meetings are mandatory."

She froze. "I didn't know about any meeting. I swear."

"Haws said Liza told you about it."

"She didn't." Tamaki shook her head. The unfairness made her want to scream. "You saw how she hates me and I didn't even do anything. Please, I want to be part of the Alchemists."

Gavin nodded. "I believe you."

Those simple words released a knot inside her chest.

"How are you feeling? Haws said you're cleared for light activity."

"I'm better, but I still need the cane sometimes for balance. And being in the dining hall isn't overwhelming anymore." She shrugged. "When I feel my head start to pound or my vision start to go fuzzy then I know to take a break."

"That sounds promising. Guess you'll need to move out of here, though." Gavin looked around the guest room. "There are some spots open in the cabins on the other side of the campground."

"I'll live in the greenhouse."

"Fair enough." He brought steepled fingers to his lips. "Want some help moving?"

*   *   *

Not only had Liza failed Hospitality 101, but she'd also failed to show Tamaki the community barn where extra furniture, clothing, and supplies were kept. Stoltzus' wife, Daisy, sat behind a desk and helped the community members sign out and donate items. Then she'd give a list to the Alchemists of what supplies the community needed.

Gavin laughed as Tamaki picked out two couches, one brown leather, and the other a flowered cloth.

"When I said I'd help you move, I didn't know this was going to be a major shopping trip."

"If I didn't shop then I could have moved by walking myself down to the greenhouse." Tamaki grinned at him.

Gavin snorted. "You'll need to sign out a sturdy backpack and a canteen. Daisy has them set aside for Alchemists to use on hunting expeditions."

Daisy nodded and brought the supplies out.

Then Tamaki selected new clothes. She'd been wearing what she'd 'bought' in Nippur and not only were the pants and pullover ripped from the fight with the *gallus* and Debossey, they had too many bad memories associated with them.

Scout had stayed outside to sun himself. He opened one eye to watch them carry the couch down the path to the greenhouse. *Have you noticed that Gavin only walks on the paths here? It would be a shorter distance if you two would cut across the grass.*

"I appreciate your help," she said loudly to Gavin as she propped open the door. They maneuvered the leather couch inside and took it to the back of the glass building. "I'm sure you have better things to do today."

As I don't have any hands, I'm sure you don't need my help. Scout snickered and stood up, stretching his front paws forward. *I do actually have something important to take care of while it's somewhat warm. Enjoy your home decorating.* He trotted across the grass toward the creek.

"I want you to feel welcome." Gavin frowned. "There's some animosity between the original preppers and the Alchemists, but this arrangement is going to benefit everyone in the long run and the preppers will see that."

Tamaki settled on the couch. "I could use a break." She patted the couch. "Tell me about what's going on."

Gavin sat down and faced her. "This camp belongs to the preppers. They've had it for ten years or so and became a tight-knit group. After the firestorm hit Little Rock, they felt no need to do anything; after all, this was what they'd prepared for. But then people started wandering into their hidden camp. Nguyen was already here – he can tell you more about it. But, Stoltzus was one of the first. Gerry and Nate arrived together. All the Alchemists found their way to a hidden camp except for you." He smiled at her. "You managed to catch an Alchemist and piggyback in."

Tamaki shrugged. "I like to make an entrance."

"You did." He rubbed his knee. "Anyway, by the time I arrived, some of the preppers were feeling paranoid, worried that their camp location was exposed, angry that there were more people to feed, wondering if Enlil was sending spies. There are some like Liza who are either jealous of Alchemists for their talents or mistrustful of the ability."

"How did the other Alchemists know how to get here?" Tamaki thought of Sister Addison, the Humanist back in Nippur who'd taught hobo symbols to Amil. "Were there guideposts?"

"No signs or guideposts." Gavin shrugged his shoulders. "The other Alchemists said they felt drawn here, that every time the road divided, they had a feeling about which way to go. Their stories were all the same. I don't know from my own experience because I'd already visited this community years before – Haws and I served together and he invited me up – so I wasn't operating on instinct."

"Curious." Tamaki stored the information away to discuss with Scout later. "But not everybody is angry at the Alchemists. From what I've seen at mealtimes, most people seem to appreciate your crew."

"That's because of what happened three weeks ago."

"And?" She blinked. "You want to tell me the rest, Scheherazade?"

He laughed and it made her feel like she was clever. When was the last time she'd sat on a couch this close to someone and talked? Abruptly her body grew cold as she remembered the answer. She and Scott had sat on her bed in Rachel's cabin and she'd shared about the Hotheads and then they'd kissed and he'd held her all night long, wrapped next to his long body. She'd felt special, wanted, cherished. If she could do it again, she'd never let him get out of the bed. They'd still be there, nestled together amongst a pile of blankets. She wouldn't have stopped with one kiss but demanded more. She would have rubbed the soreness out of his back and run her hands through his longish red hair. She would have looked for birthmarks and moles and maybe even a tattoo in case he'd gotten one while drinking during a night off. Maybe Smokey the Bear, if she had to guess. She would have stripped off her clothes so there was nothing between them and she would have told him anything he asked.

Gavin was still talking. "In an effort to foster relations between the two groups, we had an exhibition down at the amphitheater and the Alchemists showed what they could do with their talents. Some of the talents are more entertaining and some of my crew are better at demonstrating, but we added a description about how each talent could benefit the community. I think it helped."

Scout stalked in, dripping wet, through the propped open greenhouse door.

Gavin raised his eyebrows. "I didn't know that foxes liked recreational swimming."

Tamaki ran over and grabbed a rag. She dropped to her knees and used the rag to dry him off. "What did you think of the creek?" she asked.

It's cold.

"What does he think?" Gavin asked playfully.

"That it's cold."

He chuckled as if she'd said something cute.

My suspicion was right. Scott gave a huffy sigh. *There's a tingle in the deepest part of the creek. I'd say the ley line is deep and moves through rather than collecting. My working theory is that the Skeleton Forest back home formed because the energy comes in, but there's a blockage or something. Then the etemmu goes bad or corrupts.*

"Thank you," she whispered.

He waited for her to move away before he shook himself. Water droplets flew.

Gavin stared at Scout and Scout stared back, but Tamaki interrupted their contest. "You ready to bring in the second couch?"

"I'm always ready." Gavin let her lead the way back to the barn. "There's one more thing I want to get after the couch, though."

Tamaki looked over her shoulder at him.

"What?" Gavin made a face at her. "I'm invested in this home renovation project now." They walked down the pathway to the barn.

Daisy raised her eyebrows when Gavin walked out with the large box, but didn't say a word as she marked it down in the ledger.

Tamaki followed with the borrowed ladder. "Are you going to tell me what it is?"

"Nope."

When they were finished, Tamaki felt like the greenhouse was truly her first house. It was all hers. Gavin had let her call out directions all afternoon and then his surprise was perfect.

"It adds the right touch," Gavin said, nodding in appreciation. "Makes everything kind of brighter, but softer."

The chandelier had a gold finish and six candelabra with strands of crystals hanging between them. It had probably been on display in some residential house in the suburbs, but made its way to the campground storage and now hung from the ceiling of the greenhouse. Gavin had stood on the ladder to replace the bulb and do something with the wires that involved the Leatherman tool he kept on his belt and now it worked.

"It's beautiful in here." Tamaki twirled around. The flowered couch was by the front door, the leather couch in the back created a sitting space with a round table next to it. It needed a vase and flowers, maybe a lamp, but that was easy. Gavin had also hung hooks from the ceiling in a horizontal row. She'd hang flowerpots from them later. A high narrow table backed against the soil table to hold a notebook, pens, and some miscellaneous tools that Haws and Liza had left behind.

Scout was snoring in his special place high on top of the filing cabinet.

Gavin looked at his watch.

Tamaki felt guilty. It was dark outside because they'd worked for hours. He'd been so generous in helping her to put this place together. "Thank you. I really appreciate your help in setting up my space."

"You're one of us now and we all do what's best for the group."

Unsure what to say so she didn't mess up this moment, she nodded her head and wished for her phone so she could respond with an emoji. Words were so much harder.

"I should really get back to work." Gavin sighed. "Want to walk back to my office with me? Some of the guys hang out by the firepit outside the office. The patrols also pass by the firepit as part of the routine. It'll give you a chance to join the group since you missed today's meeting."

"Sure." Tamaki grabbed the cane. It was dark out and she was physically tired. It was nice to have something to lean on, although she wished she had her knife back. Just in case.

TWENTY-TWO

The night air was temperate and the stars sparkled overhead in bright pinpricks, one of the joys of being in the mountains and away from any cities. Daytime was so dim and muted because of Shamash's death, but night had the same colors and vibrancy as before the firestorm, maybe even more. The moon was almost full – Tamaki guessed that the moon god Nanna (Akkadian name Sin) must be alive and well. She wondered how he felt about the upcoming contest to replace his son, the sun god Shamash, on the Council of Seven. Did the gods love their children or was that all gone in the struggle for power?

They walked along the path past the dining hall and then Gavin reached into his pocket and pulled out a crushed pack of cigarettes.

"I'm not going to offer you one," he said with the cigarette hanging off his lip. "I'll say it's because I care about your health, but it's really because I don't want to share."

Tamaki waved her hand. "Fair enough."

He struck a match – the sulfur scent wafted and the orange flame flashed – and then the tip of the cigarette was lit and Gavin inhaled. He shook out the match and then tucked it in his pocket.

"Part of the training," he explained.

That clicked with the other things she'd noticed. "Like not walking on the grass. And your left hand makes the shape of a knife when you're giving instructions. And you never hold anything in your right hand."

He removed the cigarette to exhale. "You pay attention."

"My dad was in the Army, too."

"Ah."

They'd reached the end of the u-shape of community buildings. This was the farthest Tamaki had gone into the camp. The path split into three branches.

"To the right," Gavin said, "is the volleyball court, the zip lines and the archery range. That's where we meet for fitness drills."

Being included in the 'we' was nice.

"The other two paths are actually a circle. If you start left then you have cabins and playgrounds. Keep coming around and there's a basketball court and then more cabins, the amphitheater I told you about, and then more cabins and some larger buildings. My office is in one of those."

She nodded, but then realized he might not be able to see it because of the dark. They kept walking on the middle path.

"How'd you come to be a Debtor in Nippur?"

"Wrong place at the wrong time."

"Want to elaborate, Scheherazade?"

He'd thrown her joke back at her. It made her feel like he was trying to connect. "My grandmother and I lived near Dublin, Ohio. After the firestorm, the god Ba'al sent his people through my town. My grandmother and I got away, but then we ran into the Hotheads. Those red-painted people who worship Ashur?"

He nodded. "I've come across them. No humanity left."

"Right." Tamaki stepped on a loose rock and her ankle turned inwards. "Ouch, oh." She almost lost her balance as the cane slipped to the left.

"Careful!" Gavin steadied her. "Are you alright? This section is pretty rough if you aren't expecting it. They used loose gravel to fill in potholes and the gravel didn't stay contained."

"I'm fine." The slip was embarrassing. She might have skinned her knee, though, and felt a little rush of power as the blood appeared in little dots. That wouldn't have been so bad. Just a little taste. Tamaki cleared her throat. "Anyway, after the Hotheads, I arrived in the desert. Enlil's soldiers rolled up and forced me to Nippur."

"With a fox."

"Yeah. I met him along the way." She hadn't woken Scout up before she'd left the greenhouse. Hopefully, if he worried, he could feel her through their connection even though it was getting weaker. "What about you? How'd you end up here?"

"I was in Texas when the firestorm hit, but my younger brother and his family lived in Little Rock. My first thought was to get to them." Gavin exhaled and then rubbed out his cigarette, tucking the butt under his shoelace. "By the time I got there, the city had burned and it looked nothing like what I remembered. People had set up tents and were drinking from the river, trying to get organized, but it was a mess. I went to the pavilion where the injured were being brought. I checked every face."

Tamaki could imagine the scene he described. People going to bed worried about their job, their schools, paying their mortgage, and waking up to the smell of burning and the sight of everything on fire. A supernatural being emerging from the firestorm who could manipulate energy. Maybe he stood in the flames holding hands with his wife Ninlil as they announced they were the rulers of the city, their word was law, and they demanded to be worshipped. Tamaki's lips pressed together in anger.

Gavin said, "Some people reacted by helping others, but most were out for themselves. They hoarded supplies and hid anything of value. Other people sucked up to the new powers – Enlil and Ninlil." He spit to the side.

"Trying to make a deal with the gods by turning their back on their fellow humans."

Farther up the path Tamaki could see a firepit with dark figures sitting on logs in a circle around it. That must be Gavin's office building.

"Anyway," Gavin continued. "That's where I found my niece, Addison. She was one of the helpers. She'd been in school to be a speech therapist. I found her at the pavilion, helping kids stay calm and describe their missing parents, helping those who were hurt find the tent where medical supplies were stored. Addy was the only one left from my brother's family." His breath caught. He must have loved his little brother to drop everything and try to get to him.

"Addison," she said. "I'm glad you found her. That at least you knew what happened and didn't have to wonder." There was something familiar about the name and a face jumped into her memory. Tamaki gasped. "Wait." Yes, it all made sense.

"What?" Gavin stopped walking so they weren't close enough to be overheard by the figures at the firepit.

"I met your niece."

Gavin shook his head.

"No, this woman, Sister Addison came to the Debtor's prison and she was teaching symbols to the kid next to me. Hobo signs. And she showed me the symbol of being a Humanist. The DNA symbol."

Gavin sucked in his breath. "That is an unlikely coincidence in a city the size of Nippur."

"Your niece is the reason that I knew about Humanists. The reason I tried to find them in the marketplace and then found Nguyen."

"I see." Gavin nodded. "I would appreciate if you wouldn't share this connection with the others. She's my spy in Nippur and it could put her life in danger."

"I won't." Tamaki put her hand over her heart. "But, could you do me a favor?"

"Because I owe you?"

"No. I'm not blackmailing you." Tamaki rubbed the top of her cane as she tried to explain herself. "The next time you communicate with her, could you please find out what happened to the boy Amil, and his mother, to Darnell and his sister? They were with me in Debtor's prison and it would mean a lot if I knew they were able to escape."

"I can do that." They walked toward the fire to join Jamal, Hank, and Cal.

"Hey, boys, make room for Tamaki," Gavin said. "I've got work to do." He clapped a friendly hand on her shoulder and then went inside the office building. A moment later the interior light turned on. She'd have to ask about why there was some electricity – like the light in her greenhouse – and not in other places.

Cal, an older white man with a beard to his chest, slid over on the log. "You do some plant magic, huh?"

"Yes, I do the plant magic." Tamaki sat and laid the cane at her feet. "What about you folks?"

"When the power hits right, I can tell prophecies." Cal puffed out his chest.

"And when it doesn't hit, he makes wild guesses." Jamal grinned. Tamaki remembered that the young black man had said he was from California and enjoyed surfing. He had the movements of an athlete and wore sleeveless shirts often to show off his impressive arms.

"If something important is going to happen," Cal protested, "I'm going to tell you about it."

"Is anything going to happen tonight?" Jamal asked.

Cal made a point of closing his eyes, leaning close to the fire, and lifting his open palms toward the sky. "Universe," he intoned. "Send me your message."

Tamaki hoped the message was not that his beard was going to catch on fire.

She squinted as she sent power down to her hands. Her power was there, but still feeble. She didn't feel any energy coming off of Cal, but that could be because she was still recovering.

"No," Cal said, opening his eyes. "We can ask the patrols when they swing by, but I'm confident they will agree with me. This will be a quiet night."

"What about you?" she asked Jamal. "What's your talent?"

"Offensive energy. I can connect two things." He put his hand on a stick from the pile and then touched the end of a stick in the fire with his left hand. Then he removed his left hand and pulled the first stick towards his stomach. The stick in the fire moved the same two inches causing the sticks above to reposition. Sparks shot in the air. Jamal pulled his stick to the side and the other stick mirrored it.

"Nice," she said, nodding. That was what she'd done to herself and Scout by accident. She would have to talk to Jamal privately about how he undid the connection. "And Hank, what about you?"

Hank blew a raspberry. "Of-fen-sive." He was a tall, lanky white man with a tendency to throw his head up into air like a nervous horse.

Tamaki rubbed at the scar from the chisel that crossed her palm. Why did they keep saying that?

"Yeah, you are offensive, but what am I?" Cal taunted.

"Defensive," Jamal said. He and Hank bumped knuckles.

Cal muttered, "Am not."

"I can project my voice," said Hank. His voice came from somewhere behind them. "Wanna play hide'n'seek?" His Adam's apple bobbed and his lips moved but now the sound came from near the door to Gavin's office. "What's the matter? Scared you'll lose?"

"Man, that is not offensive," Jamal said. "That's lame."

Cal snickered.

"Okay," Tamaki said. "What is this 'offensive/defensive thing?"

They looked at each other.

"It's how we practice," Hank answered. "We divide into offensive or defensive talents and then we spar with our energy and we stay in the same groups for weapon work."

Cal spit to the side. "Growing vegetables isn't really defensive, but you're definitely not offensive."

"Yeah," Jamal said. "You'd be defensive."

"Interesting." It was clear which one they valued and telling that they didn't put her into that group. Tamaki picked up her cane and rolled it between the palms of her hands. This was such a simplistic view that she didn't even know where to begin. "I can understand learning by grouping people with similar talents, but what if you grouped people by personality type?"

Jamal sniffed. "What do you mean?"

"Like," Tamaki used the end of her cane to scratch at the ground, "maybe how a person interacts with the world – through discipline, empathy, or chaos – would make more sense." The fourth category, of course, was necromancy. No need to bring that up.

"What would I be?" Cal asked.

"Prophecy is opening yourself to chaos. You're working with probabilities. If a butterfly's wings flap in a certain way then what will happen?"

"Cool." Cal nodded.

Hank tossed his head up to look at the stars. "Well, what about me?"

"Discipline." She pointed to Jamal. "Same as him. You're both forcing your will onto the reality to create change. Those who work through empathy are working 'with' by connecting their energy through emotions, sensing multiple needs, and creating relationships. This would generally be talents like telepathy, healing, having an animal familiar."

"Might be something to that theory." Jamal gave a grudging nod of respect. "I force two to act in a way that is unnatural. Like the sticks. It sounds like you're saying that if I think hard enough then I could join two things that aren't the same?"

"It's a guideline not a set of rules." She shrugged. According to her grandmother, two things determined how powerful an Alchemist was: 1) how much *etemmu* they could manipulate at once and 2) the imagination of an Alchemist so that they could use their talent to accomplish their goals. For example, Hank had projected his voice. Maybe he wanted to use that to distract an enemy. Tamaki, when she'd recovered, could accomplish the same thing by having a tree in the surrounding forest move its branches. "You could have someone with animals using discipline, but would look different than someone working with animals through empathy. Maybe the animal acting as if being controlled versus doing something as a partner."

"No one's ever explained our talents like this before." Hank shook his head. "Like, you're…" he waved his hand at her, "Asian-American. How do you know about energy and ancient Mesopotamian gods?"

"Dude, that's uncool," Jamal said. "Don't be judging people. Like, what does her race have to do with it? How does any 21st century American know about ancient Mesopotamian gods?"

"No, it's okay." Tamaki licked her lips. "Ever heard of the Tower of Babel? In the story, humans built a tower reaching toward Heaven so that they couldn't be killed off by a flood again, but the Creator became angry at their arrogance, and the next day all the people woke up speaking different languages so they couldn't cooperate anymore. The project was abandoned and people matched into language groups. There's a possibility that energy gifts tend to follow the linguistic pattern. How did the Creator decide who would speak which language?" She shrugged. "The people took their stories with them." Including her matrilineal ancestors. "It raises a lot of questions, but –"

Gavin threw open the door and ran down the office steps. "Where is it? What happened?" The office door slammed shut.

Tamaki looked at the other Alchemists, but they were as surprised as she was. Then two figures appeared from the darkness, sprinting down the path toward them. Ripley and Gerry.

Ripley, a middle-aged mechanic, came into the fire's circle of light and leaned over, panting. "Something large is coming down the mountain behind the volleyball court. We can hear it crashing through the trees."

Gavin nodded. "Gerry, make the fire larger. We need to be able to see." He pointed his fingers like a knife at Hank. "Make sounds in the woods near us to attract it. We don't want it going toward the prepper cabins."

Jamal lunged forward and stacked pieces of wood around the existing fire while Hank moved his mouth. A series of whoops and hollers emerged from the forest.

There was a flash of movement in the trees to the left as something moved sideways. A moment later the creature leaped into the section of forest where Hank had projected his voice. It was large and dark, whatever it was.

Tamaki clutched the top of her cane. She needed a knife.

Gerry conjured more fire to brighten the night.

Suddenly the creature broke from the trees and ran toward the Alchemists. Firelight glinted off the black shell of a scorpion the size of a pony. It had eight legs and the front pair had grasping pincers. A narrow, segmented tail curved over its back. Poison shone on the stinger.

"Form a semi-circle and stay clear of the tail," Gavin called. "We need help. Don, run to the bell by the dining hall. Tell whoever you see to bring lights and weapons."

As the Alchemists moved into position, Gavin pivoted toward Tamaki. "Get into my office now. That's an order."

Tamaki nodded but didn't move. She should help. Reach out to roots and have them wrap around the torso of the creature. She sent power down to her hands. There was a tingle there, but it wasn't strong.

"Hey," Jamal yelled at her. "Don't stand there. Get inside."

Frustrated, Tamaki turned and hurried across the clearing. Fast-moving clouds covered the moon, dimming the light. Tamaki gritted her teeth as she stepped over the haphazard pile of branches gathered for the fire. A sound came from the woods behind. Someone screamed. Was the giant scorpion advancing? Feeling helpless without a knife or some other weapon, Tamaki glanced back. Her foot slid on a loose stick and she dropped the cane, falling to her knees and thrusting her hands in front of her. Pain from her healing wrist radiated up her arm.

"Crap," she said. "Enbu."

Angry she sat up and rubbed her hands together to roll the dirt and grass off. Immediately a familiar tingle spread through her hands. Tiny cuts released her life force and Tamaki thrilled to it, feeding a hunger that she'd been denying. That helpless feeling from a moment ago was gone. The door of the cabin she was supposed to hide in and straight ahead. Instead, she turned to join the fight.

She used her fingernails to scrape at her palms as she ran around the fire pit. The night opened as the pain increased. No longer were the night sounds scary. No longer was she blind. Instead, her senses delighted as she 'saw' the energy moving. Cal, the prophet, rolled on the ground. Contaminated energy pulsed in his side. He must have been stung. Nguyen had appeared and held a machete. Gavin shouted directions, but she didn't need him. She didn't need any of them.

Tamaki pushed to the front of the Alchemists. "Stand back," she screamed. A remade pop song that used to play on the radio pulsed in her mind, a few phrases repeating on a loop.

The scorpion stood on the battlefield of grass between the forest and the firepit. It turned this way and that, its exoskeleton an armor against anything the Alchemists had thrown at it. A pincer came towards Tamaki, but she laughed, thrilling in her power. Tamaki held out her bloody hands and reached for the trees. Several strong oaks, there was a walnut with branches that would break off, sturdy maples, and a tall beech tree. Such a nice, heavy tree. She pulled, testing. The beech tree groaned. Its roots were deep, but there was a fungus inside, killing the woody tissue and girdling the tree. The scorpion's tail quivered. The tree toppled, its full weight on the scorpion. The middle branches bent around her, but the higher branches fell amongst the Alchemists. She heard them scatter behind her, but the music was still loud in her head.

"It's on fire," someone yelled.

She didn't care. She pointed to the walnut tree and then closed her fist. A branch broke off. A branch with a sharp end.

Someone struggled from behind and ran to the branch. Nguyen. She folded her arms. He held the branch like a javelin and pointed it at the tree. The scorpion's pincer emerged first, waving in the air. Tamaki imagined it waving a white flag of surrender.

It hefted itself through the tree, moving one leg at a time.

"Throw the stick," she yelled.

In the firelight, Nguyen's gaze centered on the scorpion. Nguyen's hand trembled, but he was frozen.

The tree shifted as the scorpion pushed its thorax free.

Tamaki used her right hand to keep pressing the tree down onto the creature, but she used the left hand to throw an *etemmu* connection to the makeshift javelin in Nguyen's hand. Then she threw the stick in an arc, directing it to the point where the head met the torso. Black smoke rose from the shell as the scorpion collapsed. Its legs curled up and it sunk down into itself.

Tamaki snapped her fingers as she remembered the band. "The Rolling Stones." With a smile, she pivoted to face the Alchemists.

In the distance the peals of a bell rang into the night. Don must have reached the dining hall.

Gerry and Ripley wrestled the top of the tree out of the fire. Jamal and Hank knelt by Cal. Nguyen came over to stand near her. No one was thanking her, yet, somehow, they were all watching her.

Gavin cleared his throat. "Jamal and Hank. Use the cart to take Cal to Haws. Gerry and Ripley, move this tree over to the forest line. Burn the scorpion but stay clear of the smoke." They nodded.

"Nguyen," Gavin continued. "Check in with the patrols and redistribute personnel as needed." He waited for them to obey. "Tamaki, join me by the fire."

A headache thumped in her head. There was the nausea. This fight hadn't taken too much blood, but she needed to be careful. She eased onto a log and wrapped a hand around her middle. She needed a drink of water. The logs closest to the forest had been knocked over and even the fire stones had been moved. Still, it would have been worse without her. Guess the Alchemists would know that her abilities didn't end with growing vegetables.

Realizing she was all alone, Tamaki looked around. Gavin had gone into his office and he'd effectively sent everyone else away. The door slammed as Gavin reemerged. He marched across the clearing and sat down next to her. One of the men had poured water on the fire, probably when the beech branches caught, and there were only glowing embers. But the clouds had dispersed and the moon graced everything with a cold light.

"I told you to get inside my office." His voice was low, but the words were clear. "You're still concussed and you're the slowest member of my team." He nodded toward the cane.

Tamaki stared at the embers as her cheeks warmed. She'd had this conversation before, only she'd had it with a god who came to congratulate her on saving a fox. Praise that turned into censor. Her stomach clenched.

"Instead, I trapped the scorpion so no one else would die."

"Cal was still alive when they put him in the cart." Gavin lit a cigarette from the embers. "What makes you think he'll die?"

The corrupt *etemmu* coursing through his body. "Maybe I'm wrong. Maybe Haws has the antidote for mutated scorpion venom." Her right hand shook and she folded it into the bottom of her sweater.

"We're a team, Tamaki, but I'm the leader and I gave you a direct order."

Wild claws ripped at the space in her chest behind her heart. She struggled to keep her anger inside, tried not to think of a black scorpion scaling her ribcage and climbing out of her mouth, ready to sting anyone who scolded her.

"You disobeyed me."

Enbu, he sounded like a disappointed father and it made her angrier.

Gavin offered something. It must be whatever he'd gone inside to get.

"A piece of paper?" she asked, turning it over. "It's blank."

"And here's a pen." He waited until she took it. "We all make mistakes. Bad decisions. Things that, after careful thought, we regret. I want you to write down what you regret and then you can burn the paper in those coals. A ritual to let go and start over."

The scorpion was walking through her head, stinging the insides of her eyelids.

He waited.

She wanted to tell him that she'd waited for years by the living room window for her mother to return. There was no way he was going to win this game.

But as she breathed through the headache, she knew what Scout would say. That she'd already blown her cover as someone who should be dismissed. That winning this battle wouldn't actually win anything.

In her imagination, she pulled apart the scorpion ravaging her insides like it was a clay model. Then her hand moved the pen over the paper. She looked at Gavin as she folded it once, twice, and nodded her head like she was agreeing to whatever this bullshit was. She stuck the paper in the embers. Immediately a black spot formed and then a flame sprang around the edges.

"Ashes of regret," she said.

TWENTY-THREE

I only took a nap!

Tamaki and Scout were alone in the greenhouse: she stood in front of a long trough of dirt and he'd curled up in a sunspot on top of stacked tarps in the corner.

"If I'd known there was going to be an over-sized scorpion, I would have woken you up first."

How do you feel?

"Tired and a little numb. I've had a headache since last night." She shrugged. "Tired of being tired, but otherwise good."

She'd told Scout that she'd pulled a rotten tree down on top of a huge scorpion with her "growing hands". It could happen. She waited to see if he could discern her half-truths.

Still, you probably shouldn't have intervened.

"It was important to let the Alchemists know that I shouldn't be written off as the girl- who-grows-vegetables." Tamaki picked at a hole in the sleeve of the red sweater she'd gotten from the community closet. At least the material was soft, some type of clingy cashmere. The sleeves also had a thumb hole and material extended to the base of her fingers, covering her scratches and scabs from falling.

I thought you were playing them.

She felt his disapproval. "I am. I was." She twirled the blue strand of her hair. "But what's the downside if I wasn't?"

I don't want to stay. There's something rotten here. Why were all the Alchemists 'called' here? Why did a scorpion, a desert animal, come charging down a mountain of the Ozarks? How did Gavin know something was wrong before everyone else?

"Everyone has secrets. That doesn't make them bad." Tamaki ran her fingers through a section of dirt. Then she picked up the fluffy-headed dandelion from a patch that Liza had grown and blew. Seeds parachuted down into the dirt. She sprinkled water on top. "They like us here. And it's safe. Maybe this was where I was supposed to end up the whole time. With the Alchemists."

Dammit! It's not SAFE, there's nowhere left in the world that's SAFE! And the places that make you feel safe are the worst because they make you forget that fact. He sneezed twice. *And what if they find out you use blood magic?*

"They won't because I've stopped." Except for that small incident twelve hours before. "I've been here for almost two weeks, right? I'm healing, and not only the concussion. Every choice I made to cut myself was when I didn't have another option." She looked around the greenhouse. "This is a retreat, a special place, and I'm back in alignment with my destiny. This is what Obaa-chan would have wanted."

What about going back to An's territory? You said you needed Saki's egg.

Tamaki sighed. "Part of healing is realizing that you were right. I'm not going to be able to sneak into a god's territory. I'll always be angry about it, but I have to let the dream go. Same with revenge against Debossey and Mr. Wilson. I'm not going to forget, but I'm not going to actively seek them out. See? I've matured."

Sure, everything's fine... until you become frustrated again. Addictions don't just go away. You have to deal with the anger inside of you, the root cause.

"I can. When I'm calm, I can remember Obaa-chan's stories and how she taught me."

But you don't live in a vacuum. You can't only be calm when external factors 'allow' you to be. You have to control yourself in the middle of a storm. That's where your power is. Not giving up your life – and that is what you are doing when you give in to blood magic, you are using years off your life – to let chaos unfold. Then you are only a vessel.

"Do I have wrinkles and crow's feet yet?"

You're like Oscar Wilde's Dorian Gray. You're aging on the inside, full of scarring and blood clots, but beautiful on the outside.

He still thought she was beautiful? Her face was too square; she wasn't delicate. Or her body. She was strong and athletic, but she liked to eat. And, she didn't have an hourglass figure like conventional models of how women should look. That, at least, was one positive change from before the firestorm. More emphasis on who people were rather than how they looked.

She was too sarcastic when she said, "Wow, aren't you the literary one. I didn't know park rangers had time to read."

He sniffed. *What you don't know is that park rangers do read and we are also the ones who start revolutions. It's park rangers and poets.*

"Cool."

He stood up and stretched his front paws out in front. *All joking aside, you know what I'm saying is true. I told you I would hold you responsible, and I meant it.*

"Okay," she said so he'd stop talking. Tamaki stared at the pots. Gentle warmth gathered in her hand. Tamaki imagined the planted lima beans splitting open and the new plant emerging. The soil shivered and then part of a tiny green stem breached the surface of one pot and then the next. Satisfied, Tamaki shifted her attention to Scout. "I remember Obaa-chan's hands covering my own and plunging them into the soil. This smell, I think, brings back the memory."

She placed the pots into the rectangular bin with the others. "In my earliest memory, Obaa-chan scooped a handful of loam and held it right under my nose so I had no choice but to sniff. Sand. Clay. Nutrients. It made me cough because it was so pungent, but she told me to remember and I do. So the loam and my grandmother and the plants in her sunroom all combined," Tamaki waved her hands in the air, "into something more, something like 'home' or 'good' or 'real.'" She let her hands drop. "I understand what you're saying. Centering myself and crap."

Scout huffed out a breath and then settled back down into napping position, facing away from her.

"Sorry to bore you." Tamaki leaned against the black-topped chemistry table, probably salvaged from a high school nearby, and drifted back into her memory. Obaa-chan urging her to "feel," as Tamaki made a pincer-like grip, pretending her fingers were chopsticks, hovering in the air before stroking the flower petals. If she stroked too hard, the petals would bruise and her grandmother's lips would thin. The bun of white hair on Obaa-chan's head would quiver with disappointment. Without being told, Tamaki would do it again. At that time, as a child, she'd been so impatient, but now Tamaki appreciated her grandmother. It was so different post-firestorm though. Her grandmother had been teaching her how to play with matches and now, with such potent *etemmu*, Tamaki was trying to control gasoline.

You don't bore me, but you are difficult to talk to.

She didn't want to start a fight, but this seemed a good time to talk because Scout didn't seem able to read her thoughts today, but he was also being open. "I know you're angry I didn't ask consent before I forced you into the fox's body." She turned over her palm. The scrapes from the clearing were still pink and puffy, but the wound from the chisel had healed, leaving behind a scar that paralleled what in palmistry would be considered her lifeline. "I'm sorry, Scout."

He uncurled and sat up to face her. *I forgave you while we were back in Ekur Temple.* Scout shook his head. *I understand your decisions, but I don't agree with them.*

"That means a lot to me." His forgiveness felt like setting down boulders that had been strapped to her back.

He looked at her and then the fur rose along his back and he snarled.

"Hey," a familiar male voice called as the greenhouse door opened with an irritating squeaky sound. "Is this a good time?"

Doesn't he have something to do or somewhere to go? Scout stared past her shoulder at the door.

Tamaki felt her cheeks warm. "Be nice," she whispered. Turning to the open doorway, Tamaki straightened the boat-shaped neck of the sweater so it wasn't slipping off one shoulder, the calluses on her hands catching at the material.

"Gavin told me you moved in here. I like the decorating." Nguyen ducked as he came into the greenhouse and leaned against the wall. "How's the concussion?"

"Recovering." Tamaki didn't want to admit to weakness, to being overwhelmed with loud noises and too many people. Being more emotional than she'd been before. Haws had told her this was natural, part of the healing process for her brain. "I spend a lot of time alone and that helps. Haws credits the fact that I have no access to screen time with a phone or television."

"Yeah, I've noticed that you don't really hang out with the group very often." He held out the cane she'd dropped last night. "Do you still need this?"

Tamaki took it and leaned it against the wall. "What do you mean?"

"You were limping around camp since you got here and then suddenly you didn't need the cane and pulled down an entire tree by yourself. Some of the others were talking about it. It's a little confusing."

"It's not confusing. When I need a cane, I use one and when I don't, then I don't. I don't need anyone policing how or when I use a tool to help me get around. It's like pre-firestorm people who judge who gets to park in a handicapped spot instead of minding their own business."

"Noted." Nguyen was almost as tall as Scott had been and a lean physique showed off his muscles. Even in the middle of a campground, his clothes looked perfect. A blue button-down shirt under a black sweater over khakis with creases. Even the front of his hair looked styled.

I'm taller.

"Not now, you aren't," she whispered.

"What's that?" Nguyen cocked an eyebrow.

"Oh, nothing." Tamaki waved her hand in the air. "Talking to the plants."

Nguyen pushed off from the wall to stand next to Tamaki and examine the plants. "What are you growing?"

"So, dandelions here." She pointed to the seeds she'd planted a moment ago. "Kind of funny that before the firestorm everyone used to call them weeds. Homeowners would yank them out or even pour chemicals on them. Now I'm trying to grow them because every part of the plant is edible. Salad. Stir-fry. Soup."

Nguyen grinned. "I know about the value of dandelions. All preppers do."

"Right." She exhaled. "You don't look like a prepper, though. Your vibe is game designer meets academic."

"I do miss video games," he conceded. "But now I'm an Alchemist in a prepper community. Same as you. It's like we're in a video game, right?

Because we're the resistance. We're fighting for human rights against these beings with incredible power who act out of pettiness and a need to be worshipped. We'll win, of course, because we are the beloved underdogs." He laughed, embarrassed. "But please go one with your garden tour."

"First let me make a note about being a beloved underdog." She waited for him to acknowledge her joke and then pointed to another bin. "These are lima beans for the kitchen. Also, Haws asked me to encourage the aloe." The aloe plant had grown as tall as Tamaki's hip, sprouting seven arms. She didn't really like working with it because the pulp that filled the arms made her feel slimy afterward, but she wouldn't say 'no' to the doctor.

Nguyen picked up a pot with a green stem sticking out. "How do you like the camp?"

"I'm glad to be here," she said. "Crossing into Enlil's territory was a disaster." She shuddered, remembering.

We didn't exactly choose it. Scout stretched into a seated position. The tip of his tail tapped against the tarps.

"But it turned out for the good." Nguyen set the pot back down onto the table. "We're gathering everyone who knows how to use energy here and we'll have the first academy to learn and teach other humans. No more divisions based on age, gender, race. We're all humans against gods."

"You say 'energy' but my grandmother taught me to say *etemmu.* It's a Mesopotamian word that was altered by ancient alchemists to be a close play on the word for soul or animating spirit. Alchemists, like the gods, could manipulate the most basic spiritual fabric of the world."

"Huh. I'd never heard that before. We should write a questionnaire and make a book with all of our versions of how we understand what happened or is happening. Could be the start of our school's first textbook."

She smiled at his idealism as she moved the pot back with the others. "Are you a student or a teacher?"

"Uh, both?" He made a goofy face and ran his hand through his hair. "What about you?"

"Same."

They laughed.

So funny. A laugh echoed in her mind from Scout and she looked up at him, widening her eyes to remind him to be nice.

"That was some wicked *etemmu* with the tree last night, though." Nguyen's hair fell across his forehead again. "I haven't seen that before. We thought your superpower was making us eat spinach and sprouts."

"Yeah." Tamaki nodded, trying to think of something to say that didn't involve blood magic or ley lines or anything else she should hold back. "I was kind of improvising."

"Will you tell me how your talent works?"

Tamaki shrugged and adjusted the sweater neck. "My Obaa-chan also had growing hands. She taught me to learn the roots, the stalks, the leaves of a plant. I remember watching when she showed me a rose petal with an insect-made hole. Her thumb and her third finger made these little circles over the petal. I felt a tingling in my own fingers. When she removed her fingers, I clapped because the petal, like playdough, had been pulled back together." Tamaki shook her head. "She was teaching me, but I thought it was some kind of trick. Later, she stopped teaching me."

Her thoughts tangled as she remembered Scout's challenge to think about other people. I thought she quit teaching me because she didn't think I was good enough, that she blamed me for my mother's lack of interest, but maybe I was the one who lost interest when I became a teenager, maybe I rolled my eyes when she asked me to follow her traditions. Maybe I was the one who moved away from her.

It was unsettling to reinterpret a story that Tamaki thought she knew and so she pushed it away. There was no way to ask Obaa-chan for the truth now.

Families are difficult. We tell ourselves stories to survive the moment and have to examine them later.

Tamaki glanced at Scout and nodded. He had a lot of integrity, telling her the truth when she needed to hear it. They were psychically linked, but there was still so much they didn't know about each other. If only there had been more time and she hadn't cursed him into a fox's body and then lied to him ten minutes ago about using blood magic. She sighed. Relationships were so hard.

"My talent is different." Nguyen looked around and then grabbed the spiral notebook that Daisy had given her to catalogue the plants. "May I?" Without waiting for an answer, he ripped out a blank page, folded it into an airplane, and held it with one hand. With the other, he pointed to an old watering schedule written on an index card and taped to the wall near the hoses. "Three, two, one." He drew back and released the paper airplane. It flew toward the index card and performed a loop-the-loop over and over again.

Tamaki grinned. "How'd you do that?"

"My family is third generation Vietnamese and my parents taught me about the elements: water, fire, earth or metal, void, and air." He tapped his chest. "My affinity is for metal and air. So I picture the parts that make up what I'm holding and then increase the air aspect. The more I increase the air, the faster and higher I can make the object go. I think it helps that we're in Enlil's territory, but that's speculation."

Nguyen motioned with his hand and the plane flew in a different direction, heading for Scout. The fox leaped into the air and caught the paper airplane in his jaws, landing lightly on the floor and spitting the paper airplane out before coming to sit at Tamaki's feet and glaring at Nguyen.

"I don't think your fox likes me."

"Do you need to be liked by everyone you meet?"

Nguyen stepped closer and lowered his voice. "I hope we can continue becoming friends."

Oh, yeah, he really wants to be friends. I don't think he can actually get any closer to you.

"It's time for dinner." He touched her elbow, thumb circling as if brushing away a piece of dirt. "I thought we could walk over together."

"That sounds good." Tamaki looked down at his hand and then over at Scout. "Before we go, though, you said you'd tell me about the missing Alchemists."

"Ahh," Nguyen ran his hand through his dark hair. "There isn't much to tell. Gavin sent four of our guys on a mission. Even I don't know what it was about. They never came back."

Ask if they took backpacks and supplies.

She asked and Nguyen said, "Yes, they all had full packs. They were supposed to be back in a week."

"That's very mysterious."

"We all trust Gavin. Our crew breaks down if we don't have a leader." Nguyen shrugged. "But it was really bad for morale. For some of the guys, it was the first time they realized that our patrols and the hunting parties aren't a game. This is real. And learning how to use energy isn't a party trick. It's what will help us survive."

"That's grim."

"It's true. The gods want to use humans. We know this." He pointed toward the camp buildings. "We're the only thing standing between them and human domination."

TWENTY-FOUR

The next morning Tamaki watered the plants and then wiped her wet hands on her pants. "I'm off to train with the Alchemists."

Great. I'm going to take a nap.

"That's ambitious."

Fine. I'm off to conquer the world. After I take a nap.

Tamaki rolled her eyes. Scout had wandered the camp and surrounding woods through the night. She suspected he was miffed about missing the scorpion.

Unsure how physical the training would be, Tamaki took her cane and left the greenhouse. She followed the path past the dining hall and then veered right toward Gavin's office. A wooden sign with an arrow reading "Archery range" pointed at a footpath, but even if it hadn't, Tamaki could hear the men laughing. She took a deep breath and followed the footpath to the range.

When she stepped into view, the conversations lagged. She looked for Gavin, but didn't see him. Jamal, however, gave her a look and glanced at the cane. "Got your prop today."

"My prop?" She locked eyes and didn't flinch. He could decide whether to call it part of a costume or whether he meant to prop her up, but if he tried to take it, she wasn't going to fall down.

"Let's go!" Stoltzus, Gavin's second, raised his voice. "We'll warm up with stretching. Nate, it's your turn to lead."

"Ugg," Hank said. "I'm tired of doing high school soccer warmups."

"That's all I know," Nate protested. "Until two months ago, I was a high school soccer player. Varsity, by the way."

Ten targets with bright blues and reds were staggered at various distances. The Alchemists spread apart with Nate at the front. Tamaki recognized most of the stretches from her cross-country practices. It felt good to be outside and move her body. After being in Debtor's prison, she wouldn't take this for granted. As she clasped her hands behind her back, her shoulders popped. When she did lunges, her knees did too. If Scout had been here, she would have made a joke about her body acting older than a nineteen-year-old's should, and then he would have blamed it on blood magic the way he always did. She sighed. Standing in the middle of these men she suddenly felt very lonely.

"Tamaki, you can sit out and watch, if you want."

Embarrassed, Tamaki shook her head. "I'll participate as part of the team."

"Alright." Stoltzus rubbed a hand over his shaved head. "You know what to do. Divide into pairs. Then, you'll move between here and the climbing wall. After that we'll have sprints followed by meditation and then I'll assign patrols and we'll break for lunch." He looked at each person. "Move!"

Tamaki gripped the head of her cane and forced a smile. This was like middle school gym class. Jamal ignored her as he paired with Hank. Ripley and Gerry. The pairs moved away, deciding whether to do archery or climbing first. Stoltzus motioned to Don and then noticed Tamaki standing by herself.

"Ah. With Cal in the infirmary, we have an odd number."

"She'll be my partner." Nguyen appeared. He looked like a model in a designer athletic shirt and matching sweatpants. "Nate's going to join another group."

Relief swept through Tamaki. "If you're sure," she murmured.

"I am." He grinned, full of confidence. His expression was so open and honest that she felt her shoulders relaxing. "Where do you want to go first?"

Remembering how she used to love parkour, Tamaki said, "Climbing course." They followed the footpath to two obstacle courses made of ropes.

"I'm not going to let you win because you're new," Nguyen said.

"And I won't let you win because I'm afraid your head would get too big and you'd float away."

When Stoltzus shouted, "Go," they both sprang towards the ropes.

*   *   *

Scout crouched in the woods outside of Gavin's office and watched as Tamaki and Nguyen flirted. She had this habit of looking down and chewing on the inside of her cheek before tipping back her head and saying something snarky. She'd put on a couple pounds since being here and it looked good on her – the gauntness from the prison was gone. Tamaki folded her arms across her chest. Silly to wear long-sleeves in late summer. As if he wouldn't notice the scratches on her palms and the way she cradled her wrist. The same way he recognized the way her brow furrowed when one of her headaches was coming on and she should get away from people and go to the greenhouse to rest.

He didn't try to overhear her conversation. It was none of his business. His tail twitched. He couldn't care about her well-being more than she cared about it. Really, the best thing to do was get away from this place. She didn't trust his instincts so he'd followed her here, knowing that the

Alchemists would be busy. That would give him time to search Gavin's office. Unfortunately, he hadn't seen the former soldier.

Scout crept through the underbrush to the cabin's door. The screen door was warped so it was easy enough to insert a paw and slip in. There was a larger room to the side, but the office was straight back. The room was sparsely furnished: desk, bed, both a lantern and a lamp. An open closet with hangers and boots lined along the bottom. A half-eaten breakfast sandwich sat on the edge of the desk next to an ashtray. A map with pins hung on the wall while rolled up papers littered the space between wall and desk. Scout balanced on his hind legs to read the print on the map. There! The Alchemists' camp was clearly marked and north of it was a ring of mountains. In the middle were several pins. Scout pressed his nose right up against the map. DO NOT ENTER. Next to it, in what was presumably Gavin's handwriting, was a sticky note with the question: What happens to the soldiers we sent in?

What the hell?

Scout dropped down to all fours and walked over to the desk. He pushed the chair out of the way and propped his two front paws on the desk, nosing around to move papers. Here was one that read ORG CHART. It had columns with each Alchemist's name, their talent, pros and cons, and plan for utilization. Tamaki's name was at the bottom. Scout blinked as the letters swam out of focus. He shook his head.

That half-eaten sandwich smelled really good. Egg and cheese. Saliva filled his mouth. But he was supposed to be doing something. Oh, the paper. He pulled his head back slightly and found Tamaki's name again. Her talent read: *plants*, under cons: *doesn't follow orders* was followed by an exclamation point. Well, Scout could see that. Under the pro column: *female*. This was followed by a smiley face and the word "finally". In the column for plan for utilization, Gavin had written: *Try Nguyen first. She seems to have an affinity for him.*

Noise from outside made Scout's ears swivel. Instinct made him leap into the closet. Two humans entered. Male. Familiar. Leaders. They had names, but words were gone. One male went to picture on wall and pointed to a dirt mark from Scout's paw. Not stealthy. Not secret. Mistake.

Scout shook his head. A breeze blew and then scent of the sandwich drifted to him. Scout bounded from the closet and grabbed the sandwich. Men shouted, but Scout was already out the door, tail streaming behind as he gulped the food. Tastes good. Happiness. Good thief.

There was something he was supposed to tell someone. Birds sang around him and the moss was soft underfoot. Whatever it was…was gone. Lost in the now of fox-thought.

*   *   *

By the time they broke for lunch, Tamaki was covered in sweat and happy. Walking toward the dining hall in a group, it was less obvious that she was being isolated.

"Hey, Tamaki," Nate called from the front. "Is that your fox in the woods?"

Tamaki glanced to the side of the path. There was a fox there, but it had normal brown eyes. She touched Nguyen's arm so he'd stop walking.

I'm hungry.

The fox blinked and his eyes were full golden. A trick of the light? Tamaki shook her head. The rest of the group had continued on, but Nguyen waited.

"Am I being hazed because I'm a girl, because I sometimes need a cane, because I am able to grow plants and figure out which ones are rotten, or for some other reason.?"

Nguyen opened his mouth and scratched his cheek. "We're a close-knit group and I told you those other guys disappeared. Then you appear from nowhere and know more about energy, or *etemmu*, than anyone. It's hard for them to trust you because they don't know you."

"And you?" She lifted her chin. "Do you find it hard to trust me?"

"No." He smiled into her eyes. "I do, however, find you difficult to beat on a rope's course."

"You did win!"

"You made me work hard and I'm half a foot taller than you." He laughed. "Come on, I'm hungry." His words echoed Scout's. She looked in the forest, but the fox was gone.

Tamaki and Nguyen hurried into the dining hall to find that people were standing aside as Gavin finished at the buffet line.

"You missed the announcement," Nate whispered. "The preppers said for the rest of the week we get to eat first in gratitude for killing the scorpion."

"Did Haws decide that?" Nguyen asked.

"I haven't seen Haws. I guess he's still with Cal at the infirmary." Nate frowned. "Cal didn't look too bad. I'm not sure what's taking so long for him to be released. Haws got your concussion fixed pretty quickly."

Tamaki ran through several statements explaining that her symptoms weren't consistent and that was normal when a brain was injured, but she decided against all of them.

Nguyen got in line at the buffet and Tamaki followed. Gavin was smart. He'd established himself and his crew as essential to survival. The citizens of Little Rock had been so quick to accept Enlil when he promised benevolence and wind power. For the same reason, the preppers would look to the Alchemists because the new dangers were outside of their understanding.

Inching up in line, Tamaki could smell cornbread, green beans cooked with onions, and the sweet smell of barbecue. She craned her neck and saw meat that had been slow-cooked in some type of tomato-based sauce.

"That smells delicious."

"Yeah," Nguyen said, grabbing a plate from the stack. "Timmy and Paul are a married couple from Florida. They do most of the cooking by using what the Alchemist parties bring back from raiding stores or by trading with some of the farms down in the valley. Another benefit of being part of our community."

She speared the meat onto her plate, adding another helping for Scout in case the fox decided to appear. "Nice."

Watch it, you lugs. Scout dashed through the multitude of legs around the buffet and paused in an open spot in the room to flick his tail and glare over his shoulder. *How hard is it to avoid stepping on one's tail?*

"Come on, Scout," she said for the benefit of those around. They went to the Alchemist's table and she took the end seat, preparing Scout's plate and setting it on the floor. He gave a suspicious glance around before sweeping his tail close to his body.

Nguyen sat down across from her. "Are these assigned seats?"

"I don't like a lot of attention and Scout needs space to eat."

"You really like that fox. Gavin said," Nguyen glanced over at the leader sitting farther down the bench. "Never mind."

"Tell me." Fear ran down her spine and she had to blink away the overwhelming feeling. Stupid concussion! She couldn't get her emotions under control. She gritted her teeth. "Now."

"It's nothing." Nguyen waved his hand. "He just said that your fox doesn't always act very fox-like. In fact, he was in Gavin's office this morning and it almost looked like he was pawing through maps."

"Interesting." She made her tone as bored as possible so they wouldn't linger on this topic. Scout hadn't mentioned anything to her. He was probably trying to build a case against the Alchemists and was embarrassed when he couldn't find anything horribly wrong. "Maybe there are mice in the office."

Further down the table, Gerry knocked over a glass of fruit punch. Quickly people threw down napkins and moving plates out of the way.

"Why is everyone at the table acting so nervous?" Tamaki asked.

"We pull cards today."

She remembered her first day at the camp. "I see."

"It's an exercise in energy, or what you call *etemmu*." His fingers were long, nails neatly trimmed as if it wasn't the end of the world. "Gavin's idea is that we need challenges to increase our skills, right?"

"He's a military man," Tamaki said.

"Formerly Army."

"Got it." She motioned him to continue.

"So, we infuse our card with either positive or negative energy to influence whether our card is chosen or not. Some at this table are eager to get out of here and bring back supplies and others would rather stay in camp and make plans for how to deal with the newest announcement about the empty seat on the gods' council."

She remembered Don's unhappiness when she'd chosen his card.

"And how do you infuse a card?" She frowned. "When I make a seed grow, I either see the stem emerge or it doesn't."

"That's a very straightforward approach." He smiled. "You need to learn nuance. I've noticed that about you."

Was he being condescending?

Scout's voice filled her mind. It was noticeable after the absence while he was eating. And while he was in the forest on the walk over here.

One hundred percent he's being condescending. He's about to explain to you how to manipulate energy. You know. To you. The person who took on Mrs. Debossey channeling Ninlil.

"It's difficult, but learning to use a nuanced approach can give you more tools in your toolbox." Nguyen nodded his head as if giving her sage advice.

He's a tool! He's the tool in the toolbox. They all are. Please, Tamaki, let's leave. There's something…but I can't see to remember.

She looked down at Scout, sitting by the empty plate. His eyes begged, but she had to use this opportunity to learn as much as she could. Her grandmother wasn't alive to teach her anymore.

"When you pick a card, decide whether you want to go on the hunting mission or not. Holding it in your hand, feel the elements that make up the card. For me, I hone in on wood, which goes with earth, and air because of the lightness. Then you add either positive or negative to that."

"Very nuanced." She kept her expression neutral. "What supplies are being brought back?"

"This was Arkansas, home to Walmart headquarters." He'd managed to eat the BBQ without making a mess, which Tamaki found notable because she had to keep wiping her hands. "Each team that goes out has a list of supplies that are most important and we compare maps to what Gavin is compiling to see if anything has changed. As long as we plan and conserve, we're in a good position."

"What about raiding parties? Once the Walmarts and stores are out of supplies, won't people come here?"

"We get Hotheads in the area and random groups, but the mountains act as natural barriers. There are only a few ways to get out of camp and they have traps, set up pre-firestorm by this community."

"I see." That meshed with what Gavin had told her the first day she'd regained consciousness.

Gavin's chair scraped back with an obnoxious squeal. "It's time for the cards."

He passed around the deck and this time no one stopped Tamaki from drawing a card. She chose the queen of diamonds. Unsure about the whole element-thing, she tried to push *etemmu* into the card. It failed. She could feel the warmth gathering in her hands, but it couldn't exit into the paper.

Glancing around the table, Tamaki saw Don sweating as he gripped the card. Nguyen was confident as he passed his card to Gavin. Then the man to Tamaki's right suddenly cried out and dropped his card, on fire, onto the table.

"Sorry," he said sheepishly.

"That's the third time, Gerry." Gavin sighed and handed the deck to him to choose a new card.

"I'm a fire starter," Gerry protested. "That's what I do."

Gavin collected the cards and offered them to Don. "You went on the last hunting party, so you're excused."

Don nodded and fanned the cards out for Gavin to choose. Gavin's hand hovered. Then he selected the first one.

Jack of hearts.

"That's mine," Nguyen said.

Tamaki couldn't tell whether he was pleased or not.

Gavin looked at Tamaki as he put his hand on the second card.

Scout whined. *He knows that one is yours!*

Don smirked as Gavin held up the red queen.

"That's mine," she said. Her heart beat faster and she wasn't sure if it was because she was glad to get out of here, glad to have a mission with Nguyen, or because she had a suspicion about Gavin.

Before anyone could take their trays up, Haws approached the table. His face was haggard and his eyes were sad. "I'm sorry," he said. "Cal passed away. There was nothing more I could do."

"I know you tried everything," Gavin said, his voice calm. "Thank you, Haws. This camp is lucky to have you. We'll have a service of remembrance for him."

Haws sighed and walked over to the table where his wife was waiting.

One by one the Alchemists pushed away and took their trash up until only Tamaki and Gavin were at the table. Scout crouched underneath.

Impatient, Tamaki said. "You sense energy. That's how you knew the scorpion was coming and that's how you pick cards. It's deceptive to say that it's the fault of an individual Alchemist as to whether they can 'infuse' the card or not."

That makes sense. He senses some big energy around this campground and he's trying to find it. That must be what he sent the missing Alchemists to find.

"Is it?" Gavin frowned. "There has to be energy to read."

"If you can read energy, then you know that Nguyen and I are the strongest Alchemists you have. Why would you send us both out at the same time?"

"We're a family here. You're part of it now, but I heard there was some trouble this morning." Gavin narrowed his eyes. "I'm giving you an opportunity to prove yourself." He stood up to leave. "And, Tamaki? Stop questioning my decisions. If you're going to fit in, you have to follow the chain of command."

TWENTY-FIVE

The morning of the hunting mission, Tamaki looked down at the list she'd made with Scout's help: Virginia creeper, creeping thistle, atropa belladonna, sheep's sorrel, and oleander. She needed plants that could guard the camp's perimeter and make both poisons and medicines. She slid the notebook into a drawer.

Nguyen and Gavin arrived at the greenhouse together. Nguyen wore hiking boots the exact right combination of new and broken in and Gavin carried a camo jacket. Their expressions were serious. Apparently, this was a big deal.

"I brought you a coat. It'll help you blend in." Gavin's message was loud and clear. Today's mission was partially marketing. She'd scared some of the guys who couldn't even control their own talents. She had to rehabilitate her image by showing how she could contribute beyond the greenhouse. And that pissed her off.

She said, too sweetly, "I've decided to embrace more of a hedge witch aesthetic. Do you have a cape? Preferably one that attaches at the throat with a brooch? Maybe in the shape of a sprig of rosemary? It has, according to one expert, both culinary and magical properties."

Am I the expert?

She nodded once.

"What are you talking about?" Gavin frowned at her. "It's not magic. It's energy. You know that."

"I mean…Gerry sets things on fire with his mind." She blinked her eyelashes. "Sounds like magic."

Gavin gritted his teeth and Nguyen jumped in, "She's kidding. Making jokes because she's nervous." Nguyen shot her a look.

"Ah." That explanation seemed to make sense to Gavin because he nodded and moved into a more soothing tone, allowing his Southern accent to roll through the words. "Nothing to be nervous about. We don't anticipate trouble," Gavin said. "But I want you both to be prepared. There are mutations out there, Hotheads, and desperate people."

"I've been on the road," Tamaki said, losing interest in baiting him. She and Obaa-chan had traveled through Ohio after the soldiers from New Babylon came through. Not all mutations were bad, though. She'd found Saki the turtle-penguin during her travels. And she'd met Rachal and Adam. And Scott.

"Now you're a part of the Alchemists and we want you to return." He held out the jacket as he eyed her athletic, but short, frame. "This is the smallest size we have."

She shrugged into the jacket. It fit well enough though the fabric was rough to the touch. Durable.

"You and Nguyen will each carry your own packs. He has the list of priorities." Gavin opened the flap of one of the packs and reached inside. "Last, here's a Bowie knife." He slid the blade out of the leather case. "Fifteen inches of handmade Damascus steel with a bone handle." He turned the blade back and forth. "Do you know how to use a knife?"

I'm a very clever fox, but I'm at a loss for words.

So many possible answers. She said, "Yes."

Gavin must have seen something in her expression because he handed it to her, handle-first, and stepped back as she secured the case onto her belt.

When she and Nguyen had their packs on, Gavin made eye contact with each. "Return by sundown, soldiers." He left the greenhouse and Nguyen followed.

Scout got up from his spot on the tarps and stretched in a yoga downward facing dog. Then he straightened and walked over to Tamaki. *You know that sending only two people out on a patrol doesn't make any sense. There are a lot of people in this camp. You need at least four to have the ability to break into pairs and have enough people to bring back a quantity of supplies to make it worthwhile.*

"How do you know that?"

Haven't you watched the old Star Trek? *Four person teams including essential characters and a redshirt.*

"Let's make sure we're not the redshirt." Tamaki shut the greenhouse door and followed Nguyen, who moved counterintuitively away from the beach area. She'd been sure they'd follow they ley line.

"Stop here." He pulled a folded cloth from his pocket.

"A blindfold? Really?"

"You're still new." Nguyen gave an apologetic smile. That didn't stop him from pulling the cloth so tight that it cut into her nose. His fingers checked the gap under her eyes and smoothed her hair over her ears so it wasn't pulling.

"Take my arm."

She didn't want to, but she hadn't brought the cane and it was challenging to navigate with the small loose rocks underfoot. They were moving uphill and zigzagging in what she assumed was a pattern to either confuse her or miss the booby traps around camp. At one point, Nguyen slipped his arm around her waist. "Step over."

A picture of the scenery popped into her mind. *Does this help?*

It did. She could see the rotten log she'd gone over.

"This is far enough."

Nguyen's personal scent of burning sugar made Tamaki inhale as he came close to untie the blindfold.

She rubbed the marks on her face and looked around. They were in the middle of the forest midway up the mountain. Rock formations jutted from the ground, so it was as much hiking uphill as it was climbing. Evergreen seedlings sprang from cracks inside of the rocks. She was breathing hard from exertion when they came to what looked like a natural keystone arch of rock.

"Watch where I step," Nguyen said. "Only on the rocks with no lichen. Otherwise, you'll trip the hazard."

Was it a mine or tripwire? Nervous, Tamaki looked around for Scout. He'd been bounding away and exploring, circling back and then leaving again.

There's a bundle of cut logs held with a rope. They must have it somehow secured to specific rocks.

Tamaki nodded and then stepped in the same way that Nguyen had done. Scout watched from atop the arch.

Once they were through the arch, it felt like they were the only people in the world. A pair of red birds squabbled through the branches of a bush with purple berries. Trees filled her line of sight and they had the choice of going up on the left or going downhill on the right.

"Oh, look over there." Tamaki pointed to a group of trees near a boulder. Yellow and orange leaves decorated the branches. "I think they're sugar maples."

They are. Scout bounded over. *The inner bark can be eaten raw or cooked. Even the seeds and young leaves are edible.*

"Do you have something to collect sap?" As they approached, she could see that each of the trunks had split open, the bark peeling back like the edges of a wound. Inside, the tree was damp and it smelled fermented.

Scout sniffed at the wound. *This is what happened to the Skeleton Forest back in An's territory. Too much* etemmu. *The rot isn't as advanced here.*

Tamaki pulled on a piece of bark and it came off in her hand. Exposed, a hundred or so small glowing bugs scurried for another place within the tree. Some flew to other branches and others tried to get back under the remaining bark. They couldn't stay away long, though. Soon the glowbugs were coming back to the damp wound in the trunk and gathering around. Together they created a high-pitched humming sound that was almost like music.

"They have a sugar high," she laughed.

Fascinating. An important part of the post-firestorm ecosystem. They glow because they're absorbing the etemmu. *I wonder if certain tree species are more susceptible. Will you write this down when we get back? We can make a new brochure of ecology and see if anyone else will do the same in their territory.*

Tamaki grinned. Scout sounded so happy now that he had a project.

"They're giving off a pretty nice light. Is this the new version of a lightning bug? We can collect them in jars and set them along the paths at night." Nguyen looked up at the glowing bugs walking along the upper branches and gave the nearest one a shake. "Ouch." He recoiled and shut his eyes, rubbing frantically.

"Are you okay? What happened?" Tamaki looked up at the tree and then all around to see if they were under attack by the bugs or something else.

The fox made a strange chuffing sound. *A piece of bark fell into his eye.* Scout fell over laughing. *What an idiot!*

"Okay, stop." She meant it for both of them. "Let me help." Tamaki moved closer to Nguyen and pried his hands away. Tears streamed from his right eye. She opened the lids and saw a black splinter. "Hold still." Catching the edge with her fingernail, she pulled it out. "All better."

"Thank you." He wiped his face with the edge of his shirt. "Well, that was embarrassing. Thanks for not calling me a dummy."

Scout had managed to get himself under control and prowled around, sniffing at the leaves. She was pretty sure, though, that she saw his shoulders shake every few breaths and a ghost of laughter flitted through her mind.

"I wouldn't do that," Tamaki assured him. "I mean, if anything, I would have asked if you found what you were looking for. Or I could have said the tree was all bark and no bite. I could have asked if you saw that coming."

"You have a warped sense of humor."

"Yeah." Those were all Scott-style jokes.

"You know, I wasn't really the outdoorsy type."

Never would have guessed.

"Really?" Tamaki said. She licked the piece of bark in her hand.

Nguyen cleared his throat. "Yeah, I was your typical academic overachiever. Ton of AP classes, top percentage of my class, Honors college, and all that. I'm twenty-three and I'd mapped out the next steps for my career path with a timetable."

""This is delicious. We should come back with a tap and bucket." She'd had natural maple syrup before, but this sap was tangy and more subtle. She savored the taste. This was the closest she'd had to candy in months. "Want some?"

One quart of maple syrup requires ten gallons of sap. And you have to cook the sap down so it's generally done outside because of all the steam.

I like it the way you're doing it: eating the sap as is. It has a lot of health benefits and you really only need to give it a quick boil to kill any bacteria.

"Maybe later." Nguyen pulled on one of the backpack's straps. "Are you listening to me?"

"Yeah. You were a nerd."

"Uh, yes."

"Cool." She glanced at Scout. She definitely had a type. "I like nerds. How'd you end up in Arkansas?"

"Research for my Ph.D. I don't want to bore you, but I examined alternative energy sources that were more environmentally friendly. How we can deconstruct the socio-economic systems around oil, coal, etc." He shrugged.

"Light reading, huh?" Tamaki licked another piece of bark. Glowbugs landed on her arm. Their legs tickled as they marched down her wrist toward the bark. She hoped they weren't about to bite her and turn her into a giant Glowbug. "And why did that bring you here?"

"It brought me to the prepper camp for research. I was here during the firestorm."

"What about your parents?"

"They were in Vietnam visiting family." Nguyen pressed his lips together. "I have no way to reach them. To know what happened. That's why I'm so dedicated to the Alchemists. Once we gather other members there will be a way, somehow, to set up worldwide communication again. Longwire radio maybe? Cell towers working again? Humans are nothing if not inventive."

Check out this five-leaved plant. It's your Virginia creeper. Ask me how I know it isn't American ginseng. They are often confused.

Scout was showing off for her, distracting her from Nguyen's attempt to deepen their connection. She didn't hate it. "Hey, look at this."

Nguyen looked at the plant. "Poison ivy?"

Leaves of three, let it be. Can this boy not count? Virginia Creeper has dark blue berries and ginseng has red berries. This is September according to the calendar in Gavin's office. But, the petiolules give it away.

No way to ask Scout what in the world a "petiolule" was, so she set to work digging up the plant.

"I'm allergic to poison ivy," Nguyen said.

"Virginia creeper can cause an allergic reaction, too. Better step back." Tamaki tucked the plant in her backpack as she tried to segue into what she really wanted to talk about. "That announcement about competing for the seat on the Council of Gods. Humans and other deities will be allowed to compete. That was pretty shocking."

"I've been talking to Gavin, but we're just speculating. Hopefully, there will be another announcement soon."

"Hmmm." Tamaki nodded. "We're technically still in Enlil's territory. Will his priests be doing the testing to choose who will represent the entire territory? And, would the Alchemists…" She licked dry lips as she rephrased the question. "How would we decide who to send to Ekur Temple to compete? Would we only send one? They'd have to hide that they were a Humanist."

"Good questions. Uh, I don't know the answers yet." Nguyen turned away and shrugged his backpack off. "I guess we'd send the strongest candidate, whoever it was."

He's lying. Scout stood on an overhanging rock, sticky syrup making the fur on his snout clump together.

She nodded in agreement. As much as she hoped the Alchemists would base it on merit, the whole 'chain of command' thing might play a larger role. She thought about telling Nguyen that she wanted to represent the Alchemists, just to see what he'd say.

"Today's priority is to fill in the local maps." Nguyen pulled out a notebook and then shrugged back into the backpack. "We won't be heading down the mountains into an urban center."

"We're in the Ozarks, right? Don't you guys already have maps?"

"Yes, but we want to mark changes and stay updated. And we want to make sure there are no more scorpions or other mutations."

He started up the path to the left.

"Fun times."

"You've got plenty of trees to drop if one appears." He smiled at her. "And, you could always climb a tree. I've seen you scamper up a ropes course."

"You know, if a giant scorpion attacks, you don't have to be faster than the scorpion." She winked. "You have to be faster than the guy behind you."

TAMAKI! Scout's voice screamed in her head. *Hotheads. Three of them. Right around the curve.*

TWENTY-SIX

Tamaki's hand dropped to her knife and she whistled to Nguyen. When he looked back, she put her finger to her lips and pointed.

Sounds reached them: leaves crunched underfoot, the slap of body against rock, a high-pitched voice mumbling.

His eyes widened. "Hotheads. Do you know about them?"

Tamaki swallowed as bitter memories surfaced. She'd been kidnapped by a group of Hotheads and their handlers while traveling through the Appalachian Mountains. If it hadn't been for Rachel and her son Adam, Tamaki would have been sacrificed to their god, Ashur.

"Yeah, I know about them."

"They are too close to our community. We'll have to kill them."

Why are Hotheads wandering through the mountains?

She didn't know if Scout had experience with Hotheads while he traveled as a spy for the god An, but she'd guess he didn't. The problem was that Hotheads retained enough memory or consciousness that they could be unpredictable. And they didn't register pain as ordinary humans did.

"It's not like killing a person," Nguyen said, eyes searching hers. "Their minds are already gone."

"I know." She'd seen what happened when the New Babylon soldiers burned the Hotheads back in Ohio: a black smoke released into the air. Same as the mutated *etemmu* inside the oversized scorpion and the two-headed moose back at Rachel's house. The Hothead handlers were different. They served Ashur, but they were still conscious.

The Hotheads came around the corner, moving in uncoordinated motions. Tattered clothing hung off their emaciated bodies. Shuffling forward without apparent purpose, no handler in sight. Used to be two men and a woman, based on clothing, although the bright red paint covered any distinguishing marks. They could be anyone. Or no one.

Just let them go. They aren't hurting anything.

Tamaki shook her head. She knew more than Scott did about this. And she also knew this was a test from the Alchemists. Nguyen would be reporting back to Gavin whatever happened in the next five minutes. Having her future threatened made Tamaki realize that she not only wanted to be an important part of the Alchemist's future school, she wanted to be their candidate for the Council of Gods. Maybe that was too ambitious, but it was what she wanted. It would take away the pain of her grandmother's refusal to teach her. It would show everyone, objectively, that she deserved a place in power. She would represent all the humans against the petty power games of the gods. And if she made it to the Council and had a god's power? First, she would demand Saki's egg from An, then fix Scout, and, finally, destroy the Debtor's prison in Enlil's territory, including Debossey and Mr. Wilson. It was a hell of a fantasy, but if there was anything she'd learned since being exiled by An, it was that she had to stop believing that others were smarter, stronger, and more experienced. She was as capable, if not more than, any other Alchemist in that camp.

Nguyen looked at her. "Are you ready?"

"Yes." Her voice was steady.

No, please no. There's a mystery here that we need to figure out. We should follow them instead. Tamaki, remember Cooter. Remember that this is your second chance.

It was her second chance. And she wasn't going to screw it up.

The foremost Hothead bounced off a tree, hollow eyes staring at nothing. He shuffled forward in a different direction revealing a dirty ball cap shoved deep in his back pocket.

Picking up a long stick, Nguyen used his knife to sharpen the tip. Then he launched it into the air. His hand remained pointing and his eyes squinted. Tamaki watched as the stick veered left and then down. It plunged into the back of Ball Cap.

"Nice," she whispered.

Ball Cap gargled and hissed, hands pushing at the stick. Then it stopped and its head snapped to look at Nguyen. The Hothead in the skirt was at one of the trees with the glowbugs, scratching at the bark.

The other Hothead began jumping up and down in place. His mouth opened and words came out in rapid-fire repetition. "Gonna eat good tonight. Neighborhood. Gonna eat the neighborhood. Good neighbor. Farm is there. In the neighborhood. Won't you eat my neighbor? I will eat my neighbor."

Tamaki pulled out her knife with one hand. With the other she reached down and touched the ground, searching for the roots of the tree with the glowbugs. She could sense roots under the earth, but they were tangled and she couldn't "see" which ones belonged to which tree.

"A little help, please?" Nguyen's voice was panicked.

While Tamaki was distracted, Ball Cap had charged Nguyen. Now the two of them grappled, Nguyen on his back, the Hothead snapping teeth at Nguyen's exposed throat. Tamaki sprinted over and plunged her knife into Ball Cap's back. Black smoke spiraled out when she yanked the knife back.

She skipped back several steps so the corrupted *etemmu* wouldn't touch her.

Scout barked a warning and then rushed at the Hothead who'd stopped jumping and was focused on her. The Hothead, still staring at Tamaki, picked up a stick and struck Scout's shoulder with the sharp end.

The fox whined but kept trying to distract it.

"I got it," she said.

Leaving Nguyen to roll out from underneath the inert body, Tamaki ran forward, ducking away from the Hothead's outstretched arms, and grabbed its shirt to spin herself around and stab the knife into its back. Then, knowing she needed to make this good, Tamaki stepped around the other side of the tree where the last Hothead, Skirt, was still messing with the sap and glowbugs.

Tamaki placed her hands on the tree and sent energy down to the roots. They responded by pulling up from the earth and wrapping around Skirt's legs and torso. They squeezed until the black smoke issued.

Tamaki stepped back and looked at Nguyen. He was brushing leaves off his khakis.

"All good?"

"Yeah," he said. "It takes me a minute to recharge after expending so much energy on a projectile."

"Sure."

"You moved the roots." He sounded plaintive. "You didn't actually project them."

Tamaki tilted her head. "I also stabbed the other two."

"Let's head back. It's almost dark." Without making sure she was following, he stomped toward the path.

Awww, you hurt his pride.

Catching up, Tamaki reached out and grabbed onto Nguyen's pack so he couldn't keep climbing. "Whoa there, buddy. I saved your life today. Now you owe me one. Tell me about the maps."

Nguyen tried to pull away, but she held on tight.

"It's just a theory," he said.

"I love theories."

He looked up at the darkening sky and sighed. "We think Enlil and Ninlil settled their capital in the south because that's where the Tigris-Mississippi and New Euphrates come together. We think it might be an energy thing so if any missions go any direction other than north, they note where they feel power or see mutations or plants thriving. Maybe strange rock formations or water that doesn't flow quite right. That way we can figure out how the gods will store the energy or access it."

Ley lines. Scout limped along. *But he's an idiot.*

Nguyen shrugged. "Since we went north, though, it's not that important."

Tamaki reached out a hand to touch Scout's back in acknowledgment. "Why doesn't north matter?"

Up ahead she could make out the natural arch that bordered the camp's plateau. A wave of appreciation swept through her and Tamaki realized how much she'd come to like the decorated greenhouse, the guaranteed food, and the idea of belonging with the Alchemists.

"Because you go over the mountain ridge and the trees disappear, animals disappear. Within ten minutes you're in a desert." He shook his head. "There's nothing there."

That sounds intriguing. Scout's ears pricked up. *If I was going to hide something that's exactly where I'd put it.*

TWENTY-SEVEN

After Nguyen waved goodnight, Tamaki followed Scout into the greenhouse and slammed the door before settling onto the flowered couch. "Well, that could have gone worse."

It could have gone much better. He looked back over his shoulder at her, tail flicking like an angry metronome.

"Why are you pissed?" Tamaki was hungry from using *etemmu* against the Hotheads, but she was too tired to raid the kitchen in the dining hall. "You should be happy." They'd learned how to get out of the camp and learned the local geography. Knowledge was power and today had been a good day.

I'm not angry. I'm disappointed in you.

"Well, that sounds like something a mature person would say." His condescending tone made Tamaki grit her teeth so that she had to speak past the tightness. "But go ahead and say whatever you need to."

Hotheads seek etemmu. *We should have followed them to see what they were attracted to, or where they were attracted. Maybe whatever Gavin is sensing with his talent or whatever is 'calling' the other Alchemists here.*

"Okay, I didn't know all that when, in the middle of the fight, you start chatting about how we should follow them. And, I don't know that they seek *etemmu*."

It makes sense. Their lifeforce is corrupted and they want more, but their humanity is gone so consuming other lifeforce won't actually save them.

"So, it's your guess." She ignored the comparison between what he was describing and blood magic. "What I do know is that Hotheads are braindead. They bartered their consciousness to Ashur and he fries them. And, as I've experienced, they are dangerous and want to kill living things."

We'll never know, now, why they were up here. The fox leapt up to his favorite spot on the stack of towels and stared down at her. *The people here are liars, they're hiding something, but you won't analyze it because you like what Nguyen is selling you.*

She picked up a pot of dandelions. They were growing nicely. Like weeds, even. "There was already a prepper community using this campground! What is so suspicious about Alchemists starting a school and me being a teacher? This is something I'm actually good at. They don't understand Mesopotamian mythology or how to manipulate *etemmu*, but that's how I was raised."

Gavin sent you out hunting today on purpose to test you.

"Who cares?" Tamaki shrugged. "I don't mind being tested. Gavin is military. He wants to know the strengths and weaknesses of each of us."

Scout growled. *You have an answer for everything, don't you?*

"Just acknowledge the fight with the Hotheads proved that Nguyen and I are a good team."

You started off weak. And you didn't notice when the second Hothead was about to attack you. She wanted to clap her hands over her ears, except that it wouldn't help because his words were inside her head.

"No blood magic and I still held my own," she whispered through the anger boiling inside. "How about some credit for that?"

I'm glad you didn't use blood magic. His tone changed and he blinked amber eyes, the normal gold tempered with brown flecks. *That means you've accomplished your goal, right? You've learned how to use power without losing control and now we can leave.*

Tamaki scoffed. "You keep saying you want to leave. Where, exactly, do you want to go?" She sat up on the couch and punched the cushion into a better shape. "Can we agree that Ba'al's territory is out? He likes infant sacrifice. Marduk is a military god and his New Babylon soldiers already killed you. An kicked us out and Enlil put us in jail."

This isn't helpful.

"It's the most helpful thing I can do since I don't know any real estate agents or have my phone to pull up pictures of houses and check out school listings and HOA fees." She took a breath and adjusted her position on the couch. "So, Inanna has territory somewhere around here because Amil's mother mentioned her. Inanna is the goddess of sex and love. That wouldn't be too bad, but I don't know where she is. Shamash, also called Utu, is Inanna's twin brother, but he's dead and his lifeforce is what's causing mutations. What about Enki? He's the god of wisdom who helped humans before, like when Enlil made the Great Flood. He's probably too smart to like us. Ereshkigal is Inanna's older sister, but she's in charge of the Underworld so I think we'd have to be dead. I don't know, but if Geshtinanna had a territory, that might be a place to go. She's the goddess of wine. Maybe she firestormed herself to Sonoma. But, there's a story about how she -"

Would you stop?

"Why? We're trying to decide where to go because you think being in a camp with people who recognize that the gods are petty and vindictive isn't the safest place. I'm growing my talent here and then I'll know how to give you a new body and you can leave. Without me, you'll have a lot more options."

I've been thinking about being a park ranger again. Traveling through territories, staying away from cities, but meeting up with other people interested in how the natural world has changed. Making a guidebook for what is dangerous and what isn't. Scout stretched out his paws and then brought them back in. *And you'd stay here?*

"Maybe? Remember how much you liked Rachel and Adam and they became a family for you? Well, maybe that's what I could have here."

You're being emotional instead of rational about Nguyen because you're romantically drawn to him.

"I'm not interested in Nguyen. He's just the easiest to talk to right now and he knows what's going on." Except, maybe that wasn't quite true. She remembered laughing as they'd raced to scale the rope wall. How much she enjoyed their banter in the dining hall. And the expression on his face when he concentrated before using *etemmu*, as if writing physics expressions on a chalkboard in his mind. He was so smart, maybe that was what he was doing. "What do you care? Are you jealous?"

His eyes gleamed gold. *I'm in a fox's body!*

"You're a human in a fox's body."

You know it's more complicated than that. He looked away from her. *We haven't even discussed your blindness where Gavin is concerned. Your family history is causing you to trust the wrong people because of the story you're telling yourself.*

"My family?" Scout's words were bullets in her brain, hurtful bursts of pain. They made no sense. "My story? I'm an orphan. I don't have a family anymore."

You need to confront the memories or you'll keep carrying them around. You're the one who told me that maybe you had it wrong about your grandmother and her reasons for not teaching you. Maybe you were a difficult teenager. Maybe she didn't think you had enough discipline.

Tamaki clenched the dandelion pot in her hand.

You are understandably disappointed by your mother's abandonment. It makes you go to extremes to not feel alone. Like bringing me back from the dead.

"You said you forgave me. Why are you bringing that up again?" He was so cruel.

I have forgiven you and I'm not trying to make you feel guilty. But, you never examined why you brought me back. We didn't even know each other, so don't tell me it was love. You created a relationship between us that didn't exist yet.

She pressed a hand to her heart. It felt like the organ was breaking into pieces. "Stop it," she whispered. The night he'd held her…it meant nothing to him?

When Rachel and Adam left for the hospital and I was killed, you felt like your mother had left you all over again. Sitting in the Empress Paulownia tree was like sitting at your grandmother's window, waiting for someone to come. That's why you feel like you have to be useful to be loved. That's why you don't want to show weakness. You believe that you have to be the best or you will be left behind. And, that's why I'm worried that you will keep coming back to blood magic unless you stare your fears in the face. At some point, he'd stood up so he stared down at her as if to show his intensity. *You are worthy of love, Tamaki, just the way you are.*

Her breath quickened and her jaw ached from keeping it clamped. Instead, she stroked the leaves of the dandelion and the tight bud popped open into a yellow sun. She set the pot down and licked her lips. Acid washed through her stomach. "You are neither a therapist nor an expert on my life. I'm sorry you thought I fantasized a meaningful relationship with you after one date."

And you're doing the same thing with Gavin.

"That's not true. He's making us into a family."

He's not. He's creating an army. I wanted more proof so you couldn't deny it, but I think I figured out the secret of this camp. The desert on the mountain top. The energy calling people sensitive to it — whether Alchemist or Hothead. Scout used a paw to scratch his nose. *The headwaters of the Tigris-Mississippi start here and spring from pure* etemmu. *The maps in Gavin's office were the final clue. He knows it's here, but he doesn't know where and there's something guarding it, something that killed the search party he sent.*

"Okay. I don't see why this is so bad."

Because Gavin is staking a claim on that power for Humanists. He's starting a war with the gods.

Tamaki swallowed. Sure, the gods were petty and cruel, but humans weren't ready for a war. They didn't know enough yet. This entire camp could be swallowed by Enlil's maw or destroyed by one of An's powerful storms. "It's a negotiating tactic or maybe a way for us to improve our talents by being nearby."

Scout looked up at the greenhouse ceiling in a semblance of a human seeking divine help for patience. *You're going to make me say it, aren't you? To avoid any type of self-reflection.*

Tamaki looked down at her hands. Somehow, she was holding the stupid dandelion again. "Say it," she whispered.

Fine. He seemed to take a breath. *You're conflating Gavin with your absent father. You always felt like your dad chose the military over you. Now, with Gavin, you are getting the attention you wanted from your dad. You want to impress him and every time he hangs a light for you or even scolds you, it makes you more determined to impress him again. But he doesn't love you. To him, you're nothing but a soldier. And, because you don't feel worthy of love, that makes you want his approval even more.*

The pottery shattered against the wall next to Scout. Dirt and plants fell into his fur.

"I hate you," she screamed, again and again until her throat burned and someone was banging on the door asking if she was okay, and still she screamed.

TWENTY-EIGHT

Tamaki channeled her anger at Scout – who'd fled the greenhouse after their fight and hadn't come back this morning – into wrestling the PVC pipe she'd gotten from Daisy. Using zip ties, Tamaki had built a layered triangular structure taller than herself for the new hydroponic section. Once she had it established, she'd mount it to one of the walls to save space.

Hearing the gritty scrape of the door against the floor, Tamaki's lip curled. "Come back to apologize?"

"Um, no." Gavin's voice was laced with amusement. "Although, in fairness, I'm sure I've done something wrong."

"Ahh, crappity-Mccrap. Sorry." Tamaki spun around, cheeks pink. "Thought you were someone else."

Gavin set a brown paper bag on the table behind the front couch. "Your fox is outside, skulking around near the tree line."

Remembering what Nguyen had said about Gavin's suspicions about Scout, Tamaki acted like she didn't make the connection between the two sentences.

"Haws said there was some screaming from inside here last night. Then you missed breakfast this morning." Gavin's southern accent made it difficult to tell if there was a tone to his statement. "I said I'd check on you."

"Everything's fine." She feathered her hair behind her ear. "You can tell him that."

"I thought you might be hungry. Go ahead and eat." He knocked his fist against the table. "The hens will slow their laying as it gets colder so you should enjoy the eggs now."

The bag smelled like cheese and sausage. Her stomach growled. Tamaki wiped her hands on a towel and opened the bag to find a breakfast sandwich inside.

"Nguyen told me y'all encountered three Hotheads." Gavin walked around the greenhouse, examining how she'd arranged the plants. "I'm glad no one was hurt."

Tamaki bit into the sandwich. It was still warm and cheddar cheese oozed out the side.

"Hotheads don't scare me," she said, after catching the cheese drip. "I'm ready to go on another mission. We didn't actually bring anything back besides the Virginia creeper." She used the last bite of sandwich to point to the outside of the greenhouse where the vine was growing into a privacy screen on the wall that faced the Haws's house. "The creeper uses suction cups not tendrils, so it won't break the glass. Unless I want it to." She waggled her eyebrows and twirled an imaginary mustache like an old-time villain.

"No, you didn't retrieve supplies." His expression suggested amusement rather than judgment. "But it wasn't a total failure. Now we know that you and Nguyen can use energy while in a live situation."

She wondered if Nguyen had mentioned that she'd saved his life and then imagined Scout's bark of laughter.

Wanting Gavin to see her as a leader, Tamaki said, "Nguyen is strong with what he does, but I have my own techniques."

"Interesting." Gavin nodded his head like he was agreeing with something. "You have your own ideas for how to manipulate energy."

"My grandmother taught me." She'd kept it a secret for so long, first from the kids at school and then because she hadn't believed her Obaa-chan, that it felt wrong to share. "Before the firestorm."

"I believe you." It's the same thing he'd said after the confrontation with Liza and it made Tamaki stand up taller.

"My mom and my grandmother and all my direct female relatives knew how to manipulate energy. We have growing hands – a sensitivity to plants." She touched the blue streak in her hair. "There was a ritual they taught me as a teenager. And this was the result."

"Your hair changed color and it's permanent?"

"Yup."

"May I ask – you're of Japanese descent, right? Why would your family know about Mesopotamian gods?"

"Fair question." Tamaki snorted. "According to my grandmother, the world was filled with magic when the gods walked."

"Magic is what we call energy and what you call lifeforce. *Etemmu*."

"Right. The Misbegotten came from the Tigris-Euphrates valley, but the gods were not contained there. They have always wanted more. Humans who could manipulate energy also traveled, either in service to the gods or in opposition to them. Trade routes were established throughout the old world. Then, The Misbegotten's battles became too much, especially between Marduk of Babylon and Nammu of the watery deeps."

"Hold on," Gavin had settled onto the couch for his story. "You mean Babylon like in the Old Testament of the Bible?"

"The Hebrew Bible, yes."

"And you grow plants. Your whole family does."

"Yes."

He narrowed his eyes. She'd seen him do this before, when he was synthesizing information. "Wasn't one of the Seven Wonders of the World called the 'Hanging Gardens of Babylon'?"

"My ancestors helped with that. We went, learned, and brought back the knowledge to our island." She exhaled. "That's why I'm so excited about having a school here. It'll be the same thing. A multicultural place of learning where we use mental energy instead of coal, natural gas, etc."

"This is a lot to take in." He stood up. "Mind if we move outside so I can have a smoke?"

She followed him out the door and when he was ready, she finished the story.

"Dust from the gods' battles covered everything and created an inability to grow crops. Famine swept the land and humans cried out. The Creator intervened by locking the Misbegotten into a prison in the sky. Shamash, the sun god who also enacted justice, agreed to trick the others into the prison. His body was used as the lock. That was close to 539 BCE, when Babylon, without Marduk to protect it, fell to Cyrus the Great. With those gods gone, a great deal of energy disappeared as well. Then, on the Summer Solstice a few months ago, the Mesopotamian gods got free and Shamash's body was destroyed, his life force exploding onto our world, creating energy storms and stagnant pools that cause mutations."

Gavin blew out a plume of smoke. "Which humans can manipulate energy?"

"Everyone. Each person is born with the ability, but there are important factors like interest, talent, training, etc."

He continued leaning against the glass, tapping the ash with a practiced movement.

Impatient, Tamaki shifted her weight. Why wouldn't he say anything? She'd said too much, kept it all bottled up, and then, when she'd decided to share, she'd word-vomited and now he hated her.

"Maybe I could teach some of the other Alchemists what I know? I can work with different people. Except Don. Please don't pair me with Don.

He always whines during our training exercises." She cleared her throat. "Kidding." Uggg, She had to stop talking.

"You're a very unique woman, Tamaki Hayashi." He turned away to exhale and then rubbed the butt on the ground to put it out, tucking it under his shoelace. Straightening up, Gavin dropped a hand to her shoulder, a heaviness that didn't feel intrusive. "I'm glad you found the team in Nippur and claimed sanctuary. And I appreciate how you are willing to bring your knowledge to our team. A good soldier knows how to obey orders. It's important to put the needs of the community above the needs of the individual."

"I understand," she said. "I'm ambitious and I'm strong."

"I get that," he said. "We're going to have a strategy meeting soon to decide our answer to the competition for the seat on the Council of Gods, but I'm waiting on information from Addison in Nippur. I'll remember this conversation." His gaze settled on something outside the greenhouse walls. "I need to go talk to Haws. We'll hold Cal's funeral later today. For now, though, you need to get to the archery range for training."

Tamaki nodded and they walked out of the greenhouse together, Gavin veering off toward the medical center. She continued past the dining hall and then to the right, down the familiar path to the firepit outside of Gavin's office. The clearing was enlarged from burning the scorpion. The tree had been shoved off to the side. Chopping it into usable pieces would probably be one of their training tasks.

She hurried down the footpath to the archery range where the Alchemists had finished stretching and were on break before the next activity. Tamaki planted a smile on her face, determined that she wouldn't show them she cared when she wasn't chosen as a partner. Gerry the firestarter saw her first.

"Hey. Nice job with the Hotheads."

Nate looked over and grinned. "Yeah. That's an adventure on your first time out. I would've peed my pants."

"Good job." Jamal gave her a nod.

The approval was overwhelming. It made her uncomfortable so she blurted out, "I wasn't pretending with the cane. It wasn't a costume. I was hurt in Nippur."

Jamal's eyes widened. "Hey, I shouldn't have given you a hard time. Want to be partners today?"

She blinked. This whole morning was what she wanted. "I –"

"Trying to steal my partner?" Nguyen was there, swooping between her and Jamal and pulling her away. "Not today."

"Oh, I'm your partner?" She noted the way he grabbed her, how comfortable it felt.

"Yes, today is our re-match, but instead of ropes we will be competing with bows and arrows." A tight black t-shirt flattered his flat stomach and toned arms. He interlaced his fingers with her other hand as they stood face-to-face. Damn, he really did have an engaging smile. Part joking, but a little hint of vulnerability.

Stoltzus whistled. "The point of today is to incorporate your talent with the activity. For example, Gerry, light your arrow on fire."

Everyone turned to look at the clean-shaven man with the hangdog expression. His whole face turned bright red as he stared at the arrow in his hand, but nothing happened.

Stoltzus cursed. Then he walked over to Gerry, got right in his face, and yelled, "Now."

Gerry jumped and the arrow burst into flame. He dropped it and stamped it out, cracking the blackened arrow in half.

Stoltzus sighed. "That's the idea, but just the tip next time, alright?"

Nguyen and Tamaki exchanged looks and her cheeks hurt from holding in a fit of giggles.

"Stop it," Nguyen whispered, leaning close to her ear. "You're going to get me in trouble. Don't you know I'm the 'golden boy'?"

She shook off her twinge of sadness when he dropped her hands – giving them a secret squeeze first. They took their places at the station on the end. Two recurve bows and a handful of arrows hung off a post.

"Have you ever shot a bow before?" he asked.

"No."

"Well, it goes something like this. Place your feet here, perpendicular to the target with square hips." Nguyen stood behind her and placed his arms around her. "Twist the arrow so the off-colored feather is in position. Hold steady. Now draw it back like this." His long fingers were on hers so they moved together. Physical awareness rushed through her. Her arm shook from the tension.

"We can adjust the draw weight."

She shook her head. "It's fine," she managed, more focused on him than what he was saying.

"And we let it fly." The arrow flew toward the target but was high. "A little correction." Nguyen moved his hand and the arrow adjusted its trajectory by pointing its nose down. It thudded into a white circle.

"You picked the wrong partner, if you want to win," Jamal called cheerfully.

Tamaki gave him the finger and Jamal laughed.

"One more minute of practice and then we'll count points," Stoltzus yelled. "Three rounds of three arrows each."

"Need a practice shot?" she asked Nguyen.

"Nope. I'm all ready." He winked. "Should we make this more interesting? Place a bet?"

Was he flirting? Being competitive? Maybe another woman would know how to react, but she had no idea what to say. This competition was tailored to his talent.

"No big deal." Nguyen shrugged. "Beating you can be enough. You can go first."

Tamaki chose an arrow. She put herself into position, nocked the arrow, and let it fly. It went straight over the target. The second arrow hit the white circle and the third hit the target, but not the circle. She stepped back and Nguyen took his position.

He used *etemmu* to make all three arrows hit the bull's eye. Nguyen did a victory dance, making sounds like a roaring crowed. The rest of the Alchemists looked over.

"Aww, Tamaki," Nate said. "We were hoping you could take him down. He's going to be insufferable if he wins."

Stoltzus yelled. "All clear. Recover the arrows."

Stepping up for the second round, Tamaki hefted the arrow. It was made of wood, but there was nothing living for her to connect with. She aimed and released three times.

"Better," Nguyen said. "All three hit the target and two were in circles this time."

"Yeah," she said. "I decided to go defensive this round." She enjoyed the possible flirting, but she wasn't going to throw the competition. He should know that by now.

He gave her a quizzical look, then aimed his first arrow. Tamaki pushed power into her hands until they tingled. She wanted the nice long branches of a willow tree, but they weren't by water. Ahh, the redbud would do. It was on the edge of the forest, in front and to the left of the target. She reached for the heart-shaped leaves and pulled the thin branches straight. This put them in the path of the arrow.

Nguyen frowned as Tamaki shook the branches and the arrow caught in the leaves and fell to the ground.

He released the second arrow, but this time he was ready. The other Alchemists had all stopped to watch as Nguyen moved his hand through the air trying to find a way through for the arrow and Tamaki did the same with both hands, moving flexible branches until Nguyen punched and the arrow got through, yet didn't have enough momentum for the tip to pierce the target. It fell down.

Clapping began and there were wolf whistles from the audience.

The third time, Tamaki could see Nguyen gather himself. He tucked his chin and pulled his elbows to his chest. Seconds passed as he held the position, like he'd created locks in his body allowing the energy to increase. Tamaki watched him, her hands ready to move the redbud branches, but without blood magic she couldn't see his energy. Suddenly he hinged forward, picking up the last arrow with his right hand and throwing it. His left hand shot forward, pointing. The arrow followed; there an audible thump as the gust of wind propelled it.

Tamaki moved her arms, but she was too late.

The arrow plunged into the second ring of the target.

Stoltzus shouted. "By points, Tamaki wins that round."

No one was even pretending not to watch them now. Both Nguyen and Tamaki took drinks of water and walked around. She could tell he was tired by the way he pressed his hand into his side like he had a cramp. She didn't hurt so much as she was empty, like a pitcher that had been poured out. But she really wanted to win to show the Alchemists that she was a worthy member of the group.

A sound from the main pathway made them look over. Gavin led a horse pulling a cart. There was a body with a sheet over it in the back. Gavin tied the horse and walked down the dirt path.

"One more round to go," Stoltzus said.

Gavin nodded. His eyes were tired, but he clasped his hands behind his back. "Finish the exercise and then we'll gather for Cal's remembrance."

Tamaki glanced around. No one else moved. Right. She and Nguyen were the exhibition and Gavin was watching, too. She picked up the bow and arrow, aimed, and then dropped it a quarter inch since she kept shooting over the target. It flew through the air and hit the outer circle.

Murmurs behind her and Jamal whispered, "C'mon. Don't let the pressure get to you."

She steadied the bow and shot again, hitting the outer circle a second time.

"My bet?" said Don. "Nguyen's gonna win again."

Pressing her lips together, Tamaki aimed her last arrow. Blood thumped in her ears and she could feel Gavin's presence, the air smelled like cooked beef, like someone had left the dining hall door open.

She released and the arrow flew straight toward the bullseye. A sense of joy filled her chest and then the arrow nosed down, straight down, and Nguyen's hand was in her peripheral vision. The arrow dived into the grass in front of the target.

Pivoting to face him, Tamaki smiled. Her teeth were showing and she tried to rein in her competitive spirit, but Scout wasn't here and he was her conscience. "That's okay," she said to Nguyen as the Alchemists around them groaned and began to move apart, thinking the game was over. "You know I play defense, too."

He smiled back, the air between them charged. While he picked up the bow and first arrow, she bent down and untied her boots, ripping them off. She needed her feet to touch the ground. Tamaki wriggled her toes in the cool grass, feeling the sharp little spikes on the end and pushing her heels down until they made divots in the mud.

She would win; she deserved it. Tamaki reached, pressing past her empty reserves. It was like running. You thought you were done, but you had to dig deep for the home stretch.

Nguyen stared at the redbud trees, expecting the branches.

He released.

Power surged through her. Tamaki pulled the redbud's roots toward the surface. They erupted from the ground and curved around the edges of the target. She yanked.

The target fell face down.

In the stunned silence, Tamaki kept herself from throwing her arms into the air, but she couldn't help punching Nguyen's arm.

His mouth gaped open.

Cheering erupted behind her. "Never seen that before." "Now that's a strategy." "Is that even a legal move?" "Yeah, Stoltzus said we could use energy."

"I concede." Nguyen composed himself. "And I owe you."

"I never agreed to the bet."

"Nevertheless, you can call in a favor with me whenever you want."

Tamaki glanced at Gavin. He held her gaze and nodded once. A thrill rushed through her.

To the group, Gavin said, "Follow me to the forest line for the ceremony. Nate, bring the horse and cart."

When they'd been left behind, Nguyen reached out and wiped under her nose. "You okay?"

Tamaki's smile flickered. His finger was red.

While he wiped it on a handkerchief, she sank to the ground. He held it out to her. "You're still bleeding."

"I'm fine," she said mechanically, her thoughts racing. She hadn't cut herself or even decided to use blood magic. She'd just wanted to win, to press past her reserves. Pressing the handkerchief to her nose, Tamaki made herself sit up straighter. She could control this. Everything was fine. Next time she'd listen when her power was depleted.

"Do you need your cane?"

Tamaki looked up. She'd almost forgotten Nguyen was waiting for her. "No," she said. He offered her a hand up. After working so hard to win, she couldn't look weak in front of the others.

"Must be the dry air," she said, taking his hand. "Too bad we don't have any humidifiers around here." She wadded up the handkerchief. "I'll wash this and get it back to you."

Together they followed the path to where the Alchemists had gathered for Cal's burial. Hank and Nate separated to make room. Gavin said a few words and then all the Alchemists held hands as Gerry set Cal's body on fire. Hank had a surprisingly pleasant voice as he sang a hymn.

Tamaki sank down into the grass. The space behind her heart throbbed and her vision darkened. Nguyen squeezed her shoulder in sympathy, thinking she was upset about Cal. Gulping for breath, Tamaki reached her fingers into the grass as her insides burned. It hurt, but she deserved it. The pain was hers. Shards of glass slicing her.

Heat emanated from the fire and then the stench of burning flesh.

Tamaki was glad that Scout wasn't here to see this. That's what they'd done to his human body.

TWENTY-NINE

A week passed and then another until it was October. The routine became comfortingly normal: waking up, dining hall, exercise with the Alchemists, afternoon in the greenhouse, dinner in the dining hall, either patrol in the evenings or hanging out by Gavin's firepit.

This afternoon Scout lay in a patch of sun, head tucked into tail, as Tamaki watered the rows of plants. Scout kept his thoughts out of her head and, in fact, was often gone. She'd feel if their psychic bond was stretched too thin and then he'd come slinking back in without a word. They hadn't spoken since their fight.

When Nguyen knocked on the greenhouse door and then entered, Scout's ears flicked at the sound, but his eyes stayed closed.

"Ahh, there's the fox. Haven't seen your pet around lately."

"He's not my pet."

"You never told me. What's the connection?"

Deciding to take a break, Tamaki settled on the flowered couch and pulled her knees into her chest. "I rescued him from a carnivorous plant a while ago. Now he travels with me, but he's still wild."

"I see." Nguyen sat down on the other end of the couch, angled towards her. By mutual accord, they hadn't chosen each other as partners during the exercises since the archery tournament. "Hey, you look very punk rock gardener in that black turtleneck." Nguyen grinned. "Super smart, but with fashionable hair, too. I like the way you have it pinned up."

Tamaki braced for a sarcastic comment from Scout, but there was nothing but an absence in her mind. "Do you mean 'and'?"

The fox opened his eyes at the sound of her voice. From here they looked almond brown. Tamaki frowned and leaned forward for a closer look. That was strange. It must be the way the sunlight was hitting them or something.

"What's that?"

She looked at Nguyen, at his smile and the way he balled his hands into fists, but then didn't know what to do with them.

"You said 'but' like I could be either smart or fashionable." She looked back at the fox who'd risen to his feet and stretched his hips into the air. "I choose both."

Suddenly a flash of brown darted out from behind the stacked bags of mulch and then disappeared in the chaos of potted plants in the corner. Tamaki twitched in surprise before registering that it was a mouse.

A feeling of curiosity mixed with hunger passed through her mind, but it wasn't her own thought. And then Scout trotted over to the plants and sniffed. He batted at a potted pear tree's container and the little brown mouse ran out, zigzagging back toward the bags of mulch. With an almost lazy movement, Scout leaped into the air and pounced, nose like an arrow. His teeth snapped on the mouse and he shook his head back and forth.

"Scout!"

The fox looked at her with the mouse still in his jaws.

"Drop it."

Tamaki's stomach clenched. She'd been assuming that Scout was ignoring her, but there was no voice in her head now. A horrifying suspicion occurred to her. A suspicion that accounted for a change in eye color and the gentle tugging at their psychic link like it was doing the work of an invisible fence for an animal. She grabbed a gardening glove and slipped it on before kneeling beside the fox. She didn't want to touch the blood of the mouse.

"You could probably let him eat it," Nguyen said. "Some of the other people around here are annoyed that he's eating cafeteria food with winter closing in."

Tamaki kept her face down to hide her automatic snarl. She touched Scout's snout. "Let go," she whispered. She couldn't speak to him telepathically, but she stared into his eyes, trying to reach past the animal part. Then she yelled, "Now," the way Stoltzus had yelled at Gerry.

For a moment she thought Scout was going to turn away, but then his shoulders relaxed and his jaw opened. She rubbed the top of Scout's head. "Good."

She frowned at a patch of crusty fur on his shoulder. Lifting it, she saw the puncture wound from the Hothead's stick still hadn't healed.

He jerked away and then stopped as if he didn't know where he was going, came back to sniff at the pear tree, and then stood in a puddle of refracted sunlight. She'd shocked him out of the animal mindset for a brief second. How much of Scott was still inside the fox?

Tamaki threw away the mouse and removed the contaminated glove, tossing it in the cleaning solution.

"From before," Nguyen said, standing up from the couch. "I didn't mean–"

"What?" Worried about Scott, Tamaki had forgotten about whatever Nguyen was going on about.

"I was sloppy," Nguyen gave her a self-effacing look. "I was trying to compliment you and instead I gave offense. I didn't mean it that way."

Tamaki glanced at the fox. She'd have to shock Scout again. If she could do something beyond yelling that would create an emotional response, then maybe the human part would resurface.

"No," Tamaki said, stepping closer to Nguyen. She could see the fox over his shoulder. "I know you didn't."

"I was wondering," Nguyen wiped his hands on his pants. "Would you like to get our dinner from the dining hall and then take it outside for a picnic? I have a blanket and we could enjoy the autumn weather."

There was no way that Scout wouldn't mock that. Tamaki looked at the fox, but he was pawing at the greenhouse door to get it open. Angry, Tamaki turned back to Nguyen. "No, I don't want any dinner."

"Oh, well, I thought you could use a break. You work so hard in here."

"Stop talking." Tamaki took one step closer until only inches separated them. She grabbed Nguyen's shirt and pulled him in for a kiss. Their lips touched. She smelled burned sugar. His hand came against her back, settling between her shoulder blades.

WHAT THE ACTUAL HELL! The words echoed in her head, a pleasurable pain.

"Yeah," she said to Nguyen, patting his shirt back into place. "I'm good now. Off you go."

"But –" he gripped her hand. "Come to my cabin tomorrow night. There's something I want to talk to you about. Promise?"

"Sure." She gave him a little push toward the door.

He had a dazed look on his face as he left the greenhouse.

"Glad you're back," she said when Nguyen was gone.

The fox shook his head as if to clear it. *It's like I wasn't in the driver's seat of my brain anymore. I was in the backseat. And maybe asleep.*

She decided not to ask whether he remembered fighting with her over the mouse. "Yeah, I wondered if you were gone for good."

I don't know if I'll disappear again. You have no idea how hard it is trying to stay together. The fox instincts grow stronger and I'm not sure what belongs to this body and what belongs to Scott. I forget what it was like not to have four legs, not to leap and sniff for mice. The words for plants and animals, words I've known since I was a child are blanks in my mind. I picture them, I know them, maybe even more intimately than I knew them as a human, but the words. He whined. *The words are a struggle. Instead, I stay in the now of fox thought. So, when I see you I have these emotions, but the nuances are fading.*

Tamaki stood in front of the PVC pipes. Dandelions had filled in each of the levels, the distinctive leaves cascading down while the yellow heads looked like miniature suns. "Emotions bring you back," she suggested. "You were present during our last fight."

You don't always bring out the best in me. It wasn't snide or sarcastic. Instead, there was a sadness to the thought that made Tamaki turn around to look at the fox.

"Why? We could've been… I wanted to…" She struggled around a lump in her throat. "When we were at Rachel's cabin and you were on the swing with me…it was so easy to talk to you. I could see your loyalty to Rachel and Adam. I liked your stupid jokes and the way you laughed at yourself."

I was curious about you, too. I thought you were beautiful and fun and I wanted to know what made you happy and how you had a turtle-penguin.

"I could imagine us together. That we'd be able to talk through anything. Maybe we'd move into one of the abandoned houses near the ley line and I could design our house with trees growing as the timbers."

But we didn't have time to develop a real relationship. What you imagined… we didn't experience that. It was in your head. You had a fantasy and then you plugged me in. I didn't even know about it.

"I would have told you, but then you were murdered by New Babylon and my daydream was ripped away. I was so alone and it was like when my grandmother was murdered and my mother left. She wasn't murdered, but she left me all the same. And I thought I could bring you back, but you hate me."

Your bringing me back was about you, not about me. And it wasn't about love. It was about your fear.

Gods, it hurt to hear that. Tamaki clenched her fists, the empty spot in her chest pulsing with how much she hated what he was saying. It was getting hard to think, but she forced herself.

"I agree we didn't have time. That's why I tried to give us more and it backfired."

We don't even know each other. Not really.

"Fine." She rubbed her chest, anything to make the burning go away. "Tell me something I don't know about you. Something from before the firestorm. Before you met and worked for An, before you stole from New Babylon and died in a clearing with a two-headed moose. Talk about that."

Will you remember me after my consciousness dies and this body is nothing but fox?

"Don't say that."

Why not? I – the human part – am growing weaker even as this body is aging. Aches in the hip. Perhaps a dislocation at some point? My nose is still keen, but it's harder to see. The wound from the Hothead hasn't healed.

"That's not right," Tamaki said, frowning. She'd seen that wound, though. "May I look at it?"

He stood still as she peeled back the matted fur. Immediately there was a sour smell and a tingle in her hands. "Crap in a cat pan."

Yes, that's what I thought.

"Hold on." She used a clean rag dipped in the water from the creek to clean the wound. "It's from a ley line."

Thank you, it feels soothing.

"Let's not waste another moment." She made it sound positive, but Tamaki wanted to scream that this situation wasn't fair. Even if she used blood magic, she couldn't control it and there wasn't a way to reverse time. There was no telling what the magic would do to him if she allowed it to flow through her.

The fox looked to the left and then almost seemed to shrug, a liquid movement of the shoulders. *I spent a gap year in Costa Rica. It changed my life. I love the Appalachians, but it can be a harsh, unwelcoming environment. In the cloud forest, in the rain forest, even by the Pacific Ocean in Costa Rica you are surrounded by life, by biodiversity, by organisms fighting for sunlight.*

Tamaki nodded. This was Scout. He was speaking in her mind faster and faster as his excitement increased. "Go on."

You know those movies where Tarzan is swinging on vines through the jungle? That could never happen. Vines can't support the weight of a human male. Scout turned to face her. *You know what can? Roots. Aerial roots from the epiphytes.*

She let herself smile as a bitter joy flooded through her chest. "I have no idea what an epiphyte is."

It's a plant that grows on another plant. Like the seed catches high in the branches and grows down. Like orchids and ferns. He stood up and paced, triangle ears pointed to the sides as if listening for sounds outside the greenhouse. *You would love to see the plants there. The walking palms that actually shift over so that their branches can get more light, the strangler fig. That's another epiphyte. It takes over a host tree by sending long roots down to the ground and encasing the host. When the host tree rots, it leaves this hollow space surrounded by a magnificent cylinder of roots. A perfect habitat for bats, birds, and larger mammals.*

"I'd like to see that one day." Tamaki swallowed. "If Costa Rica still exists."

There's this one orchid that I'd give you, if I could. It's called a monkey face orchid.

An image appeared in her head. White flower petals surrounding a brown center. Two black dots, yellow inside the brown. An easily recognizable monkey face with surrounding hair on a white background.

"No way that it grows that way."

It does.

"It looks hand-painted."

Each petal, each monkey face, is a little bit different. Like tropical snowflakes.

She searched for something as spectacular to share with him, something with meaning from her own life, but she didn't want to share her grandmother's dark house with the superstitious placement of bowls and pictures. She didn't want him to see her at high school, never quite fitting in. No friends to share the weekend with except the cross-country runs. She hadn't even been allowed to have a pet. Maybe that's why she'd loved Saki the turtle-penguin so much.

The vital thing, Scout sat across from her and wrapped his tail around his legs, *is that the country kept no standing army. Instead, the military budget was diverted to education, health care, and environmental protection. I got to see it working down there.* The tip of his tail flicked back and forth. *That was the dream, you know?*

"Thank you for telling me that."

Tamaki wrapped her arms around herself. He'd been right. Maybe. She'd been enamored with her idea of who Scott was, not with the actual man.

"And you're right. I didn't bring you back because I loved you." She let out a shuddering breath. "I mean, I thought I did. But the magic knew what I wanted." She pressed her shaking hands together. "I was terrified of being alone. That's the truth. I'm sorry, Scout."

I knew the truth before you did and I've already forgiven you.

It was so unfair that they were finally growing closer. And his body was dying. Again.

THIRTY

All through dinner Nguyen seemed nervous. Too much smiling and then throat clearing. Staring into her eyes and then looking away. Even the other Alchemists at the table seemed in on some secret.

Tamaki reached out for Scout, but he wasn't there. The connection was a dying battery with only quick charges from intense emotion.

"I said," Nguyen leaned forward, "are you finished with dinner?"

Gavin and Stoltzus pushed away from their seats in the center of the table.

Tamaki looked down at her empty plate. "Yes, sorry."

"Let's go back to my cabin for dessert." Nguyen shoved his chair back. "Then I'll tell you what's happening."

"Sure." She reached for her plate, but Nguyen jerked his head.

"Nate, can you take care of clean up tonight?"

"Uh, yeah. I've got it." The young Alchemist smirked.

Nguyen led Tamaki through the sunset to a cabin on the left side of the horseshoe. It occurred to her that he'd always come to the greenhouse and she'd never seen an Alchemist cabin. Minimalist for sure. A single lantern hung from a nail on a post. Three cots centered on each of the walls while ragged curtains covered dirty windows. She thought about making a nervous joke about this being a rustic bachelor pad, but managed to swallow the words. Nguyen's area was obvious – his bed at least had the blankets neatly tucked. His clothes were folded on the shelves next to his cot, boots lined up in a row.

He took out two miniature plastic bottles of wine and handed one to her. "Dessert." Then he sat down on the cot and patted the space beside him. "Come here."

Tamaki's palms were clammy and she hesitated. This felt less romantic and more convenient for Nguyen. She wanted someone to make her feel special, to make her feel like they saw the real her.

"What did you want to talk about?"

He took her wine, twisted off the lid, and handed it back to her. Then he did the same for himself and took a long swig. Ah. Apparently no savoring the notes tonight.

"There's going to be an important meeting tomorrow night for all of us." He rolled the bottle between his hands. "We're going come up with a strategy for what to do about the contest for the Council of Gods."

Tamaki straightened and took her own swig of wine. It was really happening. Humans were going to fight back. Excitement sparked in her belly.

Suddenly two faces pressed against the dirty window beside Nguyen's bed. Tamaki startled; her hand dropped to her knife. Don and Nate grinned as they banged on the window. Don thrust out his tongue like he was French kissing the window. Tamaki wished she could yank it out of his mouth. Nguyen leaned over the cot and pulled the curtains closed.

He moved around to the other set of windows. "Go on," he said as the pair outside sprinted around the cabin to these windows. "Get out of here." He waited until Nate dragged Don away before shutting those curtains too.

"Sorry. You know the guys." Nguyen shrugged and gave a sheepish grin. "They like to tease."

Something wasn't sitting quite right. Tamaki moved around the cabin to give herself time to think. Had the other men seen them walk in here? Was it a coincidence or had Nguyen been bragging that they were…what were they? Dating? Hanging out?

Misinterpreting her silence, Nguyen pulled a heavy trunk in front of the door. "There. No one will barge in now. We'll have privacy."

"For what?" she asked bluntly. "Is this like hanging a tie on a college dorm room?"

"For…whatever we want," Nguyen said. He looked uncertain. "Are you okay? You seem mad."

She didn't know how to explain. She wished she had someone to talk it over with, a girl friend like in books, but there had never been one in real life. Or Scout, although he would tell her to get the hell out of the cabin if she wasn't one hundred percent comfortable.

Then Nguyen was standing beside her and his fingers caressed her jawline. "You're so beautiful," he said, mouth close to her ear. "It makes me want to kiss you all night."

Shivers ran through her and Tamaki smiled. This was better.

"The first time I saw you." His hand moved to her lower back, making circles, while the other rubbed the outer edge of her ear.

"Yes?" What had he thought? Did he mean back in Nippur or here at camp after she was cleaned up?

"It just. It made me want to know you."

Tamaki fought a flash of irritation, but kept her face soft. Maybe he wasn't the romantic type. Or particularly good with words. Maybe post-firestorm courtship didn't mean flowers and candy and grand gestures. One more reason to hate the gods.

Then his mouth covered hers and his tongue flicked until she opened her mouth. Oh, yeah. His kissing made up for a lot.

The hand on her back brought her lower body closer and he was still kissing her, making her head swim. She was losing her breath, but in the best way. Tamaki wrapped her arms around his neck, standing on tiptoes so they wouldn't stop touching. And his hand moved away from her ear into her hair and he knotted his hand, gently pulling. Tamaki moaned in pleasure.

He kept going with the scalp massage and she clung to his shoulders, knowing she would fall if she let go. Nguyen broke off the kiss and her head dropped back, still supported by his hand. He leaned down and kissed her exposed neck, working his way around to the side.

"Do you like this?" he murmured.

"Uh huh," she managed.

He chuckled, satisfied, and kissed the spot at the base of her neck where her pulse beat out of control. One kiss lower. And then another and he reached the vee of her shirt. Nguyen moved her backwards until the cot pressed into the backs of her knees and she sat down.

He gripped the hem of his shirt and pulled it off. Tamaki swallowed. He was hot, no question. Smooth skin, wide shoulders that came down to a narrow waist, defined muscles. She kept her gaze above his belt.

"Lick here." Nguyen stepped forward between her legs and circled his nipple.

Tamaki didn't need another invitation. She leaned forward and pressed her mouth against his chest, working at the nub and finishing with a gentle bite.

"Damn." He ran his hands through his hair and then interlaced them behind his head.

Tamaki moved to the other one, sucking it.

"Alright. Fair's fair." Nguyen pressed her shoulders down to the cot and grabbed the pillow to place behind her head. Then he unbuttoned her shirt, his hands moving methodically, giving her time to anticipate. One hand supported her back so he could slide her arm out of the sleeve. Then the other side and he wadded up the shirt and tossed it to the floor. She didn't have time to feel chilly before Nguyen lowered to his knees, still between hers, and lowered his mouth to her chest.

Unsure what to do with her hands, Tamaki put one on his back and used the other to grip the blanket.

His mouth closed on her right nipple and Tamaki almost passed out. It felt so good that she closed her eyes to heighten the sensation. For a moment she wasn't mad at her body; instead, she was thankful for pleasure. He moved across to the other one. A line of desire ran from her nipple down to her belly. She arced her back.

"Yeah," Nguyen murmured.

Hearing the snick of a zipper, Tamaki's eyes flew open. Nguyen stood upright, his belt unfastened. He eased his pants down his hips. His erection was obvious.

Tamaki's cheeks flamed. "No," she blurted out. "I'm not ready." Sure, Tamaki had seen movies, read Webtoons, but she didn't have any firsthand experience. She'd grown up with her traditional grandmother.

Nguyen's eyebrows pulled together in what would have been a comical expression if Tamaki wasn't so embarrassed.

"I thought you liked this," he said, finally.

"I do. I am." She wanted to cover her naked chest, her nipples still at attention, but he'd tossed her shirt. It lay on the dusty floor. "It's just happening a little fast." Oh gods, her face was burning.

"What's the big deal?" His expression lightened. "Is this your first time?"

She propped herself on her elbows and tried to move her legs, but Nguyen was still standing between them.

"I thought – you were so confident. And you were captured at Nippur. I mean, I'm glad you didn't have to do anything sexual there."

What in *kur* did that mean! Angry, Tamaki pivoted her hips up for leverage, but then Nguyen's hand was on her shoulder, rubbing her bare skin.

"Hold on, okay?" Nguyen removed his hand so he could hold his pants taut with hand and rezip with the other. She looked away, but heard the jangle of his belt as he refastened. "Relax. You can trust me." He lowered to his knees again and pulled apart the arms she'd crossed over her chest. "We good?"

She met his eyes and nodded. She'd asked him to stop and he had. Everything about this situation was making her feel out of control and she wasn't sure if she was overreacting or not. She needed time to think.

Nguyen switched his position and unbuttoned her jeans.

"No," she said, "That's enough. I don't want any more."

"What's the problem now?" He raised his head to look at her over her navel. "I'm doing this," he glanced at the juncture of her thighs, "for you. Relax, babe."

That was too much. He was doing her a favor? "Move back," she snapped.

He looked down at her jeans again as if deciding whether to listen or not. "It's uncomfortable for a man –"

"Don't care."

Tamaki, where are you? I can feel your anger. I'm on my way.

Scout's familiar voice, absent for so long, brought clarity. Tamaki pivoted her hips, placed the ball of her right foot on his shoulder and pushed Nguyen back. Unbalanced, his grip on her inner thigh loosened.

"I said, 'No!'"

She used the ball of her left foot to strike square in his hairless chest. Nguyen fell over and Tamaki jumped up, grabbing her shirt off the floor. She shrugged into it, shoved the trunk out from in front of the door, and was halfway down the cabin's steps before Nguyen made it outside. The screen door banged behind him.

Scout sat in the middle of the gravel road, staring at them both.

He paced beside her in silence until they reached the dining hall.

Are you okay? Did he hurt you?

"He didn't hurt me." She gave a bitter laugh. "Or, he hurt my pride."

I don't understand.

"Is it weird for me to talk to you about this?"

It's always weird to experience telepathy with a fox. Go for it.

"He was pressuring me. It was out of character and I didn't like it. Or," she bit her lip. "I liked it, the making out, but I didn't like that it felt like it wasn't about me. It could have been any woman in there." She shrugged. "I didn't think I was a romantic, but apparently I require a little more effort. We didn't even kiss."

I'm sorry that he pressured you. No one deserves that. Making love is a very personal decision. Scout glanced away. *And if he knew you, he would have brought you flowers.*

They reached the greenhouse and Tamaki opened the door for Scout.

"I get it," Tamaki said. She licked her lips. "I get why you were mad that I didn't ask consent about your body."

THIRTY-ONE

The next evening Scout lifted his head from where he'd been resting it on his paws. His triangular ears swiveled toward the greenhouse entrance. A moment later Nguyen pushed the door open, but he stopped near the couch by the entrance like he was waiting for a special invitation. He'd found a button-down shirt to go with his khakis and it was too easy to imagine him as an associate professor. Then he flicked his black hair and gave her a half-smile and now he looked like a model…for professional clothing.

"Yes," Tamaki said with a raised eyebrow. She made a circular gesture in the air to encompass him. "What's the attitude?"

"Trying to suss out who I'm dealing with today. The amazing fighter who killed two Hotheads without blinking, or the competitive Alchemist, or the woman who kicked me in the chest after making out with me."

"I'm a complicated woman." She glanced at Scout, but there was no reaction. She pressed her lips together. He must be struggling with his fox nature. "Sometimes insecure men have a problem with that. Like men can do whatever they want, and their behavior gets a pass, but women have to be likable."

"I like you. Sometimes you scare me, but I like you." Nguyen cleared his throat and straightened. "That's not why I came though. Gavin sent me to tell you it's time for the Alchemists' strategy meeting tonight. I'm supposed to escort you there."

She needed Scout to be on point for this meeting. It was important. She needed to get on track to become a goddess so she could give Scout a new body before he lost his humanity.

Tamaki looked at Nguyen. She crooked her finger until he walked across the greenhouse to her. Then she closed her eyes, came up on her tiptoes, and kissed him.

The first kiss had been such a spontaneous move followed by Scout's mental shout that she hadn't really registered it. Then, in the cabin, she'd been unsure. Now, Tamaki felt the press of Nguyen's lips and smelled the subtle scent of burned sugar. Her hands went to his chest and she shifted closer. It felt good to touch another human. A spark of excitement lit in her belly. His hands came around her waist as he deepened the kiss. He wanted her and that was a turn-on.

When she opened her eyes, it was to see his dark eyes looking down at her. "You're quite the mystery wrapped inside a riddle, aren't you?"

Humph. A riddle wrapped inside a mystery inside an enigma. That's a Winston Churchill quote and he didn't say it right.

Tamaki smiled. "I'm ready. Let's go."

*   *   *

The Alchemists' meeting was in a side room of Gavin's office building. It smelled like stale cigarette smoke. Mismatched chairs and couches had been shoved together. The good chairs in the audience – the ones with cushions – had already been taken by the first Alchemists to arrive. High up on the wall was one of those cheap round clocks like schools used, with the second-hand lagging and then speeding up as it circled the numbers. Gavin, Haws, and Stoltzus sat behind a table at the front, like a row of judges in one of those old reality shows. Gavin was leader of the Alchemists, Haws must be representing the preppers, and Stoltzus, was in charge of the field exercises for the Alchemists. Tamaki wondered who would be the mean one, who the nice one, and who would be the deciding vote.

"Go ahead and sit down, guys, we're about to start," Gavin said. His camo jacket hung open and he seemed relaxed as he rocked on the chair's back legs with his thumbs tugging on his belt.

Stoltzus leaned over to whisper something to Gavin, holding up his hand to cover what he was saying.

Tamaki sat on a metal chair and saw Nguyen grabbing one from the back so he could sit next to her. Scout had come in as well. Wrinkling his nose as he looked for a place to perch, Scout settled on top of some stacked boxes.

Someone tapped on her shoulder. Tamaki looked behind her to see Don and Hank.

"Well, Tam-a-ki, did you have fun visiting with Nguyen in his cabin?" Don leered at her. "Not hiding in the greenhouse like always."

He exchanged a look with his neighbor, but Hank had the grace to shake his head.

Everything about this man was annoying. She snapped, "My name is TaMAKi and I'm at all the practices. If you don't see me, maybe there's a different reason."

Don's face scrunched his face like he'd sucked on a lemon. She'd never been partners with him during an exercise, but she recognized his expression. His talent was increased strength. She had time to brace herself before Don put his hands on her chair and lifted it off the ground, giving it a hard shake. "How do you like that, princess?"

"Knock it off," Nguyen said, settling into his chair. "We're all on the same team. Hey, Nate. Great job today."

"Thanks. Too bad I can't be a projector like you." Nate grinned.

Don let her chair down with a thump. Sweat broke out across his forehead and he gave off the cloying odor of ammonia.

Tamaki wished she was a cat so she could cough up a hairball on him.

Nguyen's retort was cut short by Gavin bringing his chair upright.

Stoltzus banged his hand on the table. "Call to order."

Everyone went quiet.

"This is an exciting night because it's time for the next step in our plan." Gavin stood up and paced as he talked. "We've survivors. We're planners. We've built a community." He gestured around the room. "And we're amassing talented who can manipulate energy with their minds."

He had to stop while the audience cheered. Tamaki golf clapped as she looked around.

This feels like a political rally.

"We have knowledge that the priest caste in Nippur is so greedy that they are willing to sell information about manipulating energy." He looked at Tamaki. "They call it *etemmu* there. But we're going to beat them at their own game. We know that contestants from this region will compete for the chance to represent Enlil's territory in the upcoming battle for the seventh seat on the Council of Gods. We have to get an undercover Humanist in that seat so that we can establish a new order where people don't have to worry about being fed to a maw, sold as a Debtor, or anything else these gods can think of."

The cheering erupted again. This time Tamaki joined in.

"We – the combined preppers and Alchemists – are going to pay to send someone in this room to be trained by Enlil's priests in the art of *etemmu*, things that we don't know here. But this person has to be mentally strong, tough enough to remember who they are even when they are in a foreign temple. We need someone who intends to bring down the reign of the gods."

Butterflies fluttered in Tamaki's chest. This was what she needed so she could fix Scout and make sure that humans had a voice on the Council.

"We're a team here, a family," Gavin said. "And we're going to act like one. Think about who in this room is our best candidate. This person will have to compete against the representatives from every other territory, so we need to take our best shot."

Laughter made Tamaki wrap her arms around her chest. Had Gavin chosen that word on purpose to point to Nguyen or was she being paranoid?

Gavin sat down and Stoltzus stood up to announce in a deep voice, "In three minutes, we'll open the floor for nominations. State the name and then a reason why this person is the best candidate. We'll vote. Majority wins. Easy."

Tamaki looked at Scout. He must have been able to read her nerves because he'd picked up his head and his ears were turned to her. Or maybe her heart was beating so hard that he could hear it.

After what seemed an eternity, Stoltzus made a show of looking at the clock. "Do I have any nominations?"

Down the row, Nate stood up. He cleared his throat and had to take a deep breath. His voice still came out squeaky. "I'd like to nominate Nguyen because he's already done so much for this community by being a leader and going out on missions. Also, his talent with projecting will help him win the competition with other candidates."

Several of the men reached across Tamaki to slap Nguyen on the shoulder or mutter their support.

"Do you accept?" Stoltzus asked.

Nguyen smiled as he shook his hair back. "It would be an honor to represent you guys."

Tamaki clapped along with the rest of the room. Gavin was smiling. She was so nervous she couldn't stand it. She knew how powerful she was, that she'd been born for this, but who would stand up for her? What would they use as the reason?

The ticking of the clock filled the room. Tamaki kept her head down. Nguyen tugged on his shirt, still grinning from his own nomination.

She elbowed him. "This is it."

"What?"

"The favor you gave me."

At his blank look she prompted, "For winning the archery match. You said –"

He narrowed his eyes and shook his head.

"If there are no more–" Stoltzus began.

"Wait," Tamaki jumped to her feet. The force of the combined stares was like a physical blow. She chewed the inside of her mouth as she gathered her thoughts. It had been instinct to stand up, but she wasn't ready.

"Yes?" Stoltzus said, not cruelly. "Did you want to nominate someone?"

"Yeah." She balled her hands into fists. "Myself."

Don actually snorted and several men broke into smiles as if this were a joke. She kept staring at the men behind the desk. Gavin's expression was hard to read.

"Crap. Uh." She pressed on. "You've seen how I've changed the greenhouse to the hydroponic system, built arches for the vine plants, even decreased growing time despite the lack of a consistent sun." If they'd listen, then she could explain the ideas she'd jotted down in her notebook. "I also have ideas about how plants can be used to defend this community."

"Plans for your plants? Watch out for the killer carrots!" Don said. The men in the back chuckled. "Sit down! The other territories will die laughing."

"Then they'll underestimate me. Fine." Tamaki turned to face the audience as she remembered who she was. "My name is Tamaki Hayashi and I'm the best candidate because I've fought *gallu* demons and Hotheads. And I killed the scorpion that invaded this camp."

"You didn't kill it. Nguyen did." Jamal shook his head. "I'm not trying to be harsh, but this vote is serious."

Tamaki swallowed. "I won the archery contest."

Stoltzus gave a small nod, but someone – she thought it was Nate – said, "Because you cheated."

"It wasn't cheating! It was using my talent." Tamaki glanced at Stoltzus and saw him nod again.

Stoltzus banged his fist against the table. "Looks like we have two candidates. Nguyen and Tamaki, please leave the room while we vote."

They stood in the hallway not looking at each other.

"I'm sorry for what happened in there," Nguyen said, finally. "I didn't know you were serious."

"I don't just grow potatoes." She felt the space under her heart awakening as the force of her emotions grew.

"I know that." He held up his hands to deflect her anger.

"Then why didn't you stand up for me in there?" Her voice was rising and she hated that, but this wasn't fair. "You're smart. You're popular. You love this community. But the competition? You aren't strong enough. I have the killer instinct that will get me onto that seat."

"Diplomacy and teamwork are important."

She shook her head. "I get that you want to be the representative, but so do I."

"May the best human win." He held out his hand.

She bit her tongue to keep from saying anything, but not enough to draw blood.

They've voted. Nguyen won. Unanimous. They're about to call you in.

Tamaki closed her eyes and let the pain and shame wash over her.

The door opened and they were led back inside. Tamaki sank into her chair and glared at Haws. At Gavin. She looked over her shoulder as some looked away and others stared back. This wasn't about talent or ambition. This vote was a popularity contest for sure.

Stoltzus stood up to announce Nguyen and then Nguyen made a speech, but it was all garbled to Tamaki. She twisted her fingers around each other.

Warmth filled her brain, a message from Scout, but she didn't look at him either.

Someone said something about raiding the cafeteria for celebratory drinks and the whole noisy pack filed through the door leaving only Tamaki, Scout, Gavin, and Haws.

"It was close," Gavin said, "but Nguyen edged you out. I know you're disappointed."

"I'm more than disappointed." Tamaki forced herself to look at Gavin. "Everyone always talks about being a team, you said we were a family, but the others never even considered me."

"It's over." Gavin shrugged his shoulders. "Feel what you need to feel and then move forward. That's what they taught me in the Army and it's served me well."

"How could we send you to Nippur as a mole when you escaped from there?" Haws asked. "You think the temple people won't recognize you? Your damn hair's blue!" He cleared his throat. "There's another role –
"

"We know," Gavin interrupted the other man, "that psychic gifts are often genetic. In fact, you shared your story with me about your mother and your grandmother."

She nodded, wary.

"We need multiple plans to resist the gods. Nguyen going undercover is one." Gavin tapped on the table. He looked almost nervous.

"Another is to increase our number of Alchemists. That's where you are uniquely gifted."

"You want me to be like a recruiter?" Tamaki frowned. "Work with your Humanist spies and get people to come here instead of going to Nippur?" She played with the idea. It wasn't what she'd planned, but that position sounded important and would give her a sense of belonging. It wouldn't help her learn more about *etemmu* to help Scout, but maybe after she'd figured out how to fix him then it would be a possibility.

Haws and Gavin looked at each other.

"Not exactly," Gavin hedged.

"What's my 'special' project?" She sat up in the chair and folded her arms across her chest.

"It's more of a biological gift," Haws said. "Not to be indelicate, but you're the only female among us."

A shock of cold washed over Tamaki like a bucket of ice water.

"We're a team," Gavin said, "and we aren't going to like every job that's required, but this is more important than the individual. This is about the survival of Alchemists."

Oh, shit. Scout leaped down from the boxes to a chair and then to the floor.

Tamaki couldn't seem to think. Part of her was noticing that Scout was still limping from the Hotheads attack. And part of her was working through what Gavin was saying. He'd taken the story of her magical heritage – the one she'd entrusted to him – and twisted it to his own use.

Her body pulled in, pulled away, her breathing quickened.

"Are you asking me to be a breeder?" Tamaki's voice came out stronger than she thought it would. She stood up and pushed the chair back. "Because if you think my role in this community is to grow food and make babies on command…" She shook her head as words failed. "That you've discussed this without me. Did the whole group of men talk about me and my body and what I would or would not do?"

"Don't be ridiculous." Gavin reached out a hand as to calm her. "Yes, Haws and Stoltzus and I have an org chart and yes, we determine how everybody can best contribute, but this isn't personal."

This is the most personal thing I've ever heard.

"Screw your chart," Tamaki sneered at the men hiding on the other side of the table, "And if you think I am sleeping with any of you, you are irrevocably wrong."

THIRTY-TWO

Later, Tamaki didn't know how she walked out of the building and across the community to the greenhouse. She knew Scout was trotting beside her because of a warm presence in her mind, but as she walked more emotions blossomed through her body. She remembered finding the fox's skeleton with the vines wrapping through it and that was her. Hate curled up through her ribcage, humiliation encircling her femur, betrayal sprouting leaves that trailed through her hair.

"I trusted them," she said. "Gavin told me I was part of a family. Guess I should have known how well family treats me. I thought I could please him, that I could fit into this community.

"Gods! Nguyen was manipulating me this whole time on Gavin's orders. That's why he was so pushy about having sex. They were trying to get me pregnant."

I'm sorry. If I'd been able to fight the fox part of me then I would have been able to spy on their conversation and let you know.

"Don't you dare blame yourself! You're a saint not to say I-told-you-so. You've told me since we arrived that this place wasn't what it appeared." She ground her teeth. "All this talk about a new world. Racism is gone; it's human against god. The criteria are supposed to be whether you can manipulate *etemmu* or you can't. And I can." She flipped off Liza's house as she passed it. "Bullshit! I should have let the scorpion kill more of them. And then climbed on the scorpion's back and ridden it through this camp."

That…would have been something.

They arrived at the greenhouse and Tamaki wrenched the door open. "They chose to be sexist. They chose to see me as an object rather than a person. They chose not to make the post-firestorm world be better than it was before."

Scout jumped up on the couch with his head tilted.

"You know what's funny?" She reached into the drawer where she'd hidden her notebook. "I never got to explain how I could add a layer of security to the entrances of the community. Why I'm growing Virginia creeper over there and sheep's sorrel. They wouldn't listen to how my ability with plants was more comprehensive than Nguyen's ability to project something."

I know you wanted to stay.

"Apparently it's not about what I want." She slammed the notebook on the counter and walked to the other couch, grabbing her backpack and shoving the full water bottle inside. Looking around, she made a mental list. She had her knife, her clothing, and Scout. The Alchemists could keep the rest of their crap. "They want to see someone who can use *etemmu?* I'll give them a show."

She stepped to the hydroponic pipes she'd set up for the dandelions and pulled an entire plant out. "My grandmother had this passion for detail work, an inner drive to fix, like she was a seamstress or surgeon. But here's a secret," she looked at Scout. "I've always found destruction more fun."

That's not a secret to me.

Tamaki touched the golden petals of the dandelion. She'd been working with the plants for weeks, had grown them from seedlings, and knew them intimately. It wasn't hard to see the yellow flowers and imagine them as the ruff of a lion. She dug out the needle from the toolbox on the workbench.

She pricked her finger. A tiny drop of crimson formed a bubble. Tamaki smeared it with her index finger and then wiped it on each petal, pulling as she hummed, until each petal culminated in a tip, sharp as a lion's tooth. It was so easy to connect to the *etemmu* in the plants.

Tamaki, what are you doing? He sounded alarmed.

"Don't worry." She rubbed her forehead and scrunched her hair. Her scalp was so sensitive. Her skin could feel everything. She shivered in pleasure; no more fighting to be good.

Then she wrapped her hands around the exposed roots. Roots that, if thickened, could look like legs. Flowers with sharp edges couldn't do very much, but a marching army of golden-headed dandelions might be useful. She extended the stalks so each plant was two feet high.

These men aren't your friends. If you attack, they will attack you back.

"I'm counting on it." She felt light-headed, although that couldn't be from the small amount of blood she'd used. The fear and humiliation she'd been shoving down, down into the hole behind her heart, was churning. It was going to come out like a burst abscess. Did the *etemmu* get stuck in her instead of flowing? Was she like the Skeleton Forest?

You don't think they'll let you leave. He sounded resigned.

"I know they won't. Because I know where the community is. Because I could betray them to the priests in Nippur. Because they want me to make baby Alchemists and I won't."

Methodically she moved down the row of dandelions, creating sharp petals and legs from the roots. It wasn't enough. She needed more power. She needed more blood.

There are lights out there coming toward us.

Tamaki peered through a space in the vines that encircled the greenhouse. "Lanterns."

Use my blood.

"What?" She whipped around. His offer was a complete shock. "You hate when I use blood magic."

I hate when you're threatened more and I don't want you to hurt yourself. He limped toward her. *Go ahead. I free you from your promise to create a new body. It was a sweet offer, but neither of understood the cost.*

The lantern group stopped at Haw's house. The door opened. She was pretty sure she recognized Haws standing in the doorway before his light joined the group and the door shut.

"Doesn't matter," she muttered. They were creating a mob against her like she was Frankenstein's monster. Each new betrayal shouldn't hurt. Her heart should be hardened.

Scout's cold nose pressed against her hand. Tamaki knelt down.

She peeled the crusty fur away so she could see. The puncture wound from the Hothead was still open, the size of a half-dollar, open all the way down to pink muscle. A thin stream of blood flowed when he moved his shoulder.

"This is worse than when I treated it yesterday! Why didn't you tell me?"

He looked at her with an expression so human that her breath caught. She touched the thin line of blood, her hands shaking.

Etemmu flowed like a steady drip and with it a certainty. "You're dying. I thought we had more time, but you knew that the *etemmu*-water was a temporary solution."

Yes. This body is breaking down, not because of age, but because it is unnatural, held together with etemmu.

"Enbu." She'd failed the one person who hadn't wanted something from her. Who'd been honest with her, even when she didn't like it. "You're my one friend in this world."

I know. He leaned his head against her knee.

"I have to confess something." Tamaki's chin quivered and she had to swipe at her nose with the back of her hand. Self-hate bubbled inside her stomach like toxic stew. "Maybe An psychically linked us as a punishment. But I don't think he was clever enough to think of that. I think maybe I accidentally did it, either when I saved the fox – which explains why he followed me around – or when we were flying through the air. I don't even know what I do when I give in to blood magic. I've gotten better at it." She gave a bitter laugh. "So good that I gave myself a nosebleed the other day in order to win an archery contest."

That shouldn't surprise me. Scout sighed and he raised his vulpine eyebrows at her. *You're so terrified of being abandoned that it drives most of what you do.*

"I mean, no. I'm not fearful; I'm determined." She straightened her posture and took a deep breath. "I initiate things, I hate being talked down to, and I will not tolerate chauvinism." Tamaki's voice grew stronger. Her hands burned as *etemmu* pooled. "This camp is the corruption."

Slow down! Scout barked. *I'm probably going to die escaping this place, but preferably not before we even get out of the greenhouse.*

"Ah, sorry." As she'd grown more resolute, she'd grabbed Scout's life force. "I didn't mean to do that. I got excited."

He backed away from her and licked his wound.

"Tamaki?" A figure stood outside the greenhouse door. "We'd like to talk to you." It was Gavin using his Southern accent to make himself sound calm and reasonable.

"Ready?" She didn't want to make a promise that everything would be alright. Or that either one of them would even survive this. All she had was justified anger, mutant dandelions, and a dying fox. "Look around outside and let me know what vegetation we have available? I'll keep Gavin talking while you assess. Then we'll make it up as we go along until we burn this place down."

We don't have matches. Scout's mouth dropped open in a blend of fox-human smile. *But we had worse odds of escaping Ekur Temple. That was quite the spectacle, wasn't it?*

"I don't think the Alchemists are going to save us this time." Tamaki shrugged into her backpack.

No, I wouldn't think so.

"Tamaki," Gavin sounded impatient. "We're coming in."

"Don't bother," she said. "We're coming out." She whistled for her dandelions and walked forward.

THIRTY-THREE

The greenhouse door made a screeching sound as she wrenched it open far enough that it would stay that way. Gavin and Nguyen stood there with Haws and the other Alchemists spread out behind. Based on the beer smell, the crew had been in the middle of a party to celebrate Nguyen's election.

"What's up, boys?" She leaned against the door jamb and gave them a half-smile.

Vines – the Virginia creeper is on the outside of the greenhouse and the squash vines are intertwined. At the base of the woods there is a carpet of pine needles.

"You were pretty upset earlier," Gavin said in his Southern drawl. "We wanted to talk. Make sure you weren't going to do anything… unreasonable."

"I'm leaving tonight." Tamaki threaded her hands through the backpack straps. "I consider that reasonable."

"You know we can't allow that." Gavin's expression hardened. "You're one of us, Tamaki. You belong here."

"Allow? Are you saying that you intend to keep me here against my will?" Tamaki looked out over the group. Jamal and Hanks were confused, looking back and forth between them. Nate was taking his cue from Nguyen.

Haw's face was blank and Stoltzus had moved into a flanking position. Don looked gleeful.

"Good thing I'm not asking your permission." She moved aside and watched their eyes go wide as fifteen huge dandelions, one for each Alchemist plus an extra for dear old Haws, marched out of the greenhouse, their petals spiked instead of rounded. The dandelions walked with a bit of a tilt, like happy drunken sailors, as their roots pressed against the ground.

Lanterns were lifted high as the men leaned forward to see. Muttering began.

Tamaki released her grip on the backpack straps and stretched out her hands so her fingers pointed at the men. The flowers advanced.

"What is that?" Nate, the youngest Alchemist, backed away. "What does it do?"

Stoltzus said, "This is what she meant about turning her plants into weapons, but it's still a weed." He used his lantern to pummel the nearest one, knocking it to the ground like they were wrestling.

Tamaki concentrated, opening her senses to each connection. Finding the one that hurt, she traced it and manipulated the petals.

"Ow! What the–" Stoltzus jumped back, but the knife-petals had closed around his hand like scissors. The cuts were shallow, but they were enough. The plant drank the *etemmu* and grew taller. Part of the energy fed back to Tamaki. The plant's roots wrapped around Stoltzus's leg and pulled him to the ground.

Men started shouting.

"Stop it." Gavin was in her face, hands on her shoulders, shaking her, but she didn't care. "Think about what you're doing or you're going to regret it."

When he shook her the abscess inside her broke open and her fury and embarrassment and hurt feelings poured out.

"I trusted you and you turned my secret about my magic heritage against me. It's ironic because I would have been the best soldier you ever had. Your talent is sensing energy, so you know I'm stronger than Nguyen, but you didn't tell anyone that secret." She wrenched away from him. "You know that night after the scorpion attack when you had me write on a piece of paper? Want to know what I wrote?"

"Yes," he said, acting gentle. "I want to know about you."

She lifted her face to the night and screamed, "I REGRET NOTHING." The sound echoed off the mountain.

The dandelions attacked.

She had fifteen extensions. Stoltzus still wrestled with one and the match was even. He sawed at the base of the flower with a knife, but the roots wrapped his legs together. The other dandelions chased the men, petals slicing and feeding, making the plants taller and stronger.

Gavin took two steps back. Scout was savaging the man's leg.

Free from Gavin, Tamaki turned her attention to the carpet of pine needles that Scout had seen. She knew the scent, the feel of the long brown needles, the way they held together at the end, sticky, and then elongated to points. She understood the way they were green and then dried, became brown, became flammable. *Etemmu* flowed: connections established.

She squinted through the chaos of men and plants. Nguyen had gotten the Alchemists more or less organized with their backs to each other so they could fight facing outwards.

"Use your energy," he was yelling. "Use your power."

"Fabulous idea," Tamaki muttered as she found her target.

Her mind reached for bunches of the dry pine needles. "Catch," she screamed, as she threw them at Gerry.

The Firestarter shrieked. The needles burst into flame.

"Thanks, Gerry," Tamaki called as she moved her arms like an orchestra conductor to summon more needles and spread fires around the community.

"Get water from the creek," Nguyen screamed. Half the men bolted. That freed up dandelions and she summoned them in a defensive ring around herself.

Glancing around for Scout, Tamaki saw Gavin reach to his hip, but she didn't understand until Gavin pulled free his Sig Sauer.

"Stop," she yelled. "Put the gun down or I'll destroy the greenhouse and all the camp's live food."

Gavin looked at her and then he pointed the gun at Scout. The shot rang out. There was a bang and then acrid smoke wafted past mixed with the smell of Scout's blood. Scout yipped and fell to the ground. Tamaki sent a dandelion to scoop him up while she lunged at Gavin, shoving him off balance so he couldn't shoot again.

Gavin was taller than her and trained. She summoned two six-foot-tall dandelions to wrap their leaves around his arms.

"Look at what you've done." She pointed toward the greenhouse where the Virginia creeper squeezed the glass so tightly it was creating cracks in the panels. "I, at least, am woman enough to admit that this is personal." The large leaves of the squash plants reached around the base of the greenhouse, the tendrils of the vines digging into the cracks produced by the Virginia creeper. It was truly elegant the way they worked together.

"Nate," Gavin called to the small group still fighting dandelions. "Go ring the bell for help." A figure peeled off and ran toward the camp. Gavin glared at her, chest heaving as he strained against the plant guards. "You were a mistake," he said. "An unstable, unliked, freak."

"I know you are, but what am I?" Giddy, Tamaki stood on her tiptoes. Her blood was champagne; she was a giant balloon of golden fizzies. "This is for Scout." She put her left hand on Gavin's cheek like a caress and then she stabbed her right thumb into his eye. "You better hope it wasn't a kill shot." Her thumb pulled out with a pop.

Gavin screamed, the cords of his throat standing out as blood ran down his cheek. The dandelions let go and he fell to the ground, hands pressed to his face. "Don, take her out."

She pivoted in time for a gut punch from the burly fighter. He was about a hundred pounds heavier than her and his talent was increasing his strength.

"I've been waiting for this," he sneered. He cracked his knuckles.

Tamaki's eyes watered as she staggered and tried to catch her breath against the pain in her middle. She lost her connection to the dandelions, the needles, and the vines squeezing the greenhouse.

Don made a fist and swung again.

Tamaki ducked to the side and held up her right arm as a shield.

Don's blow struck her elbow, making it go numb and spinning her body clockwise.

Scared, Tamaki made herself remember the fight with Obaa-chan's murderer. She'd replayed the scene in her head a thousand times. Now Don was taking the place of the other man.

Stay calm.

Scout's voice in her head – the knowledge that he was somehow still alive – galvanized her. She danced around to face Don. He leaned forward, expecting her to back away. Instead, Tamaki rushed into him, burying her face into his chest and clasping him in a bearhug. Her left foot snaked around his left ankle and she let her body weight fall into him.

Unbalanced, Don fell backward, tripped by her foot. Tamaki scrambled up his prone body to sit on his chest. Her right hand still tingled from his punch, so she used her left hand to pull her knife out.

Don kicked his legs and turned over underneath her to shield his face and heart. "You coward." Rage moved through her. She plunged the knife into his back; the blade slid in like cutting meat. Tamaki yanked it out and did it again. Don's feet stopped kicking.

Tamaki hurried over to the plant making a nest around Scout. The bullet had gone at an angle into his neck and down into the muscle of his chest.

Use what's left of me so you can be free. They will kill you. If they don't, you'll wish they had.

Tamaki shuddered at the mental picture of being blinded and kept in a cage, her body used to produce babies while her mind went mad. Nope, not an option.

Little fires were everywhere: on Haw's house, at the treeline, by the cafeteria. Smoke wove itself into the night air. The men would be back from the creek soon and she didn't know how to heal Scout. So, she pulled out her knife and placed the blade against her forearm.

"I give my blood to you, my friend, with no cost attached."

The knife was sharp, but she still had to press, still had to cut.

Power released as crimson stained her arm.

Tamaki squeezed her bleeding arm and then caught the liquid running down her fingers in her cupped hand. When her hand was full, she poured it into the flesh ripped apart by the bullet shot at such a short-range. "Magic, I will be your vessel."

Scout whined.

The night became clear. She reconnected to the plants and heard the sounds of the needles crackling and the creaking of the greenhouse vines. Stoltzus alive on the ground, but wrapped in dandelion leaves. Gavin slumped over while Nguyen tried to help him. This moment was so beautiful, so crystalline, that she didn't want it to stop. Part of her knew she should pull back and regulate, but she couldn't seem to. She didn't want to.

And then a tugging, not from her plant minions, but through her connection with Scout. His wounds pulled her energy into his body.

His snout opened and Scout's body rose into the air. Golden light poured from the inside out, shining through the hole where the Hothead had pierced him, through the bullet hole, and through his eyes.

Dizzy, Tamaki shook her head. "Too much," she whispered. She fell to her knees and grabbed at the air in front of her as if she could grab onto the energy leaving her. She had to break the connection.

Suddenly, the golden glow faded and Scout floated back down. He stretched his healed neck and made a horrible racking sound before coughing. A bullet shot out of his mouth and onto the grass.

She leaned forward to rest her head in the cool grass.

Sorry to interrupt. Scout stood beside her, one paw on her head. His tail drooped with exhaustion. *But I think Nguyen is going to shoot you.*

The bell outside the cafeteria began to ring, a signal that the community was under attack.

Sitting up, Tamaki felt the chill starting from her use of blood magic. All of her lovely dandelions were gone except the six-foot one chasing Hank toward the camp. She tugged on the connection. No, that one was gone, too. Bits of vegetation littered the area.

Only Nguyen stood there, facing her with gun in hand.

His hair was disheveled, his expression grim. She wasn't used to seeing that. Even his immaculate khakis had green stains.

Maybe bring the vines from the greenhouse to attack?

Tamaki met Nguyen's eyes as she walked forward, one measured step at a time.

The bell kept ringing, but the sound was muffled as more of the blood magic reaction set in.

"Don't come any closer," Nguyen said. His hands were shaking. Like hers did when she realized that Scout was dying. Poor, sweet, Nguyen, nothing but a stooge for others.

She walked forward. "You never told anyone that it was me that killed the scorpion; instead, you were the hero and you took full credit, even when I was scolded for not getting inside."

"I wasn't sure – I was holding the javelin and then it flew through the air. That's my talent, not yours."

"You thought you killed the scorpion without even realizing it?" She tilted her head. "Wow. That is some messed-up thinking."

"I will shoot you. I'm serious."

Tamaki stepped until the gun touched her breastbone.

His eyes were wide as his finger half-pulled on the trigger.

The scar on her thigh throbbed with phantom pain.

"If you have to say you're serious," she said, placing her right hand on the gun and pushing it to the side before pulling it out of his grip, "then you aren't."

His hand fell by his side and she pivoted, launching the gun into the vine mess of the greenhouse, the structure groaning under the plant attack.

That was too dangerous, Scout railed in her mind. *He could have grabbed that mid-flight and brought it back.*

"This is why I should have been elected to represent this territory and not you."

Nguyen dropped his gaze and Tamaki walked toward the tree line, her legs growing numb. Scout limped beside her.

Behind them, the bell continued to toll.

THIRTY-FOUR

Empty, Tamaki followed the path away from the camp while the greenhouse continued crumbling behind her, the glass crackling as it broke into smaller and smaller pieces from the force of the wrapping vines. Burning pine needles scented the evening like an over-productive candle. Voices shouted, but it was all muffled. The gap under her heart was so cold she imagined her ribs covered with frost, the white spreading through her body. The betrayal by the Alchemists followed by releasing all the emotions she'd stuffed down for weeks meant nothing was left. Nothing but one last plan.

Stopping at the forest line, Tamaki shook her head. She'd had a blindfold on when Nguyen led them away.

I didn't. Scout's voice was gentle. *Follow me.*

Entering the forest should have made her feel surrounded by life force, but Tamaki only felt the darkness. She began shivering; her teeth chattered. Scout's bright tail flitted ahead like a flag. She focused on it.

You can do this. We have to get a little farther. Go around that pile of evergreens. There's a pit beneath.

She moved to the right, remembering the zigzag she'd done while blindfolded.

Now duck. More. There's a log that is tied back and will smash through here if you don't.

Not bothering to look over her shoulder to check, she stared at the red fox tail beckoning her forward, bringing her through the darkness.

Then they reached the arch.

Where to now?

"I've finally learned my lesson," Tamaki said. "I can't win this game the way it's set up. The gods are all horrible and the Humanists are just as bad. I've tried so hard, but I can't be good enough." She stared at the glowbugs shining as they feasted on the excess *etemmu* that rotted the trees. "And I don't care anymore."

That's not true.

"It's true enough." She waved her hand as if swatting away his comment. "But I have something else to do now. I didn't heal your body."

No. It was another temporary fix. She could see him thinking. *You want to find the source of* etemmu.

"We have to follow the ley lines, right? Back to their source." She was so tired. "Where would you hide the source if you were a Mesopotamian god?"

Where no one could find it. In the desert at the top of a mountain. Scout turned his nose north. *Perfect place to hide the headwaters for the Tigris-Mississippi.*

Tamaki nodded. "That's what I was thinking, too."

Remember that the group of Alchemists sent to find it never came back.

"Yeah. I remember."

The climb grew steeper until even Scout was panting. Sweat formed on Tamaki's forehead. It felt like moving through a fever as her insides were frozen while her outside sweltered. She shrugged off the pack and removed her coat before pulling out a bottle of water. She poured it for Scout first.

The fox lapped it. Then she poured for herself. For brief seconds the water washed away the residue of smoke that coated her throat. But the dryness returned before the bottle even went back in her bag.

It should have been darker as night settled, but the trees had thinned, the rocks underfoot becoming smaller, the picturesque boulders all but disappeared. Instead, Tamaki's boots couldn't find purchase in the grainy sand. She lunged for the thin trunk of a lonely tree to haul herself to the top of the rise.

Scout barked in encouragement. He stood silhouetted at the top: triangular ears rotating as they tuned into the night's sounds, his tail horizontal, the fur ruffling in a slight breeze. He was so beautiful that tears formed in Tamaki's eyes. One each spilled down her cheek. It wasn't something she could control. And then it was gone.

"I'm so broken," she muttered.

Tamaki heaved herself the last foot, hands scrambling in the sand until she landed next to Scout and looked over the top. And then she wanted to cry again, but not for the beauty. They'd climbed to the top of the mountain and spread below was a bowl of endless sand lit by unobscured moonlight.

"There's nothing here."

Sand.

Clenching her hands in the sand, Tamaki asked, "Are we sure about this?"

No.

They were face to face as she lay on her side. She could see how his fur was thinner where the shoulder rubbed against his body. The curve of his paw-knuckles and the black claws at the end. The whiskers on his snout. The golden sheen to his eyes had dulled to an amber hue. Already her *etemmu* transfusion was wearing away.

"We will die out here and no one will notice or care."

Speak for yourself. He used his hind foot to scratch his nose and ruined the noble effect. *I have a fan club.*

"Who?" She frowned at him as she tried to figure out the cryptic remark. Someone at the camp who fed him scraps? Someone from their time at Ekur Temple?

This woman who brought me back from the dead and shoved me into this stellar vulpine body.

A surprised laugh bubbled out of her and Tamaki lay on her back and laughed until the soreness of her throat made her stop. She reached for the bottle of water. "And then you got pissed."

She should have asked.

"You're right." She took a swig. With her emotions, including pride, drained away it was easier to acknowledge. "But I have apologized a thousand times."

He nodded and they sat in silence, letting the wind touch their hair with careless fingers.

I'm sorry that Gavin betrayed you. And Nguyen.

"I didn't really like that guy anyway." She screwed the cap back on. "Bad kisser."

Was it all for show?

Images of Nguyen flicked through her mind. His playful grin at the table in the cafeteria, his stupid paper airplane flying around, his panic when the Hothead attacked, his finger moving away from the trigger.

"Doesn't matter now. I think they've rescinded my Alchemists' membership."

* * *

They walked through the night, Scout slowing until Tamaki finally stopped to pick him up. His body had collapsed like an empty bag.

Not how I imagined being swept off my feet. His voice was tired.

Together they sat to watch as clouds covered the sky and morning broke, sullen and grim.

"When I'm the sun goddess," she said, "I will make sunrise spectacular again."

That going to be your campaign slogan?

"I think it has a certain ring." She closed her eyes and opened her senses to any living plant, to any source of *etemmu*. Like every other time she'd tried since entering the desert: nothing. She stood up and shouldered her pack. "That was the last of the water."

A feeling of acceptance entered her mind, but it wasn't hers. She looked at Scout. "Say something. With words."

He blinked his eyes, but no thought filled her mind.

"Enbu," she said. She shrugged off the backpack, keeping only the canteen strapped across her chest, and dropped the pack in the sand. No use carrying it around anymore.

They walked on.

The heat, the monotony, and the complete boredom made her want to laugh, but the lack of hope was the worst because this was all for nothing. There were no cacti to change the scenery, no little creatures popping their heads out of the sand, no spiders staring at them with eight eyes. She couldn't even look up at the sun to judge its position and know how much time had passed. In fact, it was only as the clouds cleared to reveal evening and a faint moon hung in the distance that Tamaki looked over her shoulder to see how far they'd walked. There was nothing. There was no slope to climb to return to the camp and there was no way out.

She stopped walking and gathered her thick hair, twisting it up in a knot so the breeze caressed the sweaty nape of her neck. "Wish you could do that too, huh?"

Scout flicked his right ear at her. The desert heat had to be bothering him with all that thick fur, but he didn't complain. He never did. She wanted to say something momentous. Instead, she said, "I think we are squarely in a trap."

Scout's amber eyes were listless, his tongue sticking out from between his teeth. The white patches on his muzzle looked like they'd spread, as if they'd been walking for years.

She released her hair and it unthreaded, spilling past her shoulders.

A stronger breeze blew and Scout lifted his snout to sniff and then his eyes widened. His triangular ears turned one way and then the other. He cocked his head, crouched, and then sprinted forward. With a bound, he leaped into the air, nose downward, and began digging into the desert.

Sand flew.

Hoping this meant something good, and not that he'd scented some desert mouse, Tamaki followed. The fox disappeared into the hole with only his hindquarters still visible.

Then it wasn't grains of sand landing at her feet, it was clumps. Wet clumps of sand.

Scout backed out of the hole he'd made with short hopping motions. *Look.*

Leaning over, Tamaki saw that three feet down was a teaspoonful of water. Immediately she laid on her stomach and lowered her canteen to scoop it up. She poured it into her cupped hand and offered it to Scout. It barely coated his tongue.

Impatient, Tamaki leaned down and repeated the action for herself. Cool drops that brought little relief.

"Oh, I probably shouldn't let you do that." The voice was mocking and seemed to come from all around. "But I'm so curious. Will you have the self-control to sit there and collect drops of water for hours or will you desperately thrust your hand in there and end up swallowing as much sand as liquid?"

THIRTY-FIVE

Tamaki scrambled to her feet as a creature manifested nearby. He was so bizarre that she couldn't take in everything without gaping. A humanoid male roughly six and a half feet tall. He had golden skin, a bare chest, and a six-pack of abs leading to tight leather pants. Very tight. Two ram horns sprouted from the top of his head: one thick and spiraling and the other a third of the size. One wing with iridescent feathers opened behind his right shoulder. Perhaps the most disturbing feature, however, were his large eyes and red hourglass pupils.

"Didn't your mother tell you that staring was rude?"

"What," she managed, "are you?" A thrill of fear ran through her exhausted body. She thought she'd made it past the point of caring about anything, but her body recognized the power radiating from the being.

"I suppose you'd call me a demon. I'm from Kur, after all."

Of course he was. She wanted to laugh because what else was there to do? But how could she laugh when looking into his red eyes was like staring into the stars: glittering and unknowable. For all the demon took a flippant tone, he'd been around when the Nephilim walked the earth the first time. He was both impossible and standing right in front of her.

The demon touched the smaller horn. "Don't mind that. Bit of an accident. The missing wing as well." He chuckled. "And by 'accident' I mean that I will kill Emesh the next time I see him. Slowly and painfully. In the meantime, I am stuck here keeping people like you away from where you are trying to go."

"People like me?" Tamaki said. "Do you mean Alchemists?" It didn't really matter at this point. She and Scout were both going to die in this desert, but it would be nice to solve the puzzle.

"That word used to mean something different. These were but pale imitations." The demon gave a half-shrug. "Still, they tasted delicious."

There it was. They'd reached the fearsome guardian of the Tigris-Mississippi headwaters and he was mercurial and opinionated and very, very powerful.

"I made them wait much longer before I showed up, but," the demon gestured at her, "honestly? I didn't think you two were going to last that long. Look at you! You're hacking yourself to bits to release *etemmu* like a butcher. What's next? Cut off a foot and throw it at someone because it's too difficult to pick up a rock? In my day, the necromancers had nuance and skill. Rituals. Festivals even. If you're going to sin against the Creator with forbidden practices then go big."

"I don't know," Tamaki said. She had no cleverness left.

"You build up the *etemmu* with locks inside your body and then you make the tiniest slice with a special blade. It's a metaphor, really. The blood is real, but you know what I mean."

"Why are you telling me this?" Tamaki asked.

"Oh," the demon widened his eyes. "Because you're about to die so why shouldn't I mock your complete ignorance? Besides, it gets lonely here so when I see another sentient being, I can't help myself. I even made a scorpion to be my audience, but the silly thing ran away."

Water. It was a whisper. Scout looked rough, crouching on the sand, his eyes a light brown. Even though it was evening, the sand still probably burned the pads of his paws. Tamaki took off her outer shirt, leaving on her camisole, and spread it over the sand. "Stand on there." Then she dipped the canteen into the water and offered him the tiny sip.

OH, LOOK. THE HUMAN AND THE FOXIE HAVE SECRET LITTLE CONVERSATIONS.

Tamaki threw her hands over her ears even though the telepathy was inside her mind, and Scout shook his head and whined.

"I'm Azag, in case you don't recognize me," the demon chattered on. "Would you like to see me dance while you wait to die? It isn't going to take that fox-man very long." He wrinkled his nose as he stared at Scout. "The host body wasn't properly prepared, was it? Who was the necromancer? Shoddy work. Probably the same one who hacked you to pieces." He made a tsking sound. "So embarrassing."

Scout sighed and settled onto Tamaki's shirt, closing his eyes and falling asleep. It was so hot here, her skin was burned and aching and her mind kept picturing a tall glass of water so cold that condensation ran down the sides.

Azag cleared his throat to get her attention and then folded his hands and nodded his head. The desert floor parted as a dancer pole emerged. "So, this is a little different than I'm used to, but similar to the columns in the temples that I used to visit." He raised thick eyebrows. "I only went to the best. I'd name drop, but honestly, would you even recognize it?"

Tamaki tried to save the water so Scout could have a decent amount when he awoke, but if she dipped the canteen to get more water, what was in there would pour back out. Because this place was hell.

Azag gripped the pole with both hands and then launched his body around it, circling with legs around the pole and right arm and wing extended until he came to the bottom.

"It's the closest thing to flying." He retracted his extended wing. "Also Emesh's work. Well, he begged the south wind for help in ripping my wing off, but I'm holding him responsible. Actually, the fault really rests on Sharur. Do you know it?"

"No. I don't know any Sharur." She made sure to pronounce it with the rolling 'r' sound like he did. She would definitely remember if her grandmother had told her about a demon who pole danced.

"It's a talking mace. And it shamed Emesh into coming back to start round three with me. The first round was with my army of stone warriors. The second was so fun. I'd love to… what does your time call it? Hollywood it." He sighed with pleasure, his eyes drifting half-closed as he imagined. "I used the Tablet of Destiny to reverse time. Imagine Emesh standing there like a fool while his arrow shafts turn back into canebrake, the feathers turn back into birds, and the arrowheads return to the quarry." Azag belly laughed. "I love thinking about that. And then he runs away like a little crying baby. Ha! What else could he do?"

"Hmm." Only half-listening, Tamaki lay down next to Scout. Maybe they should leave the demon and go back into the lonely desert, fall asleep together, and never wake up.

"I'll melt Sharur back into its components when I find them." He leaned against the pole and stared at Tamaki. "You're not too bad looking for a human. I like all that anger inside of you. Scrumptious." He flexed his fingers and glanced at his painted nails. "Do you want to make out before you die?"

"No, thank you." She scooped water into the canteen. It wet her tongue.

"I could teach you to pole dance, although you probably wouldn't be any good." He placed his hands behind his back and stalked back and forth like a stage actor. "I've spent thousands of years deciding how I'm going to punish Emesh. He's not even that brave, you know. He'd quit when stupid Sharur piped up talking about honor and how he'd be written into epic poetry. Then, after everything, Emesh gets credit for shoving the remains of my stone warriors into mountains designed so that the lakes and streams flow into the Tigris and Euphrates rivers, making them useful for irrigation and agriculture." He stopped pacing and looked at Tamaki. "Do you think that pretty boy thought of all that on his own? No. No way."

"Go away." Exasperated, Tamaki looked up at the demon. "Seriously. Poof back into the sand or whatever."

"Well, I would except that, due to a misunderstanding, the Council has me trapped here." He pulled at the velvet choker on his neck with a miniature silver mace. "They thought it would be ironic that I had to guard the headwaters of the new Tigris-Mississippi, especially since I am essentially working for Enlil. You know, the father of Emesh." He spit in the sand.

Frustration gripped Tamaki. The demon had gone through his whole monologue and she was as thirsty as when they'd arrived.

He leaned over her shoulder to look in the hole. "I told you it wouldn't work. You think you're smarter than the gods? They've had a lot of time to think up dead ends. They let you get close to something and then," he snapped his fingers, "take it away."

"Well, there have to be ways to get around the gods." She glanced over at Scout's prone form and then stood, wiping her hands on her pants. "What, exactly, are you supposed to keep people and creatures from doing here?"

"No one is allowed to steal the water from the oasis."

She looked around. "What oasis?"

He rolled his red eyes, the hourglasses slipping sideways and then back. "The invisible one behind me. Don't," he held up a hand as she started forward. "Walk around and try to feel it. It's always behind me. That's how magic works. Duh."

"What if I said that I don't want to steal any water?"

"I'd call you a liar." But she saw interest in the way his eyebrows moved, the way the demon's forked tongue flicked out and licked his lips. "But   keep   talking."

"I want to use it, yes, but not steal. I'm willing to pay." She held her arms out to the side as if to be frisked by a police officer. "Search my mind. I know you can."

Immediately she felt something inside her mind. There was an uncomfortable sensation, like an expanding sinus infection, but it grew into more than that. The physical ache made Tamaki grit her teeth. Then she groaned as the demon sorted through her memories, picking through her private thoughts and memories. She wanted to hide, to cover herself from his view. Tamaki squirmed, resisting the urge to fight back. This was for Scout. She'd gotten him into the body of a dying fox and she'd get him out.

"I see," Azag said, pulling his presence out of her mind. He tapped his index finger against his mouth. "Do you understand what you are offering?"

Her shoulders slumped in relief at being the only one inside her mind again. "I think so."

"No," Azag shook his finger at her. "It has to be more than that."

She closed her eyes and swallowed as she considered the full weight of her choice. Even in this hopeless place, some part of her looked for a loophole, for a hero to ride in on a winged horse, for a divine goddess to swoop in with a reprieve. But no one ever came for her.

"You never asked what the misunderstanding was about."

"What?" Tamaki looked at him in confusion. "Oh. The fight between you and Emesh?"

"I stole the Tablet of Destiny from Enlil. It might have been because I wanted the ability to predict the future or to reverse time, but it wasn't." He cocked an eyebrow at her. "It was because I wanted it."

Glancing to where Scout still rested on her shirt, Tamaki asked, "Is that important?"

"Shouldn't you know who you are dealing with?"

"Fine," she snapped. "You're a demon thief and I'm an unskilled necromancer. I'm asking for your help; you've seen what I'll pay." Tamaki straightened her shoulders. "I will stay here in exchange for the chance to use the headwaters to give Scout a new body made of pure *etemmu*. I would help you get free of this place too, but I don't know how to do that."

His red hourglass eyes glowed.

"Do you want me to beg?" she said. Her throat hurt so much, but she pushed the words out. "Azag, demon unfairly treated by the gods, majestic pole-dancer of the desert, future killer of Emesh, will you please let us through?"

Azag stepped to the side and bowed as he gestured her toward a hill of sand. A hill that hadn't been there a second before. She shook her head. Of course, there was a hill. She picked up Scout and cradled his limp body against her chest as she trudged up the hill, leaning forward to find purchase in the shifting sand. She remembered this same sensation when bringing the fox out of the Skeleton Forest back at the cabin. She'd made so many mistakes. But, at the top of the sandhill, Tamaki looked down and wanted to let out a tired whoop of victory.

An oasis spread below them.

A pool of clear water and beautiful palm trees nestled in the bowl created by sandhills. Tamaki set Scout down. "Can you walk?"

There was a feeling of approval that she accepted as a 'yes.'

"Be careful, old man."

Scout walked down the hill, head hanging from exhaustion. Tamaki scrambled after him, rushing toward the water and then into the cool liquid. It soothed her sunburned skin. Tamaki slid down, the water coming up to her ribcage. She cupped her hands and drank until her belly hurt. A consistent tingle pervaded the water, but it was gentle.

Scout jogged into the water, submerging and then popping up with water sluicing off, red fur slicked back and mouth opened in a grin. He zoomed around, gamboling like a lamb as he leaped and twisted through the water with joy. Tamaki laughed as the cool water splashed over her with each lap he made. Then he, too, plopped into the water, making a commotion as he drank.

Tamaki stood and took off her wet clothes, spreading out the pants and shirt to dry. The air smelled like coconut. Naked, she stepped back into the water. Only her belt hung across her slim hips, knife against her scarred right thigh.

Scout stared; his head tilted.

"Like what you see, fox?" Tamaki asked in a sultry voice. She ran her hands over her flat stomach and across her breasts. Then she laughed and dropped the pose. "Want to keep you feeling something so you don't lose your humanity when we're this close."

He thought a questioning feel to her.

"Yes, I have a plan," she said. "I'm looking for something. The skin is the most important organ when one is trying to find the invisible." She moved through the water, little waves lapping at her thighs. The bottom of the pool was soft sand against her toes. It was a pleasant sensation, but she was starting to doubt her intuition when she felt pressure under her foot. Tamaki crouched down in the water. Yes, they'd found the headwaters for the Tigris-Mississippi.

Her voice came out rougher than she'd intended. "Well, fox. Your choice. Come over if you want me to try again. I've learned more since the first time." She fixed her gaze on the nearest palm tree, tracing the pattern in the bark on her skin while she let him decide. One good thing about Scout losing his words was that he couldn't ask how she was going to pay for this *etemmu*. There wouldn't be any guilt or any last-minute trying to talk her out of it. They'd come full circle. She'd given him freedom to leave the clearing and she'd have to pay for it by giving up her freedom and staying at the oasis.

The same questioning feeling tickled her mind.

"Why did you think we came here?" She kept her voice light, teasing. "I'm going to fix my mistake if you'll let me. There's enough power for me to try to reshape your body."

Submerged in the water, Tamaki waved her hands as if this were a giant bubble bath. At the touch of a cool snout on her shoulder, she let out a breath she hadn't known she'd been holding.

Back in the camp, she'd made a connection and been able to heal Scout's body temporarily. But then she'd run out of power. If she could be a conduit instead of the battery, then it wouldn't matter how much energy it took to give him a new body. The trick would be to stay present, to keep directing the *etemmu*, and not get lost in the flow.

Tamaki inhaled and connected to the *etemmu* inside of her. When she felt her hands tingle like she was going to manipulate plants, Tamaki allowed it to keep building. The tingling filled her body, made her belly warm, filled her hips. Feeling like she would burst, Tamaki pulled out the knife.

To alter plants into new creations, she'd only needed a small drop, but this was complicated. And it was Scott/Scout. Her only chance to make things right with her only friend. This was going to be the right way: not out of fear, but out of love.

She'd chosen her left palm. The slice went on a diagonal from bottom of the index to the heel of hand, right across both her life and love lines. Crimson appeared, then the pain. Tamaki nudged Scout over the stream of *etemmu* and rubbed her hand along his neck, peeling off the scab so that her blood touched his wound. Tamaki recognized the jolt of their connection. Then she peeled away the scab that held her arm together and thrust her arm into the concentrated *etemmu*-water.

As her power drained into the fox, power sucked in through her arm. The feeling was unsettling and uncomfortable. Cold, but hot at the same time. A halo formed around the fox. His eyes shifted from brown to amber to golden. She created a mental picture and held on to it as she forced herself to relax into the flow. Part of her screamed that she didn't know if she was doing it right, that this wouldn't work, but she shut that part of her mind down. She was Tamaki Hayashi. She could do what others couldn't even dream.

Her stomach clenched and her hands cramped into claws, but Tamaki gritted her teeth. None of the other Alchemists would have been strong enough to do this. She superimposed her image of Scott onto Scout and lengthened him here, pushed there like she'd learned while working in the greenhouse. It was hard, mental work, but she sculpted each detail until there was a ringing in her ears and her eyes closed without her permission.

Gasping, she sent him to shore.

Exhausted, she let her hand drop into the water. A tugging sensation made her eyes peel open. Blood colored the water around her. Her blood. Being sucked out by the *etemmu* spring. Tamaki moaned as she fell forward into the water. The shock of liquid made her sit up and yank her hand into the air so that both wounds were clear of the pool.

Her heart beat against her ribs as she scrambled to her feet, arm still held in the air, and waded toward shore. A human body lay curled in the sand, back to her. She wanted to see his eyes open, make sure he was safe. Make sure that he was happy. See if his hair was the same shade of red. She wanted to tell him how much his friendship meant.

"Don't bother getting out, my sweet child." Azag shimmered into existence in front of her, blocking her path from the pool of *etemmu*. "What a nice oasis." He made a show of looking around. "I saw it briefly when I was sucked back into position as guardian of the headwaters. But I can't be in here unless someone has gotten past me so I just stand in the desert and fantasize about killing Emesh."

"Move," she said, sinking into the water to hide herself and too tired to play games. "I won't try to escape, but let me say goodbye to him. Then I'll sleep for a hundred years and you can show me some more pole dancing or whatever."

The demon loomed over her and cracked his knuckles. "That's not quite right." He had a half-smile that didn't reach his otherworldly hourglass eyes. "I told you I was a naughty demon."

Scout – Scott? – moaned and sat up on one arm, still facing away.

"I am sorry, but this is going to hurt," Azag said, claws extended.

"What?" Tamaki's focus snapped back to Azag as she tried to understand the new danger. She stood up, hand on knife. The old bitterness flooded through her. These powerful creatures bullied her, changed agreements, did whatever they wanted because no one could stop them. "Why?"

"Because you want to be a butterfly. I read your mind, remember?" Azag's expression was terrible. "So many people think a caterpillar turns into a butterfly the way a child grows into an adult. In reality, the caterpillar, wrapped inside its cocoon, dissolves into a goo of DNA. Just a puddle of itself and then that puddle reassembles into a completely different thing. The caterpillar dies and the butterfly gets born. It's death to everything the caterpillar knew and a fierce hope for a miracle that something worthwhile will emerge."

Maybe this could be averted if she could make Azag understand. "No." Tamaki shook her head. "I don't want to be special anymore. Fixing Scout was enough. That was the deal. I understand the cosmic irony. To free him, I have to give up my freedom. That's what I want."

"Liar."

Half a second later his body slammed into hers. Azag's weight forced her deeper into the water. His claws ripped open triple gashes along one side of her ribcage. She screamed as pain sizzled. Azag grabbed her by the left shoulder and lifted her into the air. Then he ripped down, leaving three more bloody gashes on the other side.

Tamaki reached for power, but she was losing too much blood too quickly. After the battle at the Alchemist camp and the trek through the desert and being a conduit to create Scott's new body, she had nothing left.

"I still remember what it felt like when the south wind ripped my wing," he said. "They say what doesn't kill you makes you stronger. I wonder if that's true for humans."

He dunked her in the pool, hands remaining on her shoulders. Through the water, she could see Azag looming over her. His face filled her vision: the red hourglass eyes, the thick eyebrows, the half-smile.

She twisted one way and then the other, but his hands were large and strong. The blood in her shoulder, in her ribcage, everywhere in her body strained to escape flesh, the *etemmu* in her human blood strained to combine with the concentrated *etemmu* in the water. Her blood pressure dropped and faintness washed over her. It was so hard to see, so hard to focus.

No, no, no. She'd come so far across the desert, found the spring, maybe saved Scott and she was going to die here. She still had a war to wage against An, revenge against the Alchemists to achieve. Her body sparked as if she'd been struck by lightning.

Desperate, she opened her mouth. Water rushed in. She gulped and drank and gagged, body convulsing.

Her hands grabbed at the sand on the bottom of the pool and she kicked, not up to where Azag was, but to the side. The pressure on her shoulders disappeared and Tamaki surfaced, choking and gasping for breath. She couldn't see, couldn't hear, but then a long-nailed hand touched her shoulder and she threw the sand where she thought Azag's face should be.

"Tsk, tsk, tsk." Azag reappeared with his face right against hers, her knife in his hands.

"I'm doing this for you. For Scout. For me. Take one for the team, Tamaki. If this works, it will be delectable. If it doesn't…well. You were about to die anyway."

Tamaki jabbed her thumbs at his face, but he pushed her hands away. She fell to her knees, the water splashing around her.

Azag grinned as he shoved her back underwater, one hand clamped on her shoulder. Through the distortion, she saw her knife angling down. She couldn't move except to scream, bubbles erupting. Azag dragged her knife across her throat. Pink clouded through the water as her eyes went dim.

Tamaki. She didn't know if she heard his voice or imagined it. There was a muffled splash as if someone leaped or was thrown into the water. Too late, she thought. Someone was finally coming to save her and it was too late.

She was dead, murdered by a demon. Fire burned out her heart, flooded her veins, scraped her from the inside out and Tamaki couldn't see, couldn't hear, couldn't taste. She might have still been screaming, but she didn't know. The pain went on and on, not something that could become familiar, but waves of agony. Obaa-chan's sweet wrinkled face floated in front of Tamaki, hands cupped around an orchid with spectacular blue flowers. The perfume scent hit her and then diffused as the image dissolved into Tamaki sitting on a familiar wooden chair, curtain shoved aside to stare out the window at the back of her mother, slightly hunched over and hair pulled into a tidy braid. Next to her, inches taller, the ramrod back of her father. A cigarette dangled from his left hand; the smoke smell was in her hair, a singular indication that they'd been in the same space.

Her bones melted, splintered from within, and fused together. Her feet disintegrated into ash, washing away in the water. She was burned alive as she floated in the water, skin blackened to a crisp and peeling open to reveal her gleaming white skeleton, only to be knit back together and go through it all again. The main Hothead screamed at her, teeth yellow against the plastic red of his skin. Then she was running, out of breath, she had to get to the clearing by the cabin or she'd be too late. Panting, she arrived as the rope tightened around Scott's neck. The New Babylon soldiers morphed into the Alchemists.

As one, the group turned and fanned into a circle. She wasn't allowed to leave. They would rip her apart. They were ripping her apart. Leaves on bushes moved in the surrounding forest. The vines that she'd attacked were ready for revenge. Fear stung at the crush of bodies as the circle tightened around her. Vines clenched her feet. They wrapped to her knees, to her hips, to her ribcage. Tamaki lifted her head, but the vines climbed to her shoulders and then settled in loops around her face. A green cocoon.

I'm here. Scout's voice pushed through the cocoon. *You're not alone.*

She moaned or tried to moan. She'd thought her freedom would be enough to sacrifice, but now she was truly like Scott. She was consciousness without a body, trapped in a hidden oasis.

Steady. Choose your own thoughts. Remember Saki. Show me how you met her. Show me how we met. Show me everything wonderful.

Tamaki grabbed onto his voice. It was the only sanctuary from the pain. Scout whispered to her. He asked questions and told her stories, anything to keep her nightmares away. Gradually, Tamaki became aware of the green cocoon loosening. Gaps appeared in the torture, the waves lost power, the fire waned.

Pull free. Nothing can hold you.

Tamaki opened her eyes and broke the surface of the pool. Water rushed down her body; her scars had faded to thin jagged white lines along her ribs, her arm, her palms. She touched her throat. Yes, there as well. There was something different about her skin, though. Still the color of a cherry tree's bark, but now it was harder, almost like porcelain. And she was taller, her muscles more defined. She'd always been athletic, but now her body was cut. Her subconscious had guided her new body, making her less fragile. No one would call her "little girl" now.

Her gaze settled on a human form curved on the sand in the shade of a palm tree. He'd stayed. In this moment before he awoke, Tamaki caught her breath and let it out with a shudder. His chest rose and fell in natural sleep; his red hair had grown past his shoulders.

She'd wanted to undo his death. And then saved him from the fox's death. This, then, would be their third chance.

She wasn't going to waste it.

ACKNOWLEDGEMENTS

I've shared the story of how I wrote *Flames of a Falling God (*formerly titled *Walking Through Fire)* while in a hospital room at Johns Hopkins as a love letter to my son while I stayed with my two-year-old daughter, recently diagnosed with leukemia. It was based on my fear of what happens if the world ends and you are the mother of a child with cancer. This book is different. Tamaki demanded that her story be told. She's 19 years old and she's angry about the world she's inheriting. She's angry about the chaotic gods and the power structure and what seems like arbitrary decisions that directly affect her life.

First, I'd like to thank Lyn Webb. It is no exaggeration to say that this book would not be here if she had not encouraged me again and again. She's the type of person you want to sit with in a coffee shop and listen to her stories and her advice and you leave feeling like maybe, just maybe, you should go for your dream too.

This novel, despite Tamaki's demands, was difficult to write because there was so much of the altered world that we needed to see. So, thank you to Nancy Kress and Walter Jon Williams of Taos Toolbox for helping to frame this story instead of letting it be a series of episodes. Thank you to Harrison Lee for constructive feedback. Thank you to Amanda Rutter and Bob Greenberger for editorial work on this book. Any mistakes are my own.

And, most important, thank you to my readers: involuntary and voluntary. A big thank you to the spectacular group of eleventh grade students who stayed after school to read the first chapter and gave me honest (and opinionated!) feedback.

Thank you to my sister, Tammy Day, who reads the roughest drafts and to Tory Popp who kept asking when the next book was coming. Thank you to Eric Guy who read so many versions of this story that it is hardly recognizable anymore. Thank you to Kazmin Gainey for caring about the characters enough to threaten me if I didn't hurry up. And thank you to Jennifer Greenleaf for reading my work – and making Wayne listen to it! Alicia Fisher came in for the final polishing. And, a big thank you to Mike who has the stamina for pushing through all the pesky details that I would forever ignore. Finally, thank you to Sylvia who read bits and pieces when I emailed her throughout the day and then demanded that she read more before she fell asleep at night. If anyone likes Azag – know that the pole dancing was her idea!

Much love, friends. Keep fighting for a better world.

EXCERPT FROM
FLAMES OF A FALLING GOD
(BOOK 1, THE MISBEGOTTEN SERIES)

Chapter 1

Photos spread across the oaken dining room table, but Rachel Deneuve's focus was on the window overlooking the driveway. She knew her son Adam would be mortified if he saw her watching for his return. Worry, a mother's natural instinct, was magnified in Rachel by the cancer cells made deep in Adam's bone marrow and held in check only by thirty months of grueling chemo. She wanted Adam safe and she wanted him home. From outside, a sustained rumble of thunder sounded a warning, the heavens ripping open with an anguished groan like a woman with birthing pains.

With a determined air, Rachel turned away from the window and the sounds of a summer storm toward her project: coloring in the phoenix at the top of the scrapbook page. The firebird's long tail feathers flowed down the side, framing the photo of baby Adam first brought home from the hospital.

Adam was eleven now, so she was years behind on this project, but this seemed the right time to create a graphic story of their family—before the details became muddled. In light of the separation, the responsibility to be fair was heavy across her shoulders. As if she should count each time she or Craig appeared in a photo and the tally should be exactly even. It complicated the job of chronicling from Adam's birth, through his cancer treatment, and into their new formation, whatever that would turn out to be.

The pencil's red tip broke with a snapping sound. She'd pushed too hard. Irritated, Rachel threw down the pencil and shoved a strand of thick hair back behind her ear. Her bangs were cut straight across to draw attention to her large eyes, but right now the sensation of hair touching forehead was annoying. Everything was annoying. She wanted to take a shower and go to bed, but didn't want to be in pajamas when Craig dropped off Adam.

Tires rolled over gravel. Finally, they were here. Rachel automatically checked her appearance. Peacock colored tank top under a sheer white shirt, dangling earrings, a flowing skirt and bare feet. Her features were sharp, her neck long, her collar bones jutting. All speaking to a flapper aesthetic from an earlier century in New York City rather than the suburbs of northern Maryland. Craig liked tidy. Rachel resisted the urge to smooth the auburn curls she'd piled into a loose bun and opened the door to her husband and son.

Craig stood with his hand raised as if to knock on the door. Her door? A moment of confusion. This was all new. He was tall, relaxed, wearing a collared shirt. A small scar stretched down the left side of his neck from a childhood accident. Grey-green eyes that seemed to hold so many emotions at once. Nearly just as he'd looked in college when they started dating. More lines on his face, though. Being the parent of a child with cancer had done that to both of them.

"Sorry we're late. Adam wanted to take a shower."

Adam's brown hair was wet. Pale and small for his age, he looked scrawny standing next to Craig. He clutched an overnight bag with both hands. A wet beach towel lay behind his neck, soaking the edges of his t-shirt.

"You took him to the pool?" Rachel tried to keep her tone even, but all she could think was: *You let our immunocompromised son swim in a cesspool of germs.*

Craig rocked back on the balls of his feet. "It's the first official day of summer. Thought it would be fun." He nudged Adam's shoulder. "We had fun, didn't we?"

Adam nodded. He yawned. His eyelids drooped, covering the irises. The color—a thin circle of brown around grey-green—always made Rachel think of Craig's genes and her genes battling it out for dominance. Businessman versus artist, extrovert versus introvert.

A gust of warm wind made Rachel cross her arms over her chest. Branches on the maple trees lining the driveway rubbed against each other with an unsettling creaking.

"I should get Adam in bed."

"Yeah." Craig took a step back. "I'm heading to Boston for work. I'll have my phone."

"This late at night?"

"Any reason not to?" His question was a challenge, both confrontational and hopeful.

Rachel swallowed. Her heart cramped. They needed this break, but it felt so wrong for him to leave. She made a small shaking motion with her head, but couldn't think of anything to say other than, "I can't—."

"We'll talk when I get back," he promised.

She licked dry lips and Craig seemed to take her silence as assent.

Adam brushed past her to get into the house, but Rachel stayed to watch the taillights fade as Craig drove away. The stars looked different tonight, closer to earth, as if blinking an urgent message to the planet below. Atmospheric winds blew away the clouds until a gravid red moon dominated the sky. Rachel shivered, the night sky's vivid colors making her feel unsettled. It was as if, she thought whimsically, the air was vibrating at a frequency beyond human range.

She felt both dizzy and nauseous at once. Rachel recognized the familiar symptoms of an oncoming panic attack. Whether from imagining something horrible happening that had made Adam late, or the conversation with Craig, or the strange moon, it didn't matter.

"Breathe," she coached herself. She leaned against the outside of the door and closed her eyes, counting until her heartbeat slowed and her shoulders relaxed. Taking one more breath, Rachel opened the door and went inside with a fake smile. She needed to be strong for her son.

"Alright, buddy. It's just you and me." Rachel called as she shut and locked the door.

The bright kitchen lights dispelled some of the negative feelings of watching Craig leave, of the strangeness from the outside sky.

Adam was slumped over the kitchen table.

"Come on, no sleeping down here." Rachel put her hand on Adam's back to get him out of the chair.

"I don't feel good."

Adam's forehead burned against the back of Rachel's hand.

"You've got a fever," Rachel said. "I'll call the hospital." She hit the preset on her phone and put it on speaker so she could keep moving. In an oncology patient anything over 101.4 meant an immediate trip to the emergency room. Years of chemo battling his leukemia meant Adam had no immune system to fight bacteria or germs.

Rachel grabbed the overnight bag that stood ready and ripped it open to find a tube of ointment. She helped Adam lean back in the chair and lifted up his shirt to expose the quarter-sized bump under his skin that was a medical port. Rachel squeezed a glob of white onto his chest to numb the spot where the winged needle would go in, covered it with a clear adhesive, and then pulled his shirt down.

Her phone was still ringing; the hospital's service hadn't picked up. That had never happened before, but it didn't matter. She and Adam had been through this drill many times.

Rachel said, "This won't be a long visit." But she moved to the dining room, sweeping photos, the scrapbook, and colored pencils into the emergency bag for herself. Better to be prepared to stay and then sent home than the other way around.

Grabbing her phone and wallet with one hand, Rachel put her other around Adam's waist and helped him out to the car.

"Don't forget the charger. It's in my bookbag," Adam whispered.

"Okay." Rachel left him leaning against the car and rushed back inside. After she'd retrieved the charger and come back to the front door, Rachel's heart sputtered. Adam was gone. A smell was in the air, at once electrifying and strange. The hair on the back of her neck stood at attention. Force gathered, invisible but tangible, and, with a crack, lightning struck the nearby maple tree. The topmost branch burst into flame. In the sudden light, Rachel saw Adam crouched on the ground underneath.

Rushing forward, Rachel threw herself to her knees beside her son. Oblivious to her presence, Adam stared down at his cupped hands. "I caught it. I caught the falling star." Fire reflected from the branch above seemed to glow in Adam's cupped hands, bright as if someone shined a flashlight from beneath them or from within. A disconcerting illusion.

More brusquely than she intended, Rachel pulled Adam to his feet and away from the tree. The branch fell from the tree to the lawn, the flames dying out with rebellious snaps and hisses. Rachel looked up at the deformed tree and kicked at the blackened branch with her booted foot again and again, not wanting to return from the hospital to find her home burned down by a spark in the grass. Her foot tingled and she ground the boot heel to erase the sensation.

Using the wet towel from around Adam's neck, Rachel wadded it into a ball and put it against the window for him to use as a pillow. She started the Ford NewWave with voice recognition and then glanced in the rearview mirror. Adam's cheeks were pink and his lips were chapped. She remembered the countless other times he'd been in this same position from eight years old until now as they'd rushed to the emergency room. She knew Adam better than anyone else in the world because of what they'd experienced, the absolute raw moments that no one else would understand. Like when he was younger, on his monthly steroid protocol, how he'd be angry and sad, full of energy and then crashing. How she'd be so frustrated with his mood swings, and then he'd put his arms around her neck, hot moist breath on her skin as he buried his face into her shoulder. They'd cry together, sitting on the carpet, arms wrapped around each other.

A sudden gust of wind slammed against the car. The maple tree, stripped of its leaves by the unseasonable wind and now missing its top branch, stretched skeletal hands into the sky. Purple swirled like a bruise through the blackness overhead. It was so dark. Where was the moon?

Rachel told the navigation screen to pull up the parking garage at the hospital. Overhead, sudden lightning arced and danced. *Tornado? Hope it holds off until I get Adam into the hospital.* The car's navigation lit up a yellow path. Less than an hour to get there. Not that Rachel didn't know the way, but she liked to see the miles tick down as they got closer.

Adam slept in the backseat. Her leg jittered because of the coffee she'd gulped to stay alert. They were making good time to I-95. Rachel tapped on the screen to get the radio on, anything to distract her from Adam's soft moans of pain. No local channels would come in so she hit 'scan.' Up ahead, at the exit onto I-95, a police cruiser slanted across the way, the officer turning people away.

Rachel gritted her teeth. It would take another twenty minutes to backtrack to Route 1. She drove along the right shoulder of the road right up to the cruiser. The officer waved his arms, a silhouette with blue and red pulses behind him. She had to stop or hit him.

He rapped on her passenger window with knuckles, shined a flashlight into the interior. Rachel squinted against the light and rolled down the window. The smell of something burning wafted inside.

The officer sounded angry as he said, "What don't you understand, Miss, about a police blockade!"

"This is a medical emergency. My son's life is in danger." Rachel grabbed at her bag and shoved papers at him. Papers that, in a few spare sentences, told their story. Two and a half years ago she'd taken Adam to the pediatrician for strange bruises, then to the local ER for a blood test, then to Johns Hopkins in Baltimore, all in the space of three hours. A scream that lodged in Rachel's throat and didn't release until she sobbed in the hospital shower that night. ALL. Acute Lymphoblastic Leukemia. She and Adam had been immediately admitted and then stayed for thirty-one days in the pediatric wing where the rooms have a hospital bed for the patient and a pull-out sofa for a parent.

The officer flicked his flashlight, read the diagnosis, saw the doctor's orders, and spotlighted his flashlight on Adam in the backseat. Rachel felt more than saw the officer's uncertainty.

"I've got to get him to Hopkins," she said again.

"There's a storm coming. Big one." He stepped back, "Turn around and take cover."

Rachel nodded. "I understand." She did, but the officer didn't. Without knowing what caused Adam's fever, every minute mattered. Rachel eased her foot off the brake and slammed the gas pedal. Tires squealed. The officer waved his arms in her rearview mirror.

Behind him she saw the sky rip open. A flaming meteor fell and an orange glow lit the horizon. The world was on fire.

<u>The Misbegotten Series</u>

Flames of a Falling God (Book 1)

Embers of New Babylon (Book 2)
     (forthcoming 2023)

<u>The World of The Misbegotten</u>

Ashes of Regret

www.SearbyGrayBooks.com
www.MudHousePublishing.com

www.ingramcontent.com/pod-product-compliance
Lightning Source LLC
Chambersburg PA
CBHW021435310726
48971CB00005B/1371